Praise for Layne Fargo's
"Addictive" (*BookPage*) Novels

THEY NEVER LEARN

"Sizzling with rage and wit, Layne Fargo's *They Never Learn* will delight fans of Karin Slaughter, *Dexter*, and *Killing Eve* with its deftly drawn portrait of a woman on fire and her unquenchable lust for revenge. Sensual, breathlessly plotted, and thoroughly unputdownable—this tightrope thriller feels a bit like getting away with murder."

—Amy Gentry, bestselling author of
Good as Gone and
Last Woman Standing

"A fierce, provocative thriller that grabs you by the throat and doesn't let go. Revenge has never looked so good—or so appealing!"

—Samantha Downing,
USA Today bestselling author of
My Lovely Wife and *He Started It*

"Searing . . . Fargo shocks and entertains while delivering a scathing takedown of campus rape culture. Fans of Chelsea Cain will appreciate this fiercely feminist twist on serial killer fiction."

—*Publishers Weekly*

"Dark, shocking, and utterly satisfying!"

—Kathleen Barber, author of
Truth Be Told and *Follow Me*

"With stunning, dagger-sharp prose and a deliciously satisfying plot, *They Never Learn* is the feminist revenge thriller we need and deserve."

—Megan Collins, author of
The Winter Sister

TEMPER

"A twisted tale of what happens when violence, ambition, and the taste for blood take center stage . . . Fargo's first novel will be well received by fans of Gillian Flynn and Tana French."

—*Booklist*

"Utterly compelling. A fascinating look at our willingness to accept the destruction of others for the sake of artistic genius."

—Victoria Helen Stone,
bestselling author of *Jane Doe*

"A suspense novel paced to make readers twitch in their seats waiting for the final curtain. Sexy and sinister."

—Lori Rader-Day,
award-winning author of
Under a Dark Sky

"Addictive . . . The novel's violently sensuous suspense careens toward a chilling conclusion you'll never see coming."

—*BookPage*

"A completely compelling read in which anger and passion fizz off the page."

—Araminta Hall, author of
Our Kind of Cruelty

"Fargo maintains a scalpel-like control over her characters, even when they themselves are out of control."

—*Chicago Tribune*

"The kind of debut people are going to remember: intense, well crafted, and emotionally blistering."

—*CrimeReads*

ALSO BY LAYNE FARGO

Temper

THEY NEVER LEARN

LAYNE FARGO

SCOUT PRESS

NEW YORK   LONDON   TORONTO   SYDNEY   NEW DELHI

Scout Press
An Imprint of Simon & Schuster, Inc.
1230 Avenue of the Americas
New York, NY 10020

First Scout Press trade paperback edition April 2021

SCOUT PRESS and colophon are registered trademarks of Simon & Schuster, Inc.

For information about special discounts for bulk purchases, please contact Simon & Schuster Special Sales at 1-866-506-1949 or business@simonandschuster.com.

The Simon & Schuster Speakers Bureau can bring authors to your live event. For more information or to book an event, contact the Simon & Schuster Speakers Bureau at 1-866-248-3049 or visit our website at www.simonspeakers.com.

Interior design by Michelle Marchese

Manufactured in the United States of America

10   9   8   7   6   5   4   3   2

The Library of Congress has cataloged the hardcover edition as follows:

Names: Fargo, Layne, author.
Title: They never learn / Layne Fargo.
Description: First Scout Press hardcover edition. | New York : Scout Press, 2020.
Identifiers: LCCN 2020000147 (print) | LCCN 2020000148 (ebook) | ISBN 9781982132026 (hardcover) | ISBN 9781982132033 (trade paperback) | ISBN 9781982132040 (ebook)
Subjects: GSAFD: Suspense fiction.
Classification: LCC PS3606.A685 T47 2020 (print) | LCC PS3606.A685 (ebook) | DDC 813/.6—dc23
LC record available at https://lccn.loc.gov/2020000147
LC ebook record available at https://lccn.loc.gov/2020000148

ISBN 978-1-9821-3202-6
ISBN 978-1-9821-3203-3 (pbk)
ISBN 978-1-9821-3204-0 (ebook)

For Emily

THEY
NEVER
LEARN

1

SCARLETT

I'll know it's working when he starts to scream.

But for now, I wait. I snuck into the garage an hour ago, when it was still pitch-black outside. I'm dressed to match the shadows, a hood pulled up to hide my vivid red hair, face scrubbed clean of makeup. No need to look pretty for this.

There aren't any vehicles in here, just some old exercise equipment sitting on scraps of carpet, stale sweat and mossy body spray hanging in the air. I'm pressed into the back corner behind a set of warped metal shelves. Enough to conceal me, if I stay extremely still. I keep my breathing steady, focusing my gaze on the peeling red vinyl of the weight bench, the small gashes in the material like open wounds.

Footsteps slap the pavement, and the side door to the garage swings open. Right on time. A young man comes in, swabbing the sweat off his brow with the hem of his T-shirt.

Tyler Elkin. Star athlete, and one of the worst students I ever taught in my Intro to English Lit class. As starting quarterback, he took the Gorman University football team all the way to the conference championship last season. That was before the rumors started.

He tugs his earbuds out and swipes his thumb across his phone screen. Music starts blaring from a small speaker set up on a crate beside the weights, a screamy white-boy wannabe punk rocker whining about some girl who broke his heart. *That bitch, how dare she.*

It sets my teeth on edge, but I don't move a muscle. I can't risk Tyler seeing me. Not yet.

Tunelessly humming along, Tyler walks to the dented mini fridge in the corner and removes a glass bottle. He tosses the cap onto the floor and takes a long pull of the liquid inside. It's an energy drink he makes himself, with activated charcoal, cayenne, and several raw eggs. Smells awful, and tastes even worse. I tried it myself, after brewing up a batch based on the instructions on his Instagram. Then I added my own special ingredient, mixed right in with the rest of the bitter grit at the bottom.

He made a video on his "kickass morning routine" too. He starts his day the same way, even on weekends: up at 5:00 a.m., hours before his fraternity brothers, for a brisk run along the path by the river at the edge of campus. He always pauses to take a photo of himself with the sunrise saturating the background. Then he comes back here, to the garage behind the frat house, for weight training. He'll down half his energy drink now, the other half once his workout is done, while he captions his sunrise selfie with some inane motivational message. *Rise n grind. Make 2day yr bitch.*

Tyler polishes off another gulp and wipes his mouth. He has full lips and long eyelashes, which renders his face almost feminine from certain angles. He could be a model, one of those sun-burnished Abercrombie boys tossing a ball back and forth in matching madras shorts. It's clear from his social media he considers that his backup plan if the whole football thing doesn't work out. A boy like Tyler, he could have any girl he wanted. But where's the fun in that? It must get boring after a while. Not that that's any excuse.

Tyler lies back on the weight bench and starts raising and lowering the barbell in time with the music. Until his rhythm slows, stutters. His fingers wrap tighter around the bar. Then they spasm, and he almost lets go of the weight, dropping it on his catalog-perfect face.

My breath catches. That would ruin my whole plan.

He barely manages to keep ahold of the barbell. With quivering hands, he sets it back on its stand and shuts his eyes for a second. He sits up, shaking out his wrists, his arms. But now his legs are spasming, his calf and thigh muscles clenching and unclenching like fists.

Tyler stands, trying to walk it off, rolling his neck, cracking his vertebrae. I shrink deeper into the darkness. It's almost time, but not yet, not—

"Fuck," he says, raking a hand back through his sweat-soaked blond hair. He picks up the bottle again, taking another swig, Adam's apple bobbing as he swallows.

Still holding his drink, Tyler leans against the weight bench, trying to stretch out the strange cramps in his legs. It's only a few seconds before he seizes all over and collapses. The bottle goes with him, landing beyond his outstretched hand. The glass doesn't break, but the remaining contents flow out onto the concrete floor.

That's fine. He's had more than enough now.

Tyler's body is no longer under his control. He's twitching, contorting, spine arching, lifting his back off the floor so he's supported only by his head and heels. He finally lets out a scream—throaty, guttural at first, then keening higher, turning into a sob.

If it weren't for his obnoxious music, someone might hear. If he gets much louder, they might anyway. I step out of my hiding place, but he's in so much pain it takes him a few seconds to put it all together—to recognize me in the first place and then to wonder why his literature professor is standing over him in his own garage at six in the morning, smiling while he screams.

"Please," Tyler manages to choke out. "Help me, please h—"

Another convulsion takes hold of him. Soon he won't be able to speak at all. This is the most I've ever heard out of Tyler Elkin's mouth. When he bothered to show up to my class, he grunted one-word answers, slumping down in his seat with his legs sprawled across the aisle like he didn't give a damn how much space he took up.

They never do, men like him. Well, he's more of a boy, really. The garage's fluorescent overhead light emphasizes all the still-adolescent features of his face: the downy excuse for a mustache on his upper lip, the pimple swelling in the crease between his nose and his cheek.

He's a boy, and he'll never become a man. Because in a few more minutes, he'll be dead.

It's risky for me to be here. I know that. I could have left the tainted drink in the fridge for him and slipped away while he was still out running. But the truth is, I enjoy this too much to miss it. It's my reward for all the hard work. Besides, there's one more step in my plan.

I pick up Tyler's phone and hold it in front of his face. At first, the device doesn't recognize him, his features are so twisted with agony. I wait for the convulsions to ease again, his body giving up the fight even before he does. After a few more seconds, the lock screen blinks away.

I open Instagram and crop Tyler's latest selfie so only the sunrise in the background is in the frame, applying the filter he uses for all his posts. For the caption, I imitate the appalling grammar and spelling he employs.

last run last sunrise, so sorry 4 everthing

Tyler lies there panting, soaked through with sweat, blinking up at me as I methodically wipe all traces of my fingerprints from the device.

"Why—" he starts, but his throat is too constricted to speak.

I put the phone in his twitching hand and lean over him, my body casting his in shadow.

"Megan Foster," I say.

Tyler's eyes widen—and *this*, this is my favorite part. The abject terror that takes over their faces. That's how I know they're finally seeing me, realizing what I truly am.

I imagine what Tyler might say, if he were still capable of forming words. *It wasn't just me*—that's probably where he'd start. He wasn't the only one who held Megan down on that filthy frat house mattress. They all did it—Tyler and four of his closest friends, half the starting lineup of the football team.

I didn't start it. Who knows, that might even be the truth. Maybe Tyler was the second to take his turn, or the third, or the fourth, or the fifth. Maybe by the time he got there she'd given up fighting back, so he could almost pretend she was willing. He didn't have bruises and scratches on his arms afterward, like his teammate Devin Caldwell did. But the police didn't do a damn thing to Devin Caldwell either. They claimed there wasn't enough proof.

For me, what Megan said was more than enough proof. True justice would have been bolting the fraternity house doors and setting the whole place on fire, burning every one of those boys in their beds. I might not even have needed to douse the place in kerosene first, considering every surface is sticky with spilled alcohol. But I can't kill them all, not unless I want to get caught. I've spent the past sixteen years murdering men who deserve it, and I'm not about to get sloppy now.

So I made the logical compromise: pick one man and make an example of him. Tyler was the clear choice. Not because he's the quarterback or the alpha male or any of that macho bullshit, but because, even though he and his four teammates all did something abhorrent that night, Tyler's sin was the worst.

It was his Instagram that tipped me off, actually: photo after photo of Tyler at parties, leaning against walls and doorjambs and tree trunks, holding a bottle like the one oozing out on the floor beside his soon-to-be corpse.

Tyler believes clean living means a stronger game. So while his frat brothers got wasted on cheap beer and skunk weed, Tyler restricted himself to sipping his homemade energy drinks. Five boys raped Megan Foster, but only one of them did it while stone-cold sober.

Looking back, the signs were there from the first week of class—the way Tyler always picked the seat right behind Megan's, flicked her curtain of brown curls back while she was trying to read. Told her, even as she shrank away from him, *You'd be so pretty if you smiled.*

He's seizing again, but he's gone silent now, eyes rolled back into his head. I crouch down beside him, careful not to touch anything else. It's just a matter of time. No hospital could help him at this point, not with that much strychnine in his system.

There. Finally. Tyler's body goes through one more bout of clenching convulsions, and his lips stretch back from his teeth, fixing his too-handsome face in a gruesome parody of a grin.

Who's smiling now, motherfucker?

2

CARLY

I've been counting down the days all summer, but now that we're here, I feel like I can't breathe.

The heat isn't helping. It's scorching outside, and for the whole drive from our small central Pennsylvania hometown to Gorman University, the air-conditioning in my parents' Nissan barely reached the back seat. Sweat streams down my spine, pooling in the waistband of my jeans.

My father glances in the rearview mirror, trying to catch my eye. We have the same eyes: smoky blue with dark shadows underneath. That's about the only thing we have in common.

I avoid his gaze, peering through the car's tinted windows instead as he steers onto the paved drive that curves around Whitten Hall, my new home. I was expecting, I don't know, something more like a dorm. But Whitten looks like an old manor house, with columns by the entrance and grasping fingers of ivy crawling all over the red brick.

My mom waits until my father punches the hazard-light button and gets out before she twists around in her seat to look at me. "Do you want us to come inside with you?" The hope in her voice is like a knife in the heart. "Help you unpack?"

I taste blood and realize I've been gnawing on my bottom lip again. "No, that's okay."

She took me out for a farewell meal yesterday—at lunchtime, when she knew my father would be at work. Nothing fancy; we just split some chicken nuggets and a large Frosty at Wendy's. The whole time, she blinked too much, like she was trying not to cry.

She's doing it now too, her eyelashes fluttering, fingers tangling in the gold cross necklace at her throat. Her hair is dark like mine but stick-straight instead of wavy, and she wears it in the same sleek curtains around her cheeks she did back when she and my father met. He thinks all women should keep their hair long or they aren't "feminine." My junior year of high school, I hacked mine off to shoulder-length with a pair of kitchen shears, and he wouldn't speak to me for a week. Now I wear it even shorter, skimming my jawline.

The trunk slams shut, and my mom and I both jump, shoulders stiffening.

She gets out of the car first. I take a deep breath before I follow, unpeeling the backs of my arms from the seat. My father stands on the curb beside my luggage, hands on his hips like we've made him wait for hours instead of a few minutes. I only have two bags—a duffel and a hard-sided suitcase—while most of the other arriving students seem to have a whole moving van's worth of stuff, plastic milk crates and IKEA bags and cardboard boxes labeled with Sharpie.

Next to the car ahead of ours, there's a petite black girl standing on her tiptoes to hug her dad goodbye, tears streaming down her cheeks. He's crying too but trying to hide it, clenching his jaw tight, squinting his eyes shut. I can't imagine feeling that way. I can't imagine feeling anything but relief at saying goodbye to my father.

I let him hug me, though, because I know it will be worse if I don't. It's important to him that we appear to be a happy family, even if there are only total strangers around to witness the charade. He still looks displeased—at the stiffness in my arms maybe, or the way I tensed up when he squeezed my shoulders.

He steps back to stand beside my mom, putting his hand on her hip—the spot where he knows her sciatica hurts the worst.

"Call us once you get settled," she says, smiling wider to cover her wince.

I hug her too, and then I pick up my luggage and head toward the front door. My bags are heavy, but I feel so light, almost giddy with relief. I'm not going to turn around. I'm not going to watch them drive away.

Entering Whitten Hall feels like stepping into a sepia photograph, everything a different shade of brown. In another lifetime, the entryway might have been a formal parlor. Now it's crowded with slouching sofas from multiple eras, plus a bulletin board showing a chaotic assortment of flyers for sorority rushes and intramural sports and LARPing clubs. A pop song from this summer drifts down from one of the rooms above.

Just inside the door, a girl wearing a red Gorman University tank top and denim cutoffs sits on a folding chair, a clipboard balanced on her lap. There's a boy next to her, crouched down on the nubby tan carpet with a Steelers cap pulled low over his eyes. He touches her bare thighs, fingertips brushing the shredded hem of her shorts.

Oh my God. He's grabbing her. I should—

But then she grins and ducks under the brim of his hat to kiss him. And keeps kissing him, like I'm not even here, like I've faded right into the beige walls.

I let my duffel bag thump to the floor. The girl separates from the guy's face with a suction-cup pop and finally looks at me, her lips twisted in annoyance. "Yes?"

"I'm, um—moving in?" I should have let my parents come inside with me. I have no idea what I'm doing. Maybe I'm in the wrong place. Maybe I shouldn't be here at all.

"Name?" the girl demands, looking down at the clipboard.

Her boyfriend gets up and saunters toward the door, pulling a pack of cigarettes from the pocket of his nylon shorts.

"Carly," I say, my voice scrabbling upward at the end as if it's trying to hang on to a ledge. "Carly Schiller."

"Welcome to Gorman University, Carly Schiller," she says, flat and bored like she's reading from a script. "I'm Samantha, your resident advisor. Looks like you're on the second floor, with"—Samantha motions to a girl who just came down the stairs—"Hadley!"

The girl is gorgeous, with glowing pale skin and corn-silk blond hair pulled into a low ponytail. I'm suddenly aware of how flushed and shiny my face must be, how heavy my clothes feel with sweat, while her retro sundress—the same shade of blue as her eyes—looks fresh and breezy, perfect as her cat-eye liner. I bet my own black eyeliner is all smeared. I shouldn't have bothered with it this morning, but I wanted to look . . . I don't know. Like someone else.

"Meet your new roommate," Samantha says. "Carly, this is—"

"Allison Hadley."

Allison sticks her hand out for me to shake. Her nails are shiny, painted bright red, and there's something sophisticated, almost grandiose, about the way she carries herself. It reminds me of the actresses in the 1940s movies my mom loves. Allison says her name like I should know it already.

"Where's the rest of your stuff?" she asks.

I look helplessly at my two shabby bags, slumped against each other on the floor. "This is everything."

Allison tilts her head, perfect ponytail swishing. "You didn't bring a fan or anything?"

I shake my head.

"That's okay," she says. "I've got a couple, and I've had them all on full blast since this morning, so it's slightly less sweltering up there. Here, let me help you with that."

"Oh, no, you don't have to—" I start, but she's already lifting my suitcase, carrying it toward the stairs. I catch up with her, hoisting the duffel onto my shoulder.

The curving wooden banister is grand, but the steps are covered in the same dingy carpet as the entryway, strips of duct tape stuck over worn-down patches on the treads. Upstairs, the music is louder, syncopated beats vibrating the walls.

Allison stops on the landing, letting the suitcase drop. "Damn, girl. What did you pack in here?"

I'm hoping I'm too red-faced already for my blush to register. "Just . . . books. A lot of books. Sorry. I can—"

"It's okay, you're saving me a trip to the gym." She continues down the hall, dragging my suitcase behind her like it's a disobedient dog. "Bathroom's there," she tells me, gesturing with a point of her chin. "And this is us."

The door is propped ajar, and Allison bumps it the rest of the way open with her hip. She's already moved in to the right half of the room; the bed is made with a red-and-black comforter, and there's a row of Broadway musical posters—*Wicked*, *Rent*, *Phantom of the Opera*—hanging above it. As she promised, there are multiple fans, all switched on high: two slowly oscillating between the beds, and a box fan stuck in the window, blowing stagnant air out through the ivy.

"If you don't like that side," she says, "we can switch. I just took the same one I had last year."

"No, it's . . . this side is fine." I set the duffel down on the bare mattress. "Wait, you're not a freshman?"

"Sophomore," she says, sitting cross-legged on her own bed so her skirt drapes over her knees. "My roommate from last year transferred to Penn."

"Hey, Allie, you ready—"

A boy walks right into the room like he lives here too. Once he sees me, though, he stops, suddenly awkward.

"Oh, hey," he says. "Sorry. You must be—"

"This is my new roommate, Carly." Allison gestures between us with a dramatic roll of her wrist. "Carly, this is Wes."

Wes is slightly built, with narrow shoulders and brown hair that flops over his forehead, skimming the edges of his wire-rim glasses. He must be her boyfriend. Although she didn't introduce him that way, and he's not quite the type I would have pictured her with. I mean, I only met her a few minutes ago, so I don't really know her, let alone her taste in guys. But I can tell just by looking at Wes that he's like me: a fade-into-the-background person. Whereas Allison . . . she shines like a spotlight's pointed on her.

"Nice to meet you, Carly," Wes says, before turning his attention right back to Allison. "Did you still want to—"

"Yes!" She springs up off the bed. "Yes, sorry, I lost track of the time, but I am ready!"

Allison slips on some sandals and grabs a lanyard holding her keys and Gorman ID. She doesn't look back at me, but Wes does, pausing in the doorway to cast one sidelong glance my way before following Allison out.

The low roar of the fans makes it seem like the room is breathing. My parents are probably only a few miles away, heading west on Route 422, but I feel like I'm on a separate planet, finally free.

I can be happy here. I know I can.

3

SCARLETT

"Don't kill me."

I swivel around in my chair. Dr. Andrew Torres stands on the conference room threshold, holding up his chipped Shakespearean insults mug with a guilty smile.

"I took the last of the coffee," he says.

I salute him with the cup of dark roast I picked up at the library coffee cart on my way to work. "I've got it covered."

He laughs and slides into the seat on my right. "You always do."

After taking my leave of Tyler's corpse, I still had time for an abbreviated version of my morning routine. Shower, mascara, lipstick, hair styled into soft waves. But I had to grab breakfast on the go. I'm always starving after a kill, even the ones that don't require physical exertion. I finished my cranberry muffin before I even made it across the Oak Grove to Miller Hall.

I was one of the first to arrive for the staff meeting. The rest of the faculty are filing in now, chatting amongst themselves, but none of them acknowledge me. Drew is the only coworker with whom I have anything approaching a friendship, and that's because he finds the rest of the English faculty almost as tedious as I do.

"How was your summer?" Drew asks, as we both flip to fresh pages in our notebooks. He's used the same plain narrow-ruled style as long as I've known him, buying a new one to commemorate the start of each semester. "I hope you didn't spend the whole time working on that fellowship application and studiously avoiding fun."

"Not the *whole* time," I say. "Thank you again for the letter of recommendation."

Drew waves me off. "Your work speaks for itself. If they don't choose you, they're idiots."

He's the one who told me about the Women's Academy fellowship in the first place. The academy is a private archive, dedicated to preserving the work of lesser-known female writers. They recently obtained a collection of previously undiscovered letters from Viola Vance, the turn-of-the-century poet who's been the main subject of my scholarly research for the past several years. Whoever wins the fellowship will have exclusive access to the letters for twelve months, as well as a flat around the corner from the archive in London.

And it's going to be me.

"Rafael and I would love to have you over for dinner next weekend," Drew says. "He brought a truly obscene amount of wine back from our trip to Paris, and if you don't help us, we'll be forced to drink it all ourselves."

I smile. "Can't have that."

Drew's husband, Rafael, is as vivacious and outgoing as Drew is serious and scholarly. They seem like an odd match, but somehow it works; they've been married for more than twenty years now.

"If you want," Drew says, "you could even bring—"

"Oh God, did you hear?" Our colleague Sandra Kepler slides into the seat next to Drew, her long silver earrings jangling like wind chimes. I lay my palm over my notebook page. Force of habit—I haven't written anything yet besides today's date.

Drew takes a sip of his coffee, shooting me a look. Sandra can be equally histrionic about topics ranging from devastating departmental funding cuts to copier paper jams. But I have a good guess about what might be upsetting her this morning.

"Hear what?" Drew says.

Sandra drops her voice even lower. "Tyler Elkin."

I furrow my brow, like I'm trying to place the name. It would seem more suspicious if I recognized it right away—I only had Tyler for a single one-hundred-student lecture class, and I notoriously don't follow Gorman sports.

"The football player?" Drew says. "What about him?"

"He was found this morning . . ."

Sandra leans toward us, so close I can smell the burnt faculty-lounge coffee on her breath.

"Dead," she says. "At his fraternity house."

That was fast—even in a town this size, where gossip travels at the speed of light, I thought it might take a few more hours for word to circulate.

I widen my eyes, holding my mouth in a little *o* of shock. "How did he—"

"I don't know. The police are still there, I saw the cars on my way to campus."

One of the downsides to committing murders outside the school grounds: the police are called in right away, while the evidence is still fresh, instead of campus security bumbling around the crime scene first. But I already weighed those risks when making my plans. Tyler would have been too difficult to get alone on campus; he always traveled with a pack of other football players and hangers-on.

The police don't worry me much anyway. A few of the Gorman Township officers aren't entirely inept, but they still have only rudimentary forensic training and laughably outdated laboratory equipment. And if a death is written off as a suicide, a random fall, a freak accident, they only look into it as much as they need to file their bureaucratic reports. Some days, I almost miss the challenge of evading the Chicago Police Department.

"Everyone's talking about this Instagram post he made, though." Sandra holds out her phone to show Drew and me the sunrise picture at the top of Tyler's feed. It has a couple thousand comments already.

For the benefit of Sandra and Drew, and anyone else who might be paying attention, I press my mouth closed again and arrange my face in a studied mix of concern and consternation.

"How awful," I say.

"I know." Sandra shakes her head. "He was so young."

"Even younger than that boy last year," Drew says. "The anthropology major?"

Sandra presses her hand to her chest. "Such a shame."

Twenty is young. But if Tyler was old enough to gang-rape a girl and try to get away with it, he was old enough to pay the price. And as for the boy last year, he got off easy, considering what he did to his poor girlfriend. He beat her bloody for months on end, but after I pushed him into the river from the county's most popular suicide-jumping bridge, it took him mere minutes to drown.

I can feel hardness bleeding into my eyes again, so I look down at the table, hoping it appears that I'm overcome with emotion. Then our boss sweeps into the room in a cloud of English Leather cologne, and it's time for a different sort of dissembling.

Dr. Kinnear is more than ten minutes late, even though he called the meeting. He always acts like he's terribly busy, running from one important engagement to the next with hardly a chance to catch his breath. He probably just took too long to jerk off in the shower.

Kinnear takes up his position at the head of the conference table but doesn't sit down yet, bracing his hands against the high back of the chair. He gives us all a weary smile, with a hint of sadness crinkling his eyes behind his tortoiseshell glasses. He must have practiced in the mirror.

"I'm sure you've all heard the tragic news by now," he says.

Everyone nods somberly, myself included. The department's youngest adjunct is actually crying, dabbing at the corners of her eyes with one of the brown paper towels from the bathroom. Kinnear takes a moment to give her a comforting squeeze on the shoulder. Rumor has it they slept together after the last faculty holiday party. At least she's more than half his age, if only by a few years.

The young man seated next to her takes a handkerchief out of his pocket and offers it to her. Dr. Stright—he's Kinnear's favorite, because he's basically a younger version of Kinnear. They even look alike: sandy hair, blue eyes, pretentious eyeglasses, and simpering *everyone-please-like-me* smiles. Now that Kinnear is well into his forties, Stright has the dubious distinction of being the sole good-looking young male professor in the department. He has all his students call him by his first name, like he's one of them. A pathetic ploy, but the undergrads—especially the girls—seem to eat it up with a spoon.

"I don't know any more than you do now, I'm afraid," Kinnear continues, "but I'm sure more details will be made public as soon as the police feel comfortable sharing them."

"So we don't know yet?" Sandra asks. "How he was—"

"From all indications," Kinnear says. "Mr. Elkin took his own life."

Good. If they're at all competent, the police should soon determine that the strychnine he drank came from the box of rat poison sitting right on top of the shelves that served as my hiding place this morning.

I didn't even have to plant the poison. I found it during one of my preparatory stakeouts of the garage, probably left over from some rodent infestation years prior. I took what I needed to doctor Tyler's drink and put the box right back where I found it. Perfect for my purposes: it supports the story that poor Tyler, wracked with guilt, decided to put himself out of his misery with the nearest thing at hand.

"Now," Kinnear continues. "As devastated as I know we all are, we still have business to attend to. Classes will be commencing as scheduled on Tuesday."

There's a low murmur of assent around the table, and everyone less prepared than I am—which is, as usual, the vast majority of my colleagues—readies paper and laptops for the meeting.

Kinnear takes his seat, looking directly at me with a smile. "Scarlett?"

Not *Dr. Clark*. Never that. It was somewhat less infuriating when we were both just faculty. But then he glad-handed his way to the interim department chair position after Dr. McElhaney retired last year, and now he thinks he can treat me like his fucking secretary.

"Yes?" I say, although I already know exactly what he's about to say.

"Would you mind taking notes again? You're so good at it."

I force myself to return his smile and click open my pen.

For the next forty minutes, Kinnear drones on about term dates and lesson plans and the orientation of new students (which ones, I wonder, will he try to fuck this year?). I write as he talks, filling the lines of my notebook with impeccable cursive. I chose my seat at the back corner of the table carefully, so no one can look over my shoulder and see what I'm writing, not even Drew.

Because I'm not just writing meeting notes. I'm jotting down dates, times, and places and events where Kinnear mentions he'll be. Weaknesses I can exploit, ways I might be able to get him alone, humiliate him, make him suffer, make him scream.

Now that Tyler's dead, it's time to turn my attention to my next target. And unlucky for Dr. Kinnear, he's risen to the very top of my list.

4

CARLY

I creep through the darkened room, trying not to make a sound.

My first class on Mondays is early—well, too early for Allison anyway, and I'm doing my best not to wake her. Even asleep, she looks glamorous, her hair splayed artfully across the pillow. I sleep in faded plaid pants and an oversize T-shirt, but Allison wears a satin nightgown to bed every night.

I slip off my pajamas and replace them with a pair of jeans as quickly as possible, then wrangle my bra on without fully removing my shirt. I still feel weird getting dressed with someone else in the room, even if that someone is unconscious. Our schedules seem to be totally opposite, so Allison and I have barely spoken since move-in day. I'm in bed by ten, just like back home, while she stays up way past midnight, studying by the soft glow of the string lights wound around her headboard.

As I'm zipping up my backpack, Allison shifts positions with a soft sigh. Her nightgown slides down to reveal the tops of her breasts, and suddenly it seems as bright as midday in here. I avert my eyes, hurrying toward the door.

It isn't until I'm halfway across the lawn that I realize I forgot to put on my hoodie. I had it laid out on the bed and everything: my favorite one, the black fabric faded to dark gray with too much washing, ragged holes in the sleeves where my thumbs poke through.

I'm still early enough I could go back for it. But I don't want to disturb Allison. I hunch my shoulders so my backpack straps almost touch my earlobes, hugging myself as I continue my trek into the heart of campus. Whitten—or "Whit," as everyone seems to call it—is right at the edge of Gorman, near the woods that border the university's property. It's a bit of a walk to get to class or the dining hall, but at least it's nice and quiet.

Campus is nearly silent at this time of the morning. There are only a few other students in the Oak Grove: a group of boys in running gear stretching on the steps of the library and two girls sharing a steaming cup of coffee on one of the squat red benches lining the path. Everything here seems to be red: the school's official color is crimson, and most of the buildings are the same red brick as Whitten.

This morning's class is the only one in my schedule I haven't attended yet: a Monday writing seminar that didn't meet the first week of the semester because of Labor Day. It's in Miller Hall, the same building as all my other English classes. Miller is red brick like the rest, but with a sloping slate roof and charming arched windowpanes. I've heard other students complain about how musty it is in comparison to the newer construction buildings on campus, but I love it. It feels like an old schoolhouse, right down to the wooden desks with decades of carvings from former students.

I have to wander the halls for a while before I find the right room number, and even then I'm not sure I'm in the right place. This doesn't look like a classroom. The space is tiny, made even smaller by the bookshelves lining the walls and the brown loveseat sitting in the corner, and there aren't even any desks, just a bunch of folding chairs set up in an uneven circle. A few of them are already occupied, though, by a dark-haired girl with purple glasses and a severe pixie cut, a tall guy in an argyle cardigan sweater, and—

Shit. Not only is Allison's boyfriend here, he's smiling at me. Once I make the mistake of meeting his eyes, Wes scoots his bag away from the chair next to him.

I pretend not to notice his gesture of goodwill and take the seat farthest away from him instead (which isn't very far, anyway, in this cramped room). Now I'm overheated, sweat gathering between my shoulder blades as more students fill in the circle. I don't know what I'm so freaked out about; Wes seems like a nice enough guy. And Allison doesn't seem like the type to get jealous if another girl talks to her boyfriend, the way my dad does when my mom speaks to any man who isn't him.

As if someone like Allison could ever be jealous of someone like me.

The sound of furniture legs screeching against the floor startles me to attention. A young man with sandy-blond hair picks up the last empty chair and flips it around so the back faces into the circle.

"I think this is all of us," he says, "so why don't we get started?"

This is the professor? He barely looks older than we are. He sits astride the turned-around chair and pushes his rectangular black glasses higher on his nose.

"Okay!" he says. "Well, welcome, everyone. Those of you who've taken my classes before know I like to keep things casual, so please call me Alex, none of that 'Doctor' or 'Professor' stuff. Some of us are already acquainted, but let's go around the circle and introduce ourselves anyway."

He looks over at Wes. "Mr. Stewart, you want to kick us off?"

"Sure." As he looks up to address the class, Wes's gaze catches on me again. "I'm Wes Stewart, junior, English/theater double major. From Indiana originally."

That means Allison must be from Indiana too. I knew they went to high school together because Allison has their prom photo tacked up above her desk, Wes standing behind her with his hands on the waist of her spangled velvet dress.

The introductions continue around the circle. I barely hear them; I'm too nervous about mine. I rub my sweaty palms against the faded denim on my thighs, but it doesn't seem to help any. When it's finally my turn, there's an awkward pause that's probably only a second or two but feels like an eternity. I swallow and force myself to speak.

"I'm, um, Carly Schiller. I'm a freshman. Also majoring in English."

"You're a freshman?" the girl with the purple glasses asks. She looks to Alex, her mouth twisting sourly. "I thought this was an *advanced* seminar."

"The writing samples in Ms. Schiller's application impressed me so much," Alex says, "I made an exception. We're very glad to have you here, Carly."

His smile is so sincere, I think I might be sick. I try to smile back and mumble something that sounds like *thank you*, but I can barely hear myself over the roar of blood in my ears.

Alex spends the rest of the period going over how the course is structured—required reading, how grades will be assigned, the daily journal we're supposed to keep in addition to our weekly writing assignments. Despite my detailed notes, my head is spinning. Maybe that girl is right; I don't belong here.

After class, I take my time packing my stuff while the other students file out. Wes lingers the longest, hanging in the doorway, and for a second I think he's waiting for me to catch up with him so we can walk out together. But he's just pulling headphones out of his beat-up canvas messenger bag, untangling the cord before plugging them in.

I wait until Wes is gone to approach Alex. "Professor—"

He turns around and hits me with that aggressively friendly smile again.

"'Alex' is fine," he says. "Something I can help you with, Carly?"

"It's just . . ." I trail off, wringing my backpack strap. "Well, *should* I be in this seminar? I didn't know it was for upperclassmen."

Alex sits on the edge of the desk and laces his fingers. "Do you *want* to be here?"

He doesn't seem annoyed, only curious. Like he finds *me* curious. I shouldn't have tried to talk to him. I should have just left, gone straight to the registrar and switched into a different class. *Stupid, so stupid.*

"I'm not sure . . . I mean, I don't want it to be—"

"Because you absolutely deserve to be here," he says. "Your application essay was one of the strongest pieces of writing I've read in years."

I glance down at the toes of my sneakers, my cheeks coloring.

"How about this?" he says. "Let's give it a few weeks. If you're struggling with the assignments, or have any questions—if you need anything at all, I have office hours every Thursday and Friday. Sound good?"

"Okay," I tell him, even though none of this sounds good at all. "Thanks, Prof—"

"Alex."

He pushes off the desk and stands up. The room feels smaller than ever.

"Alex," I say. "Th-thank you."

Tears are already pricking the corners of my eyes as I hurry out into the hallway. I am *not* going to cry, not here where people can see. Back home, I'd go to my bedroom, lock the door, and let this all pour out of me in private. But for all I know, if I go back to Whitten now, Allison will be there, still asleep. Or worse, awake and watching me with those sparkling, too-blue eyes.

The Oak Grove is teeming with students now, and sunlight streams through the trees, turning all that red searing. I wish I could disappear, but all I can do is hunch my shoulders again and duck into the flow of foot traffic. If I can't be happy here, at least I can be invisible. After all, anything's better than going back home.

5

SCARLETT

The sultry music thrumming through my study is almost, but not quite, enough to drown out the Friday night revelries from the student housing down the street. That's the price I pay for living so close to campus.

The house itself is nothing special: a tiny Tudor with sloping floors and a roof that leaks every spring. I bought it when I first took the teaching position at Gorman, and this study is the room that sold me. It's the largest room in the house, with built-in bookshelves lining two entire walls. Now that it's October, the weather is finally cool enough to ignite the gas fireplace set into the corner between them.

As soon as I got home after my last class, I changed out of my work clothes and put on my favorite black satin nightgown and matching robe. My feet are bare, my hair tumbling loose over my shoulders. The glow from the fire turns the copper waves almost crimson.

My application for the Women's Academy fellowship has been all but complete for weeks, but I'm reviewing it one last time prior to submitting—still more than a month ahead of the deadline. I have to make sure every detail is perfect. Getting this fellowship could change everything.

When I hear the front door open, I don't bother looking away from the laptop screen. Only one person other than me has a key to this house, and I've been expecting him.

My graduate assistant, Jasper, takes the steps two at a time but comes to a stop on the study threshold, rapping his knuckles on the open door. I make him wait until I've reached the end of a page before shutting the computer and motioning him inside.

He has to bow his head to avoid hitting it on the doorframe. Jasper's height is unusual even now; back when this house was built, it was practically unheard of. He's carrying a stack of library books in the crook of his slender arm.

"These five came in." He sets the books down one by one on the corner of my desk, adjusting them so all the spines line up. A lock of light brown hair falls over his cheekbone, emphasizing its sharp slant. "But the volume of correspondence you wanted is still in transit. I'll follow up with PALCI if it doesn't arrive next week."

I exhausted the relevant texts in the Gorman library years ago, so now most of my research materials have to be shipped in via interlibrary loan. Even then, it's difficult to get hold of what I need. But if all goes according to plan, I won't have to content myself with the Pennsylvania academic library system's paltry selection for much longer. I'll be able to go right to the source, review the primary materials. The Women's Academy archive has boxes full of actual letters between Viola and her contemporaries, in their own handwriting.

It's enough to make me salivate—but it's not the only reason I'm so keen to win the fellowship and spend a year in London. I need to get out of Gorman, at least for a while.

Not that there aren't enough deserving men to murder here. That's the problem: there are plenty, but to avoid attracting attention to myself in a town as small as this one, I have to sit on my hands for months at a stretch, wait until sufficient time has passed between deaths. Watch them keep hurting people without consequence, until the time is right.

When I was in graduate school in Chicago, I could probably have killed a man every other week and gotten away with it. London is three times larger. It would make the perfect hunting ground.

Jasper finishes straightening the books and looks at me. The flickering firelight turns his green eyes darker. "Will there be anything else tonight, Dr. Clark?"

Holding his gaze, I push my chair back from the desk and part my legs. The satin slides away from my skin like water.

Every time I fuck Jasper, I feel a pang of guilt over my hypocrisy. But I'm nothing like Kinnear. Jasper is a grown man, less than a decade younger than I am, not a wide-eyed teenager who doesn't know any better.

Besides, back when our affair started, he wasn't even working for me. During the first year of his PhD, he was Kinnear's assistant; after Kinnear took the interim chair position, Jasper was passed along to another professor—and he made sure it would be me. I had my doubts about the arrangement, but he's proven himself professional and discreet thus far. Besides, this is the closest approximation of a relationship I can risk, given my secret.

By the time we're done, Jasper's careful stack of books has toppled across the desktop. He reaches over to right the pile, lining it up perfectly again, then gathers my robe from the floor and hands it to me.

"I'll see you tomorrow morning," he says as he's tucking his shirt back in.

"Tomorrow's Saturday."

The classes Jasper TAs for me meet Mondays, Wednesdays, and Fridays, and we often see each other on Friday nights, but rarely later in the weekend. I have no idea what he does when we're not together. I figure it's not fair of me to ask. After all, he's entirely in the dark about my extracurricular activities.

"The meeting." He looks at me again. "Haven't you checked your email?"

I tie the sash of the robe closed. "You distracted me."

"Sorry." He grins and pulls his cell phone out of his back pocket, showing me the calendar invite on the screen.

An emergency all-staff meeting, Saturday at 11:00 a.m.

"I bet it's because of that whole thing with Tyler Elkin. Figures they only give a damn once it's the king of the jocks who offs himself." Jasper scoffs, combing his hair into place with one smooth pass of his long fingers. "*If* that's even what happened."

A cold fist of dread clenches in my chest. "The police said—"

"Oh, I know," he says. "I just find it hard to believe that guy would kill himself. He seemed like too much of a selfish prick to me."

He grins at me again, showing more than a hint of wicked teeth. I've always found him more pretty than handsome, but it's a harsh beauty. Slightly feral.

I used to suspect Jasper might be like me. There's a coldness in his eyes sometimes, a ruthless focus I recognize. But after spending so much time with him, I've come to the conclusion it's all words with him—cruel comments, gallows humor. He could never do the things I do. Still, he understands me better than any other man I've met. I can't show Jasper everything, but at least I don't have to pretend to be nice or sweet or accommodating when I'm with him. He's attracted to my cruelty.

"So I'll see you at the staff meeting?" he asks.

I nod, tapping my fingernails on the stack of library books. "Yes. Thank you for your assistance as always, Mr. Prior."

"My pleasure, Professor."

He leans in to kiss me. I tilt my head just in time, so his lips only catch the corner of mine. It's been a while since he's tried that; at least he didn't make another attempt to sleep over.

As soon as he's gone, I log in to my email so I can read the calendar invite for myself. But there are few details beyond what I saw on Jasper's phone. All Gorman faculty and staff are required to attend.

I tug the robe's sash even tighter, until it digs into my waist. I try to resume my review of the fellowship application, but my mind is racing. Even the slow beat of the music and the crackle of the fire are too much stimulation now. I get up and turn them both off, then pace back and forth across the rug, trying to impose some order on my thoughts.

But I don't have enough information to devise a plan. And I won't—not until the meeting tomorrow. I tap my fingertip at the corner of my mouth, the spot where Jasper kissed me.

I fucking hate surprises.

6

CARLY

"Are you making friends?"

It's a full month into the semester, and this is still my mom's first question when she calls me—which she does every other day, at minimum. This morning, she sounds bright and unhurried, so my father must not be home. Though she seems a little tired too, a rasp in the back of her throat. I bet they were up late again, arguing. I'm not going to ask. I'm *not*.

"I've been hanging out with a few other freshman girls in my dorm," I tell her. This is technically true, though the only major social event I've attended with them was a candlelight vigil for some student I've never met. Some of the other girls were crying, even though they couldn't have known the guy either, since he died before the semester started. I guess I can understand why: it's strange when someone our age dies. It makes me feel young and ancient at the same time.

"That's great, sweetie. I know how hard making friends can be for you."

I burrow into the bedcovers, pressing the phone harder to my ear, like that can somehow close the miles between us. A month ago, I wanted nothing more than to get out of my parents' house and never go back, but now, hearing my mom's voice provokes pangs of homesickness so sharp they're like needles twisting in my stomach. If only my father would move out again. I've lost count of how many times he's left. The first time, my mom sobbed for days, but I was so relieved.

I cried when he moved back in.

"So how are classes going?" she asks. "You like your professors?"

I immediately think of Alex—his infectious smile, how he adjusts his glasses as he speaks, the intense focus on his face when he listens. He's the only professor who's paid me any attention, besides writing *Excellent Work* in blue ballpoint at the top of my papers. Getting good grades is easy for me; it's everything else that's a struggle.

"My professors are okay," I say.

I hear a soft creaking sound on the other end of the line, and I picture her sitting in her blue rocking chair in the den, one foot tucked underneath her, the other pushing rhythmically off the flowery rug. The den is windowless, but she's decorated it with artificial bouquets and paintings of scenic landscapes. It's the one room of the house in which my father rarely sets foot, so it's our favorite.

She's waiting for me to elaborate, share more about which professors I like and why, but the words stick in my throat. I want to be convincing. I want her to think I'm happy, having the time of my life at college. I definitely don't want her to worry about me.

"What about your roommate? Are you two getting along all right?"

As if on cue, Allison comes through the door. She's fresh out of her post-workout shower, steam rising from her skin.

"Yeah, she's . . ." I'm trying my best not to stare, but it gets even harder when Allison whips off her towel and bends over to wrap her hair up in it. "We're . . ."

"What's wrong, honey?"

I drag my eyes back to the wrinkled gray comforter over my lap. "Nothing. I'm fine. I should probably get going, though. Talk to you soon?"

"Okay. Your father and I send our love!"

"Love you," I mumble, then end the call.

Allison is wearing a bra and panties now but nothing else. She thumbs through the dresses stuffed in her side of the closet. She's got quite an assortment of them, in every color of the rainbow, while my half of the wardrobe is all black and gray with the occasional drab olive green.

"Was that your mom?" she asks.

"Uh, yeah." I pass the phone back and forth between my hands, just to have something to do with them.

Allison turns around with a smile, holding up a sweater dress striped with different shades of purple. "It's so nice that you guys are close. Hey, I didn't wake you up last night, did I?"

"No," I tell her. "I'm a pretty deep sleeper, so . . ."

A complete lie. Even as a child, I woke up multiple times a night with my heart pounding, my shoulders tight, startled by the slightest sound. When she came in last night sometime between midnight and dawn, I only pretended to be asleep, lying very still and keeping my breathing low and steady. I don't know where she goes when she stays out so late. Probably to see her boyfriend—though she hasn't brought Wes here again. I just see him—and avoid talking to him—every week in writing class.

"Okay, good," she says, slipping the dress over her head. It looked baggy on the hanger, but the fabric clings to her body. "So what are you up to today?"

"Um . . ." I start, but then I'm briefly mesmerized by the sight of her wet hair spilling over her shoulders as she tugs the towel loose. This is the most she's ever spoken to me. "Probably just homework."

"All day?" Her eyes widen with theatrical alarm. "On a *Saturday*?"

"I have to write a story. For this writing seminar I'm taking."

"Oh, with that young guy professor, right?"

I nod. Allison sighs, picking up her hairbrush from the dresser.

"He's so gorgeous," she says. "How the hell do you concentrate in class?"

Even if Alex is young for a professor, he's way too old for me. The other girls in the English department talk about him like he's a movie star, and they're all obsessed with getting into his honors fiction intensive next semester. I'm just trying to survive this class.

"I wish I'd had him for my freshman lit requirement," Allison says. "I got stuck with this female professor instead—she was *so mean*, oh my God."

She laughs, and I force myself to laugh too, but suspicion worms through me. I don't understand why she's being so friendly all of a sudden. Not that she's been *un*friendly before now, but she's pretty much ignored me beyond saying *good night* and *have a good day* if we happened to be awake at the same time.

I don't know how to do this: make friends, talk to girls, talk to anyone my age really. In high school, kids only acknowledged my existence if they wanted something, like help studying for their AP English final.

But I should at least try. Allison is making an effort, so I can too.

"Actually," I say. "Your boyfriend is in the writing seminar with me."

Allison's brow furrows in confusion. Shit. I said something wrong.

"My boyfriend?" she asks.

Maybe she has more than one, so I need to be more specific. Maybe she and Wes have an open relationship and she's sleeping with lots of other guys. She's so sophisticated. I bet she's only talking to me because she feels sorry for me.

"Yeah," I say. "Wes?"

Allison bursts into laughter, and I want to die. She's making fun of me. *I knew it.*

She drops onto the edge of my bed, falling back onto the mattress, the ribbed material of her dress stretching over the slight softness of her waist. "Oh my God, I'm going to tell him you said that."

"Sorry." My face must be flaming. "I—I mean, I thought— I didn't mean to—"

"Oh, no!" Allison sits up again and reaches for my hands. "No, it's just—Wes is *not* my boyfriend. He's more like my brother. We've known each other forever. Besides—"

She leans closer, amusement still shimmering in her eyes.

"I'm kind of over dating boys at the moment."

7

SCARLETT

The emergency staff meeting is held at the theater building, Riffenburg Hall, since it's the one place on campus with enough seating to accommodate the entire faculty and staff. Well, aside from the football stadium, but I suppose that might seem a bit disrespectful, given the circumstances.

Even though I'm a full fifteen minutes early, most of the seats in the auditorium are already taken, the low buzz of voices filling the space like a swarm of hornets. I spot a single open chair near the front and start moving toward it. Someone touches me on the elbow, and I spin around, face already sharpened into a glare.

It's Jasper. He doesn't even flinch at the vicious expression on my face.

"Hey," he says. "I saved you a seat."

I shrug my elbow out of his grip. We've talked about this—him acting too familiar in public.

He motions toward the center section, a few rows back, where his leather satchel and houndstooth coat are draped over two adjacent chairs. Drew, Sandra, Stright, and several other members of the English faculty are in the same row, though Kinnear is strangely absent.

Drew waves to me, holding a flyer printed on garish green paper. There's one waiting on my seat too, with the clasped-hands logo of the campus counseling center and big block letters spelling out *SUICIDE PREVENTION: A Community Effort*.

So Jasper was right: this is about Tyler Elkin. Perhaps I've been worried for nothing. Whatever else this meeting means, it's a clear indication his death has been accepted as a suicide, publicly and officially. Which means no one will be looking for his killer.

Kinnear appears, but not in the audience with the rest of us. He strides onto the stage, wearing one of his seemingly endless collection of scarves wound around his neck in a way he probably considers rakish. I let my mind wander again to one of my favorite fantasies: tugging the silk so tight around his neck his eyeballs pop like pimples.

I haven't strangled someone in ages. I save certain methods for when it's personal, which it so rarely is these days. Most of my victims are like Tyler: men to whom I have only the most tenuous connections. Murdering someone in my social or professional circle requires much more care, precaution. Finesse. I've wanted to kill Kinnear for years, but I've forced myself to hold off: for the right opportunity, for the perfect time. If I get the fellowship, though, I'll be leaving Gorman in a few months, so time is running out.

A woman joins Kinnear onstage, taking up a position a few feet away from him. She's gorgeous, wearing an impeccably tailored pencil skirt and a satin blouse the same shade of red as her lipstick. Dr. Samina Pierce, the head of the psychology department.

I've seen Samina around campus—she's impossible to miss—but it's rare to find her in the same room as Kinnear, despite the psych and English departments both being headquartered in Miller Hall. Rumor has it that she and Kinnear used to be married—though what a woman like her could possibly see in him is beyond me.

Kinnear taps the microphone. The crowd falls silent.

"Dean Whitmyre sends his apologies," Kinnear begins. "He wanted to be here with you today to discuss this important new campus initiative. But I hope I'll be an able substitute."

I guess all his sucking up is really paying off. Shouldn't be long now until his interim chairship turns permanent. That position should belong to Drew. He's more qualified than Kinnear by every conceivable measure, and he has years of seniority. But Drew refuses to engage in the political games and petty sabotages that are Kinnear's specialty.

Last year, I had everything in order for my tenure application—until Kinnear took my spot on the committee I needed to complete my service requirement, then barely bothered to show up for the meetings. Meanwhile, Dr. Stright, despite being hired three semesters later than me, sailed through the tenure process, thanks to Kinnear's full-throated recommendation. Men like them are the ones who really get away with murder.

"As you all know," Kinnear says, "Gorman lost one of its own recently. Tyler Elkin was amongst our best and brightest, and he was taken from us far too soon."

Jasper leans in to whisper in my ear. "Well, maybe not our *brightest* . . ."

Drew glances over at us. I shift in my seat, crossing my legs to put some additional space between me and Jasper, and pretend to give Kinnear's speech my rapt attention.

"—prevention begins with each and every one of us, but we can't do it alone. To that end, Gorman University is establishing its first-ever suicide prevention task force."

Murmurs thread through the crowd. The past few years have seen a spate of suicides—not all my doing—and the school's leadership has always done their best to sweep them under the rug before word got to Gorman's wealthy alumni network. It's the same *nothing to see here* approach they take with student sexual assault reports. Their obsession with protecting the university's reputation has allowed plenty of misdeeds (my own included) to go unpunished, while the administration keeps waving their hands, pretending everything is fine.

Until now, apparently.

"I'm pleased to announce that the task force will be headed up by Dr. Samina Pierce." Kinnear motions to her. "Dr. Pierce, would you like to say a few words?"

Kinnear doesn't step out of the way quite fast enough, and Samina's sleeve brushes against his as she takes her place behind the microphone. I could swear I saw her shudder when they touched, but she recovers her professional poise quickly.

"Thank you, Dr. Kinnear," she says. She still speaks with a trace of her native British accent. "And thanks to all of you for taking the time to join us on a Saturday."

The agenda she outlines for the task force all seems pretty standard: increased staff at the counseling center, new suicide prevention training protocols for the existing on-campus crisis center hotline, workshops for faculty and staff to help them identify and reach out to students who might be struggling with depression or other mental health disorders.

"Finally," she says, "we'll be performing a comprehensive investigation of all deaths by suicide that have occurred on the Gorman campus over the past decade."

My chest seizes. *A comprehensive investigation . . .*

Only a fraction of my kills would be included in the campus suicide statistics. Others I've done well outside the school grounds, or made to look like accidental rather than self-inflicted deaths. Overdoses, car accidents, even an electrocution for one special target.

"I've already begun assembling a cross-departmental team to perform hands-on analysis and conduct interviews with selected faculty and students," Pierce continues. "We'll also be building a database to map commonalities in the deaths and identify personal or environmental risk factors we may be able to mitigate."

I always go to great lengths to avoid creating patterns or leaving forensic red flags, but my most useful accomplice is the negligence of law enforcement.

Samina Pierce, however, seems anything but negligent.

She steps back from the microphone, clearly meaning to end the meeting. But Kinnear seizes the opportunity to take over again. "If anyone has any questions or concerns, I'd be happy to stick around and chat—unless you have somewhere to be, Mina?"

She purses her lips but nods, acquiescing. Most of the audience heads for the exit, but a few people, including Drew and Sandra, approach the stage.

Jasper brushes his copy of the suicide prevention flyer onto the floor, then dons his coat. "You want to get some coffee?" he asks. "Discuss next week's lesson plans?"

Next week's lesson plans have been locked in for months now. He's not even attempting to be subtle.

"Another time," I say, and then I head toward the stage steps.

Samina Pierce is even more beautiful close-up, her dark hair and olive skin lustrous despite the harsh lighting. A small crowd has gathered now, but Sandra and Kinnear are doing most of the talking, something about poetry writing as a therapeutic modality for suicidal students. As soon as I step onto the stage, Samina's eyes go straight to me.

Drew steps back to include me in the circle. "Dr. Pierce, do you know—"

"Dr. Scarlett Clark," she says, extending her hand for me to shake. Her grip is firmer than I expect, but her skin is rose-petal soft. "Yes, of course."

She's clearly someone on whom I should keep a very close watch. But a task force isn't the police. They're not looking for a culprit, only for data patterns, and data can be manipulated.

Just like people.

8

CARLY

I stay at the library until dark. That way, by the time I go back to our room, Allison should be long gone, off doing whatever normal college students do on Saturday night.

Instead, I arrive to find her sitting cross-legged on my bed.

"Hey," she says. Her own bed is stripped bare. Maybe she's doing laundry?

I stop, letting my backpack straps slide down my arms. "Hey."

She's dressed more casually than I've ever seen her, in leggings and a Gorman sweatshirt with the neck cut so it hangs off her shoulders, but she's wearing her usual dramatic makeup: red lipstick, perfect feline flicks of eyeliner. She leans back on her hands, letting her feet dangle off the edge of my bed. "What are you up to tonight?"

I open my mouth to respond, but she puts her palm up before I get a word out.

"Reading is *not* an acceptable answer." She springs up, offering me her hand like she's a gentleman helping a lady out of a carriage. "Come on, I want to show you something."

A nasty voice whispers in the back of my mind: *It's a trick. She's mocking you.* But Allison doesn't seem like a mean person. She doesn't seem nice either, she seems . . . confident, I guess. Maybe I'd be that way too, if I looked like her.

I take her hand, and she smiles wider, threading our fingers together as she leads me out of our room and toward the window at the far end of the hall. She tugs at the pane until it raises, with a screech so loud it sets my teeth on edge.

"Come on," she says again. Then she climbs over the sill, trying to tug me along with her, out onto the zigzagging fire escape bolted to the side of the building.

I freeze, pulling back on her arm. "Are we even allowed to—"

"You sound like Wes," Allison says with a wink. "It's fine, I come up here all the time." She climbs a few steps, the black metal creaking ominously under her weight, then stops and looks down at me again. "Just don't tell Samantha."

Our RA mostly ignores us in favor of her on-again, off-again boyfriend, but I do *not* want to get on her bad side. But I don't want Allison to think I'm some scared little girl either, so I take a deep breath and climb out the window after her.

By the time we get to the roof, my knuckles are pale and throbbing from gripping the railing so hard, but after the rickety fire escape, the flat expanse feels like safety. It's bright and surprisingly warm up here, everything cast in a soft white glow from the strings of lights looped around the crumbling brick chimney—the same kind Allison has by her bed.

"Since you never want to go out," Allison says, "I figured I'd bring the party to you."

Her laptop sits a few feet away at the base of the chimney, all the blankets and pillows from her bed strewn in front of it. There are bowls with snacks set out too—popcorn, mini Oreos, small cubes of cheddar cheese—and a four-pack of Orangina.

She planned all of this. For me.

But why? Surely she has more than enough friends already, and way better things to do on a Saturday night.

"Sit down." She takes my hand again, leading me toward the blanket nest. "You can pick the movie."

I don't understand any of this. But it would be rude to refuse when she's gone to so much trouble. I sit on one of the pillows, and Allison stretches out beside me on her stomach. While I look through her extensive movie collection, she kicks her feet idly in the air, tossing pieces of popcorn into her mouth one by one. Her hair slides over her shoulders, the ends brushing my knee.

My eye catches on one title: *Eternal Sunshine of the Spotless Mind*. I've never seen it, but I know the Alexander Pope poem the title must come from. *Eternal sunshine of the spotless mind! Each pray'r accepted, and each wish resign'd.*

"Oh, I'm so obsessed with that one!" Allison says. "Isn't it brilliant?"

"I've never seen it," I admit.

She sits up. "*What?* Okay, we need to fix that immediately."

Allison starts the movie, adjusting the laptop screen so we can both see it, then reclines against the stacked pillows. I try to follow the action—a man walking on a snow-covered beach before boarding a train, a woman with bright blue hair chatting him up—but I'm too distracted by Allison's proximity. She keeps picking up the bowls and passing them to me, settling back down even closer than she was before.

"I want to be Clementine for Halloween," Allison says. "What do you think, could I pull off the blue?"

She runs her fingers through her hair, letting the long blond strands fan out over the pillows. I imagine her with hair like the woman in the movie, the way it would set off the afternoon-sky color of her eyes and the creaminess of her skin.

"Yeah," I say. "You'd look—"

"Oh, wait, this is my favorite line!"

She sits up again, knocking into the popcorn bowl. As the actress on screen speaks, Allison matches her words—the same pacing, diction, everything. It sends a strange little chill up my spine.

"'I'm a vindictive little bitch, truth be told.'"

She shoots me a sly look, and I want to dart my eyes away, retreat into myself, but this time I don't. I look her right in the eye and smile back.

"Thanks for doing all this," I say.

"My pleasure." She twists off the top of an Orangina bottle, taking a sip and then offering it to me. Her lipstick stains the glass. "I should be thanking *you*. You're helping me keep my mind off the audition I just had."

I take the bottle but don't drink. "Audition? For what?"

"For *Cabaret*. The theater department's doing it later this semester."

"What part did you try out for?" I ask, even though her response won't mean a thing to me. I've heard of *Cabaret* but I don't know much about it—I think it has something to do with Nazis?

"Sally Bowles," Allison says. "I want it so bad. I practiced my audition piece all summer." She flings her arms back over the pillows with a dramatic groan. "But I'm afraid I fucked it all up. If I have to watch some other girl play her while I dance around in the background . . . Like I would actually kill for this part. I would end a life."

I'm not sure how to respond to that. "When do you find out?"

"Monday. It's going to be a very long weekend." She turns to look at me, propping her head on her hand. "You ever feel so anxious it's like your stomach is trying to eat itself?"

I nod. *Yes. Every day.*

"I bet you were amazing," I tell her. "I bet you'll get it."

The wind picks up, whipping my hair into my face. I reach to smooth it down, but Allison beats me to it, tucking it behind my ear.

"You're sweet," she says.

That's the last thing I am. But she doesn't have to know that.

Allison turns onto her back again, and I stretch out too, my legs parallel to hers. We spend the rest of the movie that way, hands brushing as we reach into the snack bowls at the same time. She keeps pointing out favorite moments in the film, little observations I would never have picked up on.

By the time the credits roll, Allison has fallen asleep, her head lolling against my shoulder. The screen switches back to the movie's cover image—Clementine and Joel lying on the frozen lake, Clem's bright hair spread out on the ice like a lick of flame.

I think about turning off the computer, heading to bed. But I don't want to wake Allison. So I lie there, in the blue glow of the screen, and listen to her breathing. It's soothing at first—I feel warm and content, truly *happy* in a way I haven't in years.

But it's not long before the panic creeps in again. My throat tightening, my heart throbbing with the suspicion that happiness must be a trick, a trap, a rug about to be pulled out from under me, and any second now I'm going to fall.

9

SCARLETT

Samina Pierce wastes no time.

Mere hours after I introduced myself at the emergency faculty meeting, she reached out to schedule an appointment for the very next day so we could speak further about my offer to assist the task force. When I arrive at her office on Sunday evening, I find that she's already transformed the space into a command center. University records are stacked in neat, color-coded piles on her desk, and the whiteboard on the wall is covered with an elaborate web of photos and documents.

She ushers me inside, then asks if I'd like some tea. "I only have the caffeinated stuff, I'm afraid," she says.

"No, thank you. I'd be up all night."

"I think I've rendered myself immune." She smiles. "I could drink a whole pot at midnight and still sleep like a baby!"

Samina seems just as put-together and well rested now, at the end of what must have been a hectic day, as she did first thing on Saturday morning. Everything about her, from her glossy hair to her shiny leather pumps, seems entirely too glamorous for this cramped and dingy office space—too glamorous for Gorman in general, honestly.

"Be right back," she says. "Make yourself comfortable."

As soon as she leaves, I step closer to the whiteboard, studying the years of campus suicides she's connected with red lines of dry-erase marker. They're not all mine, of course. But the ones that are stand out to me like they're illuminated with spotlights. I remember every man I've killed, in vivid detail. His name, his crimes. His last words, if I allowed him to have any.

This is the kind of gruesome exhibition movies and television shows seem to think every serial killer has in their basement. I would never be foolish enough to put my crimes on display. I don't keep records or trophies. But there is something strangely satisfying about seeing it all laid out like this, since someone else has done it.

"Professor Clark?"

My favorite student, Mikayla Atwell, stands in the doorway, watching me. Without realizing, I've touched one of the lines on the board, smearing red marker on my fingertips.

"Ms. Atwell." I brush my stained fingers off on my black skirt. "What are you doing here?"

Mikayla shrugs, rebalancing the stack of file folders she's carrying. "The task force needed volunteers who know SQL."

Teaching herself to code is one of Mikayla's numerous extracurricular activities. She's a sophomore at Gorman and already taking my most advanced Shakespeare course. The first class session, the upperclassmen underestimated her, assuming she was as innocent as her wide brown eyes and halo of natural hair make her look. Then she argued so fiercely about the sexual agency of Juliet some of the seniors looked like they wanted to hide under their desks.

"It's such an honor to get to work with Dr. Pierce," Mikayla says. "She's brilliant."

"Am I really?"

Samina has reappeared, one dark eyebrow canted with amusement as she dunks a bag of jasmine tea in her steaming cup. Mikayla's cheeks color a little, and she busies herself distributing the folders amongst the various stacks on Samina's desk.

"You can head home for the evening, Ms. Atwell," Samina says. "Thank you for all your hard work today."

I smile at Mikayla on her way to the door. "See you in class."

Samina shuts the door, then sits behind the desk. There's a cashmere scarf draped over the chair back, covering up the utilitarian black mesh.

"She's taking one of your classes?" Samina asks.

I nod. "I'm her academic advisor too. Her freshman year, she was assigned to Uhler, but—"

"He's an *idiot*," Samina says, setting the teacup down on a matching saucer. I couldn't agree more—though I wouldn't say it out loud to a colleague, except maybe Drew. "I'm glad she's got someone competent looking out for her. Smart as a whip, isn't she?"

"She is that." I sit in the spindly wooden chair across from the desk, crossing my legs. "Thank you for making the time to meet with me so quickly, Samina."

"Call me Mina, please." The cordiality of her words doesn't match the unsettling directness in her eyes. "I was so pleased you offered to assist with our work, because I was going to reach out to you anyway."

"Oh, really?" I brace my hands on my knee. "Why is that?"

"Tyler Elkin." She pulls a notebook into the circle of lamplight at the center of her desk. "He was your student too, right? Introduction to English Literature, last spring?"

I try to get a look at what else is written on the notebook page, but her handwriting is too small to read from this distance, even more precise than my own. "Yes, that's right."

Samina picks up the teacup again and settles back. "What did you think of him?"

I can't help feeling like I'm being psychoanalyzed. She's never been a practicing psychologist—according to her CV, she went

straight from a PhD program at Penn to teaching at Gorman alongside her then husband, Kinnear—but she would have been good at
it. She swirls the tea bag meditatively through the hot water.

I lean back in my chair too. "He wasn't the best student by any
means. But he was . . ." *An asshole. A rapist. A fucking monster who
deserved exactly what I—* "Well, he was so young."

For an excruciatingly long moment, Samina says nothing. Then
she leans forward, propping her elbows on the desk. "You can stop
bullshitting me."

My mouth goes dry, and my whole body stiffens. She can't possibly know what I am, what I've done, but whatever she sees when
she looks at me, it's more than I want her to.

"Tyler was a *terrible* student." She holds my gaze for a moment
longer, before puncturing the tension with a short laugh. "All his
professors hated him—whether or not they want to admit it."

I want to laugh too, but I'm afraid the sound will come out
harsh. Crazed. Still, a small portion of the tension seeps out of my
shoulders.

"You've talked to his other professors?" I ask.

"I'm still working my way through the list." She taps her pen
against the Gorman seal at the top of the notebook page. "But so far
they've all said similar things: Tyler was a slacker, rarely showed up
to class or completed his assignments. Didn't take well to criticism
or consequences."

That certainly matched my experience. Tyler believed he could
do whatever he wanted and get away with it. His entire life taught
him that he was special, that consequences didn't apply, that he'd
pass with flying colors even if he turned in his midterm two weeks
late. Even in his final moments, I doubt he learned his lesson. But I
didn't kill him to teach him a lesson; I killed him to carve him out
of this world like a tumor. And I'd do it again.

"Listen." Samina flips the notebook shut. "I don't care about
Tyler Elkin any more than I'm guessing you do. Gorman's probably

a better place without him—though I suppose fans of the football team may disagree."

I know I should at least attempt to look shocked. But it's as if she's reading my thoughts out loud.

"But at the same time," Samina continues, "I find him fascinating."

"And why is that?" Though I spend an inordinate amount of my time thinking about them, there's nothing fascinating about boys like Tyler Elkin. They're boring, as common as rats and equally disgusting.

"He's an outlier. Most of the other suicides on campus, the person had a documented history of mental illness or substance abuse or both. But Tyler . . ." She trails off, clicking her fingernails against the crimson cover of the notebook. "He doesn't fit the pattern."

She hasn't asked a question, but she's looking at me as though she expects an answer.

"Well," I say. "I guess it goes to show: You can never tell what someone's like just by looking at them."

"I suppose you're right," she says. "But the way he died is odd too. Young, athletic men like Tyler, they usually choose a more violent, sudden method of suicide. Self-inflicted gunshot, that sort of thing."

She's correct, statistically speaking. But I don't use guns. I tried faking a suicide by firearm once in Chicago, and it was more difficult than I expected to get the angle right. That ended up being my only kill to ever attract FBI attention. The death was eventually ruled a gang-related killing, but I decided never to risk it again. There are so many less messy ways to kill a man.

"Tyler sounded awfully guilty in that final Instagram post," I say. "Maybe the suffering was the point."

Samina meets my eyes again—an intense, weighted look, loaded as a weapon—and all I can think is: *How did a woman like this put up with Kinnear for even a second?*

Maybe she's changed since they were married. Maybe putting up with him was the thing that changed her.

This investigation, comprehensive or not, doesn't have to change anything for me. Who knows, working with Samina could even prove useful to my plans for Kinnear.

If anyone has reason to hate the man even more than I do, it's his ex-wife.

10

CARLY

"I can't look."

Allison turns to me. We're outside the theater department's lounge, which they call the green room even though it's just a bunch of musty brown furniture. The *Cabaret* cast list was posted beside the door a few minutes ago, and it's already drawn a swarm of students, like flies on rotting fruit.

She grabs my hand. "Will you do it for me?"

My breath catches. I should be on my way to my afternoon poetry class right now, but Allison begged me to come for the cast list unveiling. She's been a nervous wreck all day. She changed her outfit about six times this morning, and at lunchtime, after claiming she was too nervous to eat anything, she proceeded to polish off most of Wes's Cool Ranch Doritos. He's here too, standing on her other side, but it's me she wants with her at the moment of truth.

It feels like we've been friends for much longer than a day and a half. After the rooftop movie night, she dragged me to brunch with Wes and a bunch of their theater friends. Someone smuggled a tray full of doughnuts out of the cafeteria, and we laid out on the grass in the Oak Grove and gorged until the ants got into them.

Even when we were with all of Allison's friends, somehow it still felt like it was just the two of us. And not just because Allison was the only one who really talked to me. She kept touching me too, playing with my hair, tracing her fingers over my wrist like she was trying to draw something.

She takes ahold of my wrist again now and digs her teeth into her bottom lip. "Please?"

"Of course," I say. "I'll look."

The initial crowd around the cast list has started to thin out, but I still have to push through a clump of bodies to get close enough to read the tiny print. Some of the people we pass look positively ecstatic; others are doing a poor job of hiding the tears brimming in their eyes. I don't quite understand why they care so much—but if Allison cares, I care too.

Allison slides her hand down to clasp mine. She has her head bowed and her eyes shut, waiting for me to tell her her fate.

I give her hand a comforting squeeze. Then I look at the list.

Her name is right at the top. "'Allison Hadley,'" I read. "'Sally Bowles.'"

Allison tenses, clenching my hand so hard it almost hurts. "Are you serious? Don't fuck with me."

"She's not," Wes says over my shoulder, crunching on another bag of chips. I hadn't even noticed he followed us. "Look."

He points at the list. Allison opens her eyes and reads it for herself.

"Oh my God." She squeals and claps. "Oh my *God*!"

She's jumping up and down now, yanking on my arm—which *does* actually hurt, but I don't want to dampen her excitement by complaining.

"Congratulations!" I say.

She flings her arms around my neck and kisses me on the cheek. It takes a second for me to hug her back, and by then she's already letting go of me, turning to Wes to do the exact same thing. When she grabs another girl passing by—a petite redhead wearing a *Little Shop of Horrors* T-shirt—and plants a celebratory peck on her too, my excitement starts to seep away.

Wes gives Allison a friendly little jab on the shoulder. "You're gonna be great, Allie."

I know a little more about the show since Allison's been talking my ear off about it, but she still loses me when she starts chattering about dance numbers she can't wait to do, who's playing the other characters, and which Broadway revival cast was better. I stand silent and watch her, the effervescent pop of her gestures, and suddenly realize my cheeks are sore. I've been grinning like an idiot, witnessing how happy she is.

A tall boy with dark hair saunters down the hallway, and as soon as she sees him, Allison's whole posture changes, drawing up taller, shoulders back so her chest sticks out.

"Hey, Bash." There's a syrupy sweetness in her voice I've never heard before. It makes my stomach turn.

"Hey," the boy says. He clearly isn't sure enough of Allison's name to use it.

"Congratulations!" Allison points at his name below hers on the cast list. Sebastian Waller, the Emcee.

He smiles—kind of blankly, though. Just being polite. Or maybe his eyes are always blank like that, distant and half asleep. Allison grins back, tilting her head coquettishly, tucking a strand of hair behind her ear. Wes doesn't acknowledge him at all, too busy sifting through the remnants in the bottom of his Doritos bag.

As soon as Bash has meandered out of earshot, Allison sighs dramatically. "Isn't he so fucking *gorgeous?*"

He's good-looking, I guess. But skinny, all sharp angles, and his hair is too long, the curls falling sloppily over his forehead. Everything about him seems affected, from the loping way he walks to the leather cord wound around his wrist to the artfully ripped jeans that look tight enough to cut off his circulation.

Wes shakes his head, crushing the empty bag in his fist. "I will never understand what all of you see in that guy."

Allison playfully bumps Wes's glasses higher on his nose. "You need your vision checked, babe."

Wes tosses the bag into the nearest trash can, then cleans off his glasses where Allison smudged them. I can't tell if he's mad or not. I'm just feeling stupid. Of course Allison would have a crush on a guy like that. Of *course*.

I look over at her with what I hope is a teasing smile. "I thought you said you were over dating boys."

Allison and Wes are both silent. *Shit, did I go too far?* I was trying to make a joke. But maybe it was supposed to be a secret between us, and now I've broken her trust, and—

"I am." Allison leans in, right next to my ear, dropping her voice into a sultrier register. "But Bash is a *man*. This is going to be my year, I know it."

"Your year for what?" I ask.

Wes is shaking his head again, exasperated. He must have heard this all before.

"The year he finally notices me," Allison says. "No way he can keep ignoring me when we're dancing together in our underwear."

Since I've never seen *Cabaret*, the image playing in my head now is of Allison onstage in the underwear she wears every day: black cotton panties and a lace bra sheer enough to show her nipples. I lower my head, hoping the frizzy curtain of my hair will hide my blush.

But there's no hiding from Allison. She giggles and brushes my hair back. "You're so cute when you're scandalized."

I pick up my backpack off the floor, ignoring the prickling of heat spreading across my chest. "I should get to class."

"*Or* . . ." A sly smile spreads across Allison's face. "We could ditch and go hang out down by the river."

"I shouldn't." I'm already behind on my classwork after spending most of the weekend with Allison.

"Come on, it's a gorgeous day!" She tugs on my backpack strap, her fingertips brushing the bare skin at my neckline. "Who knows how many of these we have left before winter?"

I've never ditched class before in my life. But I'm already learning that it's basically impossible to say no to Allison.

"Okay," I say. "Just this once."

Allison squeals with delight. For a second I think she's going to hug me again, but she just claps her hands together, a wicked grin lighting up her face.

"I have an hour until stagecraft," Wes says, "so I could—"

"No." Allison slips her arm through mine. "Girls only."

We leave the theater building still linked, bumping up against each other as we walk. Bash is sprawled on the stone stairs out front, smoking a cigarette. He looks up for a second, his eyes passing over me like I'm another tree in the Oak Grove. A little wisp of anger curls in my chest, but I try to ignore it, focusing on the feel of Allison's elbow curved around mine.

My high school was full of guys like Bash.

They always look right through girls like me.

But I see them.

11

SCARLETT

"Of course he deserved it," Mikayla says.

The lecture hall is meant for a much larger audience, so the twelve students enrolled in my advanced Shakespeare class tend to spread out across the room, using extra chairs to hold their backpacks or serve as footrests. As usual, Mikayla is the only one sitting down front near Jasper and me.

Ryan Cutler, a senior who always sits in the back row, shakes his head in disagreement. He's wearing the same holey *Game of Thrones* T-shirt he had on in last Friday's class.

"I just think it's messed up," Ryan says. "That they tricked Angelo into sleeping with another woman."

"Compared to what he was going to do to Isabella?" Mikayla shoots him a challenging smile, one eyebrow raised. Her angelic looks make the expression all the more unsettling. "That's *nothing*, and you know it. He was—"

"Yeah, but," Ryan interrupts her. "Isn't what they did to him sexual assault or whatever too? I mean, technically?"

The girl behind Mikayla shifts in her seat. Ashleigh Lawrence, junior. From the papers she turns in, I can tell she's smart, but getting her to speak up in class is next to impossible, especially with strong personalities like Mikayla and Ryan in the room. Ashleigh opens her mouth, then claps it shut again, chewing on her lower lip.

"Ms. Lawrence," I say. "Did you have something to add?"

"N-no." She twists her braid nervously around her fingers, the diamond ring on her left hand glinting in the fluorescent light. "I mean, not really."

Mikayla is more than happy to take the last word instead. "Angelo had no qualms about coercing Isabella into sleeping with him. So I say he got exactly what was coming to him."

Jasper grins at her. "Well, since you're such a revenge enthusiast, Ms. Atwell, I'm sure you'll enjoy next week's assignment."

He starts distributing handouts, explaining the requirements for our upcoming module on *Othello*. Mikayla's already read it; she's onto *Titus Andronicus*, which we won't be covering for weeks yet. I know I shouldn't let her dominate the discussion as much as she does, but it's hard not to play favorites when she's so far ahead of most of her classmates.

As soon as Jasper and I dismiss the class, Mikayla approaches me. "Do you still have time to meet now, Professor Clark?"

We're not even halfway through the semester and Mikayla has already been agitating to lock in her spring course load. I have to chase down most of my other advisees—or send Jasper after them. I don't know whether it's his harsh grading or his height or that unsettling gaze of his, but the students seem far more scared of him than they are of me. If only they knew.

"Of course," I say. "Although it's too nice outside to stay cooped up in my office. Coffee?"

Mikayla nods eagerly, following me into the hallway. Jasper brushes past, his long strides overtaking us. He doesn't look at me, but his fingers graze my hip. I tense, glaring after him. Mikayla doesn't seem to notice, but someone else might have.

Mikayla and I pass Dr. Stright's office just as he's ushering Ashleigh Lawrence inside. Ashleigh is in his honors writing seminar and already a better writer than he'll ever be. I sincerely hope she'll keep writing even if she goes through with her—in my opinion ill-advised—plan to marry her high school sweetheart next summer.

Stright eases the door shut behind Ashleigh, hand hovering near her spine, and my jaw muscles clench. He's not as shameless as Kinnear yet, but it's just a matter of time. In some ways, he's already worse than his mentor. At least Kinnear doesn't have a wife at home waiting for him while he fools around with his students.

"Are you still planning to apply for Stright's honors seminar?" I ask Mikayla as we exit Miller out to the Oak Grove. It's practically summery today, and the students are taking full advantage of it: stretched out on the grass with their jackets as picnic blankets, using the pretense of studying as an excuse to bask under the clear blue sky.

"I'd like to," Mikayla says. "If you think I can get in."

She can definitely get in—on the merits of her writing talent, of course, but also because Stright handpicks the seminar students every semester, and they're nearly all pretty young women.

"I'd be more than happy to give you a personal recommendation," I tell her. "But I have to warn you—"

"About Professor Stright?" she says. "Don't worry, I know all about him. I still want to try for the seminar, though."

I'm loath to praise anything Stright does, but I have to admit his seminar seems to be valuable. One of his students last year got into the Iowa Writers' Workshop. Others have ended up with internships at literary magazines, publishing houses, the *New Yorker*. I don't want Mikayla to miss out on opportunities just because Stright is a creep.

But if he touches her, I'll fucking kill him.

"I was planning to take your Victorian poetry class too," Mikayla says. "But if you get that fellowship in London, I guess Dr. Kinnear will be teaching it?"

"Or Dr. Torres." Drew's already been reviewing my syllabus, just in case. "You should consider his gender-theory course too. He only offers it in the spring."

"Do you think he'd take over as my advisor too?" Mikayla asks. "I mean, if you leave."

"I'm sure he'd be happy to. But I'll still be available via email if you need anything."

She smiles. "Good. I'll really miss you, though."

Our walk to town takes us past the cluster of dormitories sitting at the edge of campus. Mikayla waves at a student coming out of Whitten Hall—a girl I've never seen before, with frizzy brown hair, wearing a flannel and frayed denim ensemble that would have been stylish when I was her age.

"You're in Whitten this year?" I ask.

"Yeah," Mikayla says. "It's the only place I could get a single as a sophomore."

Whitten is one of the older, more run-down dormitories on campus, and so not a favorite choice of most students. But I've always thought it had a certain charm, with its white columns and leaded windows, the ivy covering the facade. In the afternoon light, the overlapping leaves gleam like the scales of a snake.

With so many students outside enjoying the sunshine, the coffee shop in Gorman's small excuse for a downtown is nearly deserted. Mikayla and I are discussing options for her global literature requirement as we wait for our drinks—plain black coffee for me, a caramel chai latte for her—when a man comes through the door and walks right up to us.

I look up, already irritated, and my annoyance only grows when I see who it is.

"Afternoon, ladies!" Kinnear says. "What are you up to?" Then, without waiting for either of us to answer, he says to me, "I figured you'd be locked up in your office, hard at work on that fellowship application. My offer to review your materials still stands, by the way."

"I've already submitted it, actually," I say. "But thank you."

As if I would ever make that mistake again. Two years ago, Kinnear read a paper of mine on Viola Vance's rumored bisexuality, gave some insulting notes on the structure of my argument, and proceeded to present a trivialized version of the exact same thesis in a talk he gave at the ALSCW conference the next semester. Kinnear specializes in Victorian literature, including the work of Viola's prominent novelist husband, Lord Douglas Vance. Even when Kinnear isn't outright stealing from me, there's an unfortunate amount of overlap in our research.

The barista sets our coffees on the counter. Mikayla picks up both and hands me mine.

"I'm sure you'll hear something soon." Kinnear smiles indulgently and gives me a squeeze on the arm. "They just reached out today to schedule my phone interview."

"Your phone interview? For what?"

"For the fellowship, of course."

Mikayla's mouth drops open. "For the *Women's Academy* fellowship?"

"It's open to all scholars in the field," Kinnear says. "The head curator is an old Cambridge chum of mine, actually. She encouraged me to throw my hat in the ring."

I don't understand. Why would he even want it? He's been gunning for the department chair job for years, and now it's almost in his grasp. Going to London for twelve months would almost certainly interfere with that—whereas it could make my career. Although I'm sure that little sycophant Stright would be more than happy to keep his seat warm for him. The idea of Kinnear in London, and Stright as my boss, no matter how temporarily, is too much to bear.

"Apparently there's some good stuff about Lord Vance in those letters too," Kinnear says. "You know, since they date from the early years of his marriage to Viola."

The thinnest of justifications. Viola's writing is already treated as an afterthought to the oeuvre of her more famous husband, and for decades now it's been actively suppressed by his estate. Her poems are full of rage and desire, unapologetic and aggressive even by today's standards. She's never been taken seriously as an artist in her own right, but my work could change that. Those letters would amount to a footnote in Kinnear's research. They could define mine. And he damn well knows it.

Mikayla watches us warily, like she's afraid we're about to come to blows. I'm trying to keep my face composed, but I can feel the rage bursting behind my eyes like firecrackers. I grip the corrugated cardboard around my coffee cup to keep from bashing his teeth in.

I can't let Kinnear get to me like this. Not now, not when I'm so close. Besides, what does it matter if they give him the fellowship, when I can make sure he's not around to take it?

12

CARLY

"'I'll always love you,'" Wes says. "'Just not in the way you want.'"

I'm trying to pay attention as he reads his latest short story in class, but I'm too nervous knowing it's my turn to read next. I pinch the stapled corner of my assignment, and one of the pages slices into the pad of my finger.

Lucky for me, Wes's story is long. It's overwritten, and sentimental too—a sappy account of a shy boy who spends years in unrequited love with a quirky, troubled girl from his hometown. But Alex seems to love it, and one of the girls sitting across from us has actual tears glittering in her eyes. I stick the papercut into my mouth, sucking some of the sting away.

Wes finally finishes reading, and Alex lays his hand over his heart. "Beautiful, Mr. Stewart. Thank you so much for sharing that with us."

Now Alex looks at me. I shift uncomfortably in my seat.

"Ms. Schiller," he says, "I believe you're—" He cuts himself off, glancing at his watch. "Actually, we're running a bit short on time. So let's end there, and we'll pick up with Carly's story first thing next week."

I make a mental note that next Monday would be a great time to ditch class with Allison again. The writing part I've been getting more comfortable with as the semester wears on, but I don't think I'll ever be okay with reading aloud in front of people. If Alex weren't so nice, I'd swear he was doing this to torture us.

Wes waits by the door, slouching in the oversize corduroy sport coat he's been wearing every day since the weather started turning colder. His eyes are naturally squinty, like he's smiling all the time even when he's not, but now there are deeper crinkles at the corners, just visible behind his glasses and the shaggy hair spilling over his temples.

"Saved by the bell," he says as we move into the hallway.

"What?"

"I could tell you were dreading it. Reading your story."

"Yeah, it's . . ." I look down at the scuffed toes of my Doc Martens. Allison found them for me last Saturday, at the Goodwill in the strip mall out by the Gorman Walmart. The boots were too big on her, but they fit me perfectly. "Well, it must be easier for you. Since you're a theater major."

Wes chuckles. "No, I totally hate it too. There's a reason I stay backstage."

He holds the door for me as we exit Miller Hall out to the Oak Grove. Autumn has fully taken hold now, turning the trees into a riot of brilliant reds and rusts.

A muscular guy in a letter jacket nearly bumps into us, and Wes moves closer to me to stay out of his way. I'm struck suddenly by the thought that people might see us together and assume we're a couple. As soon as the path is clear enough, I sidestep so I'm a few inches away from him. It's stupid; I don't know why I care.

Suddenly my vision goes dark.

Someone's behind me, covering my eyes. Their elbows digging into my shoulder blades. My pulse starts pounding, and I wrench to the side to get out of their grip. I'm shaking, my breath coming in shuddering gasps, as I turn around to see who it is.

Allison. Who else.

She's still laughing, her eyes lit up with cruel glee. But once she sees the look on my face, she stops.

"Oh my God, I really scared you!" She draws me into a hug, stroking my hair. "I'm sorry!"

I lean in, and her arms tighten around me. My heart rate starts to slow. "It's okay."

"What are you two nerds up to?" she asks as she pulls away. She's wearing an outfit from our thrift store excursion too: a men's houndstooth blazer over jeans and a black top that bares a strip of her midriff.

"We just left writing class," Wes says. "We—"

"Want to get some lunch?" Allison's asking me, not him. Her hand is still in my hair, playing with the ends.

I nod. It's not quite noon yet, but my stomach is growling, the gnawing nerves giving way to hunger pangs.

For the first month of the school year, I only ate at the main cafeteria, which serves mostly room-temperature pizza and stale breakfast cereal. Allison's the one who told me about Trocino, the dining hall on the other side of campus that's set up like a mall food court, with options from bagels to burgers to made-to-order stir-fry.

We scatter as soon as we push through the big glass doors, Wes opting for his usual sausage-and-cheese calzone while Allison makes a beeline for the burger station. I wander around for a few minutes, weighing my options before deciding on the daily casserole special. Allison's right that the food is much better here, but I find the number of choices overwhelming, and they're always blaring some aggressively cheerful Top 40 broadcast over the sound system.

Lunch in hand, I set off in search of Allison and Wes. I spot them at one of the big tables in the center of the space, surrounded by a bunch of their theater department friends. Even though I've met some of them before, I can't recall their names. They all seem to have some distinguishing, memorable feature, though: the girl with the bleached hair and nose ring, or the guy with the gauged ears and skull tattoo.

There's nothing distinctive like that about me. My hair is a boring brown somewhere between curly and straight, I'm not particularly skinny or particularly voluptuous, I don't have any tattoos or piercings besides my ears. Next to them, I feel impossibly plain, so it's no wonder their eyes skate right over me. If Allison and I hadn't been thrown together by the campus housing authority, I'd be just as invisible to her.

All the seats at their table are taken. Should I go sit somewhere else? More and more students are arriving after their morning classes, and soon all the tables will be occupied. My stomach twists, anxiety edging out the hunger. I try to catch Allison's eye, but she's too busy laughing at whatever the boy beside her just said.

It's Bash Waller. His dark hair is tucked under a knit cap today, black Henley unbuttoned partway down his sternum, and he's leaning back in his chair so far it looks like the legs might snap. Allison is contorted toward him, ignoring her food as completely as she's ignoring me.

"Carly."

Wes stands in front of me, gesturing to the spot opposite his half-eaten calzone.

"Here, sit down," he says. "I'll pull up another chair."

"Thanks," I mumble, sinking onto the warm red plastic seat. I don't know what I was thinking, getting the casserole. It looks disgusting to me now, like layers of wrinkly flesh.

Wes pushes an extra chair into the narrow gap next to me and resumes eating his lunch, his knee knocking against mine under the table as he chews. Allison flips her hair back and brushes her fingers over Bash's forearm. The girl on her other side—the one with the nose ring—rolls her eyes, but she's watching the two of them just as intently as the rest of us. They're the stars of the show.

Bash looks bored, though. This is clearly an everyday occurrence in his world: girls fawning over him, flirting shamelessly. He'll bask in her attention like a snake sunning itself on a rock, but he clearly doesn't give a shit about her.

He's already finished his food, leaving a smear of ketchup and a small pile of chicken bones behind, but he reaches for Allison's plate, grabbing a french fry without asking.

"Hey, those are mine," she says, but she's still smiling, her voice full of sugar.

As he chews, his eyes rove over her, pausing on her waist. I can't see her stomach from where I'm sitting, but I don't miss the little gasp of breath she takes as she sucks it in. My fist tightens around my fork.

"You'll be performing half-naked in front of a bunch of strangers soon," Bash says, already reaching for another fry. "Better watch the junk food."

What an *asshole*. I glance over at Wes to see if he's as disgusted as I am, but he's barely paying attention, picking at the few stray bits of calzone crust still on his plate.

Allison takes Bash by the wrist and draws his hand toward her mouth. "You're the one who has to show your bare ass onstage," she says, then bites off the tip of the fry he's holding.

He watches her lips as she chews, her throat as she swallows.

I stab my fork into the top of the casserole. I'm definitely not hungry anymore.

13

SCARLETT

My favorite thing about men like Kinnear: they're so fucking predictable.

Every Friday evening, he goes to get a drink (or several) at the Gorman Tap—the only bar in town that caters to the faculty rather than rowdy students. He sits at the same table every time too: right in the window, so I don't even have to go inside to spy on him. With the early setting of the sun, I'm another shadow in the mouth of the alley across the street.

I've stepped up my surveillance over the past few days, trailing two blocks behind him on his walk home from campus, tailing his car to the organic grocery store the next town over. Watching from the trees behind his house while his latest undergraduate conquest stumbled down the back steps this morning, her lips still swollen red, her jacket buttoned wrong.

He brought her to this place a few nights ago too, although she was almost certainly too young to be in a bar. He sat in the front window like always, didn't even try to hide what he was doing. Tonight, though, he's sipping his overpriced red wine alone. Angling his Joyce novel just right so the cover is visible to anyone who might walk by the window. I'm not sure I've seen him turn a page yet; it's a prop, part of his performance of Erudite Tenured Professor.

Kinnear doesn't really want the fellowship. He just doesn't want me to have it. The Women's Academy did finally contact me to set up a phone interview, but I can all too easily imagine Kinnear pouring poison in the ears of the selection committee during his own call, framing his work as superior to mine, undercutting my accomplishments. That's what he's been doing since the day I was hired at Gorman.

Gorman University wasn't my first choice, but tenure-track positions are hard to come by, even for someone with my stellar academic record. I worked so hard to get ready for that interview, accounting for every detail down to my outfit: a blazer and pencil skirt I'd had tailored precisely. It made me feel formidable, capable—the kind of woman I'd worked so hard to become during my years of graduate school.

But the way Kinnear stared at me as I took my seat in the interview room immediately punctured my confidence. Later I overheard him commenting on my "great legs" to one of his older male colleagues, and I deflated entirely. I took the job, but I never wore that outfit again.

I should have killed him years ago. He's held me back, tripped me up, screwed me over in more ways than I can count. I'll never know for certain where I might be today without his malicious interference in my career, but I do know that fellowship is going to be mine. Come January, I'll be in London doing career-defining research, and Kinnear will be rotting in his grave.

This murder will be riskier than most, though, especially with the task force sniffing around. I always study my victims thoroughly—I have to know them, inside and out, to know how best to kill them. But I can't wait much longer, and not only because of the fellowship.

I need to kill again. The urge seems to come harder and faster every time now, the desire building in me like a scream. Tyler barely kept it at bay for a month.

In the window, Kinnear shuts his book and swallows the rest of his wine. For a second I imagine slipping inside, sneaking up on him. Smashing the wineglass and dragging the jagged remains of the stem across his throat. If only I could kill him in such a satisfying way.

I dig my gloved hands into my pockets, hunch my shoulders so my black scarf covers my chin. This is about the time he usually leaves the bar. So far, whether alone or accompanied, he's always headed straight back to his modern monstrosity of a house a few streets away, but I have to make sure the pattern holds. Any minute now—

"Scarlett!"

My shoulders shrug even higher, because that voice belongs to the last person I want to run into right now.

Samina Pierce.

14

CARLY

"Maybe I got the time wrong," I say.

I steal a glance over at Wes, leaning against the car door next to me. He's drumming out a nervous rhythm on the dented metal, and the vibrations travel up my spine.

"No, she said six fifteen." He takes his phone out again. "I ran into her after her last class, and she said, 'See you at six fifteen.'"

This was Allison's idea in the first place, spending Friday evening in Pittsburgh. She wanted to check out this thrift store in Shadyside, eat at some new Ethiopian restaurant, maybe try for student rush tickets at the Pittsburgh Public Theater. She's been talking about it all week ("I have to get out of this town, I need some *culture*!").

But now she's nowhere to be found. "You could try calling her again," I suggest.

Wes's jaw muscles jump. I can't tell if he's furious with Allison or worried about her. Maybe both. She's usually at least ten minutes late to everything, rushing in in a flurry of *sorries*, but not showing up at all isn't like her. At least, as far as I know. I have to keep reminding myself we haven't known each other all that long.

"Yeah. Okay." Wes takes his phone out again, but before he can dial her number, the screen lights up with a text. His face falls.

"What?" I lean closer to look. When he holds the phone out to show me the message, our shoulders touch.

So sorry can't make it tonight, maybe next week?

Wes sighs and slips the phone back into his jeans pocket. I feel a flare of annoyance so sudden and hot it's like flames singeing my skin. But that's not fair. Maybe she has a good reason for canceling.

Or maybe she got a better offer from that slimy asshole Bash. He's pretty much all Allison talks about now—that and *Cabaret*. But that's about him too, I guess.

I push off the car and start to walk away before Wes can see how upset I am.

"We could still go," Wes calls after me.

I stop and turn back to look at him, my Doc Martens grinding into the parking lot gravel.

"I mean, if you want." He sounds noncommittal, but I can't tell if he really doesn't care or he's just trying hard to come off that way.

It's already getting dark. It'll take an hour to get to Pittsburgh, at least. And what will Wes and I even talk about without Allison? She usually does 90 percent of the talking.

But if we don't go to Pittsburgh, then I have nothing to do besides go back to my room and sit there alone all night, studying and waiting for Allison to come back. And she might not come back—or worse, she might come back *with* Bash. The way he looked at her in the dining hall the other day, it's obvious they're going to start hooking up soon if they haven't already.

"Okay," I say.

"Yeah?" Wes says, squinting against the glare of the floodlights in the parking lot.

"If you don't mind driving all that way."

"It's not that far. Besides, I've missed being behind the wheel. Allison and I used to drive all over Indiana when we were in high school." He runs his hand over the top of the car like it's a beloved pet instead of a rusty hulk that's probably older than we are. "Once we even drove all the way to Chicago. Her parents were so mad. Do you drive?"

I shake my head. I got my license when I was sixteen like everyone else in my class, but my hometown is so small you can walk almost everywhere, and driving fills me with stomach-churning dread. It's so much responsibility. So easy to take a life or cut your own short.

"Let's go," Wes says, unlocking the doors. "Copilot picks the tunes."

I get situated in the passenger seat, brushing some Sheetz sandwich wrappers onto the floor, and choose an album at random. Punk-pop guitar fills the car, loud enough to rattle the windows. Wes taps his fingers against the steering wheel in time with the beat as he peels out of the parking lot. As we turn onto the county road that leads out of town, he starts singing along under his breath—something about being "so tired of having sex." My face flushes.

"Great choice," he says. "This is my favorite Weezer record."

"I've never heard it before," I admit.

Wes looks over at me. "Seriously?"

I bite my lip and nod. Now that we're in the car, headed out of Gorman, it's starting to sink in that I'm completely alone with him. I've never been alone with a guy before. All my father's warnings flash through my head—*boys only want one thing*—but I can't imagine Wes being any kind of threat. He's barely over my height, way skinnier than I am. It's guys like Bash my father meant to warn me about, not guys like Wes.

"So what kind of music do you like?" Wes asks.

"I don't really . . ." I look down at my twisting fingers in my lap. "I mean, I mostly read."

Reading was my most reliable escape in childhood, the one way I could get away from my father while still trapped in the same space with him. That's why I'm majoring in English.

"Tell you what," Wes says. "I'll make you a mix."

"Oh, you don't have to—"

"Just some of my favorites, and you can let me know if you like any of them."

No one's ever made me anything like that before. No one's ever made me anything at all.

"That would be awesome." I smile over at him, but he's looking at the road, his profile glowing red in the dashboard lights.

The rest of the drive to Pittsburgh, we're silent—except when the music runs out and Wes recommends another album to play next. I like that one even more: a solo female singer with a throaty, moody voice. She's still crooning when we reach the Allegheny River. I hunch down in my seat so I can watch the bright yellow bridge girders blur by as we cross into the city.

We arrived too late to go to the thrift store, and then we can't find the Ethiopian restaurant Allison wanted to try, so we end up at an Italian place instead, with white tablecloths and taper candles and soft piano music playing.

The second we're seated, I start to feel panicky. This is totally the kind of place you would go on a date. But we're not on a date, obviously.

"You want to order some breadsticks?" Wes asks.

"Sure," I say, looking around the restaurant just so I won't have to look right at him. Most of the other diners are couples a few decades our senior, wearing blazers and sheath dresses, sipping martinis. I feel stupidly underdressed in my baggy sweater and jeans, and Wes is even more out of place with his *Star Wars* T-shirt and rumpled corduroy jacket.

A few tables away, there's one other person about our age, but she's dressed far more stylishly than we are, in a blue minidress and matching stiletto heels. The candlelight catches the highlights in her long blond hair, making them shimmer like strands of jewels.

She's so stunning, it takes me a second to notice her companion. He's at least twice her age, hair shot through with gray, deep wrinkles at the corners of his eyes. Smoky-blue eyes with dark shadows.

Oh my God, it's my father.

15

SCARLETT

I force myself to smile and drop my shoulders. "Samina. How are you?"

"I told you, call me Mina." She shivers, stamping her feet on the pavement. She's carrying a reusable bag laden with food from the market down the street. A loaf of French bread and the neck of a wine bottle peek out of the top. "What are you doing standing out here in the cold?"

The bar's heavy wooden door pushes open. A small clump of graduate students emerges. Not Kinnear. He's still at the table, nursing the dregs of his wine.

Mina follows my gaze, her brow furrowed. I quickly refocus my attention on her. "Oh, I was just out for a walk. I love this weather, actually."

That, at least, is the truth: fall has always been my favorite season, ever since I was young. All that death and decay clearing the way for something new.

"Not me," Mina says. "Give me a sunny beach and a margarita any day."

The front door of the bar opens again. This time I force my eyes to stay on Mina.

"I'm so glad I ran into you," she says. "I was planning to stop by your office first thing tomorrow."

"Oh?"

She huddles closer to me, the sleeve of her gray tweed coat brushing my arm. "Does the name Richard Callaghan ring a bell?"

I frown, tilting my head. Buying myself some time.

"You'd probably recognize him if I showed you a picture," she continues. "Big guy, buzz cut. He was a janitor—cleaned the library for almost a decade."

I steal another glance over at the bar. Kinnear's table is empty. He's not outside yet, but he will be soon.

He might not even see us. It's dark, we're all the way across the street. He's probably distracted, a little drunk. He hasn't noticed me any of the other times I've followed him.

Of course, now that I'm standing beside his ex-wife, Kinnear homes in on my location the second he exits the bar.

Kinnear smiles and waves, and Mina smiles back, and now he's stepping off the curb to come talk to us. *Goddammit.*

But instead of crossing the street, he taps his watch with a simpering, apologetic smile and takes off in the opposite direction. He's not walking toward his house, or campus—a major break in pattern. Of course, there's no way I can follow him now.

Mina watches Kinnear's back until he turns down another street and disappears from view. "You know, we've been divorced four times as long as we were married, and the dean's wife still calls me 'Mrs. Kinnear'—which was *never* my name, by the way." She sighs, her breath coming out in a puff of white steam. "What about you? Ever been married?"

I shake my head.

"Good for you." Mina's lips quirk up in a sly smile, her eyes sparkling under the street lamps. With her looking at me like that, I barely feel the cold anymore. "Then again, if I'd never met him, I wouldn't be here at Gorman, so."

"Why did you split up?" I ask.

"Men like him don't want a relationship, they want a fan club. The more members the better." Mina laughs, playing this statement off like a joke, but her voice is too brittle with bitterness. "But hey, we all do stupid things when we're young, right?"

I try to make myself smile in response, but my mouth won't cooperate. The full force of the cold settles back into my bones.

Mina's studying me again, the way she did in her office. "Have you had dinner yet?"

"No." I know what she's going to say next, and something inside me I didn't even know was open snaps shut, locks tight again. "I'd better be getting home. Lots of grading to do."

"Another time, then." If she's insulted or disappointed by my brush-off, she hides it well. "I'll have Mikayla bring you the file on Callaghan. Let me know if anything jogs your memory."

As if I could ever forget him. Callaghan wasn't a garden-variety rapist or abuser like most of my victims. He was a voyeur—and he got away with it for years, jerking off while spying through peepholes he'd carved into all the ladies' rooms in the campus library.

The stairwell I shoved him down was used so rarely, it took days for someone to find the corpse. They had to shut down the library for a week to air out the smell—and to seal up all the peepholes, which the new janitor discovered her very first day on the job.

"Of course," I say. "Have a good evening."

As Mina walks away, that same clutch of panic I felt in her office claws into my chest again. She doesn't know. She can't. All she's figured out is that some of the deaths on campus don't quite fit in with the others. She doesn't suspect there's foul play involved, and even if she did, she certainly wouldn't have any reason to pin it on me.

But she's still closer than anyone else has ever been to figuring out the truth.

After Mina leaves, I consider trying to track down Kinnear again. I don't know where he was headed, but Gorman is small; there's only so much town left in the direction he walked. I'm unsteady now, though. Distracted. Better to head home and warm up, then resume my surveillance tomorrow.

The door to the bar opens again, and two people come out. Jasper's height and pale skin make him unmistakable, even—no, *especially*—in the dark. I can't tell who the petite figure beside him is, though. They're walking away, on the other side of the street, Jasper's hand pressing into her back to urge her forward. They haven't seen me.

But then Jasper turns—a casual twist of his neck, subtle enough his companion doesn't see it—and looks me right in the eye.

He knew I was there the whole time.

16

CARLY

I'm halfway down the block before I realize I've fled the restaurant, leaving Wes behind.

My father. Touching that woman. That *girl*. She's barely older than I am. It's disgusting.

"Carly!" Wes calls after me, jogging to catch up. "What's wrong? What happened?"

My father is a cheating bastard. I wish he was dead.

I open my mouth, but the words won't come. My cheeks burn. I think I'm crying, but everything feels so removed, unreal.

Oh God, what if he saw me too? I don't think he did, but what if he noticed me when I was running outside? He could come out here and confront me. Any second now, he might—

Wes puts his arm around me, and I'm too shaken to push him away. But once he's touching me, it's surprisingly comforting. My trembling starts to subside.

"Can we just . . . go?" I say, his warmth radiating along the side of my body. "I want to go."

"Of course." Wes slips off his jacket and wraps it around my shoulders, even though I'm already wearing one of my own. "Of course, we'll go."

On the drive back, we're just as silent as we were on the way here, but now the air in the car feels heavy, a storm cloud about to burst. A few miles outside of Gorman, Wes stops at a Sheetz station for gas, then goes inside the store to get us some snacks, since we didn't end up having any dinner.

I'm not hungry. All I can think about is my father—the way he looked at that woman, the actual *affection* shining in his eyes. I knew it. I knew he was a cheater. The late hours at work, the frequent overnight trips, his insane jealousy if Mom even *glanced* at someone else herself. I tried to tell her. So many times I tried to tell her, and she refused to believe me. But I fucking knew it.

Wes gets back into the car, goose bumps stippling his arms below the wrinkled sleeves of his T-shirt. He takes a sandwich out of the plastic bag he's carrying and unwraps it but doesn't take a bite.

We sit there for a few minutes, the twangy music from the gas station speakers pinging off the surface of the car, before Wes breaks the silence.

"You don't have to tell me what happened if you don't want to," he says, still looking straight ahead, the red Sheetz sign reflecting in the lenses of his glasses. "But—"

"I saw my father."

Wes looks over at me, not understanding. He probably has a father who loves him. If he ran into him unexpectedly in an Italian bistro, he'd smile and hug him and pull up a chair.

"He was with . . ." I stare through the windshield, into the fluorescent light of the gas station. "Some woman."

"So you think he's cheating on your mom?" Wes says.

"I know he is," I snap.

Wes flinches, and I stop, looking down at my hands. I've been twisting one of the buttons on Wes's jacket so hard the thread is starting to fray. I drop it, pressing my palms down on my thighs to still them.

I wonder how he met her. At the insurance company where he works, maybe—she might even be his secretary, that old cliché. Or they met at a bar, or online, or at the goddamn grocery store. It doesn't matter. It doesn't matter how he met her, if he's in love with her or she's just one of many women he's stringing along. The important thing is, now I know for certain. I have undeniable proof of the kind of man he is. My mother has to believe me now.

"I've suspected for a while," I say. "But I didn't know for sure. Not until tonight."

Wes exhales, long and loud, and sets his sandwich down, still uneaten. "Wow. I'm so sorry, that's . . ."

"I hate him," I say, and the words sting on the way out, but it feels so good to say them, so *satisfying*, like peeling off a scab.

Wes stays quiet, so I keep going. I tell him about my father's mind games, his weaponized silences, the way he controls how my mother wears her hair, how she dresses, what she makes for dinner. How whenever she pushes back, no matter how small her rebellion, he tells her she'd be nothing without him, helpless, destitute, alone. How every time, she believes him and takes him back and tells me I ought to show my father some respect, he's done so much for us, he loves us, really. She swears.

As soon as I stop talking, my chest flares with embarrassment. Wes is staring at me now, eyes owl-wide, and I wish I could disappear. What was I thinking, spilling all that to Wes? I shouldn't have said anything at all. I wish I could rewind the whole night and walk away from him in the parking lot instead of getting into his car in the first place.

Then he reaches across the gear shift and grabs my hand.

"You're amazing," he says.

I blink at him. "What?"

"You've been through so much, growing up with a dad like that, I can't even imagine." He squeezes my hand tighter. "And you've turned out to be such a badass."

"What?" That's not a word I would *ever* use to describe myself. Allison, *she's* a badass. I'm shy, awkward, anxious. The girl everyone overlooks.

"Yeah." He smiles. "Really. The way you looked when you got up from the table . . ."

I cringe, shrinking back against my seat. God, I must have looked totally unhinged, hysterical. Like a little girl throwing a tantrum. I hate that my father has that effect on me. I wish I could have kept my cool, that I had marched right up and told him what I thought of him, instead of running away.

"You looked like you wanted to burn the whole place to the ground," Wes says.

That's not pity in his eyes, or judgment. Instead, it's something like . . . wonder. Maybe admiration, even. It's so far from what I expected, I don't know how to respond.

The air in the car feels charged now, and I almost think Wes is going to kiss me. But he doesn't. And that makes me like him even more.

The rest of the drive into Gorman, our hands stay intertwined.

17

SCARLETT

This time, I want Kinnear to know I'm coming.

I dress up for the occasion, but not too much—just slightly bolder lipstick, kitten heels that make a clicking sound on the linoleum floor as I walk across the hall toward his office.

After my conversation with Mina, I decided it was time to do something I loathe: use my feminine wiles to get closer to a target. I resorted to this with Callaghan too; luring him into the stairwell would have been impossible otherwise, since he was so much larger than me. With Kinnear, it's just expedient. As much as I hate to admit it, he's an intelligent man, and I need him stupid, thinking with something beside his brain.

The third Wednesday of every month, his secretary gets her hair done, leaving her desk in the anteroom of his office vacant for several hours in the afternoon. But Kinnear's door stays open. That's one of his policies as department chair: *My door is always open.* His door is always open, and I'm always watching.

Kinnear's head pops up as I approach, but I rap my knuckles on the doorframe anyway.

"Scarlett." He's surprised—and why shouldn't he be? This is the first time I've ever stopped by his office of my own accord, at least as far as he knows.

I smile as sweetly as I can manage. "May I come in?"

He motions for me to take the leather club chair across from him. Kinnear's office is the only one in the building that doesn't feel like a glorified prison cell. His bookshelves are dark wood rather than gray metal, and he has a gallery wall of historical photographs of the university, hung in artfully mismatched gilt-edged frames. The wide picture window behind his desk looks out on the Oak Grove, students hurrying over the paths like ants.

"How was your phone interview?" I ask.

He already seems disarmed by the lack of vinegar in my tone. I cross my legs so my pencil skirt creeps up slightly, and his gaze goes right to my thigh like there are fishhooks through his pupils. He realized long ago I was the last person on earth who would deign to sleep with him, but that's never stopped him from looking.

"Oh, good, good. It's always a delight to catch up with Judith. No matter how many years it's been since we've seen each other, when we get to talking it's as if no time has passed at all!"

He laughs, and I force myself to smile in response.

"Actually," he says, "I had a second call with her and one of the archive's major donors yesterday. They mentioned they were talking to you soon too."

"Next week." *Right before I kill you.*

"Well, don't be nervous," he says. "I'm sure you'll do fine. Even if you don't get this one, it's great practice."

I've been preparing for this interview for months, compiling meticulous notes on how I intend to spend my time at the archive and which specific resources I'll utilize, plus a chapter-by-chapter proposal for the book I plan to write based on my findings. I'm going to do much more than *fine*.

This is harder than I thought it would be—and I knew it would be hard. But I've stepped in this far. Might as well go all the way.

"I was actually hoping you could give me some advice."

Kinnear sits up a little straighter. "Oh?"

"You're just so much more . . . experienced at this kind of thing." I lean forward, and he does too. Now I'm imagining a hook piercing the meat of his cheek, reeling him in. "And your paper on gender performance in Lord Vance's early correspondence with Viola was enormously helpful to me as I was preparing my application materials."

"Thank you," he says. "I didn't realize you'd read it."

I lean in even closer. "I read *all* your papers."

This part is true—I have to know my enemy, and in academia that means studying what they study. I'm not sure what's more nauseating: Kinnear's pretentious writing style, or the way he shamelessly regurgitates my ideas and those of our colleagues. Drew is too nice to call him on it, but Kinnear's latest publication lifted, almost verbatim, a lesson from Drew's survey unit on the Aesthetic Movement. The man is shameless.

"The way you juxtaposed her letters with her husband's," I say. "That must have taken you ages, finding all those commonalities in the language."

I happen to know it was Jasper who did this. He pulled multiple all-nighters poring over those texts back when he was Kinnear's assistant, so Kinnear could meet his deadline—and, of course, claim all the credit.

"It did take a while. But it's all worth it, isn't it? To contribute to the discourse on a literary treasure who might otherwise be forgotten."

Kinnear is using his professorial voice now, the better to mansplain my own academic specialty to me. Mina was right; all he wants is a fan club.

"Caspar's annotated collection of correspondence was invaluable to me," he continues. "It includes several letters from Lady Vance that others leave out. And the insights in the foreword—well, I'm sure you know."

Typical, that he chooses to call her "Lady Vance"—replacing her name with her title by marriage. His research will do the same, make Viola's words, her life, all about her husband. Kinnear talks about Douglas Vance like he was a literary saint instead of a narcissistic prick who left a swath of emotional destruction wherever he went and undercut his wife's artistic aspirations at every opportunity. I suppose it's no wonder Kinnear is such a fan.

"I haven't read it, I'm afraid." The book he's referring to is one of the many I've been unable to obtain through interlibrary loan. At the Women's Academy archive, though, they have three copies, including one with handwritten notes from the scholar who compiled the collection.

"Really? Oh, you must! You can hardly call yourself a Vance aficionado without reading it; it will change your whole perspective on her work. I have a copy in my personal collection."

Of course he fucking does.

"I'd lend it to you," he says. "But I don't want to let it out of my sight—it's a first edition, very valuable."

"I understand."

This is precisely where I hoped this conversation would lead. And I don't even have to feign excitement at the idea of finally getting to see Kinnear's enviable home library. It's the only attractive thing about him.

"Perhaps I could come take a look at it sometime?" I say. "Under your close supervision, of course."

Now I smile at him, in the way I know makes my eyes sparkle. During my less-cautious graduate school years in Chicago, I used that look to lure men from bars and nightclubs to alleyways, pitch-black public parks, or even my one-bedroom in Hyde Park. I didn't kill all of them, but I could have.

"Certainly," Kinnear says. "Although this week is a bit busy for me, I'm getting ready for— Actually, there's an idea! Why don't you come to my Homecoming celebration on Saturday?"

I can't seem too eager. I have to make sure he thinks this was all his idea. "I wouldn't want to impose."

"Don't be silly, I'd love to have you. I would have sent you an invitation already, but I know how you loathe parties."

Kinnear used to invite me to all sorts of department functions and dinner parties when I was a new hire, but after I declined enough invitations—and he realized he wasn't going to get me in bed—he stopped. Lucky for both of us: too many of those insufferable events and I'd have lost my cool and killed him long ago.

"Well, thank you, this has been enlightening." I smooth my skirt as I stand up. Kinnear's eyes follow the motion, tracing the shape of my hips. "But I don't want to take up your whole afternoon."

I linger in the doorway and lock eyes with him, finally letting some of the hatred I feel toward him seep into my gaze. But he won't see it. They never see the murder in my eyes.

I hustle out of Kinnear's office before I really do lose my grip and run straight into Jasper. He's standing suspiciously close to the door, like he was out here eavesdropping on our conversation.

He catches my arm to steady me. "Hey. You look nice today."

I shake him off, smoothing down my sleeve where his grip wrinkled it. "Thank you."

He peers into Kinnear's office, then looks back at me. "Fraternizing with the enemy?"

"We were discussing the fellowship."

"Oh yeah?" Jasper says, keeping pace with me as I head to my office across the hall. "You know, I have a lot of friends in London. So if you get it, maybe I could—"

I turn my head just enough for my glare to land. "No."

I've been trying not to think about what I saw the other night—him with that girl, his hand splayed against her back—but I can't push the image from my mind.

We're at the door to my office now, and Jasper is obviously planning on following me inside. I stop right on the threshold and turn to face him.

"I saw you," I say.

Jasper's lips slither up into a smile. "I saw you too."

He's enjoying this too much. It almost seems like he's been waiting for me to bring it up.

"Surely you're not *jealous*," he says. "Because I could draw my own conclusions about what you were doing in there with our fearless leader. Or the other night, lurking around in the dark with his ex-wife."

So he did see me talking to Samina. I didn't notice him entering the bar with his date (or whoever she was), so they must have been in there the whole time I was watching Kinnear.

"Good thing for you . . ." Jasper tucks a strand of hair behind my ear, his fingers lingering at my jawline. "I'm not the jealous type."

I swat his hand away, all the rage I suppressed during my meeting with Kinnear threatening to spew out of me like lava. Jasper towers over me, taking up the entire doorway.

"I'll see you in class tomorrow, Mr. Prior." My teeth bite down on the words hard enough to snap bone. Fury flashes in Jasper's eyes too, as I close the door in his face. Surely he didn't think this was foreplay.

He's getting too brazen. I'll have to deal with him soon. I just hope it will be the easy way rather than the hard way.

18

CARLY

Seven minutes after three.

I flip over on my other side and tug the comforter up around my ears, trying to block out the light from Allison's digital clock. I keep waking up, every hour. Sometimes more often. Checking to see if she's back from the party yet.

It's some house party for Gorman's Homecoming weekend, which seems to be a giant excuse to get drunk and set things on fire. She invited me to come. Wes invited me too—more than once. But ever since Pittsburgh, anxiety has been buzzing around me like an increasingly angry swarm of bees. When it came time to get ready for the party, I ran away to the library instead, without telling Allison or Wes.

I turn over again, squeezing my eyes shut until sparks explode behind my eyelids. I still haven't told my mother what I saw. I should have done it right away, but I couldn't bring myself to pick up the phone. I've been dodging her calls too, letting them ring through to voicemail, then responding with vague, hurried texts. The secret feels like it's eating away at me.

I'm terrified of what will happen when I tell her. But I'm even more terrified that *nothing* will happen, that she'll ignore me and carry on like normal.

The room door opens—hard, like it's been kicked, the knob hitting the wall and rebounding. I bolt upright, clutching the covers.

There's a man standing in the doorway.

My fingers tighten into fists. He's coming in the room. He's coming to—

But then my eyes adjust, and the silhouette shrinks, and I see it's not an intruder at all. It's only Wes. Well, not *only* him—there's someone else with him, slumped against his side.

Allison. He's supporting her weight with his arm threaded under her shoulders.

I jump out of bed, letting the sheets puddle on the floor. "What the hell is—"

Wes switches on the overhead light. Now that the room is illuminated, I feel exposed, embarrassed—my pajamas aren't particularly revealing, but I'm not wearing a bra.

He isn't even looking at me, though. He has his arm braced against the doorframe, and Allison's head lolls onto his shoulder.

I cross my arms over my chest. "What's wrong with her?"

"Too much tequila. At least I think it was tequila." His eyes are a little bleary too, but he's buzzed at most. Allison seems barely conscious.

I've never seen her like this. I mean, I've never been to a party with her before, but the times we've hung out with their theater friends, Allison's had no more than a drink or two, even when other people were getting trashed.

"Why did you let her drink so much?" I ask.

"I wasn't even with her. I was playing quarters in another room."

Wes starts trying to drag Allison toward the bed. She moans a little and burrows her head deeper into his jacket.

"She was with Bash. It's his house."

He finally manages to set Allison down on her bed. She flops over immediately, burying her head into the pillow. She's wearing a minidress, with a sweatshirt that I've seen Wes wearing in class before zipped over it. Her skirt is bunched up high enough to show the black lace trim of her underwear.

Wes reaches out to fix Allison's hem, but I beat him to it, bumping him out of the way with my hip so I can tug her skirt back into place. While I'm at it, I grab Allison's legs and shift them so she's stretched out on the bed.

"They were dancing, and then—doing shots, I guess." He takes a step back, raking his fingers through his hair. It's even messier than usual and stringy with sweat. "I should have been paying more attention, I haven't seen her like this since—"

Before he can finish that thought, our RA, Samantha, barges through the door.

19

SCARLETT

"Stop talking about dead white men. It's a party!"

Rafael takes the book out of Drew's hand and replaces it with a glass of cabernet. Drew purses his lips, pretending to be annoyed, but as usual his eyes radiate pure affection when he looks at his husband.

"Literally no one needs this much Proust," Drew grumbles over the rim of his wineglass.

"We need more alcohol," Rafael says, already heading toward the hairpin-leg sideboard Kinnear uses as a bar. "Scarlett, you want anything?"

I shake my head, smiling in spite of myself. Their presence is making Kinnear's Homecoming party almost tolerable. We've been hiding out in the living room, admiring Kinnear's custom-made barrister-style bookcases—and poking fun at their pretentious contents.

Rafael pours himself a fresh glass of wine, then examines the remains of the spread on the dining table. The other guests are outside, gathered around the fire. Kinnear's backyard Homecoming bonfire is even more elaborate than the official one the university threw the night before the big game. The blaze rises almost as tall as the trees at the edge of his property, and an effigy of a lion burns at the center, lashed to a pole like an accused witch.

Rafael returns carrying a tiny plate piled high with black truffle sliders and fancy cheeses. He offers it to Drew, who takes a bit of baked Brie and pops it absently into his mouth. He must have let Rafael pick out his outfit for tonight: a cashmere sweater the same chocolate brown as his eyes, and a pair of dark jeans. Still plain compared to Rafael's expert-level pattern-mixing, but a vast improvement over his professorial uniform of tweed jackets and rumpled button-downs.

"So, Scarlett," Rafael says. "Where's your boyfriend tonight?"

Drew gives him a gentle kick in the ankle. "Time and place, babe. Time and place."

They're the only people I've told about me and Jasper. I can tell Drew doesn't entirely approve, but he's been discreet—keeping both the relationship, and his opinions about it, to himself. He and Rafael have a comparable age difference between them, though they met under less ethically dubious circumstances: Drew was doing his postdoc at Columbia, and Rafael worked at a Filipino restaurant a few blocks away from campus.

Even though Jasper has been perfectly professional since our little spat, I had some concerns he might give me trouble at the party tonight. But I arrived fashionably late, and by the time I walked in, Jasper was already taking his leave. He hates mingling almost as much as I do.

"I don't blame you, the boy is gorgeous." Rafael takes a sip of wine. "Although I'd be a little afraid he was going to murder me in my sleep."

I laugh. "That's why I never let him sleep over. If you'll excuse me just a moment . . ."

As much as I enjoy spending time with them—and they're just about the only men in the world I'd say that of—it's not why I'm here. With a quick glance back to make sure Drew and Rafael aren't watching me, I slip down the darkened hallway toward the master suite.

I've got a solid idea of the layout from my previous surveillance, but this is my one opportunity to inspect Kinnear's home from the inside before I finalize my plan.

His house is the only modern one in the neighborhood, all glass and concrete and harsh angles. It's almost as abrasive and ostentatious as Kinnear is, sticking out like a serrated knife blade amid the turn-of-the-century cottages and carefully maintained craftsmans—including Drew and Rafael's place, one street over.

Kinnear's king-size bed is piled high with coats, but the room itself is relatively spare: a minimalist headboard made of wooden slats, a bedside table holding a stack of novels, a sleek midcentury modern dresser on the opposite wall. I peek in the walk-in closet, then duck into the master bathroom to look over the sundry medications and toiletries sitting on the counter.

Back in the bedroom, I peer through the slate linen curtains into the backyard. The heat of the bonfire is palpable even through the windowpane. Kinnear stands right beside the pyre, the sparks snapping off the flames making the auburn tones in his hair gleam. He's dressed head to toe in crimson Gorman Sharks paraphernalia like he's trying to add *School Mascot* to his CV.

Dr. Stright is beside him, wearing a Gorman hoodie that makes him look even more like a student than he usually does, and they're surrounded by football players. From here I can't tell what they're saying, but I'm sure it's some variation of *That was a great game we played today, wasn't it?* Kinnear and Stright always talk about Gorman football victories with a sense of ownership, like they took to the field and sacked the quarterback themselves.

Stright guffaws and claps the boy next to him on the back. Devin Caldwell, with the scratches on his arms that the police were so quick to dismiss. I can only hope Tyler's death scared Devin and his teammates into keeping their hands off unwilling girls for a while. I know it won't last—if it's made any difference at all. I can't kill them now—not so soon after Tyler, or with Kinnear finally sitting at the top of my list, and certainly not while Samina Pierce is scrutinizing every death on campus. But that doesn't mean they're off the hook forever.

My fingers fist the curtain. I force myself to drop it, smooth out the fabric.

Stright's time will come too. Unless the sudden death of his mentor scares him into a newfound morality. Unlikely. If men like that could learn the error of their ways, I wouldn't have to teach so many of them a lesson.

I slip back into the shadowed hall, heading toward the glow of the living room. Then something blocks out the light—another person entering the hallway. Walking right toward me.

The overhead light flicks on, and I'm standing face-to-face with Mina.

"Hey!" she says. "What are you doing back here?"

I don't know whether I'm more surprised that Kinnear invited her or that she actually showed up. She must have just arrived. She's still wearing her buttoned-up coat, the same tweed one she had on when she ran into me outside the bar. No Gorman team colors in sight.

"Just looking for the bathroom." The lie comes out smoothly; I prepared it in advance, along with several other backup explanations in case I was caught skulking through Kinnear's private space.

She gestures confidently down the hall. "Oh, it's right there."

"Did you live . . ." I start to ask. "I mean when you and Kinnear were—"

"Yeah." Mina glares disgustedly at the industrial light fixture hanging above us. "He bought this place right after we got married. Isn't it hideous?"

Even in this stark light, she looks stunning, her dark brown ringlets shining, lips stained berry red. Before I can stop myself, I'm picturing her in my own warmly lit house, bare feet curled up underneath her on the worn leather sofa, a cup of tea in her hands. In my bed, curls splayed over the pillow, skin looking burnished against the plain white sheets.

"I was just heading outside." I need fresh air, even if it's heavy with bonfire smoke. "Did you—"

She raises an eyebrow. "I thought you were looking for the bathroom."

"Oh, I—" *Shit.* I can't seem to keep my thoughts—and my lies—straight around her. "I'm fine for now. What I need is a drink."

Thankfully, Mina doesn't point out the clear contradiction in that statement; she just follows me out the back door onto Kinnear's multilevel deck. My coat is still inside, piled on the bed with the others, but with the fire roaring, it hardly feels like an October night. Someone's tossed on a few fresh pieces of wood, and the flames flare up toward the black sky.

Mina shakes her head. "I'll never understand lighting shit on fire as a form of celebration."

Profanity sounds so pretty in that refined accent of hers. "Don't they have a whole bonfire-based holiday where you're from?"

Mina smiles. "Indeed. Fireworks are involved too. Makes it look like London is under siege."

"Do you miss it?" I ask.

"What, Guy Fawkes Day?"

"No, I meant—"

"Sometimes. I thought about moving back, after." She falls silent, letting me fill in the blanks. "But I planned my career around that wanker for long enough, no way was I giving up a tenure-track position just to get away from him."

She takes two bottles of imported beer out of the cooler at the edge of the deck and hands me one, then twists the cap off hers and takes a long pull. We're both looking Kinnear's way now. The football players have moved on, but he's still huddled close to Stright. They look so alike they could pass for father and son.

A girl in a short skirt bends over the cooler to fish a soda can out of the slush, and the two men don't even try to disguise their wolfish leers at her leggings. When she straightens up, I see that it's my student Ashleigh Lawrence, the golden hair she usually braids down her back tied into a high ponytail instead.

"Have you had a chance to look at that file I sent you?" Mina asks. "On Richard Callaghan?"

"Yes, I read it." There was nothing in there I didn't already know—including the fact that, before he came to Gorman, Callaghan used to work at an ice rink in Scranton, and he was fired in the face of similar complaints about his perversions. "Seems like the guilt just got to be too much for him. Same as Tyler Elkin."

"Maybe," Mina says. "But there's something about it that's sticking in my brain, you know? It doesn't add up."

My body goes cold all over, despite the heat of the flames. "What do you mean?"

"I'm not sure yet," Mina says. "It's just an instinct, I suppose. There's another case also, from a couple of years back. It wasn't in the original suicide data, actually. A graduate student who—"

"Good evening, ladies."

I never thought I'd be so happy to hear Kinnear's smug voice.

He sweeps his hand over the yard like a nobleman showing off his ancestral lands. "How are you enjoying the party?"

"It's quite the spectacle," Mina says. She nods toward the burning lion. "Wherever did you get that thing?"

"Stright helped me set it up." Kinnear nods toward him.

Stright has escalated from ogling Ashleigh to chatting her up. I can only hear snippets of their conversation—just the names of several Beat poets and the phrase "change your life."

Kinnear launches into a long-winded explanation about the Pittsburgh artisan who constructed our rival team's mascot to his exact specifications. I tune him out, instead devoting my mental energy to figuring out to which dead graduate student Mina might have been referring. Perhaps the history postdoc who had a heart attack in the rare books room after I tampered with his Adderall? Though there was also the theater student whose hanging I staged. One had been a rapist like Tyler; the other had emotionally abused his girlfriend until she attempted suicide herself. Like Callaghan, they both got exactly what was coming to them.

Stright is still subjecting poor Ashleigh Lawrence to his Kerouac spiel. She isn't even trying to get a word in edgewise, just nodding along as he speaks, ponytail bouncing, a polite smile plastered on her lips. Her gaze keeps flitting over Stright's shoulder toward the shadowed trees, like she'd rather flee into the wilderness than talk to him.

He's clearly a few beers in, swaying a little on his feet, and he uses it as an excuse to keep angling farther into her personal space. The side of his beer bottle brushes her wrist, and she flinches away from him, tugging her sleeves down. No one else seems to notice how uncomfortable she is—not even Mina, who's putting in her own performance of polite interest as Kinnear points out the finer points of the lion's wireframe skeleton.

Stright leans in even closer, splaying his hand on her shoulder. I can't stay quiet anymore.

"Dr. Stright."

He looks at me, and I smile like a razor blade buried in a candy apple.

"Where's your wife tonight?"

20

CARLY

Samantha sees Allison passed out on the bed and scowls. "Let me guess. Someone had a little too much fun tonight."

"She seems really out of it," I say. "Maybe we should take her to the hospital, or—"

Samantha rolls her eyes and pushes past Wes and me. She seems more annoyed about us disturbing her beauty sleep than worried about Allison. Unlike me, she has no shame about Wes seeing her in her pajamas.

"She just needs to sleep it off." Samantha bends over Allison and slaps her lightly on the cheek. "Isn't that right, Hadley?"

Allison squirms a little but keeps her eyes shut. Samantha smacks her again, harder this time.

What the hell? Is she allowed to hit us?

"Look at me," Samantha orders.

Allison opens her eyes, but squints against the light. Her skin looks slightly green, and there's a sheen of sweat over her whole body. With another exasperated eye roll, Samantha goes over to Allison's desk, dumps the contents of her trash can into the matching one under my desk, and brings the empty can over to Allison's bedside.

Just in time for Allison to lean over the side of the mattress and vomit. Samantha sighs and gathers Allison's hair back into a pony-tail with her fist, like she's done this a hundred times before. For all I know, she has.

Allison retches again, and Samantha tugs her hair tighter.

Wes presses his knuckles into his teeth like he's trying to keep from being sick himself. "Is she okay?"

"Ask her again in the morning," Samantha says, shooting him a glare.

Allison lies back on the mattress, wiping her mouth with the back of her hand. I peer at the vomit-spattered trash can. "Shouldn't we clean that out, or—"

"Let her do it herself when she sobers up," Samantha says. "You might want to sleep in the common room tonight, Schiller."

I shake my head. "No way, I should stay with her. She could choke on her own vomit, or—"

Samantha shrugs. "Suit yourself."

Wes steps closer to me—although he's stayed pretty close this whole time, standing right over my shoulder. "I can stay too. You shouldn't have to—"

"Now I know you don't think I'm going to let a male student spend the night in this female-only residence." Samantha raises her eyebrows at Wes. "Do you?"

She's such a fucking hypocrite. Her own boyfriend is probably asleep in her twin bed down the hall right now.

"Fine." Wes turns back to me. "I'll come over first thing in the morning, okay?"

I bite my lip. "Okay."

"Good night, Wesley." Samantha's smiling, but her tone says *get the fuck out* loud and clear.

Wes leaves, with one more guilty look back at Allison's prone form on the bed. Samantha follows him, but she pauses in the doorway. I think for a second she's going to give me some sage RA advice. But instead she says, "You better not wake me up unless she's dying."

I nod, trying to keep the anger seething under my skin from showing on my face. This is Samantha's *job*—she's supposed to take care of us.

I should have gone to the party. This wouldn't have happened if I'd been there. Allison would have been hanging out with me, not with Bash. I can see it as clear as if I had actually been present: him pouring shot after shot down her throat, dancing pressed up against her, putting his hands all over—

I wasn't there for Allison at the party, but I can be here for her now.

First, I clean out her trash can, leaving my own in its place in case she has to throw up again while I'm gone. I bring some damp washcloths back from the bathroom and move my desk chair next to her bed so I can watch over her. I can't sleep until I'm sure she's okay.

Allison vomits twice more. I stay by her side, laying fresh washcloths over her forehead and the back of her neck, until dawn peeks through the window. She's over the worst of it, settled into a real sleep, so I go wash out the trash can again. I feel disgusting, the scent of sickness clinging to my skin, but I'm so exhausted I'm pretty sure I'd fall asleep standing up if I tried to shower.

I'll go back to bed for a little bit first, then scrub myself as many times as it takes to get the smell out. Before lying down, I pull Allison's covers up to her chin, double-checking she's still breathing and everything. I'm about to collapse into my bed when she stirs.

"Hey." Her eyes are bright and dazed, but they're focused on me. "Where are you going?"

I look toward my rumpled bedding, then back at her. "I was just—"

"C'mere." Allison slides back so she's closer to the wall, leaving a spot big enough for me.

I hesitate. She's still drunk.

But the way she's looking at me . . . it makes my legs feel all wobbly. And suddenly I'm sitting down on the edge of Allison's bed.

She lifts up the comforter—inviting me in.

I stretch out beside her, my heart pounding so loud I'm afraid it will vibrate the bed frame. But Allison doesn't seem to notice. She drapes her arm across my waist, snuggling up to me. Our bare legs twine together under the covers, and the thump of my pulse moves lower.

We're face-to-face now, sharing the pillow. "Thanks for taking care of me," Allison whispers, and as her lips move, they brush mine.

It's not quite a kiss; it might have been an accident. Even though her breath is sour with liquor and vomit, it's all I can do to keep myself from pulling her in for a real one.

21

SCARLETT

Stright's usual overly friendly grin stays in place, but I can see the irritation scrawled all over his face. "What?" he says.

"Your wife," I repeat. "She couldn't make it?"

"She, uh . . ." Stright scratches the back of his neck. "She had a headache."

My smile turns sharper. "I bet."

Ashleigh Lawrence is already backing away from him, her glossy pink lips pursed. Mina's pressing her lips together too, but in her case it's a fruitless attempt to hide her amusement at Stright's discomfort.

Stright reaches for Ashleigh's elbow. "Hey, wait a—"

But she's already gone, hurrying off toward a group of party-goers closer to her own age who are playing horseshoes at the edge of the lawn. Drew and Rafael have wandered outside as well, and Drew bounces a worried look between Stright and me.

Stright's even drunker than I thought, his eyes flat and bleary—trying to relive his college glory days in more ways than one. I hold his glassy gaze, unblinking, until he looks away and drains the rest of his beer.

"Rafael and I were just heading out," Drew says to him. "Why don't you let us take you home?"

He touches Stright's arm, but Stright shrugs him off, stumbling in the direction Ashleigh headed. I grab his sleeve, much more forcefully than Drew.

"Lemme go," Stright slurs, trying to shake free of my grip.

I dig my nails in around his elbow. "You don't want to do that."

"Mind your own fucking business."

Stright wrenches his arm away, losing hold of his beer in the process. The bottle smashes against the bonfire logs, shattering into glittering green shards.

Mina gives Kinnear a look, like she's waiting for him to intervene; it is his party, after all. But he seems oblivious to the tension, sipping his drink as if nothing's wrong.

Stright turns on me, scowling. He's nowhere near as handsome without that winning smile plastered on his face.

"Bitch," he mutters—just low enough that Kinnear can pretend he didn't hear.

"Hey," Mina snaps. "That's enough."

She threads her arm around my shoulders, and I let her pull me tight against her side and draw me away from the men. Once we're far enough that I can barely feel the heat of the bonfire anymore, Mina stops. Instead of letting go of me, though, she draws me even closer. Even with the smoke in the air, I can smell her perfume. Flowers, that's what she smells like. Jasmine and something sweeter.

"You okay? I'm so sorry about that arsehole. Well, about both of them." She throws a glower back in the general direction of her ex-husband.

It adds fuel to the fire of my rage, hearing her apologize for them. Mina starts rubbing comforting circles into my back with the heel of her hand, and I want to scream. Stright is letting Drew and Rafael lead him away now, and it's taking every scrap of my will-power not to run after them, pick up one of those bottle shards, and slash the jagged edge across Stright's throat.

"You want to get out of here?" Mina asks. "Go get something decent to drink?"

I want to say yes. I really do.

But I can't. I can't get close to anyone. Least of all the woman who's nearer than she knows to discovering who I really am.

"I should . . ." I pull away. "Go home. Get to bed."

"Okay, sure," Mina says. "I'll walk y—"

"No." At the harshness in my tone, she flinches like I've slapped her. I try again, try to make my voice softer, but the edge is still there. "I mean, thank you . . . but you don't need to. It's not far."

"All right. Have a good night, Scarlett." Her voice is stiff and formal, and so is her posture as she turns on her heel and strides away—not back to the bonfire, but around the side of the house, leaving the party entirely.

I should go home, like I told her I would. But I can't do that either.

My preparations are complete. I have everything I need. I just need to finish setting the trap, and let Kinnear walk right in. By this time next week, he'll be dead.

I wait until the crowd around the fire thins out, until he stands alone, watching the flames burn down with one hand in his pocket and the other choking the neck of a fresh beer bottle. The lion effigy is nothing but ash, though the pole it was lashed to still sticks up from the center of the pyre.

When Kinnear sees me coming, he smiles and waves me over to join him by the smoldering remains. "Where did you run off to?" he asks.

"Oh, I was over there." I gesture vaguely toward the darkest part of the yard. There are a few people in white Adirondack chairs, huddled together for warmth, but most of the other guests have retreated into the house.

"Not so bad, is it," Kinnear says. He's tipped over into full drunkenness now—looking at me, his eyes won't quite focus. "Socializing with people."

"Thank you again for inviting me." I smile—trying to seem pleasant, friendly, the incident with Stright totally forgotten.

He takes another sip of beer. "I didn't realize you were such good friends with Mina."

"Oh, we're—" I'm not sure what we are, but not friends. Especially not now that I rejected her overture yet again. "I'm helping her out with her campus suicide investigation."

Kinnear points the bottle at me. "Make sure to add that to your tenure file. It's not flashy, but they like that sort of selfless community service stuff. How's it going so far?"

"Mina seems like she has it all handled," I say. "She's very capable."

"Yes, she certainly is that."

He doesn't even try to conceal the contempt in his voice. I raise my eyebrows at him, prompting him to go on. He gives a bitter laugh and takes another swig from the bottle.

"I just mean—she's very focused on her career. She'll do whatever it takes to get ahead."

And you won't?

"You should just—watch out, that's all," he says. "Mina doesn't care about relationships unless she can get something out of them. Once someone's outlived their usefulness . . ."

How bold of him to assume he was ever "useful" to Mina. He's saying much more about himself right now than about his ex-wife. If anything, his warning increases my respect for her.

"Oh, I almost forgot!" he exclaims. "You wanted to see that book."

He turns toward the house. I grab his arm to stop him.

"There are so many people here now," I say. "It will be too distracting."

"I'll grab it off the shelf, and we can go somewhere quiet."

The only quiet place in the whole house is his bedroom. Convenient.

"That wouldn't be very professional, would it?" I say. "Someone could see us going off together alone."

"People are seeing us together right now." He casts a look around to make his point, but the few guests remaining in the yard are all at least half-drunk and caught up in their own conversations. Not paying a bit of attention to us.

I let go of his arm and step even closer. "That's different, and you know it."

Kinnear stares into my eyes, a self-satisfied smile tugging at the corners of his lips. With the dying flames lighting up his face, even I have to admit the man is infuriatingly handsome. I'm sure I look alluring right now too—the firelight against my copper hair, my cheeks flushed from the mix of heat and chill around the fire.

"What if I come over another night?" I offer.

"Okay," he says. "Tomorrow?"

"I'm busy tomorrow, I'm afraid. What about next weekend?"

This can't seem too calculated; he has to think *he's* seducing *me*. I pretend to consider for a moment, then make my face light up like I've had a brilliant idea.

"What are you doing on Halloween?" I ask.

"I don't know," he says. "Probably hiding inside with all the curtains drawn to avoid the trick-or-treaters."

That's exactly what I was hoping he'd say. I had contingency plans for covering up the windows, but it will be that much easier if he takes care of it himself before I arrive.

I hold his gaze for a few more seconds, giving him time to imagine it: what I'll look like with my clothes off, spread out in his bed. The fire's dwindled to almost nothing now, but there are still sparks in his eyes.

"Perfect," I say. "Just tell me when to come over."

"How about nine? Unless that's too late."

"It's not too late. I'll see you then."

I touch his arm again—only for a second this time, digging my nails in just enough for him to feel it through the thick weave of his Gorman Sharks sweater. As I walk away, I can feel him watching me, following the calculated sway of my hips.

I count out a few steps before turning back to him. "One more thing."

Kinnear smiles. "Anything."

I move back to his side so I can whisper in his ear. "Promise you won't tell anyone. I wouldn't want to start any rumors, or—"

"Of course." Kinnear squeezes my upper arm, like I did to his. The same way he's touched me countless times, after staff meetings, in the hallway, when I ran into him at the coffee shop. Like he's placating me and putting me in my place at the same time. "It'll be our secret."

I don't believe him. If he actually succeeded in sleeping with me, he'd brag to Stright immediately, and everyone else in the English department would be well aware within forty-eight hours.

Good thing he'll be dead before he gets the chance to run his mouth.

22

CARLY

"I've never done this before."

"It's easy," Allison says. "Start at the top, smear it all over."

When she asked me to help her dye her hair for Halloween, it seemed easy enough. But now that we've got trash bags spread out over every stainable surface in the Whit bathroom, and Allison's sitting in front of me wearing a distractingly thin tank top, I'm having second thoughts.

"What if I mess it up, though?"

She twists around to grin at me. The bag draped over the desk chair we dragged in here crinkles behind her shoulder blades. "Then I'll shave my head and dress up as Dr. Evil for Halloween instead."

That doesn't exactly set my mind at ease.

Allison laughs. "It'll be fine. Just don't get it in my eyes."

I start mixing up the dye, checking the instructions on the package multiple times to make sure I'm doing it right. Allison has her laptop propped up by the sink, some Broadway cast album playing through the speakers.

Everything seems to be back to normal between us. Last Sunday, I woke up alone in her bed, the room still smelling sour. When Allison came in a few minutes later, carrying a paper bag and two giant cups of coffee, she didn't seem hungover at all; she was practically chipper. But she kept her sunglasses on—big retro ones with polka dots on the frames.

"My head is *killing* me!" she announced, after I asked how she was feeling. "Wes is on his way over to tell me what the fuck I did last night."

Then she laughed, bright and airy like this whole situation was a sitcom romp. She clearly didn't remember inviting me into bed with her, or how close we came to kissing. So I'm not going to bring it up either, even though it's all I can think about. A welcome distraction from worrying about my father and his mistress. I still haven't spoken to my mother. This is the longest we've ever gone without talking.

I take a deep breath and squeeze out the first bit of dye onto Allison's part. It looks too dark, almost navy, but the box shows a vibrant blue like the actress in *Eternal Sunshine of the Spotless Mind*.

"So—" Allison turns her head again. My hand slips, and I smear some blue on her temple.

"Stay still!"

"Sorry." She settles back into position. "You're definitely coming to the party, right?"

"Yeah, I told you I was." I keep working the dye through the length of her hair, as deliberate as if I were defusing a bomb. "Why?"

"Wes was asking me. He talks about you all the time, you know."

I stiffen. I know they hang out sometimes without me. But now I'm picturing her laughing with him about our almost kiss, making a giant joke of the whole thing. Allison with her hand on Wes's shoulder so she can catch her breath, wheezing, *Can you believe it? As if I'd ever want to kiss someone like her.*

"He's a really great guy," she says.

"Yeah, um, he seems . . . nice." *Nice* is putting it mildly. Wes is like an old-fashioned gentleman from a Jane Austen novel.

"We went to the prom together, you know," she says. "My senior year. Wes wasn't even supposed to be my date; he was in college already. I'd been going out with this guy—Justin—but he dumped me a week before the dance, so Wes drove home for the weekend to take me."

I didn't date at all in high school, or go to any school dances—not even with a group of girlfriends, all dancing in a circle with our backs toward the boys. I stayed home and read *Crime and Punishment* in my bedroom and tried not to let myself imagine what it would be like to sway against someone while a slow song played.

"Why did that guy break up with you?" I ask.

"I told him I was bi."

I almost drop the dye bottle. So I haven't been imagining things. Allison likes girls, which means there's still a chance she could—

"Wes already knew," she continues. "He's the first person I ever told. But then Justin . . . he told *everyone*." She laughs, but the pain is evident in her voice. "You can imagine how well that went over in our bumfuck town."

Allison picks up one of the strips of her hair I've already finished and holds the end to the light, getting blue all over her fingertips.

"Wes is the only one who didn't give me shit for it. Well, him and his mom. You know I even lived with them for a couple months?"

I shake my head.

"Yeah, my parents and I had some . . . differences of opinion. My dad's a Methodist pastor, so . . ."

I'm furious with my father, and I'd be perfectly happy never speaking to him again, but at least he's not a *pastor*. I can't even imagine.

We fall silent for a few seconds. The cast album has ended, so the only sound in the bathroom is our breathing. I suddenly become very aware that I've been running my hands through Allison's hair for ten minutes straight.

I don't plan to say it, it just spills out. "I'm bi too." It's the first time I've ever called myself that. The first time I've labeled my sexuality out loud at all.

"Don't take this the wrong way . . ." Allison swivels around again. My fingers were still buried in her hair, but now I let go and the damp strands slap against the plastic-covered chair back. "But I already knew."

She locks eyes with me, a sly little smile curving up her lips. My heart is pounding. Part of me feels so relieved, to finally tell someone the truth, but another part of me wishes I could pluck this secret out of the air between us and shove it back down my throat.

"R-really?"

"All the cutest girls are bi, didn't you get the memo?"

She winks at me, and I think my whole body is blushing. Like my toes are probably bright red. Allison throws her head back and laughs—and before I know it, I'm laughing right along with her, my shoulders shaking silently at first, then giving way to actual giggles.

Soon my eyes are watering, but I can't wipe them because I still have the dye-covered gloves on, so Allison does it for me. The feeling of her fingertips on my cheek snaps me out of it.

I nudge her to get her to turn back around. To stop looking at me like that. "Come on, I have to finish this. You don't want half a blue head, do you?"

"I mean, I think I could pull it off."

She probably could. Allison resumes her position in the chair, and I pick through the rest of her hair, making sure to cover any remaining blond with blue goop. There's some new energy vibrating between us, like sparks shooting through my fingers every time I touch her. Or maybe it was there all along, and I'm just now letting myself feel it.

"I'm sorry, by the way," Allison says.

"For what?" I ask, although I can think of several things.

"For . . . everything." She sighs and drops her blue-speckled shoulders. "Getting so wasted last weekend, and blowing you guys off when we were supposed to go to Pittsburgh."

"Where were you anyway?"

"Bash's place. He hosts this weekly poker game."

I figured as much, but it still stings to hear her say it. "So you guys are . . ."

Allison scoffs. "Not even. I'm shaking my ass in his face every night, and he barely knows I exist."

I find that hard to believe. Allison is pretty difficult to ignore.

"I'm gonna make him notice me, though," she says. "I have a plan: at the Halloween party, I'm going to—ouch!"

I lift my hands away from her head. I was working the last bit of the dye into her scalp, and I must have tugged too hard on her roots. "Sorry. I'm— You're done."

As I strip off my gloves, Allison goes to look at herself in the mirror, turning this way and that to examine my handiwork. The color is starting to brighten as it develops, turning as vibrant as Clementine's. Allison's blue eyes pop, and her pale skin glows like moonlight.

She tilts her chin up and licks her lips, and I have a flash of us in bed together, her mouth brushing lightly over mine. What if it *wasn't* an accident?

"'I'm a vindictive little bitch,'" Allison quotes, flicking her blue hair over her shoulders.

I step behind her and meet her eyes in the mirror. "'Truth be told.'"

23

SCARLETT

Tomorrow is the night.

So tonight I prepare: picking out the perfect outfit, shaving my legs, shaping my nails. All the things most women do to prepare for a date. But little do they know: killing a man is so much more satisfying than fucking a man could ever be.

I'm in the bathroom brushing out my hair when I hear a noise from down the hall. It sounds like the creaking of floorboards, but as far as I know I'm alone in the house.

The hairbrush clenched in my fist, I creep down the hallway to investigate. The sound seems to be coming from my study. The door is ajar, as I'd left it, and the lights inside are off.

I brace myself for a body rushing out at me. I could bash his skull in. I could push him down the stairs and break his spine.

I push the door farther open. More light spills in from the hallway—illuminating Jasper, standing behind my desk. I must have missed the sound of him opening the front door, climbing the stairs. I'm often distracted like this, right before a kill. Too busy going over every detail of my plan to notice what's going on around me.

He glances up when I enter, but doesn't look the least bit guilty. "There you are."

I'm wearing my satin robe, with nothing underneath. I feel exposed suddenly, even though Jasper has seen me wearing far less than this.

"What are you doing?" I fold my arms over my chest, still clutching the brush.

He holds up a red folder. "Scintillating reading."

It's the case file on Richard Callaghan. The other one, about the graduate student, is beside it. I had guessed right about which death caught Mina's attention: it was the Adderall-addicted history postdoc. The rapist. Unlike Tyler Elkin, he acted on his own, and the woman was his girlfriend. She stayed with him for months after, so of course when she finally got up the courage to pursue criminal charges against him, no one believed her. Except me.

I take the folder out of Jasper's hand and place it back on the desk. "I don't recall inviting you over tonight."

Jasper runs his fingertip over the seam in my robe, right along my spine. "You want me to leave?"

I don't. I hate myself for it, but I don't want him to go.

I set the brush down too, turning around so I'm sitting against the desk. "I'm busy."

"Oh yeah?" He steps even closer. He'd be between my legs if I opened them to him, but I don't. "Doing what?"

"I was going to color my hair."

Jasper studies me in the dim light, brushing a few strands back over my shoulders. The red is still vibrant, my natural color showing slightly at the roots, but I want to be at my best for tomorrow. The more I look like Kinnear's wet dream, the more satisfying it will be to transform into his worst nightmare.

"I could help," Jasper says.

I scoff and shove at him, though I can't bring myself to push him away entirely.

"I'm serious! I used to bleach my ex's hair for her."

This is the first time he's ever mentioned a previous relation-ship to me. I don't know the first thing about Jasper's life; it's better that way. He used to ask me about my past—where I grew up, old boyfriends, old girlfriends—but after I refused to answer him enough times, he gave it up.

Jasper twists a curl around his thumb and gives it a tug. "I'm a man of many talents."

"If you insist." I have an extra box of dye; if he manages to fuck this up, I'll still have time to fix it before tomorrow.

He follows me into the bathroom and strips down to his under-shirt, carefully folding his oxford button-down before setting it off to the side.

After laying a towel over my shoulders, he starts spreading the dye through my hair. I watch him in the mirror: the look of intense concentration on his face, the way his arm muscles flex. This might be the gentlest he's ever been with me. I let my eyes drift shut, con-centrating on the feeling of his fingers on my scalp, the tingles of pleasure that spread down my back.

"So you're working with the task force now?" he asks.

My eyes snap open, shoulders stiffening. Jasper's hands jerk a little, and a spurt of red liquid lands on the white fabric covering his torso.

"That guy, the janitor." Jasper hunches down to knead the color into the nape of my neck. "He was a Peeping Tom or something, right?"

"That's what the police said," I tell Jasper.

He shakes his head as he drains the last of the dye bottle into the ends of my hair. "Seems like a waste—all this time spent looking into guys like him and Elkin. As if anyone really gives a damn that they're dead."

He sets the empty bottle down on the sink and massages the dye deeper into my roots. There are multiple red streaks on his shirt now, and a few speckles stippling his cheekbone too. His hands are so strong it feels like he could crush my skull. I lean into his touch, and he presses down harder.

Sometimes I wish that Jasper were like me, that I could share my true nature with him. I try not to dwell on it, but occasionally the fantasy still creeps in: how much easier it would be to kill with his help, his powerful hands holding men down while I finish them off. Blood spraying across Jasper's skin like the dye is now.

But I can't. I might enjoy fucking him, but I can't trust anyone with the truth about what I am, not if I want to survive. I have so many more men to kill.

We sit in silence for a while, waiting for the dye to develop. My robe has shifted a bit, exposing my cleavage, but I don't bother to cover myself up again. Jasper keeps staring at me in the mirror, until I finally turn around to face him.

"That's going to stain." I reach up, and he crouches down to let me rub at the spots of color on his cheek with my thumb. The color only spreads further.

Jasper lays his hand against mine, pressing my palm into his cheek. The red looks so beautiful against his pale skin; it makes his eyes shine brighter. Hungrier. He kisses the heel of my hand, and I can feel his teeth through his lips.

I peel his stained shirt off, then let my towel and robe fall to the floor beside it. Without a word, Jasper switches on the shower spray for me, turning the water on its hottest setting. I get into the claw-foot tub to start rinsing the dye out, and seconds later he's in there with me, naked, his hands in my hair again, red oozing through his fingers and swirling around our feet.

He tilts my face up and kisses me—deep and devouring, his hands digging into my jaw. Our bodies press together, slick and hot, and the dye is running into my eyes now, running over our lips, it's burning, and I can taste it, the harsh bite of the chemicals mixing with the clean taste of mint on Jasper's tongue.

I should stop. It's too much, he's too close, I can't breathe. But this is what I can allow myself. I can't have what I really want, but I can have this.

So I wrap my leg around Jasper's to pull him even closer, and I let him press my back against the tiles, gripping the curve of my waist as he thrusts into me. We fuck until the water runs cold, and the whole time I'm imagining that the red sluicing over us is blood.

24

CARLY

"Come on, get dressed—Wes will be here any minute."

Allison brushes past me, flipping her blue hair back so it falls into the hood of her baggy orange sweatshirt. The color already looks faded, but that makes her costume all the more authentic. She even has blue striped arm warmers like Clementine wears in the movie.

"I am dressed," I say.

Allison gives me a dubious once-over. Okay, admittedly my outfit isn't that different from what I usually wear: a black sweater, black jeans, my Doc Martens. I put on way more eyeliner than usual, though, plus some earrings I got in the Halloween section at Walmart.

"It's Halloween," Allison says.

"My earrings are spiders." I tuck my hair back and tilt my head so the cheap silver catches the light.

Allison isn't swayed. "That's *not* a costume. What did you go as last year?"

"I didn't dress up last year." My mom and I stayed home, with the porch light switched off. My father had to work late, and he didn't want us opening the door to strangers without him there.

"All the more reason to do it this year!" She grabs my arm, leading me toward the closet. "I'll find something for you to wear."

"That's okay, you don't—"

But Allison's already pulling things off hangers and tossing them onto my bed. Most of the clothes she's picking out look *way* too small—like, small even for her, which means they'll be obscene on me.

I'm already regretting going to this party, and we aren't even there yet. I only agreed to it in the first place because I want to keep an eye on Allison.

She turns away from the closet and picks through the items piled on the bed. A couple of garments ooze down onto the floor, and she leaves them where they fall.

"Here." She holds out a fistful of shiny black fabric to me. "Try this on."

I shake my head. "I'd really rather—"

"Just *try* it. You can change back if you hate it."

I huff out a sigh. "Fine."

Allison watches while I slip off my sweater, kick off my boots, unbutton my jeans. I unfurl the clothes she gave me: fishnet pantyhose with a rip across the knee, and black satin shorts that are barely more than underwear.

As I tug the shorts up over the fishnets, I'm painfully aware of how the fabric cuts into the softness of my stomach. The last item is some sort of corset, with boning running up the sides. I start trying to wrap it around my torso, reaching for the laces in the back.

"Oh, you don't need a bra with that." Allison unclasps my bra with one quick motion.

The feel of her fingertips zaps my spine like a static shock, and I freeze, clutching the corset against my chest to keep the flesh-toned cups in place.

"Come on, I'll help you with the laces."

My heart is pounding, and Allison's looking at me expectantly, like this is no big deal and she has no idea why I'm standing here frozen like this. I force my arms to move enough to slip the bra's straps off and let it fall to the floor.

I press the corset back over my chest as quickly as I can, but I'm pretty sure Allison saw everything. She steps in close behind me and starts weaving the laces through the two sides of the corset, cinching it together. The boning does seem to hold my unwieldy breasts in place, at least while I'm standing still like this. I'm not sure what will happen if I attempt to walk or sit—or, God forbid, dance.

I think she's done, but then she gives the laces a big yank, almost pulling me back into her. My cleavage spills out over the strapless top, and I feel ridiculous. I feel *naked*. I can't possibly go out in public like this; it's bad enough that Allison's seeing it.

She ties off the laces and steps back to admire her handiwork. Surely once she takes in the full picture, she'll realize how awful I look and let me change back into my normal clothes.

Her eyes widen. "Wow."

I tug uncomfortably at the corset, trying to get it to cover more of my chest, but it just makes the boning jab into the flesh under my arms. "What?"

"You look *hot*," she says.

I blush. "No, I don't—I mean, you don't—"

"See for yourself." Allison steers me over to the mirror mounted above the dresser. I'm already cringing in anticipation, even before I raise my eyes to look in the glass.

But once I see my reflection, I stop breathing.

I don't look awful at all. The corset tugs my waist narrow, emphasizing my breasts and hips, turning my body into a perfect hourglass. My gaze traces each curve—all the parts of myself I usually cover up, hunch over to hide. I've never seen myself like this before.

"See, I told you." Allison leans in to whisper in my ear. "All the cutest girls are bi."

I blush again, the color spreading over the pale expanse of skin above the corset. But now all I can see in the mirror is Allison's hand resting on my waist, right where the corset cinches it in the most, Allison's mouth so close to my ear her lips nearly touch.

"Hey, ladies, you ready to—"

We turn away from the mirror to see Wes walking into the room. He stops short when he sees us. No: when he sees *me*. His eyes nearly bug out of his head.

Allison drops her hand from my waist. "Jesus, don't you knock? We could have been naked."

"Sorry." Wes flinches a little at the harshness in her voice. I wonder if he's picturing the two of us naked now, if the image in his head looks anything like the one in mine. "Are you ready to go?"

He's speaking to Allison, but his eyes are still on me. My shoulders slip into their usual slumped posture, but there's no hiding in this outfit.

I have no idea what Wes's costume is supposed to be. He swapped out his regular glasses for a pair of fake ones with thick black frames, and the rest of his costume is just a red cardigan sweater over a clashing plaid shirt and tie.

"Yes, we're ready." Allison turns back to the mirror for a second and fluffs up her hair, the blue cascading over her shoulders. She shoots Wes a teasing look. "Just make sure you wipe up that puddle of drool before we go."

Now Wes is the one blushing. He looks down at the floor, but only for a second before his eyes find me again.

My jacket covers up my chest, but my legs still feel exposed in the tiny shorts and ripped fishnets. I slip back into my Docs, half expecting Allison to shove some high heels or something at me instead, but she lets me put on the boots without comment.

We're heading for the door when Allison stops. "Wait! One more thing."

She goes back to the dresser and picks up a tube of lipstick, then takes my chin in her hand and starts swiping the color on my lips. I'm too stunned to stop her.

"Open your mouth a little," she says.

I let my lips part slightly. My throat has gone dry, and my heart is hammering again. I don't know what I'm more aware of: Allison's fingers on my face, or the heat of Allison's breath—or Wes's steady gaze on the two of us.

Allison takes off a little fleck of color with her thumbnail, recaps the lipstick, and tosses it in the general direction of her bed. "Perfect! Let's go."

She hustles Wes and me out the door, and I don't have a chance to peek at my reflection again until we get to Wes's car. I'm startled by what I see staring back from the dark, dirt-flecked windows. My lips are ripe-apple red, and it changes my whole face. I look like a completely different person—someone bold, sexy, confident.

I'm not sure who I'm supposed to be, but I definitely don't look like myself tonight. And isn't that the whole point of Halloween?

25

SCARLETT

*H*alloween. The night I've been waiting for.

The night Kinnear dies.

I'm so eager to get to his house I'm practically vibrating, but I force myself to go over the whole plan again. I've been anticipating this kill for so long, and I want it to be perfect.

As I'm plugging my cell phone in to make sure it stays on all night—at home, sitting on the kitchen counter, so it looks like I've been here the whole time too—the screen lights up with a text.

Happy Halloween.

Jasper. The phone buzzes again, rattling against the granite.

What are you up to tonight?

I almost pick it up to respond that I'm at home, working, too busy to talk to him, but knowing him he might come over and check. I really need to get his key back—or change the locks. Though Jasper knows how to pick them; I watched him break Sandra into her office once when she left her keys at home, with nothing but a quick flick of a credit card in the door. I have to break it off with him, but I'm afraid of what he'll do—and even more afraid of what I might do to him in response.

He's still typing, in fits and starts, the bubble icon appearing and disappearing. I flick the Do Not Disturb setting on and switch the screen off, examining my reflection for a moment in the darkened glass—the excitement, the bloodlust burning in my eyes.

Jasper can never know who I really am. But tonight I get to introduce Kinnear to the real Scarlett Clark.

I force myself to take a slow, indirect route to Kinnear's house, winding my way through the outskirts of town rather than cutting through the heart of campus. Even here, there are plenty of students roaming the streets in various states of costumed undress. They hardly notice me, though—too busy talking amongst themselves, taking surreptitious sips from poorly disguised liquor bottles, trying to keep their flimsy costumes secure as the wind swirls around them.

I'm in costume too: dressed up as a woman who might actually consider fucking Kinnear. Black lace trim peeks out of the plunging neckline of my dress, and my bright lipstick picks up the fresh copper tones of my hair. I've tied it back in a tight chignon the way I always do when I kill, to prevent leaving strands at the scene.

Two girls walk down the sidewalk in my direction, huddled close together against the cold. One of them—the prettier one—has shocking blue hair that licks back on the breeze like a flame. Real or a Halloween-store wig, I can't tell.

As I cut down a different street to avoid them, a shiver shoots through me, though I'm dressed much more appropriately for the weather than those girls are. I tuck my gloved hands into my pockets and increase my pace, pressing my elbow into my purse so it doesn't jostle too much against my side. There's a bottle of whiskey in there—a special gift for Kinnear.

I made him promise again, when I accidentally-on-purpose ran into him after his final class of the week: to keep tonight our little secret, so our colleagues don't start talking about us. He agreed, of course, nodding at me with a schoolboy giddiness that made me want to abandon my plan and end him right there, let his life drip out onto the linoleum for all to see.

I turn another corner, and I'm in his neighborhood. Only professors and high-level administrators can afford to live in this part of town, and trick-or-treating ended hours ago, so it's quiet here. Most of the houses are dark or lit solely by the soft flicker of a television screen. I circumvent Drew and Rafael's street entirely, though the two of them like to turn in so early, they're probably in bed by now.

Kinnear's house looks like a block of concrete, gray drapes pulled shut over all the windows to conceal him from the costumed children who trundled through earlier this evening.

Perfect.

My rubber-heeled shoes barely make a sound against Kinnear's driveway, but he still opens the door before I can lift my hand to ring the bell.

"Scarlett!" He smiles, almost as eager as I am. "Please come in."

26

CARLY

On the drive to the party, Wes keeps stealing glances at me in the rearview mirror. At first I try to pretend I don't notice. But then I find myself enjoying it a little, almost *wanting* his eyes on me.

He's playing a different Fiona Apple album than the one we listened to on our drive to Pittsburgh. This song was on the mix he made me, though, so I know all the lyrics. I mouth along with the words—*I've been a bad, bad girl*—and his gaze goes right to my red-painted lips, hands gripping the steering wheel like he's afraid he might run off the road. Allison's totally oblivious, chattering away about theater department gossip in the passenger seat.

So this is what it feels like to get the attention of a boy. It always seems like magic when I watch girls like Allison flirt. But it's so simple.

The Halloween party is at an off-campus house where several upperclassman boys from the theater department live—including Bash. The building pulses with music like it's alive, the sound thrumming through the car doors even before Wes parks in the gravel lot around back.

As we climb the rickety steps to the front porch, Allison loops her arm around me. I'm grateful for the warmth; the cold night air makes me feel even more naked. Wes trails a few steps behind us, but when we get to the door, he swoops into position to hold it open.

Inside, we're hit with a wave of heat—bodies and sweat and several different kinds of smoke. The dancing must be happening on the upper level. It sounds like the ceiling could come down at any moment from all those feet bouncing against the floorboards, rumbling like thunder.

It's so *loud*. I see Allison's lips moving as she greets her friends—a girl wearing a shiny black dress and devil horns, a guy in a Spider-Man suit with the mask pushed up so he can sip his beer—but I can't hear her, can't hear anything. Even the music is starting to sound far away now, the cacophony combining into one all-consuming drone.

Allison and Wes move deeper into the crowd, but I'm frozen, my feet rooted to the sticky floor, my throat closing up fast as if someone's squeezing it. Allison doesn't even notice that I'm not beside her anymore—she's saying hi to a girl wearing an eighties wedding gown with fake blood smeared down the front, her hair teased into an electrocuted fright—but Wes looks behind him. Looking for me.

He stops and offers me his hand. I take it.

The pressure of his grip calms my pounding pulse. We catch up with Allison again, and a boy with spiky brown hair and a fake mustache pasted to his pockmarked face—I've seen him around the theater department before, but I don't know his name—offers us all bottles of beer. Allison and Wes take them. I shake my head. "No thanks."

The boy knocks the bottle against my arm, the sweating glass leaving a cold smear of moisture on my skin. "Come on, it's a party."

Allison glares at him. "She doesn't drink."

"Why not?" He leers at me, looking down my top. "Can't be against your religion, dressed like that."

"Back off, Kyle," Allison says. "She said no."

Kyle scrambles backward, trying to disappear into the crowd to get away from Allison's glare.

"Thanks," I say.

"He just wants to get all the pretty girls wasted, 'cause that's the only way he'll get laid." Allison narrows her eyes, then tips her head back and drinks the bottle of beer he gave her in a few long swallows. "Let's dance!"

I tense, gripping Wes's hand harder. His knuckles accidentally brush against my thigh, touching my skin through the fishnet, and he jerks like he's been shocked.

"I'm not really much of a dancer," I say.

"I don't believe that. With these hips?"

Allison grabs me and squeezes. I blush, and for whatever reason, my eyes go straight to Wes. He doesn't respond, but when Allison pushes me toward the staircase, he follows us.

The second floor has slanted walls, like an attic. All the furniture has been pushed off to one side, and in the middle of the space a clump of people are—well, I guess it's dancing, but it looks more like they're all rubbing up against each other while the techno remix of a pop song blares from big speakers set up in the corners.

Before I realize what's happening, I'm in the middle of the floor, and Allison's pressed up against me. I can't see where Wes went. There's a dented disco ball hung from the rafters, throwing off strange, jagged light that distorts everything.

Allison's unzipped her hoodie, revealing a tight black tank top underneath it, already riding up to show a sliver of her stomach. She puts her hands on my waist and tugs me close so our hips smash together.

I try to stay in rhythm with the music and Allison's much more confident gyrations, but I feel totally ridiculous. Like everyone's watching me, thinking about how awkward and pathetic I am.

Like they can somehow sense the heat building between my legs as Allison rubs against me, moving to the beat.

Allison swings her head, tossing her blue hair in a wide arc, and I almost stumble over my own feet. I grab on to her to hold myself steady, and my hands end up so low I'm practically cupping her ass. I start to apologize, lift my hands away, but Allison seems unbothered. She makes a figure-eight motion with her hips, grinning, her teeth glowing as blue as her hair in the strange light. I might feel ridiculous, but Allison isn't embarrassed. She doesn't care if the whole world sees us.

Including Wes. My eyes have adjusted to the shattered light now, and I find him over in the corner near the stairs, nursing his beer and watching us dance. Allison tosses a look over her shoulder, and at first I think she's trying to get him to join us. I let myself imagine it for a second: Allison pressed against my front, Wes molded along my back, their hands tangling on my hips.

But Allison isn't looking at Wes. She's looking past him.

Bash. He has his hair slicked back, and he's wearing all black, plus what looks like liner smudged around his eyes. It makes his cheekbones appear hollow, vampiric. Maybe that's what he's supposed to be, but it's not much of a costume.

As soon as his eyes meet Allison's, she grabs me tighter, grinding against me so hard it almost hurts. I stiffen. Is that all this is? I'm just a convenient prop to try and get his attention?

Well, it's working. When the song changes to a slower one, the dance floor crowd breaks up a bit, people filtering out to get drinks or some fresh air, and Bash sidles over to us.

Allison turns to face him, her arm still around my waist. "Hey, Bash."

I want to push her off me. I want to push her so hard she hits the floor.

"Hey." He looks Allison up and down. He clearly doesn't know what her costume's supposed to be, but he doesn't ask either.

I look over at Wes again. He knocks back the rest of his beer and heads toward the stairs without giving us a second glance.

"It was so awesome of you guys to host tonight." Allison moves toward Bash, tugging me along with her. With her free hand, she laughs and touches his shoulder—the skin right below the rolled-up sleeve of his T-shirt. "Remember that night a couple weeks ago when—"

"Who's your friend?" Bash asks.

"Oh." Allison looks at me, then back at Bash. He's staring at me like she's not even there. "This is my roommate, Carly. Carly, this is—"

"Are you a theater major too? I don't think I've seen you around."

He has seen me around, plenty of times. He just didn't notice me when I wasn't half-naked.

"No," I say. "I'm—"

"She's an English major. I totally dragged her along, she hates parties." Allison smiles at me, but there's something mean behind it. As if it's my fault this asshole is ogling my boobs.

Another fast song starts up, and people begin to file back out onto the dance floor. I don't really want to dance anymore—didn't want to dance in the first place—but at least it might pull Allison's attention away from Bash.

He uses the excuse of all the bodies pressing in around us to get even closer to me. "You're having fun tonight, though. Aren't you?"

Bash smiles and the light from the cracked disco ball glints off his white incisors. My heartbeat spikes with panic. He's so close now I can smell his sweat. All I can think about, besides running outside and never looking back, is smashing my fist into his perfect teeth.

Allison drops her hand from my waist and steps between me and Bash. I'm so relieved, but my jaw is still clenched with tension. She's going to stand up for me. She's going to tell him to back off, the same way she did with that Kyle guy.

But instead, she smiles and loops her arm through Bash's elbow. "So since this is your house," she says, "I bet you know where they keep the good stuff."

He finally drags his eyes away from me. I swear I can feel an oily smear where his eyes passed over my skin.

"Sure," he says. "Come with me."

Bash starts leading her off.

I reach for her. "Wait, Allison, I—"

But they're already gone.

27

SCARLETT

Kinnear ushers me inside his house, hand hovering possessively over the small of my back. The lights are dimmed low, and the space smells like meat, a mix of char and spices wafting from the kitchen. Soft classical music streams from the wireless speakers set up in each corner of the room.

"May I take your coat?"

"That's all right." I want to keep it in my sight—and also avoid the chance of fibers transferring to the other items in his closet.

I lay the coat over the back of one of the dining chairs instead. White taper candles burn on either side of a polished wooden carving board, and there's a stack of precisely folded cloth napkins at the head of the table, but he hasn't put out the place settings yet. That's one less thing I'll have to deal with later. I can't leave any sign that Kinnear had a guest this evening.

Kinnear looks relaxed, sure of himself, the sleeves of his black cashmere sweater pushed up casually to his elbows. No glasses tonight, so his blue eyes gleam bright in the candlelight. He thinks this is just another date for him, another easy seduction. I wonder if he makes all his conquests the same meal, plays the same music, whispers the same clichés in their ears.

"Let me get you a drink," he says. "What's your poison?"

I take the whiskey bottle out of my purse and hold it up to the light.

Kinnear smiles. "You've thought of everything, haven't you?"

Indeed I have.

I hand him the whiskey. I'm still wearing my black cotton gloves, and I kept my hands covered every other time I touched the bottle, so only Kinnear's fingerprints will show up on the amber glass.

He goes to the sideboard and pours us both generous portions. I remove the gloves and tuck them in my pockets for later. I chose this dress specifically for the generous pockets at the hips—and the deep V neckline.

"Ice?" Kinnear asks.

"No, thank you." I hang the purse off the back of the chair next to my coat, then wander toward his bookcases. I'm glad of the glass fronts over the shelves, because my bare fingers itch to glide across the gilded spines. When Kinnear saunters after me, holding out my drink, I wave him away. "I'll have it with dinner."

He sets the glass on the table and takes another swig of his own whiskey. "You know, I toured this distillery when I was living abroad."

"Really?" I say. He's standing right beside me now—much closer than necessary—and he lifts the whiskey to his nose, breathing in the scent. "Is it as good as you remembered?"

Kinnear takes another swallow. I know I should smile at him, the sort of vacant, rapturous stare that will make him think I'm desperate to go to bed with him, so I watch the muscles in his throat move and think about how, a short while from now, that neck will turn purple and swollen. My lips curve upward.

"It tastes even more magnificent directly from the cask," he says. "You know they only use trees cultivated in one specific grove in the Scottish Highlands to make the barrels?"

"I didn't. How fascinating."

I was in fact well aware of that detail already, because Kinnear told the same exact story to the dean of admissions at an alumni event last year. That's why I bought this particular kind of whiskey: so he'll bloviate about the flavors and history and not keep track of how much he's consuming. He's already almost to the bottom of his first glass.

"They must have changed something, though; I'm detecting a note of . . ." He sips again, considering. "Black pepper, that's it. It's good. Adds a hint of bitterness."

I steal a glance at the clock on the wall. About twenty minutes until the drug I mixed into the whiskey starts to take hold. That's not what will kill him, but it should make him drowsy, pliable. Easier to overpower.

It's a triple dose of the same liquid sleep aid I saw in his bathroom during the Homecoming party. In the unlikely event that the police run a tox screen after his death, it will look like he took too much, by accident or on purpose.

"Dinner's about ready," Kinnear says. "I made you my famous—"

"Oh, I thought you were going to show me that book first." I peer up at the shelves, squinting like I can't find the title, even though I clocked it from across the room. *The Collected Letters of Lord Douglas Vance*, gold script stamped into pale blue cloth. It's at the top of an entire bookcase stuffed to the brim with books about Victorian writers—all men, of course.

Most of the volumes are so pristine, it's clear Kinnear has never read them. He wants people to admire them, and by extension to admire him. A man like Kinnear doesn't deserve a library like this. Maybe his family will donate it to the university after his untimely death.

He slides the glass door away, deliberately brushing my shoulder as he reaches for the book. Another volume, sitting right beside it on the shelf, catches my eye. It's smaller than the others, compact enough to fit in a pocket, and there's no title or author printed on the red spine. What's more, it looks like someone's actually read it, the edges faded and frayed from handling.

I point to it. "What's that?"

"Oh, that. Just a little something I picked up at a rare bookstore in London, years ago now." He leaves Vance's letters on the shelf and takes the small book down instead, opening the cover so I can see the handwritten inscription.

The Diary of Viola Emily Vance

My hand darts out to touch the yellowed page, but I stop myself just in time. "Is it . . ."

"Real?" He smiles. "Yes. No idea how it ended up in that ramshackle shop instead of with the Vance estate."

He's never mentioned this diary, never cited it in any of his papers. This whole time, this *whole fucking time*, he's had a one-of-a-kind primary source that would be invaluable to my research, and he's left it sitting on the shelf, buried amongst books by every pretentious asshole of the era.

"Of course, it's mostly juvenilia," he says. "Little poems and such she wrote when she was first married. But you can take a look if you want."

He hands me the diary, holding it by the corner like it's a piece of trash, like it means nothing. I want to snatch it out of his hands and cradle it against my chest. But I can't touch anything, not without my gloves.

"I don't want to damage it." I try to sound deferential, demure. Anything but full of murderous rage.

Kinnear eats it up. Any hint of perceived helplessness, and men fall over themselves to play the hero. He takes the book over to the dining table and sets it down by the stack of napkins. Then he pulls out a chair for me. I sit, spine stiff, and Kinnear leans over me, arms caging me in, to turn the delicate pages covered in Viola Vance's unmistakable scrawl.

"This one's not half bad." He reads a short poem fragment, his whiskey-soaked breath rustling my hair. On the last few words, he slurs a little, though he keeps going like nothing's wrong.

The drug is working already.

"It's wonderful," I say. It is, despite his mangling.

"You know," Kinnear says, "if I end up getting the Women's Academy fellowship, it doesn't necessarily mean you can't access the archive."

I turn my head to look at him. He's so close, he probably thinks we're a breath away from kissing. If only he knew what I really wanted to do to him.

"You could come to London." He lays his hand on my shoulder, pressing the pad of his thumb into the bone. "Spend some time with me, and I could see about getting you guest access."

Under the table, I dig my fingers into my thighs. How dare he. How fucking *dare* he. He thinks he's going to get the fellowship— the fellowship *I* deserve, the fellowship that should be mine in the first place, that *would* be mine if he weren't "Cambridge chums" with the goddamn curator—and he'll do me the *favor* of helping me with my work if I fly across the Atlantic to suck his cock.

He disgusts me. I'm so tired of pretending he doesn't.

But not for much longer now.

"That would be amazing." I force myself to hold his gaze, and for a second I think he's actually going to try to kiss me. I can't allow that, obviously—too many forensic variables, not to mention my own gag reflex. His eyes are looking less focused by the second. I think I've waited long enough.

"I know we were supposed to have dinner but—" I shift in my seat, so his hand falls away from my shoulder, but he has a clear view of the cleavage spilling out of my dress. Even with his gaze going glassy, Kinnear doesn't miss that. "I'm not really hungry."

28

CARLY

*I*t feels like Allison's been gone an hour, but it can't have been that long. The dance floor is back in full swing, and everything's swirling, all the lights and the music and the writhing bodies.

I press my back against the wall to steady myself. A guy in a zombie costume dances too close to me, the shredded sleeve of his shirt brushing my arm. I shrink closer to the wall and take a deep breath, but my chest heaves like a romance novel heroine in this stupid corset.

Someone taps me on the shoulder, and I whirl around, but it's only Wes. He jerks back, out of my reach. Oh God, I almost hit him, didn't I? I force my hand down to my side, still tightened into a fist.

"Are you okay?" He looks around. "Where's Allison?"

"She left." It's hard to get the words out; my throat feels cinched tighter than my waist.

"You want to go outside for a minute?" he asks.

Really I want to leave the party, but I don't want to ruin Wes's night any more than I probably already have. And I can't leave without Allison.

Wes offers me his hand, and I let him pull me away from the relative safety of the wall and down the staircase. We're still holding hands as we head out the back door. Despite the cold, the patio is almost as crowded as the dance floor, a thick haze of smoke hanging over all the pirates and sexy cats and glow-in-the-dark skeletons gathered there, so Wes and I keep walking, toward the thicket of cars parked haphazardly on the gravel lot behind the house.

"Who are you supposed to be, anyway?" I ask. Now that we're away from the party, my throat feels less like there are fingers around it, but my voice sounds weirdly far away, my ears still ringing from the music.

"Oh, uh—I'm Rivers Cuomo," Wes says.

I blink at him.

"The lead singer of Weezer?"

I have no idea what he's talking about. This whole night feels blurry, even though I'm completely sober.

"That band we listened—" Wes pushes the thick-framed glasses up higher on his nose.

They're a lot like the ones Alex wears. They look right on Alex, but on Wes they're a little much, taking over his face so it's hard to focus on his features.

"Never mind. It's a pretty lame costume anyway. That wasn't cool, you know," he says, lowering his voice even though we're far enough away from the house that no one's likely to overhear. "The way Allison was using you to get his attention."

My chest burns, with shame and something else, at the memory of Allison's body pressed up so close, moving against mine, the music vibrating through us. "Oh, no, that's not—"

"Trust me, she's always been like this. She never wants what's right in front of her. She wants what she can't have." He looks me in the eyes. "You get used to it after a while."

He's so close to me now, and we're all alone out here. Well, there's a Honda hatchback a couple feet away that's rocking slightly, so not *completely* alone. We're almost to Wes's car now. It's so chilly out. We could get inside, crank the heat up. Talk some more, or—

I swallow, the cold night air burning in my lungs. "Have you and Allison ever—"

"Slept together?" Wes says.

"*No*," I blurt out. "I just meant, have you ever . . . anything."

"We kissed once, when we were twelve. Spin the bottle."

He laughs. I try to laugh too, but the sound gets stuck in my throat.

"I'm not trying to rag on her," he says. "I mean, she's my best friend. But I don't want you to get hurt either."

I'm shivering harder now, even though I barely feel the cold on my skin anymore. Wes puts his hands on my shoulders and starts rubbing up and down, trying to warm me. Eventually his rhythm slows and he's no longer looking me in the eyes. He's looking at my lips, and I wonder if that bright lipstick is still there or if it's faded, smudged, red bleeding out at the corners of my mouth.

Someone over on the patio lets out a screech, echoing into the night. I can't tell if it's celebratory or a call for help, but I don't turn my head to check, either. I'm frozen, staring at Wes—focusing on his lips now too, the chapped bit in the center where he bites down when he's thinking during class.

Wes's hands press down harder on my shoulders, drawing me in. He's going to kiss me. Oh my God, he's going to kiss me, and part of me wants him to, but another part, a stronger one, wants to get as far away from him as possible.

"I'm sorry, I—" I say, and Wes stops pulling me toward him, but he doesn't let go of my shoulders. So I shake him off—harder than I needed to, than I meant to. He stumbles back, stones crunching under his feet. "I can't."

I'm already running, my boots kicking up gravel to sting my shins through the fishnets. I don't even know where I'm going, until

I find myself back inside the house. The partygoers crush around me, and a scream builds in my throat but I don't let it out. I keep pushing through the crowd until I get to the stairs and then I climb, climb, climb.

I dart down the dark hallway, feeling my way along the wood-paneled walls, looking for somewhere, anywhere I can be alone. Finally I find a knob. It won't turn, but the door isn't latched right, and it swings open when I push.

The lights are already on inside, and I'm blinded for a second, but then I blink away the stars in my eyes and see them.

Allison and Bash.

He's pressing her against the sink. One hand up her shirt, the other shoved down her unzipped jeans. Bash sees me, but Allison doesn't, because her eyes are shut.

She's unconscious.

29

SCARLETT

I let Kinnear lead me down the hall, pretending I don't know my way to his bedroom.

When we cross the threshold, Kinnear stumbles forward and grabs my waist to steady himself. The drugs have fully taken hold now, but he thinks he's drunk.

"Guess I can't hold my Scotch like I used to!" He laughs but doesn't let go of me.

I laugh too, but if he weren't so out of it, he'd be able to hear the false note in it. I'm not bothering to hide the coldness in my eyes anymore; I'm studying him like the insect he is. But he's totally oblivious. As far as he's concerned, he's having a great night: pleasantly intoxicated, about to get lucky.

Kinnear squeezes me tighter and takes another unsteady step forward, pushing me up against the bedroom wall. His hands are moving higher now, cupping my breasts. I'd hoped I could maneuver him into position without letting him touch me, but I can tolerate it for a few more seconds to get him where I want him.

"Y'know I always thought . . ." His words trip over themselves. "Ever since the first day I met you—but you held out on me, didn't you?"

Kinnear grasps at my thigh, fingertips sliding under the hem of my skirt. This dress is brand-new, picked out especially for tonight—same with the black lace lingerie underneath it. He'll never get far enough to see it, of course, but it makes me feel powerful. Armored.

I keep my hands down at my sides, but I arch my back, letting him think that I'm aroused by the way he's pinned me against the wall, stabbing his sorry excuse for an erection into my hip. When he moves in to kiss me, I turn my face away. I have to do it three times before he finally backs off, stumbling a little like he's going to keel over backward.

He looks at me, bewildered, eyes unfocused. "What's w—"

"Take off your pants and lie down on the bed."

At first he just gapes at me, and I'm afraid I've overplayed my hand. He likes women who fawn over him, not order him around. For this next part of my plan to work, though, I need him to do what I say.

But a second later, his face lights up with a wobbly grin, and his hands go to his belt buckle. "Yes, Professor."

Kinnear takes a few halting steps before managing to fully step out of his pant legs. When he reaches the bed, he more falls on it than lies down. But it doesn't matter: he's right where I want him now.

Once he's sprawled on the mattress, leaning against the wooden slats of the headboard, he shoots me what I'm sure he thinks is a seductive smile. "Aren't you going to join me?"

I stay where I am, arms folded. "Close your eyes."

"But I want to see you." He makes a suggestive little circle with his hips, grinding at nothing. "God, you're gorgeous."

I run my fingers along the neckline of my dress. "Close them."

He gives me a shit-eating grin that makes me want to rip his teeth out with pliers and jam them down his esophagus, but he does what I've asked. I wait a few seconds to make sure he's going to stay put before taking the gloves out of my pockets.

Kinnear shifts on the bed—starting to get uneasy, even through the drugged haze. He lifts one eyelid as I'm slipping the second glove on.

"No peeking," I say, moving to the closet to pull two scarves off the hanger inside the door. I pick up Kinnear's belt from the floor too and climb onto the bed, straddling him.

Kinnear keeps his eyes shut like I told him to, but he gropes around until he manages to get a handful of my ass. I grab his arm, pressing it back against the headboard. He opens his eyes just in time to see me winding one of the scarves around his wrist.

"What are you doing?"

I tug the knot tighter. "Don't tell me you've never done this before."

"Of course I have," he says, even though he clearly hasn't. "I just—"

I'm already tying up his other wrist. He starts to squirm a little, but he's not panicking.

Yet.

"I thought this was what you wanted." I grind down against him, pinning him to the bed as I finish lashing his wrists to the headboard slats. "Ever since the first day you met me."

Kinnear blinks at me, like his brain is buffering, taking a second to catch up with what's happening. He finally notices the gloves. "Why are you wearing those?"

I sit back against his pelvis and smile at him—merciless, predatory. My real smile. The one I save for these final moments. I wait until the fear in his eyes starts to roil like storm clouds, then rear back and slap him across the cheek. Hard enough to sting, but not to leave a mark.

"What the *fuck* are you—" He finally fights back, trying to throw me off the bed, but with his arms bound and the drugs in his bloodstream, he isn't strong enough.

I lean over him, holding his wrists in place with my hands too. He's tied securely, but I can't risk obvious ligature marks on his limbs. Once he's dead, I'll untie him and put the scarves right back where I found them, to support the story that he did this to himself. I can see the headline now: *Esteemed literature scholar found dead in his bed, an attempt at autoerotic asphyxiation gone horribly wrong.*

I was going to use a scarf to strangle him too, but his belt was right there, coiled up on the floor like a venomous snake, and it seemed too perfect. This will hurt so much more, and above all else, I want him to suffer. I loop the leather around his neck.

He's thrusting up against me now, a terrible parody of what he thought we were going to do in his bed tonight. I pull the belt tighter, and he's so stunned with terror he goes still.

Kinnear has never looked at me like this—*really* looked at me. In all the years I've known him, eye contact was always a brief stopover on the way to ogling my tits, my ass. Reducing me to parts. This wild-eyed fear is the closest thing to respect he's ever paid me.

Too little, far too late.

I can't finish him until I see the realization dawn in his eyes. Until I'm sure he knows exactly who I am, and why I'm doing this to him. I cinch the belt under his chin, tilting his head up so he can get a better look at my face.

"Do you remember me now, Alex?"

30

CARLY

"Don't."

My voice is so quiet, Bash might not have heard me over the music. I'm still on the threshold of the bathroom. Frozen, helpless. But not as helpless as Allison is. Her head dangles over the sink, blue hair pooling in the basin.

I take a step forward. "Don't touch her."

Bash looks up, but he doesn't stop what he's doing. He looks me right in the eyes, and he doesn't stop.

"Don't fucking touch her!"

I'm screaming now, shooting toward him. Why did I hesitate, why did I let her go off alone with him in the first place? I should have known better, I should have protected her.

Bash finally takes his hands off Allison, and, without him holding her up, she crumbles toward the floor. On her way down, she knocks over the bottle sitting on the edge of the sink, spraying smoked-glass shards over the floor tiles.

She's not just drunk. I've seen her drunk, and this is different. He must have put something in her drink. He did this on purpose, he drugged her and took her in here and shut the door. If I hadn't walked in when I did . . .

Some of the partygoers are gathering outside the bathroom, drawn by my shouts. But none of them do anything except gawk at us, my red face and clenched fists and Allison crumpled on the floor and Bash backed up against the bathtub, regarding me with those lazy, sleepy eyes like he's bored with the scene.

I get down next to Allison and try to help her up. My knees grind into the broken glass, but I barely feel it. Allison's left temple is bleeding a little; she must have smacked it against the counter. The red drips down, tracing the line of her cheekbone. Her orange hoodie is on the floor too. Bash must have stripped it off before he—

No. I can't think about that. I have to concentrate on helping her.

I shake the glass off the sweatshirt, then dab at Allison's cut with one of the sleeves. She stirs a little, eyelids fluttering—not completely unconscious, but seriously out of it. What the fuck did he give her?

He's still right next to us, close enough that I can smell his musky cologne—or maybe the scent is all over Allison.

I can't let myself look up at him. If I look at him I don't know what I'll do.

Finally, a girl wearing an angular black wig and an oversize white button-down breaks off from the cluster of onlookers. "What's going on?"

Bash gives her a lazy grin. "Hadley got wasted again."

The girl doesn't laugh, but some of the other students around her do. Mostly the guys. The low tones of their derisive chuckles vibrate down to my bones.

Suddenly I'm on my feet, facing Bash. His smile fades when he sees my expression. He takes a step backward, his heels hitting the base of the tub.

Someone moves behind me, around me. I'm vaguely aware that it's Wes, pushing his way into the bathroom, kneeling down next to Allison. I'm furious, I'm on fire with it, prickling heat exploding over my skin. But a strange calm washes over me too—a curiosity, almost. I'm wondering whether, if I shoved Bash back into the shower, I'd be able to hear the crack of his skull against the tile, or if the music rattling the walls would drown it out.

Allison gives a little whimper, smacking Wes's hand away from the wound on her head, and my surroundings click back into focus.

I crouch down next to Wes. "Help me get her out of here."

"Did you see what happened?" he asks. "Did she fall, or—"

I don't even look at him, too busy wrapping the bloodstained sweatshirt around Allison's shoulders, bracing my arm against her waist. "Grab her arms."

"Are you sure that's—"

"Are you going to help us or not?" I snap.

Wes cowers a little, blinking at me. I know I shouldn't take it out on him—he's not the enemy here—but it felt good, letting a little bit of the rage break through. Like spitting out poison.

He takes hold of Allison like I told him to, and together we haul her up to standing, then awkwardly make our way toward the door with her arms slung over our shoulders. Wes keeps looking over at me, but I stay staring straight ahead, my jaw clenched. I want to get out of here. I should never have come here in the first place— except I don't want to think about what might have happened if I hadn't been here.

The crowd parts to let us through, but there are more than a few snickers, knowing looks exchanged. I hate them all so much. Bash most of all. That smug look on his face. I wonder how many times he's done this before.

When we make it to the car, Wes leaves me supporting Allison's full weight for a second while he gets the back seat ready. As soon as he walks away, she shifts against my shoulder.

Her eyes are open.

"Oh thank God," I say. "Are you—"

"Don't tell him." Her voice is a wavering rasp, barely audible.

"What?"

She looks over at Wes, leaning halfway into the back door of the car to lay a blanket over the seats. "Promise me. Promise me you won't—"

"I'm so sorry." The words come out in a torrent, flowing like tears. "I shouldn't have let you go off alone with him, I should have—"

Allison is terrifyingly lucid now, her blue eyes sharp as icicles. She grips my shoulder hard enough to bruise. "*Promise* me."

I blink at her. I don't understand why she would want to keep this a secret from Wes. He's her best friend. If he knew what Bash did to her, if he'd seen what I saw, he'd be furious. He would want blood too.

But I don't want to upset her any more, not after what she just went through—what she's *still* going through—so I nod. "Okay. I promise."

Wes shuts the car door and circles back. "Hey," he says to Allison. "Are you okay? How are you feeling?"

"I'm fine." She's slumping harder against me, though her grip on my shoulder stays firm.

"We should take her to the hospital," I say.

"I said I'm *fine*." But she isn't—the lucidity of a few moments ago is fading, her eyelids growing heavy again.

"You hit your head. You could have a concussion." That's the thing I'm *least* worried about in this situation, but obviously I can't mention the real reason she should see a doctor without breaking my promise.

"I just wanna go home," she says. "Sleep it off. C'mon . . ."

"We could keep an eye on her tonight," Wes suggests. "Go to the doctor in the morning."

"Yeah, my head barely even hurts." Allison nods vigorously as if to demonstrate.

"*No.*"

I'm not shouting like before. The word comes out quiet, but there's a threat underneath it. *You don't want to argue with me right now.* I've never heard myself sound like this. It's as if someone else's voice is speaking through me.

Wes and Allison are silent. They both seem a little scared of me. Usually I would trip back over my words, apologize, try to make sure no one was offended. But right now I don't give a fuck.

I start steering Allison toward the car. "Come on, let's go."

Wes hesitates, worrying his keys between his fingers.

"What?" I ask.

"I'm . . ." he starts. "Well, I mean I'm not *drunk*, but I think I might have had too much to—"

I grab the keys out of his hands with an exasperated sigh. "Help me put her in the back."

Wes and I awkwardly stuff Allison into the back seat. She's gone deadweight again, her eyes shut. Whether she's really hurt or in some sort of shock, we have to get her to a doctor. I'm worried we've waited too long. Who knows what Bash gave her, what other effects it might have.

Wes slides in beside Allison, maneuvering her head onto his lap. I get into the driver's seat, and as I'm adjusting the rearview mirror, Wes and I lock eyes, the way we did on the ride to the party. But everything's different now.

My hands squeeze the steering wheel, and I wish it was Bash's throat.

31

SCARLETT

"You don't even remember my name, do you?"

Alexander Kinnear's mouth gapes, red and wet as a wound, but he doesn't speak.

"You remember what you did to me, though." I press down harder, grinding my knees into his rib cage. "Or maybe you can't remember that either, I was one of many, too insignificant to—"

"Carly."

It comes out in a gasp. I smile and wind the end of the belt tighter around my knuckles.

"B-but wait," he says. "You, you—"

His eyes rove over my face, my body. He's seeing it now: the awkward girl I used to be, with the frizzy brown hair and the too-skinny limbs, still saddled with my father's last name instead of the one I gave myself.

The first semester I worked here, I spent every day sick with dread, waiting for someone to put the pieces together—to recognize me as Carly Schiller, even though I'd changed almost everything about myself since leaving Gorman in the middle of my freshman year.

No point in telling the whole story to Kinnear, though. He'll be dead in a few minutes.

"Look," he says, squirming. "I was going through a really hard time back then."

I've been looking forward to this part too: his pathetic attempts to justify himself. As if there's anything he could say to stop me at this point.

"I did a lot of things I regret. But it was a long time ago, and—"

I pull the belt taut until Kinnear makes a sputtering sound and starts thrashing with panic—but only for a few seconds. I have to be careful with choking him from this angle. A few marks are okay; it will look like he was testing out the pressure, edging himself closer.

"Please." Kinnear gulps in air, trembling all over. "Don't—you don't want to do this."

Good. I was hoping he'd beg.

"I know you're angry with me," he says. "But you're not a murderer."

I can't help it: I laugh, throwing my head back. "I've been killing men like you for years."

Kinnear's pupils are huge from the medication, the blue almost eclipsed by black. It's remarkable he's awake; it must be thanks to all the stress hormones coursing through his veins. But I'm glad he's still somewhat lucid so I can enjoy the look on his face as he takes this knowledge in.

"You're just the next asshole on my list, Alex."

He squints. I can practically see the gears grinding in his drug-muddled mind.

"That boy," he says. "When you were a student. The boy who died . . ."

Now *that* I didn't expect him to figure out. Since what happened was ruled an accident, it's not even in the campus suicide data. My first kill was easy. It made me realize what I could get away with. What I was truly capable of.

"That boy deserved it." I lean over Kinnear's face, close enough to kiss him. "But not as much as you do."

I should kill him and be done with it. The hard part is over already; now all that's left is to loop the belt over the headboard. Wait for him to struggle and convulse and go still. It will be over in minutes.

But after all those years of hating him, all my months of preparation, I want to savor this a little while longer: the lascivious dismissal draining out of his eyes, replaced by gut-twisting fear. I'm not an object or an obstacle to him anymore. I'm his goddamn ruination.

"This is—it's absurd," he says. "You can't possibly—"

Leave it to Alexander Kinnear to attempt to sound imperious when he's prone and bound and a breath away from dying.

"You really think it's a good idea to tell me what I can and can't do?"

His eyes flash, anger burning off the fear. "You were an adult, you—"

"I was your *student*."

"You're one to judge me for carrying on with students. Don't think I don't know about you and Jasper Prior."

I yank on the belt. Kinnear seems more alert by the second, even though there's no way the drug should be wearing off yet. I shouldn't have bothered with drugging him at all—getting him in this bed would have been nearly as easy without it. I can't stand the thought that any of his suffering might be blunted. I want him to feel it all, every moment.

Kinnear writhes underneath me. He'll pass out any second now, so I have to enjoy this—the desperate, animal sounds he's making, the spittle flecking his mouth, the way his skin is turning the color of bruised fruit.

I've been waiting so long.

Then my vision goes black and pain bursts on the side of my

skull. Kinnear's hand seizes my hip. His hand—*how is it free? I tied the knot so carefully, I—*

He pushes me with all the strength he has left, and I tumble off the side of the bed. As I'm falling, I see the gap in the headboard. He's managed to snap one of the slats off, and now he's unbuckling the belt from his neck and tearing his other hand out of my restraints.

No. No. This is not the plan. This is not happening.

He tries to run for the door, but I grab him by the ankle and take him down, clawing my way up his body until I'm straddling him again. The broken slat is on the floor beside us. I press it across his throat, throwing all my weight against it, ignoring the sparks of pain in my palm as the jagged ends sting my skin even through the gloves.

All I have to do is get him unconscious so I can haul him back onto the bed, strap him back into place, and finish the job there. The damage to the headboard won't fit the narrative, but I can take the broken-off piece with me, bury it in the woods, burn it. I can still make this work.

I have to.

But Kinnear is gaining strength, adrenaline driving the drug out of his system. He bucks against me, digging his nails into my skirt. Then he gets his hands around mine and slams upward. The splintered wood scrapes under my chin, snapping my teeth together, and I'm on the floor again and he's gone, dragging himself to his feet, scrambling toward the door.

I'm right behind him, and when he stumbles a little, shoulder bashing into the wall outside the dining room, I close the distance, grabbing the back of his sweater, stretching the cashmere. He shakes me off and lurches into the dining room, reaching for something on the table.

His cell phone. I lunge at him, knocking the phone out of his hands. When it hits the floor, the screen shatters. Kinnear stares at me, gasping for breath. Broken blood vessels spiderweb around his blue eyes, and the flickering light of the candles brings out all the marks I've left on him: the red circles around his neck and wrists, the scratches on his face. Anyone looking at him, even the absolute idiots in the Gorman Police Department, will know he was attacked tonight.

He's ruined my plan. He's ruined everything.

I can't let him leave this house. But he doesn't try to run. He's not even looking at me anymore; his gaze is cast downward, gaping in horror at something by my right side.

My hand.

"Scarlett . . ."

I didn't even realize I had grabbed anything, but now I feel it there: the weight of the handle, the cold steel soaking through my gloves. The knife from the carving board in the center of the table.

Kinnear makes a clumsy grab for the weapon, and I jab the point toward his stomach. He leaps back with a yelp even though all I've stabbed is the air between us. Fucking coward.

"Scarlett, please." He starts backing up slowly. I match him, step for step. "You don't have to do this. I'll do whatever you want. Anything. I'll—you want the fellowship? You can have it, I'll make some calls, make sure they give it to you, just—"

I lift the knife. The candlelight reflecting on the blade makes it look like it's on fire. The metal is polished to such a high sheen, I wonder if he's ever used it before, or if the knife is like the books in his library. Only for show.

He trips over the chair where I left my coat and purse; it topples backward, thumping against the thick geometric rug. I step over it and keep coming. Kinnear is larger than me, stronger. He could physically overpower me if he wanted, but he thinks he can talk his way out of this. Still underestimating me.

"You sought me out." He takes another step back. "You came to see me alone, you—"

My fingers clench around the knife. "Shut up."

"No one else gave a damn about you. You know that, right? I was the only one who tried to help." He shakes his head—like I'm pathetic, like he feels *sorry* for me. "And this is the thanks I get."

"Shut the fuck up." My hand is shaking, gripping the knife handle so hard it hurts down to my bones.

"Scarlett, come on, it was *sixteen fucking years ago.*"

There it is: the anger, the disbelief, the utter indignation that I would dare to judge him, to hold him accountable. To make him pay for what he's done.

"You have to take some responsibility too," he says. "You knew exactly what you were doing. Girls like you always—"

My arm is already swinging. One slash, and Kinnear's throat blooms red.

32

CARLY

The waiting room of Gorman's only ER is filled with college students in Halloween costumes. In comparison, Allison, Wes, and I look almost normal.

Allison's lying stretched out across a couple of chairs the same eye-searing orange as her hoodie, her blue hair dangling off the side to brush the floor. Wes is a few chairs down, tapping his heel on the tiles compulsively.

I sit between them, a clipboard balancing on my lap, my thighs sticking to the plastic seat through the fishnets. I'm supposed to be filling out the hospital paperwork, but I keep getting distracted, checking on Allison. You're not supposed to let people with concussions fall asleep, right?

A nurse in mint-green scrubs emerges from the swinging doors and calls out another name. This time a guy in a Superman cape responds. He has a black eye and a bent nose, but he's not bleeding like the last patient who went back.

Allison stares up at the fluorescent lights with her jaw clenched. The blood on her temple has dried to a smear of rust. She kept arguing with Wes and me on the way to the hospital, insisting she was fine even as her words slurred together, but since we got here she's been silent.

Two girls dressed as Playboy bunnies rush together to the industrial-size trash can by the reception desk, the redhead holding the brunette's hair back while she vomits. I swallow the bile rising in my throat and bow my head over the hospital form, writing the date. *October 31*—no, it's after midnight, the first of November now. *2004.* It's technically Monday; Wes and I have Alex's writing class in a few hours.

I write my name next, then realize I should have written Allison's instead and start scratching the letters out.

"Your full name's Scarlett?" Wes says. He must have been reading over my shoulder.

Allison props herself up on her elbow. "Why do you go by Carly?"

She's seeming more lucid by the minute—which is good, of course, but I'm afraid if we have to wait too much longer, whatever Bash gave her will be too far out of her system to register. If they'll even test her for roofies, or whatever it was.

I shrug. "My parents always called me Carly."

Well, my father did—and as with everything else, my mother went along with it to keep him happy. Besides, I've never felt like I could carry off a name as dramatic as *Scarlett.*

After I turn in the completed form, it seems like hours before the nurse calls Allison's name. The Playboy girls are the only ones still left in the waiting room with us, the redhead sitting with the brunette's head in her lap, stroking her hair.

Allison pops upright, then winces. "Careful!" I say, moving to loop a steadying arm around her waist. Wes gets up to help too, but she's already shrugging me off, walking determinedly toward the double doors.

The nurse deposits us in—well, it's not quite a room, just a bed sectioned off from other similar beds by white curtains. She goes over what I put on the form, then takes Allison's vitals in a brusque, dismissive blur and tells us the doctor will be in to see her soon. I wrote down that Allison fell and hit her head, but I'm hoping if I can get Wes to leave for a little bit, I can convince her to tell the doctor what really happened.

As soon as the nurse walks away, I turn to him. "Are you hungry? I'm *starving*."

He seems a little surprised, but also relieved to have something to do. While the nurse examined Allison, Wes just stood in the corner, chewing on his lower lip. "I can go try and find some snacks. Anything in particular?"

"Something hot. Maybe the cafeteria's still open?"

He looks at Allison. She's so spaced out, it's like she doesn't even see him for a second. But eventually she shakes her head and says, "I'm good."

She's not, though. I can tell. She seemed calm in the waiting room, but now her eyes are shining, like there are tears building up but she's refusing to let them spill out. It makes my chest ache, seeing her like this. And it's all Bash's fault.

The doctor comes in a few minutes after Wes leaves. He's an older guy, deep lines etched around his eyes and silver streaks at his temples. He looks like a skinnier version of my father.

He stares at me for a second. No, not at me: at my chest. I hunch my shoulders, and the corset boning bites into my ribs. This damn costume. I should never have let Allison talk me into it. But that's the least of my mistakes tonight.

"Ms. Hadley?" the doctor asks.

Allison nods. She looks so tired, like she can barely keep her eyes open. I expect the doctor to start examining her, but instead he folds his arms across his white lab coat and says, "You want to tell me what happened?"

"She—" I start.

"I hit my head." Allison's trying to sound extra lucid for the doctor's benefit, enunciating each of her words precisely, but the effort makes her seem even more intoxicated.

"Were you drinking?" he asks.

I glare at him. "Is that really—"

"Yes. I was drinking." Allison lifts her chin, challenging him.

He flips through her chart. "We'll give you some fluids, keep an eye on you for the next couple of hours."

"That's it?" I say. He hasn't even touched her. "What about her head?"

He approaches the bed and pushes Allison's hair back—rougher than necessary. Some bedside manner.

"You're fine; that'll heal in a few days." He lets her hair fall back over her forehead. "Don't worry, you won't have a scar on that pretty face."

He's already turning to leave. I have to tell him. Surely if he knew what really happened, he'd take more than a cursory look at her.

"Wait," I say. "That's not—"

The doctor turns back. Allison gives me a warning look.

"This guy at the party," I continue. "I think he drugged her. He was—"

The doctor sighs and squints at Allison. "You know, it's really hard for me to help you if you lie to me." He poises his pen over the chart. "Tell me what you took."

"I didn't take anything," Allison says. "I had a couple drinks, that's it."

I shake my head. "He must have put it in your drink."

"No, I—nothing happened, we were just fooling around and—"

"You were *unconscious*!"

Allison stares at me, stunned, tears glittering. The doctor clicks his pen closed.

"You want a rape kit?" He says this so matter-of-factly, like he's asking if Allison would like a glass of water. He doesn't seem the least bit concerned.

"No!" She shakes her head, hair swishing over her shoulders. She's trying to sound strong, but there's a waver in her voice. I want to gather her in my arms. I want to slap this asshole doctor across the mouth. "No, I don't—"

"He didn't—" I don't know how to explain, without making it sound like I'm minimizing what Bash did. "I mean, he was touching her. While she was passed out."

The doctor looks at Allison. "Is that what happened?"

She hesitates. She looks so lost, her face blanched of all color. "I'm not— I don't—"

"You don't remember?" His voice drips with mockery. I don't want to slap him anymore; that wouldn't be nearly enough. I feel the sensation again: that eerie wash of calm over the surface, the heat roiling underneath.

Allison's eyes are welling up, but she keeps blinking the tears back. I put my hand on her arm, to reassure her, to let her know that I'm here for her, I believe her, no matter what.

She pulls away from me. "No," she says. "I don't remember."

33

SCARLETT

I've never felt so out of control before. Not even the first time. I drop the blade and a few specks of blood stipple my bare knee. The puddle of red oozing from Kinnear's throat has almost spread to my toes. I step out of the way just in time to avoid getting any on my shoes.

The blood, the broken glass from his shattered phone. The smell of liquor in the air, the flicker of the candle flames. I shut my eyes, trying to steady myself, but images start flashing across the backs of my eyelids. Not of Kinnear. Not of the easy way the blade parted the skin of his throat, the red gushing out, the way he clutched at his ruined neck like he was trying to stitch it back together.

Something else. Something I haven't thought about in years.

No, that's not true. I thought about it earlier tonight, when I saw that girl with the blue hair. Her plainer friend, walking in her shadow. That used to be me.

My knee throbs, and I swipe at it absently, trying to brush away the pieces of glass. But there's nothing there, no wound, no blood except Kinnear's. That was back then, when I knelt on the floor and clutched Allison in my arms, her blue hair spilling over me like water. When all that rage rushed up inside me. The same rage I've been trying to keep under control ever since, to sharpen and wield like a weapon so it doesn't consume me from the inside out.

Tonight I failed. There's no way I can pass this off as an accident or a suicide. The drapes are still closed, but someone could have heard our struggle, heard Kinnear screaming—did he scream? I can't remember. My throat feels raw, like I might have been screaming too.

Everything is silent now. No sirens, no noise from outside. That's good. The only good thing about this situation.

I could try to clean this up. Drag his body to the woods and bury it. But that would probably increase my chances of getting caught, not lessen them.

No. I have to get out of here. I retrieve my coat and purse from the dining room floor before the pool of blood can reach them too. There are probably some drops of blood on my dress, but my coat will cover that and the spatter on my knee until I can get home to clean myself up. After I burn my clothes and anything else that might have his blood on it, I'm going to scrub every inch of my skin until I'm certain no trace of Alexander Kinnear remains.

The taper candles are burning lower, guttering, white blobs of wax dripping on the table, and Kinnear's pale skin glows bright in the dim light. His blue eyes stare up at me, mouth hanging open almost as wide as the wound in his throat. Now that death has slackened his features, he looks more like his younger self. The affable young professor I met all those years ago when I was young and stupid. Just the way he liked us.

The police will know this is a homicide, but they won't necessarily be able to trace the crime to me. I made sure not to touch a single thing without gloves, so my fingerprints shouldn't be anywhere in the house. Definitely not on the murder weapon. And if those candles were to tip over . . . a fire can't destroy the evidence entirely, but it could certainly make the investigation more of a challenge.

I return to the bookcases, pulling down as many volumes as I can carry and dropping them on top of Kinnear, until he's covered head to toe with the words of the dead white men he loved so dearly. Then I grab the whiskey bottle off the table and drizzle its remaining contents over the covers. Destroying these beautiful books sparks more guilt in me than any of the murders I've committed, but at least they're serving a purpose.

I'm about to light my makeshift funeral pyre when I remember: Viola Vance's diary. The slim red book is still sitting on the dining table, open to the poem Kinnear read to me. It's at the opposite end from where I struck the fatal blow, too far away for any spatter to hit the pages.

To avoid transferring any blood onto the book now, I use one of Kinnear's napkins to pick it up. As I turn it over in my hands, I imagine Viola Vance running her own fingers over the cover when it was new, scrawling scraps of poetry in it by candlelight. She would be furious, I'm sure, if she knew her diary had ended up in the possession of someone like Kinnear. This book should belong to a person who cares about it, who knows its worth.

It should belong to me.

No one will even know it's missing, with the rest of his library reduced to ash. I've never been one to keep trophies, but this is different. This is a one-of-a-kind literary treasure, and I couldn't live with myself if I left it to burn with the rest.

I slip Viola's diary into my purse, and tip the candles over onto Kinnear's corpse.

I know my way through the woods, but it's harder to navigate so late at night, even with a burgeoning inferno at my back. The rug was already ablaze when I left through the back door, and by the time I reach the tree line, the curtains have caught too. If I'm lucky, the whole house will go up in flames.

The panic doesn't start to rise in my throat until I'm farther into the forest. It feels as alive as the flames I just fled, like it's chasing me, snapping at my heels. I want to run the whole way home, so fast my lungs burn, but I force myself to take a slow, methodical, indirect route skirting the edges of town. Once I'm safely inside, I head straight to my study and ignite the gas fireplace. I strip down so I'm wearing nothing but my gloves and underwear and start feeding my clothes into the flames.

While I wait for all the fabric to catch, I take the diary out of my purse to admire it again by the firelight. My plan may have gone awry tonight, I may have lost control, but I can still get it back. I can still get away with this. No one knows I was there tonight, and no one has to—

There's a sound from downstairs. I freeze, clutching the spine of the book.

The front door slamming shut. Footsteps. And then Jasper's voice, calling my name.

Goddammit.

"Scarlett?"

Jasper's halfway up the stairs now. I slip the diary into an empty spot on the bookcase next to the fireplace, then peel off my gloves and toss them into the flames, just before Jasper pushes open the study door.

I turn to face him, angling my body so it blocks his view of the fire. As he stares at me, standing there in my bra and underwear with flames roaring at my back, I can already see the questions forming on his lips. So I head him off with one of my own.

"What the hell are you doing here, Jasper?"

"I was worried about you." He clearly hasn't slept. The circles under his eyes look cadaverous, and his usually neat clothing is a mess, his shirt untucked, his collar askew.

"Worried? Why?" I have no idea what time it is, how long I was at Kinnear's. The whole night is a blur—completely unlike my other kills where, even years later, I remember every detail with perfect clarity.

"You didn't answer me." For all I know he's been texting me incessantly since I ignored his earlier messages. "I've been—"

"I had my phone off," I say. "I was working."

Jasper steps into the room. "Where?"

"Here. I was—"

"No. You weren't here. I came by earlier, and all the lights were off." He's edging closer to me now. Looming, trying to intimidate me. "You're lying."

Maybe I should feel afraid of him, but there's no room for fear with all this rage coursing through me. I killed a man tonight. I could kill Jasper too. I could push him into the fire, hold his beautiful cut-glass cheekbones there until they melt from the heat. I could do anything.

"You can't just come over here whenever you like."

"Where were you?"

"I'm going to need your key back, this is un—"

"Tell me where you were tonight."

He leans down, hair falling across his forehead. I think of all the times I've run my fingers through it, and I want to rip it out at the root. He's so close, and I have nowhere to go. The heat on the back of my bare legs is almost unbearable as it is.

But even stronger than my desire to flee is my desire to punish him. If he knew what I really was, what I was capable of, he wouldn't treat me this way. He'd be cowering in fear.

"Tell me," he says again, and he tries to grab me by the shoulders. But I'm already lashing out, pushing so hard against his chest that he stumbles back. He looks at me, stunned.

Then he looks into the fire.

All the other evidence has been reduced to ash, but the black fingers of my gloves are still visible, curling inward as they burn like they're grasping at something.

Before Jasper can ask any more questions, I slam my hands into him even harder, shoving him until he falls back against my desk, sending books and papers tumbling to the floor. Finally, there's some fear in his eyes. But he wants me too. More than ever.

I grab him roughly by the jaw and force my mouth onto his. He seizes the back of my skull, and I bite down on his lower lip until I taste blood.

Jasper pulls me down onto the floor in front of the fire, and I'm ripping open his shirt, raking my nails across his chest, drawing more blood, digging in harder when he moans. He tears at my bra clasp, the small of my back, the meat of my thighs, and all I can think is: *Yes, good, the more he marks me up the better*. The scratches Kinnear left on me will be nothing compared to the damage Jasper and I are about to do to each other.

If I don't hurt him, I'm going to kill him.

34

CARLY

We don't make it back to Whitten until after dawn. While Allison's in the bathroom, I manage to struggle out of the corset on my own and put on a sweatshirt. For the first time in twelve hours, I can breathe properly, and the relief is so intense it's almost painful.

Has it really only been twelve hours? Last night felt years long, even before we went to the hospital.

"Do you want something to eat?" I ask Allison when she comes back in. Wes brought us a tray of lukewarm cafeteria food and some vending machine snacks at the hospital, but she wouldn't touch any of it. "I can run over to Trocino, or that coffee shop you like downtown, and—"

"I'm really tired." Her voice sounds small and ragged.

"Of course," I say. "You should rest. I'll be right here if you need anything."

"Don't you have writing class?" she asks.

"Yeah, but—it's not important, I can skip it."

Allison shakes her head. "No, you should go. I'm just going to sleep."

She starts to peel off her costume, and that's when I notice the bruises. On her back, her rib cage, her waist. I don't even realize I've reached out to touch her until she jerks away from my hand, tugging her shirt back into place. But I know what I saw. All the places Bash—

"He hurt you." It's a laughable understatement; the bruises are the least of it.

"It's nothing." Allison's eyes won't meet mine. This isn't just exhaustion. It's like the light inside her has been snuffed out.

"It's *not* nothing." I can't believe I didn't notice the bruises until now. I can't believe the *doctor* didn't notice them. Fucking negligent bastard.

"We could go back to the hospital," I say. "Demand to see a different doctor. So there are medical records to back up your police report."

Allison is obviously still in shock. It's a good thing I'm here to help her through this, to make a plan. The bruises are relatively light, so they'll be healed in a matter of days. There's no time to waste.

"You probably shouldn't shower either, maybe there's some other physical evidence they can collect, like from your skin, or— oh, did he touch your hair?"

Allison turns away from me. There's a little cluster of bruises above her elbow too, like dirty fingerprints.

"I know it'll be hard," I say. "But I'll go with you. Wes will too. I can call him right now, I'm sure he'll come and get us and drive us over there. It will all be—"

"I'm not going back to the hospital," she says. "I just want to sleep. And you should go to class."

She flops down on her bed, facing away from me, drawing the comforter up over her shoulders. I stand there gaping at her for a few seconds before a shrill bell breaks the silence.

My cell phone. Allison winces at the sound and tugs the covers higher.

"Sorry." I grab the phone, pressing it to my chest to muffle it as I hurry toward the door. Once I'm out in the hallway, I answer the call without looking at the screen. "Hello?"

"I didn't wake you, did I, sweetheart?"

Shit. It's my mother.

Since I've been ignoring her calls, she's started making them at stranger times, hoping to catch me. As much as I've been dreading talking to her, as much as my instincts are screaming to make up an excuse, *any* excuse, and hang up the phone, it's unbelievably soothing to hear her familiar voice on the other end of the line. I lean against the wall across from our room and slide down to sit on the floor.

"No, I was . . . already up." I can imagine the tutting sound of disapproval she'd make if she found out I was at a party on a school night, let alone the rest of what happened.

"Okay, good. I know you have class soon, but I wanted to touch base with you about Thanksgiving."

I lean my head back. Thanksgiving. I was already dreading it, but now, knowing what I know about my father, going home will be intolerable. I wonder what Allison's plans are. Since she doesn't get along with her parents, she's probably not spending the holiday with them. Maybe she goes to Wes's house for Thanksgiving? Or she might even stay on campus. Maybe I should too.

"Do you have to go to all your Wednesday classes?" my mother asks. "Or can you—"

"I don't know if I can make it home, actually."

In the silence that follows, I can picture the exact face my mother is making—the narrowing of her eyes, the set of her jaw. Susan Schiller never raises her voice, but her passive-aggressive Midwestern silences might be even worse.

"Doesn't the whole campus shut down anyway?" There's a brittle edge in her voice now. "You might as well come home. I miss you; it feels like it's been . . ." She trails off, and I realize she's not angry with me, or at least not only angry. She's trying to keep her-self from tearing up.

Maybe I could go home for a couple of days. Maybe I could lie on my childhood bed with my head in my mother's lap and tell her everything and cry and cry and cry.

"Your father would love to see you too," she says.

Yes, I'm sure my father would *love* to see me and act like we're one big happy family. He'd love to let my mother make him Thanksgiving dinner with all the trimmings and iron his shirts and maybe even wash his underwear so it's nice and clean the next time he pays a visit to his barely legal mistress.

"What if I don't want to see him?"

"Carly, I know he can be strict sometimes, but he is your father."

"He's not *strict*, he's—"

"If you don't have a relationship with him, you'll regret it when you're older."

I have to tell her. Now's the perfect time. I know he's at work, so he won't overhear. She'll be upset, but she has to know.

"Mom, I—" I swallow and steel myself. "I saw Dad in Pitts-burgh."

"What? What were you doing in Pittsburgh? How did you even—"

"He was there with another woman."

She goes so quiet I worry the call might have dropped. I thought I'd feel better, lighter, once the secret was off my chest, but instead it's turned into a pile of heavy stones, settling in the pit of my stomach.

Finally, she clucks her tongue. "Why would you say such an awful thing, honey?"

"Mom, I saw them. They were having dinner at this Italian restaurant in Shadyside."

"He was in Pittsburgh for work a few weeks ago. I'm sure she was just a colleague."

"She was practically *my age*, Mom. They were clearly on a date, she kept touching his hand, and—"

"You're wrong." Her voice is expressionless, distant. "He wouldn't do that."

She's not listening to me. I wish I were more surprised.

"What the hell is wrong with you?" I blurt out.

She gasps at my cursing, like I knew she would. The way my father treats the two of us is fine, apparently, but swearing is beyond the pale.

"Don't you have any self-respect?" I spit into the phone. "He's *lying* to you, that's all he does, he—"

"Scarlett Christina Schiller. That is *enough*."

If this didn't turn her against him, nothing will. It's like he's brainwashed her. But it doesn't fucking work on me anymore. I'm done attempting to appease him, done pretending our family is happy or normal. We're sick to the core, and we always have been.

"I have to go," I say into the phone.

"Don't you hang up on me, young lady," my mother says. "Not after—"

But I'm already pressing the button to end the call.

35

SCARLETT

I jolt awake, the scream still echoing in my head.

I was dreaming about Kinnear—burning alive instead of dead, howling as the flames melted his flesh. I never dream about my victims. Daydreams, certainly. But not like this. Not nightmares that follow me into the waking world.

My careful hairstyle from last night is wild now, askew from Jasper's fingers tearing through it. I have no idea when he left, whether he spent the night. If we slept side by side for even an hour, that'd be more than we've ever done.

Or maybe he didn't sleep. Maybe he got up and snooped around. Maybe he's already seen something he shouldn't have. Something incriminating.

The fire is still blazing, and my whole body is slick with sweat from sleeping on the floor so close to it. I turn off the gas, and the flames cut out. Nothing I threw into the fireplace is recognizable anymore, but I need to dispose of the remains. I can't risk a single wrong move now, not after my colossal fuckup last night.

I retrieve my robe from the hook on the bathroom door, knotting the sash around my waist as I head downstairs. Jasper is in fact still in my house—and even more alarming, he's cooking breakfast. A pan of scrambled eggs sizzles on the stove, and he's measuring beans into my espresso machine.

"Good morning," he says when he sees me watching him from the doorway. He's already showered and dressed, his damp hair slicked back over his skull.

"What are you doing?" I ask.

"I thought I'd make us breakfast."

Us. I feel frayed enough as it is, and him being in my space, breaking all my rules, just makes it worse.

"Go shower," Jasper says. "This won't be ready for a few minutes yet."

He stirs the eggs. The espresso machine hisses like a snake. He's certainly making himself right at home. But if he found anything suspicious during our sleepover, he doesn't seem troubled by it. He's humming a tune under his breath, happier than I've ever seen him. I think again of the way he snarled at me last night, thumb pressing my throat as he thrust into me.

My phone vibrates against the kitchen counter, and the sound makes my whole body clench like a fist. Jasper sets down the spatula and reaches for the phone, but I snatch it up before he can, ripping it away from the charging cord.

"Hello?"

"Scarlett." It's Drew. His voice sounds strange, strung tight like a bow.

He knows.

"Is everything okay?" I ask—even though I know damn well it's not.

"I'm afraid I have some bad news."

Jasper leans down next to me to listen in. I swallow the urge to smack him away from the receiver. "What is it?"

"It's Kinnear, he's . . ." Drew trails off, taking a deep, shuddering breath. "He's dead."

Jasper tenses. I can't look him in the eyes; I'm afraid I'll give myself away.

"Oh my God, that's . . . that's awful," I say. "What happened?"

"His . . . I think his house burned down in the night. Rafael and I, we were taking the dog for her morning walk, and we smelled the smoke. There were fire trucks everywhere, ambulances, I—"

"Maybe he's okay, then." It seems like the right thing to say. I'm trying to concentrate on modulating my reaction appropriately, but Jasper is too damn distracting—the heat of his skin pressing through my robe, the smell of my bath products lingering in his hair. I have to get rid of him. "Maybe he got out in time, or he wasn't home."

"No," Drew says. "No, the county coroner was there too. And there's—well, there's no way anyone could have survived. The house, it's—there's hardly anything left."

I press my fingertips to my forehead, more to hide my face from Jasper than anything. I can't let him see the hope in my eyes: hope that the fire I set destroyed everything, that there's not enough of Kinnear left for the police to ascertain how he died.

"Should we go into the office?" I say. "Or wait until Monday?"

"I don't know. I— God, what are we going to tell the students?" He sounds like he's on the verge of tears, but then he exhales, steadying himself. "I'll contact everyone. Call a meeting for first thing tomorrow, and then—"

Their elderly boxer dog starts barking, and I hear Rafael shush her. Then silence.

"Drew?"

"I have to go," he says.

"Why?" I ask. "What's—"

"The police are here."

36

CARLY

I made it through writing class without crying.

Then Alex asks me to stay after for a minute, and the heat starts building like a lit match behind my eyeballs. I should have skipped like Wes did, tried to get some rest. But I knew I'd never be able to get to sleep after that argument with my mom, and I didn't want to disturb Allison. She was totally out by the time I got off the phone, despite the way I was raising my voice out in the hallway.

As the rest of the students clear out, I can't even look at Alex. I'm sure he's going to tell me the story I read today was terrible (*it was, I know it was*). My hands are shaking so hard I have to grip the straps of my backpack to steady them. I can't take this today. I can't take anything else.

Once everyone else is gone, it's all I can do not to bolt from the room after them.

"Is everything all right, Carly?" he asks.

This wasn't what I was expecting: the genuine compassion in his voice, the concerned crinkles around his eyes. I try to keep it all in, play it off like everything's fine, but I'm too tired. My face crumples like a wadded-up piece of paper, and tears spill out onto my cheeks.

The few times I've cried in front of guys before, they've always acted panicked, like I'd suddenly transformed into some gruesome and terrifying monster. Which is still better than how my father reacted to tears: as if they were a personal affront to him.

But Alex doesn't even seem fazed. He shuts the office door and ushers me to the nearest chair, then hands me some Kleenex from his desk drawer before sitting down next to me, his elbows propped on his knees. "You want to talk about it?"

I dab at my eyes with the Kleenex, sniffling. I have no idea what to say. But maybe Alex could help. He's an adult, an authority figure. He's way better equipped than I am to handle a situation like this. He might even know the right way to report what Bash did, to make sure he's held responsible.

"It's okay if you don't." Alex holds out the tissue box. "Here, you want another one?"

I shake my head. "I'm just really tired."

Alex smiles. "Out late partying for Halloween?"

I stiffen. He's so close to the truth, yet completely off base.

"My roommate, um . . . she got sick. We had to go to the ER. We were there all night."

His smile vanishes, brow furrowing with concern. "I'm sorry to hear that. Is she okay?"

I don't know what Allison is right now, but she's definitely not okay. But I can't tell Alex what happened last night. Allison didn't even want to tell Wes the truth; she'd never forgive me if I told a professor, a *stranger*.

"She's fine," I say. "She's back in our room, getting some rest."

"That's good," Alex says. "What about you? Are *you* okay?"

"I'm . . ." But no words come out, just more tears. This is so humiliating.

But Alex remains totally calm, like I could cry for the rest of the day and he wouldn't mind. Somehow it makes me feel calmer too.

"She's lucky," he says, "to have a roommate who cares about her as much as you do." He leans back a little in his seat, giving me space. "Freshman year is a really difficult time, for everyone. It's quite an adjustment."

It is—it *was*. I should have adjusted by now, right?

"When I first came to Gorman," Alex says, "it was a big adjustment for me too."

I find that hard to believe. Alex seems like the kind of person who could make friends with anyone, anywhere. Not like me. All my "friends" at Gorman are really Allison's friends—Wes included. They only tolerate me because Allison likes me. If Allison decides she doesn't anymore, it's over. I'll be on my own again.

"My wife was in grad school," Alex continues. "So we only got to see each other a few times a year."

"You're married?" He's never mentioned having a wife before. He's not wearing a ring either, and there are no pictures of her on his desk.

Alex nods. We're sitting so close now, I can see his eyes aren't just blue, they have little sea-green flecks at the edges.

"Look," he says, "I don't want to pry, but if you ever need someone to talk to, I'm here." He dips his head down to look me right in the eyes. "Okay?"

I nod, twisting the damp Kleenex between my fingers. Bits of tissue flutter to the floor like ash.

"Not just during office hours either. Here." Alex goes back to his desk and grabs a business card, jotting another phone number on the back. "That's my personal phone. Call anytime."

I can't imagine ever calling a professor on the phone. But I've never had a teacher show concern for me like this before. In high school, no matter how bad things got with my father, no matter how much I withdrew or unraveled, every faculty member I encountered treated me with total indifference. Alex sensed my distress immediately—and not only that, he tried to *do* something about it. His wife is a lucky woman.

"I know it might feel like it sometimes," he says, and the warmth of his smile is like sunlight on my face. "But trust me, Carly: you're not alone here."

37

SCARLETT

"Good riddance, if you ask me," Jasper says.

I twist my face into an expression of disgust (this reaction, at least, I don't have to fake) as I set the phone down beside the stove. "A man is dead, Jasper."

"Oh, come on." He reels me in by the wrist, pinning me between his body and the counter. "You hated Kinnear. If anything, we should be celebrating."

Jasper bends down to kiss me, but I push against his chest. The scrambled eggs are starting to smoke, a charred scent filling the kitchen, the air around us clouding. He redoubles his efforts, digging his fingers into the base of my skull to force my face up toward his, and all I can think about is burning pages, burning fabric, burning flesh. I shove him again, so hard he stumbles backward, almost putting his hands down on the hot stove.

"Jesus!" He switches off the burner. "What the hell is your problem?"

"You need to leave." I straighten my robe, smooth out my hair where he mussed it again.

He sighs. "Let's sit down and have breakfast, and then—"

"Now, Jasper." I take the cooling pan off the range and tip the contents into the trash. The eggs are a blackened mess, far beyond saving. "And I want your key back."

I hold out my hand. Jasper glares at me, his jaw working. I don't have time for this—his moods, his games, his childish attempts to manipulate me. I should never have gotten involved with him in the first place.

His satchel sits on the edge of the counter, next to my knife block. I grab the bag, plunging my hand into the front pocket until I feel his key ring.

"What are you doing?" he says.

My house key still has the red plastic cap I put on it before I slipped it into Jasper's student mailbox last spring, tucked in an unmarked envelope.

"Scarlett, come on."

I use my fingernail to separate the metal ring, dragging my key free. I hold the rest of the keys out to him, but he doesn't take them. He's looming over me again, eyes dark.

"You know I don't need that to get in this house," he says.

"Get the fuck out." I hurl the key ring at his chest, and he catches it, holding the metal against his sternum. I'm shaking, digging my nails into my palms to keep myself under control. He needs to leave, or I'm going to hurt him, much worse than I did last night.

Jasper grabs his satchel and stalks out of the kitchen. A few seconds later, the front door slams, and I slump against the counter with relief.

But I can't relax—not yet. Maybe not ever again.

The rest of Sunday, I spend cleaning up: disposing of the ashes from the fireplace, scrubbing my skin raw in the shower, trying to scrape the ossified remains of the scrambled eggs off the pan before giving up and chucking the whole thing in the trash with a frustrated shout. I don't bother cooking myself anything else. Usually I'm ravenous after a kill, but today my stomach is a queasy knot.

Monday morning dawns cold and gray. I barely slept, but at least that spared me any more dreams of a scorched, screaming Kinnear. I get out of bed even earlier than usual and choose a suitably somber outfit for work. After I do my makeup, I rub my eyes a bit so they water and redden in a way that approximates real tears.

I'm not good at this part—one of the many reasons I prefer to kill men well outside my social circle. Since Kinnear was a colleague, I had prepared a lengthy mental list of nice but noncommittal things I could say about the deceased in the aftermath. But I thought I would be discussing his death as a humiliating accident, not a violent crime.

One wrong move, one false note in my voice could be enough to attract suspicion. But if I can pull it off—if I can perform appropriate shock and grief in front of my colleagues, make them believe I'm just as disturbed as they are by this sudden tragedy—I'll be one step closer to getting away with it.

The smell of smoke hanging in the air during my walk to campus does nothing for my nausea. When I get to Miller Hall, there are two squad cars parked outside. Gorman Township police—a third of the local force.

I take a deep breath and school my face into a mask of concern before heading inside. The classrooms I pass by are all empty, the lights still switched off. As I get closer to the hallway that houses the faculty offices, I hear soft weeping and whispered words. Everyone is huddled together right outside Kinnear's office like some sort of awkward vigil.

Sandra Kepler stands in the middle of the crowd, sniffling into a shredded Kleenex, her eyes so swollen from crying the pupils are barely visible. She waves me over.

"Scarlett, thank God you're here!"

I let Sandra hug me, and I pat her back in what I hope is a comforting manner. While she embraces me, I peer over her shoulder into the anteroom of Kinnear's office. Drew stands just inside the door, shirtsleeves pushed past his elbows like he's already been hard at work for hours, while two uniformed police officers talk to Kinnear's stricken secretary. Stright is there too, standing right behind her, hands squeezing her shoulders like he's giving her a massage.

As the first morning class session approaches, more students fill into the hallway, trying to figure out what's going on. It's like a wave, as what happened is whispered from person to person: faces lighting up with shock, hands flying to mouths, eyes brimming with tears. When Mikayla walks in, clutching a stack of library books to her chest, Ashleigh Lawrence flags her down to share the news. In response, Mikayla just presses her lips together—resolute, like she always knew this day would come.

The officers emerge from the office, with Drew and Stright a step behind them. Kinnear's secretary stays inside, her head bowed over her desk.

"If there's any way we can be of more assistance," Drew says.

The taller of the two cops nods. "Thank you, Dr. Torres. We'll be in touch."

Both policemen look young enough to be students themselves. With a crime of this magnitude, though, it's just a matter of time before they summon bigger guns to investigate.

I have relatively little direct personal experience with the police. I was interviewed by local detectives after my first kill, but they accepted me for what I appeared to be: a sobbing college student too panicked and grief-stricken to possibly be responsible for what had happened. Several of my kills in Chicago were investigated as murders, but even those close calls weren't really: I left no DNA at the scene, and I had no relationship to the victims, so the authorities never even brought me in for questioning.

Stright starts to walk the cops out, but a female student catches him by the sleeve—the same pretty blond sophomore I saw doing a walk of shame from Kinnear's house during my pre-kill surveillance.

"Dr. Stright, is it true?" she asks.

He nods with exaggerated solemnity. "I'm afraid so."

She breaks down crying, collapsing into the arms of the girl next to her. Instead of attempting to comfort her—or any of the other openly weeping students—Stright slips his arm around Mikayla's shoulders.

"Everything's going to be fine," he says, giving her a squeeze.

She immediately shrugs away from him, brushing off her sleeve like there's dirt on it, and I feel a surge of almost maternal pride.

Drew raises his hands to get everyone's attention. "All classes are canceled today, but starting at ten a.m. there will be representatives from the campus counseling center in Lecture Hall C for anyone who needs to talk. And, of course, my door is open to you as well."

As he speaks, everyone seems to settle, soothed by his calm competence. Well, except Sandra Kepler. She presses the remnants of the tissue to her lips like she's trying to hold the emotions on her tongue until they dissolve.

Once the crowd starts to disperse, I approach Drew and lay a hand on his shoulder. At my touch, he exhales and his posture softens. He looks like he slept about as well as I did last night.

"How are you doing?" I ask.

"I just . . ." He shakes his head. "I still can't believe it."

"I know." I squeeze his shoulder, and he lays his hand over mine, squeezing back. "The police came to your house yesterday?"

"They were talking to people in the neighborhood, trying to figure out if anyone saw anything." Drew lowers his voice to a whisper. "They think he was dead before the fire started—that someone murdered him and burned the house down to cover it up. Isn't that insane?" He runs his fingers through his hair, leaving a few pieces standing on end. "I think Rafael's more upset than I am; he spent all day yesterday installing extra fire detectors. As if that would make any difference with a *murderer* on the loose."

I pull my hand away. "Well, you're doing a great job holding things together here."

He really is: he's a natural at this. Maybe now that Kinnear is dead, they'll give Drew the department chair position that should have been his all along.

"Thanks." Drew manages a weak smile. "Do you think you could help me round everyone up for a quick faculty meeting?"

"Of course," I say, mirroring the small, sad uptick of his lips. "Ten minutes?"

"You're the best, Scarlett."

This I can handle. I can be helpful, a team player, doing what I can to hold things together. Just like everyone else.

Drew and I take off in opposite directions, stopping every professor we see to inform them of the meeting in the conference room. I check the faculty lounge, expecting to find some of our colleagues there commiserating over black coffee and a box of Kleenex, but the room is shut, only darkness visible through the narrow glass window on the door.

I'm about to move on when I hear a deep intake of breath, almost a gasp. I peer through the window, looking for the source of the sound.

Mina. She's alone, huddled on the floor in the corner, her face buried in her hands. I'm overwhelmed by an urge to rush to her side and wrap her up in my arms, stroke her hair, whisper reassurances. But no matter how fraught their marriage was, I'm sure the last person Mina would want comfort from right now is her ex-husband's murderer.

I slip away before she sees me, her grief-stricken sobs still echoing in my ears.

38

CARLY

"You want some of my fries?"

I push the tray toward Allison. She flinches, like I've startled her. Her own lunch—a little paper container of tomato soup and some smashed-up crackers—sits untouched on the table. At least I got her to come to the dining hall today.

Allison accepts a single french fry off my plate. Instead of eating it, though, she starts picking it apart, flaying off the crunchy outer layer.

Wes comes up to our table, carrying his own tray. He got the same cheeseburger special I did, onion rings and barbecue sauce on top. He smiles at us, but the expression fades when he gets a good look at Allison.

Rather than her curated thrift store clothes and retro-chic makeup, she's wearing a baggy Gorman sweater with a grease stain on the front, her face bare and splotchy. I'm not sure when she last washed her hair; the blue strands have faded to a sickly swimming pool shade.

"Hey." Wes sits down next to her and tries to put his hand to her forehead to check for a fever. "Are you sick?"

Allison jerks away from him, her chair pushing back with a screech. "I'm going to the bathroom."

I start to stand up too, intending to follow her, but maybe it would be better to give her a moment alone. Or maybe she shouldn't be left alone at all.

"What's going on with her?" Wes lays his hand over mine, trying to get my attention. "Is this about what happened at the party?"

Allison's disappeared into the bathroom at the other end of the dining hall, but I keep staring at the door like I can still see her. I pull my hand away from Wes.

She finally comes back to the table just as Wes is finishing up his lunch. She looks even paler than when she left, her cheeks pink and damp like she splashed cold water on them. I've lost my appetite too.

"Hope you feel better, Allie," Wes offers as he gets up to clear his tray.

Allison tries to smile at him, but it's not very convincing. "I'm fine."

She keeps saying that. But all week she's been sleeping through classes, barely eating. She's still going to *Cabaret* rehearsal, but that means spending hours in the same room as Bash. I want to help her, but I have no idea what to do.

Well, that's not entirely true. I have one idea, but I don't think she'll like it.

"You want me to walk you back to Whit?" I ask her. "My next class isn't until two."

Allison shrugs, like she couldn't care less. But she gets up and follows me, first to the line of trash bins to toss my half-eaten lunch and her untouched, room-temperature soup, and then outside.

It's a bright, clear day, freezing in the shadows but bearable in the light. Allison's wearing her favorite coat—a vintage green brocade duster with a faux fur collar—but she still shivers as we head down the sun-beaten sidewalk toward our dorm.

Impulsively, I slip my arm around her. She stiffens at first, but doesn't pull away. I could swear her shoulders feel slighter, sharper. It's like she's shrinking out of existence.

Meanwhile, Bash is just going about his business. I passed him in the Oak Grove this morning, tossing a Frisbee back and forth with another guy from the theater department, grinning and laughing, not a care in the world.

"Allison, don't be mad, but—" I swallow, keeping my eyes focused straight ahead. "I did some research."

She looks at me. "On what?"

"On how to report . . . what happened."

Allison comes to a halt in the middle of the path. She's trembling, shaking her head, blinking rapidly to keep tears at bay. I hate seeing her upset, but after so many days of unsettling listlessness, this reaction is almost a relief.

"I'm not going to the police," she says. "No way. You heard what the doctor said, there's no proof, and they'll tell my parents, and—"

"Not the police."

I tell her what I found out during the several hours I spent at the library yesterday, desperately searching for some way to help her: There's an official process for reporting sexual assault on campus. You go to the office of the dean of students, file a statement about what happened, and then they do their own internal investigation. No police necessary.

Allison keeps shaking her head, a few tears tracking down her cheeks. We're still blocking the sidewalk, and other students split off to go around us, crunching the dead leaves gathered at the edge of the grass.

"What he did to you was not okay." I take Allison's hand. Her knuckles are ice-cold. "You know it wasn't."

She starts walking again, but she doesn't let go of my hand. I let her pull me along, heat building between our palms. When we get to the front steps of Whit, she finally turns to me.

"If I report him," she says, "will you go with me?"

I squeeze her hand. "Of course I will."

39

SCARLETT

When I arrive at the campus chapel for Kinnear's funeral, Mina is already there, sitting alone in the center of a pew.

Unlike the last time I saw her, she looks completely put together, her eyes dry and clear. I watch as Drew and Rafael approach her, their faces matching masks of polite sympathy. Mina smiles warmly at them, but as soon as they turn away to take their own seats, her smile drops and her jaw clenches.

This is the first time I've attended a funeral for one of my victims at Gorman. But I'm here as Kinnear's acquaintance and colleague, nothing more. I should be sad he's dead—and worried about the possible murderer on the loose—but not devastated.

I weave around the ostentatious bouquets lining the aisle to slide into the pew beside Mina. The flowers are stark white, same as the chapel walls, but the stained glass windows above the altar cast shards of color onto every surface—including Mina's soft gray sweater dress. She's the only one here not wearing black.

Mikayla Atwell is right in front of us—one of just a few undergraduate students in attendance, despite the extreme emotional displays I've been witnessing in the hallways of Miller for most of the week. Mikayla twists around to give me a brief smile of greeting before bowing her head over the book in her lap again.

Mina keeps staring straight ahead at the closed casket. I wonder what they even found to put in there. I've resisted the temptation to drive past Kinnear's property during the past several days, but the local paper printed a picture of the scorched husk of his house. It burned down to the foundation, even better than I could have hoped for.

I glance over at Mina, trying to think of the right thing to say. The standard *so sorry for your loss* won't work in this situation. I'm not sorry, and it's not really her loss.

She beats me to it. "I'm glad you're here," she says. "Maybe you'll scare them away."

More people are filing in by the minute—including Stright and his wife, a ghostly pale blond with a permanently pinched expression. Or maybe she only looks so sour around her husband; they seem to absolutely loathe each other. I wonder if that's what Mina and Kinnear were like when they were still married.

"Scare who away?" I ask.

"All these people who want to know 'how I'm holding up.' "

"Why would I—"

She turns to me. This close up, I can see how tired she is, the redness still rimming her eyes, the makeup not quite covering the pallor of her complexion.

"Because you're terrifying." She smiles and bumps her hip into mine. My chest prickles with heat under the high collar of my black blouse. "That's what I like about you."

A somber organ melody strikes up, signaling the start of the service. Even though the chapel is almost full, our row stays just the two of us—and the front row remains entirely empty. No family, at least none willing or able to make the trip.

The usher is about to shut the door when two more people slip in: a woman with salt-and-pepper hair in a no-nonsense bob cut, and a baby-faced black guy, neither of whom look familiar. The man keeps his hand on the door to hold it open for one last straggler.

Jasper. This is the first time I've seen him since I threw him out of my house. He never showed up to work on Monday, and he's skipped all his office hours and classes since then, his only notice a one-line email informing me he was "under the weather." He looks perfectly healthy today in a pressed black suit, his angular face no paler than usual.

Mina sucks in a breath. She's looking toward the door too, and at first I think she's reacting to Jasper's arrival. But her eyes follow the other pair, the older woman and younger man.

She turns back toward the front of the chapel. "They could at least wait until after the fucking funeral."

"Who are they?" I ask. The two of them are clearly here together, but they don't quite come across as a couple. She's old enough to be his mother, if she had him young.

"Those detectives they brought in from Pittsburgh," Mina says. "I was locked in a room with that woman for hours yesterday. If I hadn't been in my office with Mikayla at the time of Alexander's death, I think she would have slapped handcuffs on me."

I expected the investigation to play out this way, but I certainly didn't expect Mina to fall under suspicion. Thank God she has a solid alibi.

Jasper takes a seat on the other side of the chapel, while Stright and his wife slide into the pew right in front of us. Stright bumps his shoulder into Mikayla's, then tilts up the cover of her book to see what she's reading. His wife pretends not to notice, peering into her purse without removing anything.

The detectives remain standing, taking up positions against the wall. So they aren't *too* concerned with staying inconspicuous. Both are dressed in nondescript dark clothing, but they're scanning the room like they're taking in every detail. The woman especially. She has sharp, roving eyes like a bird of prey. Her gaze lands on me, and I look away, focusing on Mina again.

"Do they have any other suspects?" I ask.

"Not that I can tell." Mina shakes her head. "I mean, they should have lots of options to choose from. So many people hated him."

Her voice is dripping with contempt, but fresh tears stream down her face.

"He was such a *bastard*," she says. Then she breaks down completely.

I have no idea what to do other than put my arms around her, the way I wanted to when I saw her crying in the faculty lounge. She leans against me, sobbing onto my chest. Mikayla glances back at us, brow furrowed with concern, but Stright stays facing the front, pretending not to notice the scene playing out behind him. He's sitting much closer to Mikayla than he needs to, while leaving several inches of space between him and his wife.

As the service gets underway, Mina keeps crying, so I keep my arm around her, stroking her hair. Jasper glares daggers at me from across the room—probably his main motivation for attending the funeral in the first place. He's sure as hell not here to mourn Kinnear.

Most of the speakers are fellow academics, and they all say some variation of the same generic platitudes: Alexander Kinnear was a brilliant scholar. He cared so deeply about his students. He was taken from us too soon, and he will be missed.

When the final speaker steps up to the podium, though, I nearly gasp aloud.

It's Judith Winters, head curator of the Women's Academy.

I had no idea she would be here, and I can't believe I didn't notice her before. She looks exactly like her picture on the archive's website, her distinctive silver hair swept back in a twist.

Judith introduces herself as an "old friend of Alexander's from Cambridge," and Mina makes a sound against my shoulder that might be a scoff or a sniffle. From the way Judith waxes poetic about how funny and generous Kinnear was, I'm guessing they must have slept together at least once. Kinnear had a special knack for making smart women do stupid things.

"Years ago," Judith says, "Alexander told me he didn't want any Bible verses read at his funeral, only Shakespeare. This was his favorite passage."

She speaks the lines from memory: the "To be, or not to be" speech from *Hamlet*. Around the room, people are nodding along, their eyes gleaming with tears. All I can think is: This reading would be so much more appropriate if his death had gone as planned, and everyone thought he killed himself.

By the time Judith finishes, her eyes are glistening too. Someone in the back starts applauding, and then the rest of the audience joins in. It feels in poor taste, applauding at a funeral. But Kinnear probably would have loved it.

The service ends with a melancholy piano hymn, and Stright and the other pallbearers hoist Kinnear's casket onto their shoulders to carry it out of the chapel. I don't want to leave Mina's side, but I'm also desperate to talk to Judith. Not that I can bring up the fellowship *now*—even I know how insensitive and inappropriate that would be—but I ought to at least make my presence known.

Judith is standing by the spot where Kinnear's coffin was a few moments ago, talking to the dean of the humanities department. I'm about to make some excuse to Mina so I can go over there and speak to her, when two bodies move in front of our pew, blocking Judith from view.

Mina tenses, huddling closer against my side. It's the detectives.

The young man speaks first. "Good morning, Dr. Pierce."

Mina narrows her eyes at him. "Is this really necessary? I already told you—"

"Yes, thank you again, Samina. You were very helpful yesterday," the female detective says. "We were actually hoping to talk to your friend."

She holds her hand out for me to shake. "Professor Clark, I'm Detective Sharon Abbott. This is my partner, Detective Benjamin Flynn. We're with the—"

I take her hand. "Pittsburgh Bureau of Police. Yes, I know."

They already know who I am. They're seeking me out, specifically. But I can't show any signs of disquiet. It doesn't mean anything. Even if they suspect me of killing Kinnear, they'll need evidence, and I didn't leave any.

At least, not that I'm aware of.

"Mina mentioned that you've been interviewing our colleagues," I say. "I'd be more than happy to sit down with you at your earliest convenience."

The male detective—Flynn—takes a card out of his wallet and hands it to me. "You can get ahold of either of us at this number."

"Thank you." I take the card. "Though I don't know how helpful I can be, really. I'm afraid I didn't know much about Dr. Kinnear's life outside of the university."

"I'm sure you know more than you think," Abbott says, fixing those shrewd eyes on me. She's going to be a problem, I can tell. But I'll prepare for this interview like I prepare for everything else.

As soon as the detectives take their leave, I look for Judith Winters again, but she must have slipped out already. No matter: I'll catch up with her at the cemetery. Maybe that's better anyway. I'll find a way to stand near her during the burial and introduce myself afterward. We can reminisce about our mutual friend, then discuss my future.

I'm so absorbed in my strategizing, it takes me a moment to notice that Mina is trembling, more tears streaming down her cheeks. "I can't," she says.

"What?" I lean in, looping my arm around her.

"I can't, I can't go to the cemetery, I can't watch them—" She breaks down again, shoulders heaving, but it's silent this time.

"It's okay," I say. "You don't have to; you can go home. Everyone will understand."

Another silent sob shudders through her, and she clutches at my sleeve. "Will you come with me?"

I've refused Mina several times before, but in this moment, with those beautiful, anguished eyes staring right into mine, I can't bring myself to do it. She shouldn't be alone right now, and I'm the one responsible. Connecting with Judith can wait.

I squeeze her shoulder and smile. "Of course."

40

CARLY

I wasn't sure she'd go through with it. But the morning of our meeting with the dean of students, Allison is awake and ready to leave before I am.

She even showered, though she didn't dry her hair. On the walk from Whit to Capin Hall, the damp strands freeze into little blue icicles. It's the coldest morning of the semester so far, frost sparkling on the ground. Most of the other students we pass are bundled up better than we are, scarves wrapped around their mouths, knit caps pulled low over their brows.

Capin is the tallest building in the Oak Grove, looming over the tops of the trees. There's a little white bell tower stuck on top, but I've never heard it ring. My stomach twists as we mount the steps, but I don't know how much is from nerves and how much from hunger. Allison still refused to have breakfast, so I didn't eat anything either, in solidarity.

Halfway to the entrance, Allison stops, staring up at the building's imposing facade, the white steam of her breath obscuring her expression.

I offer her my hand. "It'll be okay. You're doing the right thing."

She doesn't look convinced. But she takes my hand, and we keep climbing.

I give Allison's name instead of my own when I check in with the receptionist, a bespectacled young man in a crimson sweater vest. Allison stands back, looking around nervously. It's almost as quiet as the campus library in here, the only sounds muted phone ringtones and the distant click of high heels.

We're the first appointment of the day, so he ushers us right into the dean's office before we even have a chance to sit down in the uncomfortable-looking chairs out front.

The university website only listed a last name, so I was expecting a stern old man, maybe wearing horn-rimmed glasses and a tweed jacket. Instead, Dean Bowman is a woman several years younger than my mother, with warm brown eyes and blond hair arranged in a neat, unfussy style that just skims the floral scarf knotted around her neck.

She stands up to greet us. "Allison?" she says to me.

I open my mouth to correct her, but Allison steps forward herself. "No, I'm Allison Hadley. This is my roommate, Scarlett Schiller."

For the first time all week, she sounds like her poised, confident self. She must be even more relieved than I am that we're meeting with a woman. The dean's office space seems designed to set people at ease too: plush carpet, soft lighting, and walls painted a soothing blue just a few shades lighter than her tailored pantsuit.

The dean smiles and motions toward the upholstered chairs across from her. "So," she says, taking her seat too. "Tell me what brings you girls here today."

Last night in our room, Allison rehearsed what she was going to say. I listened to her tell the story over and over again until she could get through it without crying. Her voice shakes a little when she starts speaking to the dean, but she gets stronger as she goes. She manages to recount exactly what Bash did to her in a clear, calm tone, not even a hint of tears.

"And then Carly—" Allison looks over at me.

I smile, encouraging her to continue. She's doing so well. She's the bravest person I know, and as much as I hate that she has to do this, I'm proud of her too.

"Carly and my friend Wes took me to the hospital," Allison says. "They thought I might have a concussion."

"And did you?" Dean Bowman asks.

"Well . . . no," Allison says. "They sent me home after a couple of hours."

The dean nods and taps her fingers on her desk. It's spotless, just a phone, a cup with a cluster of identical blue pens, and a single silver frame. The picture is facing away from us, but I assume it's a family photo. Maybe she even has a daughter of her own.

I know Allison was scared to come here. I was nervous too (though I tried my best to hide it, for her sake). But we shouldn't have worried so much. This woman understands. She'll be able to help us.

"Well, Ms. Hadley," Dean Bowman says. "It sounds to me like you were very lucky."

Allison and I both blink at her in disbelief. The dean turns to me, smiling again.

"You're a good friend," she says. "Looking out for her like that."

I'm a "good friend"? Allison is "lucky"? Is she *joking*?

"But what if—" I sputter. "I mean, if I hadn't been there, he might have—"

"But you were there." The dean folds her hands on the desk. "And nothing really happened. Did it?"

I expect Allison to be as appalled as I am by this response, but instead she looks like she's in genuine shock. Her lips are slightly parted, her eyes unfocused, the blood drained from her face. I'm losing her again.

"You're not injured," the dean continues, ticking off points on her French-manicured fingers. "You don't have to worry about STDs or pregnancy."

"He *drugged* her," I say. "She was barely conscious, and he was touching her. That's—"

"Yes, well." The dean's smile stiffens. "Maybe now you'll both think twice before accepting drinks from boys you don't know."

"But I *do* know him," Allison says. Her voice sounds so small and uncertain now, it breaks my heart. "He's in the theater department with me."

"They're costarring in a show," I explain. "So she has to see him every day."

"I see," the dean says, frowning.

I have a glimmer of hope—maybe she just didn't understand the seriousness of the situation, the urgency. Maybe now she'll agree to do something.

"Were you flirting with this boy?" she asks Allison.

Allison looks down at her hands twisting in her lap. "I—"

"Maybe he misunderstood," the dean says. "That happens sometimes, in these situations."

The calmer she sounds, the more agitated I get. My legs won't stop jiggling, my heels tapping the thick carpet. It feels like flames licking the soles of my feet, climbing higher.

"You want to know what she was wearing too?" I snap. Dean Bowman and Allison both stare at me. I'm just as shocked by the edge in my voice, but I can't stop now. I'm too fucking angry. "You think *flirting* is an invitation for him to assault her?"

"That's not what I'm saying at all." Dean Bowman's voice is as smooth and neutral as a politician's. "But you do have to be careful about the signals you send."

Allison has gone scary-still, her jaw clenched. She bows her head, and a single tear falls into her lap, darkening the red fabric of her skirt. Seeing how hard she's trying to hold herself together just enrages me all the more. She's been through enough; she shouldn't have to deal with this. The dean should be helping her, not accusing her of bringing this on herself.

"So that's it?" I'm on the edge of my seat now, muscles poised to lunge.

Allison grabs my wrist. "Carly, don't, it's not—"

"You're not going to do anything? You're not going to help her at all?"

"This can be a valuable lesson for you," the dean says, sounding so fucking reasonable I want to punch her teeth in. "There's no need to ruin anyone's life over it."

"What the fuck is wrong with you?"

Allison gasps, like she can't believe I said that out loud. I can't quite believe it either.

Dean Bowman pinches her lips together, clearly more bothered by me swearing than by the actual *crime* that took place. Just like my mother, offended by all the wrong things.

"Excuse m—" she starts, but I've heard enough.

"You're just going to let a *known sexual predator* have free rein on campus?" I say. "Seriously?"

"Ms. Schiller, I'm going to need you to calm down."

But that's the strangest thing of all: I sound perfectly calm. Not just calm, but cold, commanding, all the usual anxious hesitancy in my voice stripped away.

I stand up, bumping my chair back. Allison digs her nails into my wrist.

"Stop it," she pleads. "Just—"

I shake off her grip, advancing on the dean's desk.

"Carly, stop it!"

I don't take my eyes off Dean Bowman, but I can hear the change in Allison's voice. She's crying again. This woman, this horrible, heartless woman made her cry.

How dare she. How *dare* she.

"Please just *stop*."

The dean leans back in her chair. Trying to get away from me, because she's afraid. Afraid of *me*. I feel so alert, blood thrumming, muscles coiled, like her fear is feeding me.

"She can't talk to you like that," I say.

"It's okay," Allison says. "Let's just go. Please, I want to go."

It's not okay. None of this is okay. I want to grab that fucking floral scarf and tighten it until the dean's face turns as blue as her suit. I want to smash windows and rip doors off their hinges. I want to destroy everything in this building, everything on this entire campus.

Everything except Allison.

I turn around to look at her—to reassure her, to tell her that everything isn't okay but it will be, we'll figure this out together, somehow.

But her chair is empty, the office door swinging shut in her wake. She's gone.

41

SCARLETT

When we get to Mina's house, she heads straight for the whiskey.

After pouring herself a generous glass, she holds up the bottle. "You want some?"

It's the same brand I brought to Kinnear's. I shake my head. Mina shrugs, then knocks back her own drink in a few swallows and pours herself another.

"You should eat something," I say.

"I'm not hungry." She's carrying the glass in one hand and the bottle in the other, already swaying a little on her feet.

Her home isn't at all what I expected. There are a few personal touches—a quatrefoil mirror above the fireplace, a faux fur throw draped over the taupe sofa, a pile of art books under the end table—but otherwise it's a soulless white box. It seems transitory, like she just moved in and she might leave any day. The whole space smells like her perfume, though—that heavy floral smell like nighttime in a summer garden.

"I don't really cook," I say, "but I could go pick—"

"It's such bullshit." She kicks off her pumps and sets the whiskey bottle down on the coffee table. "All those people, acting like he was some fucking saint. He was a piece of shit."

"We . . . didn't always see eye to eye."

"Oh, come on." Mina flops down on the sofa, sloshing a little whiskey out of her glass. Her eyes are getting bleary, but they still gleam with rage. "You despised him as much as I did; I could see it every time you looked at him."

What else could you see? The question burns like acid at the back of my throat.

I sit down next to her and sigh. "You're right. He was a piece of shit."

Mina stares at the floor, gripping the glass harder. I've gone too far, I'm sure of it. I shouldn't drop my mask for anyone, not even Mina. Especially not Mina.

But then she throws her head back, her whole body shaking with laughter.

"*Thank* you!" She raises the glass. "Finally, an honest woman."

She drains her drink, swallowing the whiskey with an almost triumphant flourish. But when she looks at me again, her eyes are wet with tears.

"Hey." I lean toward her, and she folds in on herself, curls surging forward to hide her face as she suppresses another sob. I reach for her hand. "Hey, it's okay."

She straightens up, threading her fingers through mine. "I just hate that he can still affect me like this, you know?"

I nod, and for once I don't have to force my sympathetic expression. I don't feel bad about killing Kinnear, and I can't imagine I ever will. But knowing my actions have caused Mina this much pain . . . that *does* make something twist deep in my gut. It's been years since I've felt anything this close to guilt.

"And that insufferable woman from Cambridge," Mina says. "I can't believe she showed up today. You know he didn't even go to Cambridge, right?"

I've always wondered about this. Kinnear's CV lists a special certificate from the University of Cambridge, but undergrad and graduate degrees from different institutions. Yet he talked constantly about his "Cambridge days" like he was a distinguished alum.

"It was this summer program for rich American kids. They accepted anyone whose parents could pay. That's how we met, actually."

"You went to Cambridge?"

"No, I wish." Mina lets go of my hand and takes another sip of her whiskey, more contemplative this time. She's slowing down. "I was working in this little coffee shop across the street from King's College—trying to save up for tuition, actually. Alexander started coming in every day, buying cappuccino after cappuccino just as an excuse to talk to me. And then one night he snuck me into the library with him."

I picture a younger Mina walking reverently through the stacks, dragging her fingers over the spines of the books, the smell of coffee caught in the coils of her hair.

"He'd pull books off the shelf and read them to me," she says. "Joyce, Hemingway, Proust, all that shit. I was young enough to be impressed. And he was so fucking handsome."

He was—*so* fucking handsome. Walking into his classroom at Gorman when I was eighteen, I felt like I couldn't look directly at him.

Mina taps her fingernails on the rim of the glass. "I thought he was the love of my life."

She leans forward to set her drink on the coffee table. When she settles back, she's closer to me, our knees touching.

"You're so smart," she says. "You stayed single, you never let a man dictate the course of your life."

"My life isn't as together as you think." All my careful planning means nothing if I let my rage override it. I won't make the same mistake next time—assuming there is a next time.

"Don't do that."

Mina's watching me like she's looking through a rifle sight, her finger on the trigger. My throat goes dry, and suddenly I'm regretting turning down that whiskey.

"Don't do what?"

"That's not you," she says. "You know you're brilliant, you're gorgeous . . ."

And then her hand is on my knee, and my vision nearly whites out from the heat of my desire. I never thought—I never *let* myself think—

Mina leans closer, hand sliding higher. "You're too good for this place."

For a moment, I let myself imagine how soft Mina's body would be under my own, her thighs spreading, opening up, letting me in. It's been so long—too long—since I've been with anyone but Jasper, and he's all hard angles. Sex is always a battle with him, but with Mina it would be as easy as falling.

I put my hand over hers, pressing it into my leg. She's staring at my lips, eyes heavy-lidded, unfocused. I can smell the whiskey on her breath.

The same scent as Kinnear, when he pushed me against the wall, groped at my skirt. When he writhed underneath me, pleading for his life.

I can't. Not like this. Not with Mina intoxicated, the same day her ex-husband went into the ground because of me.

I take her hand between mine and squeeze it. The spell of the moment is broken, but the heat still simmers between us.

"You should get some rest," I tell her. "Take a few days off, take it easy."

Mina turns away to take another drink. "That's the last thing I'm going to do."

42

CARLY

It's been hours, and there's still no sign of Allison.

I gave up the pretense of getting any studying done a while ago, and now I'm just lying in bed, staring at the ceiling, opening my cell phone and snapping it shut again. I keep mentally rehearsing my apology, the same way Allison practiced her story for the dean, but I don't know what I can possibly say to make this right. I almost *want* her to yell at me, to vent all her rage in my direction. I deserve it.

My phone buzzes with a new text, and I sit straight up, heart pounding.

It's not from her, though. It's from Wes.

Have you seen Allison?

I type back, I think she's still at rehearsal.

Though he should be there too—running the lights or sound effects, I can't remember which. And rehearsal ended half an hour ago. Sometimes they run long, but she should be back by now. If she's coming back. Maybe she's so mad at me she decided to sleep elsewhere tonight.

No, Wes replies. She never showed.

Allison's been a wreck this week, but she's never skipped *Cabaret* rehearsal before. The show is the most important thing in the world to her. This is even worse than I thought.

I dial Wes's number, hands shaking. He answers on the first ring. "Hey, what's—"

"When was the last time you saw her?" I ask.

"Yesterday," he says. "When we all had lunch."

I fall silent, pacing back and forth beside the bed. I don't even remember standing up.

"Carly? Is something wrong?"

"I haven't seen her since this morning," I tell him. "And she was . . . upset."

"You guys had a fight?"

This is all my fault. I'm the one who talked her into reporting the assault. I thought it would help, but all it did was traumatize her more. And then instead of being there for her, trying to comfort her, I lost my temper. I can't believe I spoke to the dean that way. Even though I can remember the words I said, the way I felt, it almost doesn't feel real. I was like a totally different person.

"Something like that," I say.

"She's probably just somewhere cooling off," Wes says. "She does that. Like this one time in high school—"

"No." I shake my head. "No, there's something wrong. I'm going to go look for her."

"At this time of night? Are you—"

"Call me if you hear from her."

I rush to get dressed, pulling my coat on over my pajamas, adding gloves and a knit cap, then tucking the pants into my Doc Martens. I shouldn't have waited so long. I should have been looking for her this whole time.

I have no idea where to start, though. Wes said she's not at the theater, and there aren't that many campus buildings open this late, even on Fridays. Surely she's somewhere indoors—it's too cold to-night to stay outside for long.

I stick my hands in my coat pockets and strike out in the general direction of the Oak Grove. I've only made it a few feet down the path, though, when I hear footsteps in the distance—far away, but approaching. Fast.

I increase my pace, but the other person speeds up too, gaining on me, shouting something over the wind.

"Hey!" A hand catches me by the sleeve, holding me back.

It's Wes. He's panting, his face ruddy. He must have run all the way from Riffenburg.

"What are you doing here?" I ask.

"I couldn't—let you—" Wes stops to catch his breath, leaning his hands on his thighs. "It's not safe. Wandering around by your-self at night."

I fold my arms across my chest. "Yeah, some random guy might run up and grab me."

"Sorry," he says, but he's smiling. "Come on, I'll help you look for her."

We go into the student union first. The only entrance un-locked at this time of night is the main one, with its big arched door and antique clock that looks like it belongs in a big-city train station. Besides the bored-looking security guard, the only people inside are two girls getting Double Stuf Oreo crumbs all over the checkerboard carpet in the atrium, and a lone guy doing weight reps in the gym without a spotter, rock music blaring from his headphones.

The library proves to be even more deserted, and we reach Tro-cino Dining Hall just as they're switching off the lights for the night. I guess everyone is either back at their dorms like I would usually be, or they're off campus partying. Wes says there aren't any theater department get-togethers that he knows of tonight, though.

We head to the river next, taking the concrete path that veers off from the Oak Grove. I don't know why she'd come out here in the middle of the night—and we probably shouldn't be here either—but I don't know where else to look.

"You said she's done this before?" I ask Wes as we approach the forested area at the edge of campus. I can hear the water rushing beyond the trees. If not for the moonlight glinting off Wes's glasses, I'd barely be able to see him walking beside me.

"Yeah," he says. "Sophomore year of high school, she got in some fight with her parents. She never told me what it was about. But she disappeared for a couple days."

"Did they look for her?"

"No," he says, disgust in his voice. "They *prayed* for her."

The path curves to meet the riverbank, and we have to cross a little wooden footbridge to keep going. Halfway across, I stop, gripping the railing, watching the black current flowing by below us. Wes stops too, resting his hands next to mine.

The longer our search continues, the more tense Wes seems, but I still get the sense he's humoring me on some level. If he knew what had really happened to Allison, if he'd seen her face this morning, he'd be much more concerned.

"So what happened?" he asks. "You said she was upset."

I want to tell him everything. But I promised, and I've already fucked up enough today.

The wind whips over the water, blowing my hair across my face. Wes reaches out and smooths it back behind my ear. "You really care about her, huh?"

I nod. He's still touching me, fingertips lingering by my temple. Just like at the Halloween party, I'm sure he's going to kiss me. Only this time, I don't feel like running.

I move toward him—not a step, just rocking forward on the soles of my boots. But instead of closing the distance, he leans away, lowering his hand.

"We're not going to find her out here." He taps his fingers on the bridge railing. "We could get my car and drive around, maybe? At least then we'd be warm."

"Okay." I feel colder than ever, like a blanket's been ripped off me, exposing my limbs to the cold. Did I really want him to kiss me? We're supposed to be looking for Allison. I shouldn't be thinking about anything else.

We walk to Wes's dorm to get his car keys. He lives in the honors residence hall, Cooper. Unlike the dilapidated beige interior of Whitten, Cooper's common areas are all aggressively colorful, reproductions of classical paintings all over the walls, shelves overloaded with books tucked into every corner.

We pass a small cluster of students draped over mismatched lounge chairs, passing a bowl of singed microwave popcorn back and forth as they have an impassioned discussion about the *Star Wars* prequels. Wes nods at them in greeting, but I'm the one who draws their curious stares, following Wes into his dorm room well after midnight.

He has a single. The walls are papered over with an overlapping riot of music and movie posters—Elliott Smith, *Pulp Fiction*, *Garden State*—but the space is otherwise neat, books stacked carefully on the desk, all his toiletries lined up along the back of the dresser.

As soon as Wes shuts the door, I'm struck with a pang of alarm. It's way too warm in here, even with the window above the radiator cracked to let the excess heat out.

Wes grabs his messenger bag off the papasan chair in the corner and starts rooting around for his car keys. I yawn, leaning against the corner of the desk to keep myself upright. Until we stopped moving, I didn't realize how tired I was.

"You okay?" Wes asks.

"Yeah," I say, stifling another yawn. "You got the keys?"

He holds them up. "We can hang out here for a bit if you want, though. Get some rest."

I want to find Allison. But I can barely keep my eyes open. If Wes is anywhere near as tired, it's not safe for him to be behind the wheel.

Besides, there's nothing to be afraid of. We were just out in the woods in the middle of the night, and he didn't even *try* to start something. If there's any guy in the world who's safe to be alone with, it's Wes.

As if he can read my thoughts, he starts stammering, "I mean, you can have the bed, I'll sleep on the floor, we don't have to—"

"No," I say.

Wes flinches a little, his eyes squinting even more than usual.

"I mean, yeah, we should probably get some rest. But you don't have to sleep on the floor, that's stupid."

He swallows, seeming more nervous than I am all of a sudden. "O-okay."

I have no idea what I'm doing—no idea what I even *want* to do, except lie down and close my eyes and be warm. And I hope wherever Allison is, she's doing the same.

Before I can talk myself out of it, I shuck off my coat and boots, then climb up into Wes's lofted bed. He hesitates for a second before following suit.

I turn toward the wall, facing away from him, 'cause I figured that would be less weird, but now all I can think about is the heat of his breath on the back of my neck. Despite the narrowness of the mattress, he's careful to leave a sliver of space between his body and mine.

It's awkward and strange, and I'm not the least bit comfortable, but my exhaustion is so overwhelming I drop off almost immediately, falling headfirst into a dream about Allison. She's running along the riverbank, barefoot, the branches grasping at her hair. Calling out to Wes and me on the bridge, but we can't hear her over the rushing water.

Her foot catches on a sharp rock, and as she plunges into the current, I surface—jolting awake with a gasp, flipping over, arms thrashing out.

I almost push Wes right out of bed. He startles awake too, grabbing at me to keep himself from toppling off the edge of the mattress.

We're so close now, heads sharing a pillow, hearts drumming in time, mouths inches away in the dark. I swallow and lick my lips, staring into his eyes.

But he just pulls the blanket up over both of us, and eventually I drift back to sleep, dreaming of cutting winds and freezing water even though I'm surrounded by warmth.

43

SCARLETT

I thought things might return to a semblance of normality after Kinnear's funeral, but most of my colleagues are still using his death as an excuse to slack off, cancel class, even stay home. I at least hope Mina is managing to get the rest she needs; I stayed at her place last night until after she fell asleep, slumped on the sofa with her bare toes pressed into my thigh.

Dr. Stright is one of the only English faculty members other than Drew and me who bothered to show up to work today. Stright always leaves his office door slightly ajar, so we all have to hear his pretentious indie folk Spotify playlist wafting down the hall. As I pass by his office on the way to my own, I slow my pace so I can glance inside. There's a female student in there with him again, and this time it's not Ashleigh Lawrence.

It's Mikayla.

Her back is to the door, but that halo of dark curls is unmistakable. She's sitting in the chair across from Stright's desk, but he's not seated behind it. Instead, he's right beside her, leaning over her shoulder.

My fingers squeeze the stack of papers I'm carrying. I knew it. That fucking *creep*.

"Hey, Scarlett," Drew says, poking his head out of his own office across the hall. He looks better-rested today, back in his usual uniform of tweed jacket and dark slacks. "I was going to get some coffee—you want anything?"

I want to rip Stright's door off the hinges and rush in there to tear him away from Mikayla. Stright leans closer to point out a line in the book on her lap, and she nods at whatever he's just said, tilting her face up to smile at him.

Drew raises his eyebrows. "Everything okay?"

"Yes," I say, dragging my attention away from Stright and Mikayla. "Yes, I—"

My purse vibrates, and I shuffle the papers onto my other arm so I can dig my phone out.

It's a UK number.

Drew sees it too, and his eyes widen. "Here, here, give me those."

I shove the papers and my purse into his waiting hands, then answer the call. "Hello, this is Dr. Scarlett Clark."

"Dr. Clark, this is Judith Winters from the Women's Academy."

"Dr. Winters. Thank you for calling."

Drew grins at me, bouncing a little on his feet, and I smile back. I can't let too much excitement seep into my tone, though. I'm supposed to be in mourning for our murdered colleague, after all.

"I'm sorry I didn't get a chance to speak to you at Alexander's funeral," I say, heading into my office. Drew follows, placing my possessions quietly on the desk. "But your eulogy was incredibly moving."

"Thank you, dear," she says. "It was a beautiful service. I'm afraid I'm still in shock."

"Yes, we all are." I glance across the hall. Kinnear's office door is shut, but his secretary is still at her post outside, dabbing at her already-destroyed mascara with a tissue. She's been going through more than a box of Kleenex a day. I wasn't certain before that she and Kinnear were fucking, but her unmanageable grief seems to confirm it. "It's so awful."

There's a blast of white noise on the other side of the line, as if Judith is standing outside.

"Are you still in town?" I ask. "Perhaps we could—"

"No, I'm at the airport. My flight to Heathrow leaves in an hour. But I wanted to set up a time with you once I'm back home—to discuss the fellowship further."

I can't prevent myself from smiling now. Drew mouths, *What did I tell you?*, and pumps his fist in the air. I've done exhaustive research on all the people in our field who might apply for the fellowship, and with Kinnear out of the way, my path should be clear. While some of my competition might have tenure at elite institutions or boast other accolades I can't compete with, none of them have the specific expertise on Viola Vance that I do. But I can't get overconfident. That's how I got into the mess I'm in now.

"I'd love that," I say to Judith. "Any time that's convenient for you."

"Don't you have classes to teach?" There's a sternness in Judith's voice, like I'm a disobedient student she's chastising.

"Yes, of course," I say. "But this fellowship is my top priority right now, and I have a very capable graduate assistant."

Or I did, anyway. I wonder if Jasper will actually show up for work today, since he showed his face at the funeral. As soon as the dust settles from Kinnear's death, I'll see about transferring Jasper to another professor. Maybe I can find a way to foist him on Stright. The two of them might kill each other and save me the trouble.

"All right," Judith says. "Would next Tuesday be suitable? I'm available at three p.m. my time, which I believe is—"

"Ten a.m. Eastern. Yes, that's perfect."

"Wonderful. I'll speak to you then. And I hope you'll let me know if there are any developments."

My mind is already whirring to life with preparations for the interview, so it takes me a second to realize she's referring to developments in Kinnear's murder case.

"Certainly," I tell her. "I know we all just want answers."

Across the hall, Kinnear's secretary pops her head up like a startled doe, looking toward his office door. It's swinging open.

"You must feel so fortunate," Judith says.

The two Pittsburgh detectives emerge from the office. Flynn looks relaxed, loose-limbed, but Abbott's jaw is set. Good cop, bad cop. They stand aside to let someone else exit the room.

Jasper.

I grip the phone harder, heart pounding. "I'm sorry?"

"Fortunate to have gotten to work with him for as long as you did," Judith says. "I'm sure he taught you a tremendous amount."

"Yes, yes, of course." Alexander Kinnear taught me *so* much. I'll never forget his many lessons. "He was . . ."

Jasper smiles at the detectives, trying to act like his typical smooth self. But he's rattled, his hands shaking so hard I can see it from here. He sticks them in the pockets of his trousers.

Then he looks right at me.

"Well, I'll let you go." There's that edge in Judith's tone again.

"I'm sorry," I say. "I— It's a bit chaotic here."

"I can imagine," she says. "I'll speak to you on Tuesday, Dr. Clark."

"Yes, looking forward to it."

But she's already hung up.

"So?" Drew says. He's been so focused on me, he hasn't even noticed the detectives. Abbott and Flynn are lingering outside Kinnear's office, conferring in hushed voices, but Abbott's gaze keeps flicking toward my open office door.

"Sounds like I made it to the final round," I tell Drew.

He whoops and scoops me up into a celebratory hug. Now Abbott and Flynn are both watching us, Abbott's eyes narrowing with interest.

Jasper appears in the doorway, blocking my view. "What are you two so giddy about?"

Drew looks at me, still grinning, waiting for me to share my good news. Instead, I smooth my blouse back into place and turn the phone facedown on my desk.

"Nice of you to grace us with your presence today, Mr. Prior."

"Well," Drew says, already edging toward the exit. "I should get back to work. Congratulations again, Scarlett."

Jasper stands aside to let Drew through the doorway. Then he steps over the threshold and, before I can protest, pulls the door shut behind him.

"Don't worry," Jasper says. "I covered for you."

I'm suddenly aware of how small this space is with Jasper in it. "What do you mean?"

"The detectives were asking about you, what you were doing the night of—"

"They were asking about *me*?"

I assumed it was a good sign I seemed to be so low on their list of people to interview. But maybe they're interviewing everyone else first so they can catch me in a lie.

"I told them I was with you." His hands aren't shaking now when he runs his fingers down my arms to grip my hips. "All night."

"You shouldn't have done that."

Jasper scowls. "You should be thanking me."

"*Thanking* you? For lying to the police?"

"They're saying the crime seems personal." His hold on my hips tightens, fingertips digging in. "They think it's someone who knew him, knew where he lived. Maybe even someone who works here."

"That describes you too, you know." I push past Jasper to get to the door. "Sounds to me like you're trying to cover your own ass."

"You think *I* killed him?" Jasper looks genuinely amused.

I turn back to face him, lifting my chin and crossing my arms. "You don't have the balls."

For a second I think he's going to slap me. I wish he would; I'd love an excuse to make him bleed again.

Instead, he smiles. "I've missed you, Scarlett."

My back is against the closed door now, so there's nowhere to run when Jasper leans down and kisses me. My hands stay stiff at my sides, my mouth unyielding, but he's not dissuaded. This is still a game to him.

His hand snakes down my leg to lift my skirt up, and I shove him away. "Stop. Not here."

"Where, then?" He grips my thigh. "You told me not to come to your house anymore."

"This has to stop, Jasper." I turn around, trying to open the door, but Jasper presses against my back, pulling my hand away from the knob so he can pin it flat against the door. His breath is scorching on the back of my neck.

He wasn't trying to protect me by concocting that fake alibi. He just wants me beholden to him. If I break things off with him now, there's no telling what he'll do.

Someone knocks on the door, two sharp raps. The vibration rattles my teeth.

The detectives, I think. But then a familiar voice says my name.

"Scarlett? Are you in there?"

It's Mina. So she did come to work today.

"One second." I manage to twist around just enough to glare at Jasper. Surely he's not going to persist, with Mina right outside.

He holds on a few seconds longer before releasing me. I smooth my skirt and bump him back with my hips so I have enough room to open the door.

"Oh, good, you're here," Mina says. Her eyes aren't red anymore, but they're unfocused, buzzing with a strange energy. She has the air of a mad scientist on the verge of a breakthrough. "I need to talk to you, I just—"

Jasper has moved in right behind me again, and he plants his hand on the edge of the door, touching mine. Mina isn't looking at him, though. She's staring at my lips.

I lift my fingertips to my mouth, and they come away stained with smeared lipstick.

"Mina," I start, but something slams shut behind her eyes.

"Never mind," she says. "I can see you're busy."

44

CARLY

All night, I dreamed of Allison.

She was always running. Running through the woods, through endless unrecognizable hallways. Across the gravel parking lot behind Bash's house, barefoot, bleeding. Up the fire escape, face tilted toward the black sky.

I wake with all my muscles clenched, like I'm poised to run too. Wes is still asleep, lying on his back with his palms sandwiched between his skull and the pillow, a soft sound that's not quite a snore escaping from his lips.

I slide off the end of the bed, extending my toes until I feel the floor. It's freezing in his room now; the heater must have switched off sometime in the night. I push the windowpane down to close it, flinching at the screech it makes against the frame.

And that's when I realize: I know one other place where Allison might be.

Wes didn't stir at the sound of the window closing, so I decide to let him keep sleeping. It isn't dark out anymore, though it's still so early that the campus seems deserted my whole walk back to Whitten.

I take the fire escape steps fast, so I won't have time to think about the weakness in my knees. The metal railing is so cold it stings my palms. As soon as I reach the rooftop, I call out for her, but it sounds more like a gasp than her name. My pulse is racing from the climb—and also because Allison is sitting so close to the edge.

"Allison, thank God. How long have you been up here?"

She keeps on gazing off into the gray sky, like she hasn't heard me. She can't have been here the whole night; it's too cold, steely clouds threatening snowfall, and she's just wearing that thin coat with the faux fur collar.

I edge closer, trying not to look over the edge of the roof. "Are you . . . are you okay?"

This time, her shoulders stiffen at my question. Her skin looks like wax paper, and her faded blue hair is lank and stringy, spreading from her skull like veins. I want to wrap my arms around her, but she looks too fragile for that. She looks like she's on the verge of shattering.

"I'm fine," she says finally. She's lying to herself just as much as me.

"It's freezing. Why don't you come downstairs and—"

"Where were you last night?"

"I was . . ." I swallow. This is not at all the question I was expecting. She must have come back to our room at some point and found me gone. "Looking for you. Wes and I—we were really worried."

Spending the night in Wes's bed feels like a betrayal in a way I can't quite explain. Allison clearly doesn't want him for herself—and nothing happened between us anyway—but I don't want to risk upsetting her more.

"Let's go down to our room and talk," I say.

"There's nothing to talk about."

Allison leans forward, letting her feet dangle off the roof, and my stomach lurches.

"I told you," she says. Her heels bump against the brick below the roof line. "I told you I didn't want to do that. I told you there was no point."

"I'm sorry." I crouch down beside her. I'm trying to remember the whole speech I had prepared, the eloquent apology, but I can't think with her legs hanging in midair like that. "I'm so sorry, Allison. I was just trying to help."

"The dean was right."

"*No.*" I lay my hand over hers. "No, she wasn't, that's—"

"I just want to pretend that whole night never happened." She still won't look at me. "I barely even remember it anyway."

I can't know exactly what Allison is going through. But I know what I saw, and I know Bash deserves to be punished for it. The dean too, for making Allison doubt herself, making her feel so helpless.

She pulls her hand away from mine and slips it into her coat pocket, then draws it out again, something silver clenched in her fist.

A pair of scissors.

My pulse spikes. "Allison."

She extends the scissors in front of her like a dagger, gripping the handle so hard her whole arm is shaking. The blades flash bright even in the dreary light.

My mind fills with images of metal slicing into her pale wrists, blood spilling off the edge of the roof. I seize her elbow, digging my fingers into the same spot where Bash left bruises.

Allison stands up, shaking off my grip. I feel awful about grabbing her, but I can't let her hurt herself. I have to do something. Her eyes are welling with tears now, lower lip quivering.

"Just give me the scissors, okay?" I stand up too, holding out my hand. "And then we can figure out a plan. I want to help."

She raises the scissors and points them toward the base of her skull.

"Allison, please. Don't do this. Let me help you."

She gathers her hair into her fist, gripping so hard a few strands rip out at the root. Then in one violent motion, she snaps the scissors shut. Hacking off her ponytail.

Blue tendrils rain down on the rooftop, float away on the breeze.

"I told you." Allison tosses the scissors at my feet. "I don't need your help."

45

SCARLETT

Mina can't avoid me forever. But she's been doing a damn fine job of it for the past couple of days.

It's Sunday evening when I finally catch up with her. She's in her office on the second floor of Miller, working even later than I am. Her eyes flick up from her laptop screen just long enough to see that it's me darkening her doorstep, and her mouth pinches. She looks exhausted, shadows under her eyes, new worry lines etched between her brows.

"Scarlett." She enters a few more keystrokes. "You're here late."

"Can we talk?" I want to know she's okay. But I *need* to know what she came to speak to me about with that strange, frantic energy sparking in her eyes. "About the other day, I—"

I stop—not looking at Mina anymore, but at the wall across from her desk. The web of pictures on the whiteboard has been taken down, the lines of marker wiped into faint red smears. Written in a straight line down the middle of the board, there's now a list of names.

Richard Callaghan

Kevin Pratt

Brandon Risman

Samuel Wexner

Tyler Elkin

My blood turns to ice. They're all mine.

In chronological order, no less.

"It's none of my business." Mina shuts the laptop, finally meeting my eyes. "It just surprised me, that's all. I didn't think you were like that."

Like Kinnear, she means.

I step toward her. "I'm not."

"Really?" she says. "So you're not fucking that boy? That *student*?"

I don't want to lie to her. She's too smart, she'd see through it anyway. She sees so much it's terrifying. She may be right that this mess between me and Jasper is none of her business, but part of me wants it to be.

"*Graduate* student, and I'm ending things with him. I should have done it a long time ago. Well, technically I shouldn't have allowed it to start in the first place."

Mina purses her lips, like she doesn't quite believe me. I can't blame her.

She stands up, walking around the desk. When she crosses her arms over her white blouse—somehow still crisp and flawless this late in the day—I see the flecks of red ink marring her manicure. It feels like she's written those names in something far more permanent than dry-erase marker.

"Are you in love with him?" she asks.

I can't help laughing. "*God* no. He's . . . convenient."

At least he started out that way. Now he's a ticking time bomb.

Mina stares at me for a second, her expression unreadable. Then she puts her hand on my arm. The warmth of her skin feels like fire, even through the fabric of my sleeve. "You deserve so much better than him. You know that, right?"

Longing pulses through me again, throbbing in time with my heartbeat. Mina might be strung out with exhaustion, but she's sober now. And we're completely alone.

But I've allowed myself to get too close to her already. This woman has the power to ruin my life as surely as Jasper does. The list of names on the wall behind her proves it.

I pull away. "What was it you wanted to tell me?"

Mina blinks, almost startled—the spell between us shattering once again. "What?"

"When you came to my office." *The names, tell me about the names.*

"Oh." Mina shakes her head. "It might be nothing."

I look at her expectantly. That spark of mad-scientist energy lights up her eyes again.

"Okay, so—Mikayla and I were discussing the Tyler Elkin case," she says. "I'm assuming you'd heard the gossip about him, and that girl Megan—"

"Megan Foster, yes." With Tyler gone, Megan seems to be thriving. I don't have her in any of my classes this semester, but every time I see her in the halls of Miller or walking through the Oak Grove, she looks brighter, happier, less haunted. She's on track to graduate in the spring, and I heard she got early acceptance to a master's program at Stanford.

"Well, we got to talking, and we realized that several of the other suicides also had, well, less than stellar reputations." Mina points at the list on the whiteboard. "These men all had complaints against them, either around the time of their death, or in the year before. Sexual harassment. Domestic abuse. Rape."

If this is all she has, I'm not concerned. The allegations against these men were an open secret, if not a matter of public record, when I killed them. No one cared at the time of their crimes, so why would they give a damn now?

I pretend to consider what she's said as if it's brand-new information. "Wouldn't that be a risk factor for suicide? Facing criminal charges like that?"

Mina shakes her head. "That's just it: none of them were facing actual charges. Only complaints to the school. Accusations. That kind of thing."

"Rumors."

"Exactly," Mina says. "Like this guy—" She taps one of the names. "Did you know him?"

Kevin Pratt. Sophomore from Kentucky. Spent most of his time barricaded in his dorm room, playing video games or recording YouTube screeds bemoaning the stuck-up bitches on campus who spread their legs for football players while refusing to fuck him. I spent hours watching those vile videos when I was planning his death, and I always felt like I needed a shower after.

"Not well," I say. "I think he was in one of my first-year survey courses?"

"A female student tried to get a restraining order against him, said he was stalking her. But the judge dismissed her request. Two weeks later, he's dead in a field at the edge of town."

For such a skinny little worm of a boy, Kevin gave me much more trouble than I'd expected. Luring him to a remote location was easy enough: I made a fake Facebook account, pretending to be a cute girl his age who couldn't *wait* to meet him in person. But once he realized I wasn't Ashley G. from Blairsville, he pulled a hunting knife on me and put up a hell of a fight. I had to drag him to a new location before finishing him off so the police wouldn't find signs of a struggle and drops of my blood next to his still-cooling corpse.

I used his own knife to slit his wrists. No one ever suspected it was anything other than a suicide. Kevin Pratt absolutely seemed like the type to kill himself—though if not for my intervention, he might very well have taken his own life after taking out who knows how many of his classmates with the cache of weapons they found when cleaning out his dorm room.

"Mikayla's working on a more in-depth report for me right now," Mina says. "Looking at social media, newspaper reports, student forums. As you can imagine, it's hard to confirm a lot of facts. But you have to admit, it's an interesting pattern."

"Have you told anyone else about this?"

"No. Just you and Mikayla. I can't take it to the administration until I have more to go on. They'll think I'm some hysterical bitch with a conspiracy theory." She turns away from the whiteboard, running her fingers through her hair with a sigh. "Do *you* think I'm crazy?"

I know I should say yes. *Yes, this is insane, you're overworked, you need to sleep, you're seeing things that aren't there. You should drop this, get some rest. Leave well enough alone.*

But I can't help respecting Mina for figuring even this much out. It's only a small fraction, really, of the men I've killed. And she has no proof whatsoever that they were murdered, only that they were all creeps who deserved to be. I don't want to get caught, of course, but it *is* nice to finally have someone recognize my handiwork.

"No," I tell her. "I don't think you're crazy at all."

46

CARLY

Even in the dark, I can spot Allison at a distance.

The windows in the first-floor reading room of Thiede Memorial Library provide a perfect view of the Oak Grove—and Allison, walking to *Cabaret* rehearsal. This afternoon, she had one of the other girls in our dorm even out her DIY haircut into a sharp chin-length bob, and then she dyed over the blue remnants with glossy black. It makes her skin look full-moon pale, her features sharp as claws.

She stops to greet the students smoking on the steps flanking the front entrance of Riffenburg Hall. Bash isn't part of the group; he went inside a few minutes ago.

It makes me sick, thinking of him in there with her for all the hours of rehearsal, smiling and laughing and dancing like there's nothing wrong, like he's not a fucking rapist.

My hand throbs, and I force myself to set down my pen. I pressed it so hard into my notebook that I ripped through several pages again. I shake out my wrists and crack my knuckles one by one. The sound echoes like gunfire in the silence of the library, and the boys studying at the next table over glare at me.

I want to leap out of my chair and lunge at them, teeth bared like a wild animal. Ever since my outburst in the dean's office, I've been having these urges. I can't act on them, of course. But just imagining lashing out sends a little surge of satisfaction up my spine.

"Carly?"

I twist around in my seat to find Alex standing right behind me, hands buried in the pockets of his leather jacket. I immediately feel like I need to explain myself—but as far as he knows, I'm just here studying, like any other student. He's the one who shouldn't be here; it's a Saturday, and he's not even carrying any library books.

"How are you?" Alex asks. "Your roommate's feeling better, I hope?"

My eyes dart back to the Riffenburg steps—empty now. "Yeah. Much better."

I know it's wrong, following Allison, watching her like this. But I don't know what else to do. She won't talk to me. Since our encounter on the rooftop, she won't even look me in the eyes. But with everyone else, she's acting like she's totally fine, back to her effervescent self. Like nothing happened at all.

Alex sits down next to me. "You *sure* you're okay?"

I bite my lip. I'm not going to cry in front of him. Not again.

"It's just, you seem really stressed out." He looks me up and down. "You've definitely lost some weight."

I shrink into my chair, pulling my hoodie closed across my chest. It weirds me out, thinking of him noticing my body in any way, even out of concern. But at the same time, his attention is like a drug rushing into my bloodstream. The longer he looks at me, the more my heartbeat slows, my muscles unknot. It reminds me of the strange sense of calm I felt when I faced off with Bash on Halloween. I wish I could feel that way all the time.

Alex leans in, elbow propped on the table next to my notebook.

"Remember what I said: I'm always here if you need to talk." He smiles. "I really want to help, Carly. If I can."

Rehearsal just started, so I could talk to Alex for a while and still make it back in time to ensure Allison gets home safe.

"Can we go somewhere else?" I ask.

"Sure," he says. "I know just the place."

Alex and I don't talk the entire walk downtown. I figure we're headed to the coffee shop next to the courthouse; that's pretty much the only decent hangout spot that's not on campus.

But he turns in the opposite direction, leading me across the train tracks. I've never walked this way before, so it takes me a second to realize where he's taking me.

The Gorman Tap. Allison's told me stories about sneaking in there, but I don't have a fake ID like she does.

I look up at the flickering neon cocktail glass above the bar entrance. "I'm sorry, I'm not old enough to—"

"It's fine," Alex says, holding the door open for me. "They know me here."

I hesitate. This feels wrong. But he's my teacher; he wouldn't get me in trouble.

The Gorman Tap is bigger than it looks from the outside, but it still feels claustrophobic, shadows and lingering cigarette smoke pressing in on all sides. Alex weaves around the tables to a booth tucked into the corner by the bathrooms, then backtracks to the bar to get drinks for us.

There's practically no one here except us and the bartender, but I still feel conspicuous. The song playing over the speakers seems too loud, the singer's pleas of "don't look back in anger" ricocheting off the tin-tiled ceiling. As soon as I'm alone at the table, the urge to run becomes almost unbearable. *This was a mistake.* I should go back to the library and wait, like I planned.

Before I can think of an excuse or make a break for the exit, Alex returns, carrying a small glass filled with amber liquid in one hand and a soda with a striped straw in the other. He settles in across from me and takes a sip of his drink, closing his eyes to savor the taste. The low sound of pleasure that rumbles in the back of his throat makes my cheeks heat, but hopefully he can't tell since the stained glass lamp over the table casts everything in shades of red.

He really *is* good-looking. Definitely the best-looking guy who's ever given me a single moment of attention in my whole life. It's just because I'm one of his students, and he's worried about me. But still, it feels nice, sitting here with him. Better than staring out the library window obsessing.

I take a tiny pull of the soda, teeth sinking into the tip of the straw. It's a Cherry Coke, so sweet it makes my head swim. I skipped dinner again tonight so I could set up in my spot at the library as early as possible. Alex is right, I have lost weight; I keep having to notch my belt tighter to keep my jeans from hanging loose around my hip bones.

"So." Alex sets his glass on the table. "You want to tell me what's really going on?"

I do. I really do. But it's not my story to tell. Allison is mad enough at me already.

I stare into my soda. Alex dips his head, trying to catch my eye.

"Boy trouble?" he asks.

"No!" I blurt out. He raises his eyebrows, more amused than concerned now. I look down again, tracing my fingertip through the condensation on the soda cup.

Alex straightens his glasses, the way he does in class when he wants to make sure we're paying close attention. "You know what always makes me feel better?"

I shake my head. I believe he genuinely wants to help, but there's no way he can understand what I'm feeling right now—the shame, the helplessness. If he'd been at that party, he probably would have socked Bash in the jaw. He'd have insisted on calling the police right away, instead of panicking like a pathetic little girl.

"Writing about it." He leans over the table. "It always helps. Like a few weeks ago, I got into this big argument with my wife."

"What about?" I want to bite my tongue off the second the question comes out. It's none of my business.

But he doesn't seem the least bit bothered by my prying. "Oh, the same stuff we always fight about. I'm too dedicated to my students, I don't have enough time for her."

His wife might have a point there. It's after 7:00 p.m. on a Saturday, and he's sitting in a bar with me. But maybe she had plans of her own tonight. It's not my place to judge. I know nothing about being in a relationship. I've never even dated anyone, and my parents haven't exactly been a positive example.

"Anyway," he continues, "I went to my office—just to cool off, you know? And I ended up writing a short story about it."

I furrow my brow. "About the fight?"

"Sort of. More like . . . how I was feeling, what I really wanted to say to her. It poured out of me like water, washing away all those bad emotions."

I stab my straw down into the crushed ice at the bottom of my glass. "Did you tell your wife?"

"Oh, no," he says. "She wouldn't have understood. She's not artistic like us."

Allison's the artist, not me. I've never written anything that wasn't required for school. It might be worth a try, though, if it could help me make sense of these violent urges I've been having. But I'm terrified to open the door to them any further. What if I can't shut it again?

As though he's read my mind, Alex slides his hand across the table and says, "You can't keep all this stuff you're feeling bottled up inside forever, Carly."

He's not touching me, but if he moved another fraction of an inch he would be. I don't know if I want him to. I don't know what I want. Lately I've been feeling so many different things, I swear my muscles will tear from the strain of trying to contain it all.

"You don't have to show me what you write. You don't have to show anyone." Alex smiles at me, and the stained glass light makes his teeth shine crimson. "But trust me on this: you have to let it out sometime."

47

SCARLETT

"'Hark, villains! I will grind your bones to dust.'"

Jasper's voice echoes off the high ceiling of the lecture hall. He finally showed up today, so I'm putting him to work, reading a scene from *Titus Andronicus* aloud to the students. It's only a little bit of a punishment.

He finishes the passage, then steps back to cede the floor to me. Even with the growing tension between us outside the classroom, I have to admit he and I still work well together.

I've always preferred the research side of my academic career, but right now teaching feels like an oasis. I'm forced to stay in the moment, my worries about the police and Mina Pierce and her list of names dialed down to a low buzz in the back of my brain.

"Thank you, Mr. Prior. So tell me"—I turn my attention to the students—"do you think Titus is justified in his treatment of his daughter's rapists?"

"I mean . . . it just seems kind of extreme?" Ashleigh Lawrence says. She's speaking up more and more, without any prompting from me (though the majority of her comments are inflected like questions). "Baking them into pies and feeding them to their mother. It's so gross."

Ryan Cutler nods his agreement, the brim of his Pittsburgh Pirates hat bobbing. "Yeah, like, I know what they did to Lavinia was bad. But I don't know if they deserved to die for it."

Mikayla scoffs. Not under her breath; she wants everyone to hear it. I haven't seen her with Stright again, but there's something going on with her. She skipped class last Friday, which is completely unlike her; in the past, she's shown up even when feverish, and protested when I sent her back to her dorm.

I turn to her. "Ms. Atwell, I take it you disagree?"

"I think Chiron and Demetrius got off easy," she says.

"Seriously?" Ashleigh gapes at her. "He sliced their throats open and ground them up."

"They only suffered for a few minutes. What Lavinia went through was so much worse. They chopped off her hands, they cut out her tongue, they left her to—"

"I mean, yeah, I guess," Ashleigh says. "But at least they left her alive, right?"

"They left her alive to hurt her *more*." Mikayla doesn't even try to conceal her exasperation. "It's all the same crime anyway. It's about power, not sex."

Ashleigh goes quiet, but Ryan is getting more and more worked up, shaking his head, feet bouncing against the floor.

"Okay, sure, fine," he says. "But like, we can't go around killing every rapist and baking them into pies?"

"Why not?" Mikayla twists around to glare at him. "You scared?"

Their classmates erupt into uneasy giggles and whoops. I sweep a glare over the room to subdue them, but a hum of disquiet hangs in the air.

Ryan leans forward in his seat. His face darkens with a mixture of embarrassment and anger—perhaps the most dangerous combination of emotions in a man. Mikayla is a fierce debater, and she often gets into heated arguments with her classmates, but this is different. It feels like she's spoiling for a fight.

"Is that what you'd do if you were raped?" Ryan asks her. "Just slit the guy's throat?"

"Hey now," Jasper interjects. "Let's keep this academic, shall we?"

Ryan backs off, putting his hands up in surrender. But Mikayla doesn't.

"If someone raped me," she says, "no one would ever find his body."

The room falls silent, everyone looking a little queasy—except Ryan, who rolls his eyes and mutters under his breath, loud enough to make sure Mikayla hears, "Psycho bitch."

She's on her feet in an instant, her notebook and copy of *Titus Andronicus* crashing to the floor. "Come down here and tell me that to my face, you fucking douchebag."

Ryan laughs, but he's shrinking as far away from her as he can get, his spine pressed flat against the chair. Mikayla looks like she's about to scale the seats and throttle him. I know I should do something—the students and Jasper are all looking at me, waiting for me to intervene, regain control of the class. But part of me wants Mikayla to do it. The little shit deserves it.

Jasper grabs Mikayla by the elbow—gently, but she reacts like he's given her an electric shock.

"Don't fucking touch me." She glares at him and wrenches out of his grip. Jasper backs off, a strange smile canting the corners of his lips.

"Ms. Atwell," I say. "Why don't we go speak in my office?"

Mikayla's face is still twisted with rage, but before the tears have a chance to spill, she turns on her heel and walks out, leaving her things scattered across the floor. Her classmates stare after her, then exchange *Can you believe that?* looks.

"Finish up without me," I tell Jasper as I follow Mikayla out.

He'll never be able to get their attention back to finish the lesson, but maybe they've all learned something else today.

The hallway outside the lecture hall is completely silent, Mikayla already long gone. I head toward the nearest ladies' restroom—maybe she's in there crying, that's what I would have done at her age—but I'm stopped by the sound of my own name.

"Dr. Clark." Detective Flynn strides toward me. "I've been looking for you."

48

CARLY

"Excuse me."

A girl in a dingy slip and ripped fishnets pushes past me, pulling her hair into crooked high pigtails. They're doing a dress rehearsal for *Cabaret* tonight, so the basement of Riffenburg Hall is packed full of people, most of them wearing little more than underwear.

Two skinny guys in pinstriped shorts brush by me next, already smeared with pasty white makeup from their hairlines to their hips. I press myself against the wall to let them through. Then I decide to try going the other way, toward the end of the hall with slightly fewer people, and I nearly collide with Allison.

She's in costume too: black shorts, a corset, and boots. It looks a lot like what she made me wear to the Halloween party, except the corset has thin straps to hold it in place, and the boots go all the way up to her knees.

"Hi!" Allison says. "Did you bring it?"

I hold up her makeup bag—a vintage train case with pictures of classic starlets decoupaged all over the lid.

"*Thank* you!" She takes the case from me, clutching it against her stomach. "I can't believe I forgot it."

"No problem," I say. When I got her frantic text asking me to bring her makeup to the theater, I was glad of the excuse to get out of our room for a little while. I've spent all day working on my next story for writing class—or trying to, anyway. I attempted to take Alex's advice and write about my feelings, but it all came out a mess, just a bunch of whining about what an asshole Bash was. It made me feel worse, not better.

Speak of the devil. Bash appears next to Allison, his hand already squeezing her waist.

"Sally, *darling*." His costume consists of low-slung black shorts and garish red lipstick staining his mouth. He looks like a leering clown, finally as grotesque on the outside as he is inside. "You ready for this?"

Allison doesn't push him away. She doesn't even flinch at his fingers digging into her side. Instead, she smiles and bumps her hip against his. "But of course, darling!" she says, putting on an even more exaggerated version of the British accent she does for the show.

Bash winks at her, then saunters off. I glare after him, but for all he cares I might as well be part of the fucking cinder-block wall. I wonder if he even remembers me from Halloween.

"I should go get my face on," Allison says. "But if you want to—"

"Are you okay?" I ask.

She tilts her head, black hair slashing over her jaw. "What do you mean?"

"He just came up and *grabbed* you, like—"

Allison presses her lips together. "It's not a big deal."

"Seriously?" I stare at her. "After what he—"

She grabs me by the arm and drags me down the hallway. I raised my voice more than I meant to, and now everyone is looking our way—including Wes, who's just come out of a supply closet with a coil of cables wound around his arm.

Wes smiles when he sees me, starting to approach. Then he notices the angry expression on Allison's face, and he stops in his tracks, letting the cables fall slack.

"You need to calm down," Allison says in a harsh whisper.

"I-I'm sorry." I focus on the spot where her fingers dig into my sleeve, because I can't look her in the eyes.

"I don't need this right now." She lets go, already turning away. "We have a show to do."

She heads toward the dressing rooms. Bash has joined a pack of male dancers loitering outside the dressing rooms, and as she passes him, his hand snakes out, patting her on the ass.

I want to slam him back into the wall, grind his blood into the gray bricks. But Allison doesn't react at all. Doesn't even slow her pace. She's clearly used to it. He must do it all the time. Every damn night.

"What's wrong?" Wes asks me.

He didn't even see it. Bash just groped Allison right in front of everyone, and I seem to be the only person who's not totally fucking oblivious to it. What else has Wes missed during all these weeks of rehearsal?

So many times, I've imagined Allison and Bash onstage together: smiling and winking and sliding their hands over each other's skin. But it was always choreographed, controlled. A performance. I didn't imagine this—how casually he puts his hands on her, his appalling *possessiveness*.

Of course Bash feels entitled to touch her however and whenever he likes. He got away with it. He drugged her and assaulted her and hasn't faced a single consequence. What he did to her might not meet the legal definition of rape, but I'm certain he's done worse to other girls. He'll do worse to Allison if he gets the chance.

I imagine prying his fingers off her body, one by one. Then I imagine bending them back until they snap.

"Carly?" Wes says. "Is everything okay?"

The details rush into my mind so fast I feel dizzy: the bone sticking out of Bash's skin, the angry red of his blood, the way his screams would vibrate through me.

"I have to go." My voice has dropped into that same icy monotone it took on during the meeting with the dean.

Wes takes a step back. "What? Where are you—"

But I'm already gone. I run out of Riffenburg Hall, straight across the Oak Grove. My usual table at the library is already taken, but it doesn't matter, because I'm not here to watch Allison this time. I slide into a seat in the corner and pull a notebook out of my backpack, my heart pounding as I turn to a fresh page.

He wasn't afraid of me, I write. *That was his first mistake.*

49

SCARLETT

This is the first time I've seen Detective Flynn or his partner in days, but that doesn't mean they haven't been skulking around, turning over rocks to see what's crawling underneath.

"Detective Abbott and I would love to sit down with you," Flynn says. "Pick your brain."

"Of course," I say. "Just let me know when—"

"How's right now?" He smiles in a way I'm sure he intends to be disarming. Too bad for him, that sort of thing doesn't work on me anymore.

"I'm teaching," I say. "I just stepped out for a second, but I should be—"

"Oh, don't worry," he says. "This'll only take a few minutes."

A sneak attack. And I know how bad it will look if I attempt to evade it.

So I let Flynn usher me toward Kinnear's office. His secretary has gone home for the day, so at least I don't have to deal with her curious stares as well. Abbott is already inside, sitting in Kinnear's chair. Everything in here is just as he left it, except for the laptop and assortment of Sheetz coffee cups cluttering the desk. The curtains have been pulled shut, blocking the scenic view of the Oak Grove.

"Dr. Clark," Abbott says. "Thank you for making the time."

She motions for me to sit across from her. Flynn stays standing, moving behind the desk. He looks like a bodyguard, hands clasped behind his back so the gun strapped to his side peeks out of his jacket—though it's pretty clear Sharon Abbott is a woman not in need of any guarding.

"Of course," I say. "I hope I can be of assistance."

Abbott leans back. "Nice office, isn't it? Much more comfortable than the station in Pittsburgh, I'll tell you that." She rocks a bit, the plush leather creaking. "Say what you will about the man, but he had good taste."

"I suppose he did."

She's warming me up, easing me in gently. I'd much rather get this over with.

"Did you ever go to his house?" Abbott asks. "Back when it was still in one piece, I mean."

I cross my legs and fold my hands. "Once."

"It was nice too, wasn't it? I saw pictures. All that furniture from the sixties, such a shame." Abbott straightens up, the chair snapping back to attention. "And when was it? The one time you were there?"

"A few weeks ago. He threw a party."

Abbott checks her notes on the laptop screen. "For Homecoming, correct? Saturday, October twenty-fourth."

I nod.

"And that's the only time you've ever been there?"

"Yes." This is getting tiresome, but I can't let my annoyance show. I have to be pleasant, compliant, cooperative. They have to believe I want to help.

Abbott taps her fingernails against the edge of the desk. "So the other times you've met with him, it wasn't at his house."

My amiable mask falters for a second. "I'm not sure what you mean."

"You live at"—she checks her notes again—"1489 Beacon Street?"

"That's right."

"So Dr. Kinnear would meet you there, instead of going to his residence?"

"He's never been to my house." That's the truth. In all the time I've worked at Gorman, Kinnear never set foot there. Few people have, besides Jasper.

"That's strange." Abbott looks to her partner for backup.

"Very strange," Flynn agrees.

Sweat prickles between my shoulder blades. "How so?"

"Well," Abbott says. "Some of your colleagues seemed certain that you and the deceased were dating."

I'm unable to conceal my disgust. "*Dating?* Absolutely not."

Abbott smiles. "Maybe *dating* is the wrong word; I was trying to be polite. What they really said was that they thought you two were—"

"We weren't doing that either, I assure you."

Abbott tilts her head, studying me. "Sounds like you couldn't stand him."

"No, that's not—" I try to swallow my anger, but it's still too close to the surface, straining at the back of my throat. "It's just that, we were colleagues. I only thought of him in a professional context."

Flynn nods. "I guess that explains why you don't seem too broken up about his death."

"I'm . . ." Calm. I have to stay calm. I wasn't prepared for the previous line of questioning, but this one I've practiced for.

"Well, of course I was sad to hear about it. And shocked, like everyone else. But we weren't close. We didn't really socialize outside of work."

My pulse seems to slow with each word. I can still take control of this situation.

"May I ask who told you that Dr. Kinnear and I were . . . involved?"

"We can't divulge the details of our other interviews," Flynn says. Abbott is silent, her face maddeningly unreadable.

"Well," I say. "I can assure you, our relationship was entirely professional."

The scent of Kinnear's cologne hangs in the recycled air; I don't know how I didn't notice it before. It's like he's still here, breathing down my neck. The smug bastard.

Abbott leans forward, resting her elbows on the desk. "What about your relationship with his ex-wife?"

"Samina and I are colleagues as well."

"Not friends?" Abbott asks.

"I'm assisting with her work on the suicide prevention task force, perhaps you've—"

"You seemed awfully friendly with her at the funeral."

I press my lips together. I refuse to give them anything that could implicate Mina.

"You went home with her afterward too, and stayed for quite a while." Abbott looks to her partner again.

Flynn nods. "Several hours."

"You *followed* us?" The rage slips right through my teeth this time.

Abbott's face is entirely readable now: she looks delighted, eyes shining with glee. "Dr. Pierce was a potential suspect at the time, but we've cleared her."

The implication is clear: *I* am very much still a potential suspect.

"She has an alibi for the night of the murder," Flynn says. "Just like you. Mr. Prior told us you two were working quite late that night."

The smirk on his face says he knows exactly what Jasper and I were doing. But it doesn't matter. As long as they believe the alibi, they can make all the innuendos about my sex life they want. Maybe Jasper's ill-advised lie will be to my benefit after all.

"Did you or Mr. Prior happen to see your colleague Dr. Andrew Torres on Halloween night?" Abbott asks.

"No, I believe Drew stayed in with his husband. They're homebodies."

Abbott nods. "That's what Dr. Torres said. Well, he said *he* was at home that night."

"Rafael Torres was at a party," Flynn confirms. "At a nightclub in Pittsburgh. Witnesses place him there until at least two fifteen in the morning on November first."

I vaguely remember Drew mentioning this, complaining that Rafael wanted to go out dancing like they were still in their twenties. I figured they'd both decided against it.

Surely they're not trying to drag *Drew* into this, of all people. But if he was alone all night on Halloween, just around the corner from the scene of the crime . . .

"When did you and Professor Torres first become acquainted?" Abbott asks.

"My first term teaching at Gorman."

"That was about seven years ago, correct? You were hired right after you got your PhD?"

"Yes."

"And you like it here?"

I nod. Abbott sounds almost bored now, staring at something on her laptop. Flynn focuses on it too, peering over her shoulder, and they share a conspiratorial look.

"I guess you must," Flynn says. "To come back to the same place you went to school."

My stomach drops.

Abbott turns the laptop around. "This is you, right? Scarlett Christina Schiller."

On Detective Abbott's laptop screen is a picture of my old Gorman University student ID. My former self, with the frizzy dark hair and the long dour face, my eyes too big for the rest of my features.

"Did you know Dr. Kinnear when you were a student here?" Abbott asks.

There's no point in lying; if they know who I really am, they can look up my transcripts. Maybe they already have. "I had one class with him."

"Did he recognize you? When you came back to interview for a job?"

My undergraduate degree is from Swarthmore. My CV omits the single semester I spent at Gorman, and my staff records contain no trace of my original surname. Which means they dug deeper than that—but how deep?

"I'm not sure I would have. You look so different now." Abbott gestures at the photo. "We stared at this for such a long time, didn't we?" She looks up at Flynn, smiling; he smiles too, like this is all some enormous joke. "Trying to figure out if it was really you."

I can't stand it, the sad, sullen expression on Carly Schiller's face, the overwhelming fear in her eyes. I'm not that person anymore.

That girl is dead.

Abbott isn't even pretending to look at her notes anymore. "Clark, that's your mother's maiden name, right?"

"That's right." The response comes out shaky, the way I used to speak all the time.

"And you both started using the name shortly after your father's death." Abbott fixes her bird-of-prey gaze on me again. "How did he die, exactly?"

"He . . . it was a heart attack." My hands are shaking too; I press them against my thighs to still them. I feel like I've been plunged right back into my old anxiety-ridden body, where everything was too intense, too much.

"I'm sorry to hear that," Flynn says. "It must have been hard on you and your mother."

On my mother, yes. She never got over it. Never forgave me, even though she couldn't prove I was responsible. She still doesn't know what I did, how I swapped out his heart meds, slowly, methodically, over the several months I spent living at home between dropping out of Gorman and transferring to Swarthmore. But she saw the satisfied expression on my face when he was lying on the kitchen floor, clutching at his chest, gasping for his last few breaths, and that was enough.

The detectives wouldn't have looked so thoroughly into my past unless they had strong suspicions about me. But they also haven't arrested me yet. For that, they'll need much more than sordid rumors and unflattering old photos. If they had anything real, I'd be handcuffed in a police interrogation room, not sitting in my dead boss's office having a casual chat about my college days.

If they try to pin the crime on Drew, though . . . I can't let him take the fall for what I did. I'd have no choice but to turn myself in and confess everything. Unless they decide we were in on it together. I remember the look in Abbott's eyes when she saw Drew and me in my office, celebrating my call from Judith Winters. Smiling and laughing and embracing each other less than twenty-four hours after Kinnear's funeral.

"Well." Abbott lays her hands flat on the desk. "This has certainly been enlightening. But we don't want to drag you too far down memory lane. We know how busy you must be."

She stays seated while Flynn ushers me to the door and holds it open for me. What a fucking gentleman.

"Thank you for your time," Flynn says. "Dr. Schiller."

I flinch visibly when he uses my old name—which, I'm sure, is exactly the reaction he was hoping for. A violent fantasy flashes across my mind: driving my knuckles into the bridge of his nose until I hit raw cartilage. I blink it away, but not fast enough.

"Oh, I'm sorry." Flynn smiles. "Dr. Clark."

50

CARLY

Alex's eyes sweep around the room, and I could swear he lingers on me longer than the other students. "I think we have time for one more."

This time I don't look away, praying he'll ignore me, the way I usually do. This time I stick my hand straight up.

Alex looks as surprised as everyone else that I'm volunteering to read my work. "What do you have for us today, Ms. Schiller?"

"It's a new piece." I pick up the stapled printout. "Just a work in progress, but . . ."

I spent all night working on this, typing away while Allison tossed and turned on the other side of the room. Like Alex promised, the words had poured out of me. But not like water. More like molten lava.

I clear my throat and start reading. "'He wasn't afraid of me. That was his first mistake.'"

I'm surprised by how calm and confident I sound. It's safer somehow, because it's my character's voice, not mine. Maybe this is why Allison loves acting so much.

The story isn't about her and Bash. It's about a woman who's catcalled by the same man every day on her way to work—until she can't take it anymore and decides to murder him. At first she's planning to kill him quickly, cutting his throat with a butcher knife. But she can't let him get off that easy, not after he's harassed her for years on end. So first she lures him into an abandoned building, ties him to a chair, and puts duct tape over his mouth to muffle his screams while she peels his fingernails off one by one. *Then* she pulls out the knife.

"'The weapon felt good in her hand,'" I read. "'Heavy, grounding. The blade was so sharp, it would only take one stroke to—'"

"Oh my *God*."

Along with the rest of the class, I turn to look at the girl who spoke.

Mallory Russell, the senior girl who questioned my presence here on the very first day. She hasn't gotten much friendlier in the intervening months.

Mallory glares at me, her oversize purple eyeglasses making her look like a judgmental beetle. "What the hell is wrong with you?"

My cheeks heat, but I'm not blushing this time. I'm not embarrassed; I'm furious. I'd love to see the look on Mallory's face if she knew Alex personally asked me to write this story.

"Mallory," Alex says. "You know we always hold our feedback until the end; let's just let Carly—"

"We shouldn't have to sit here and listen to this. It's *sick*!"

Mallory looks to our classmates for support. A couple of them nod—though they seem a little scared. Of her or of me, I'm not sure. Wes shoots me a small smile, trying to be supportive. But even he can't quite look me in the eye.

She turns back to me. "I mean, Jesus. Are you a straight-up sociopath, or—"

"Hey," Wes says. "It's just a story. Fiction. It's not fair to assume it says anything about the author."

Mallory scoffs. "No way. Only someone with serious mental problems could write something like *that*."

"Yeah?" My fist closes around the pages. "Well, only someone with massive daddy issues could write the shit you do, *Mallory*."

Her mouth snaps shut, eyes already filling with tears. Clearly I've struck a nerve. She looks at Alex, but he's totally at a loss for how to wrest back control of the class.

Wes takes it upon himself to try to play peacemaker instead. "Why don't we all take a—"

"Save it," I snap, and Wes flinches like a kicked puppy. "I can stand up for myself."

"That's enough." Alex is smiling, and I want to slap him. This was his goddamn idea in the first place. But he cares more about everyone liking him than about standing up for me. "Let's pick back up next time, shall we?"

The other students file out, giving my seat a wide berth. I try to catch Wes's eye—I know it was wrong to bite his head off like that—but he ducks out with his notebook clutched against his chest like a shield.

Mallory bumps my desk with her hip as she passes. "Freak," she mutters—just loud enough for me, but not Alex, to hear.

I shoot to my feet, chair legs screeching against the floor. Alex catches me by the elbow, holding me back.

"See you next week, Ms. Russell," he says, and Mallory practically runs for the exit. She looks terrified of me.

That feels even better than writing the story did.

Once we're alone, Alex shuts the door. "That was . . ." He trails off, folding his arms across his chest. "Very creative."

I bristle. "I was just doing what you told me to do, you *said*—"

"You're right," he says.

He sits in the chair right next to mine. Alex doesn't look mad at all, and I'm almost disappointed. I wanted the excuse to argue with him, to stoke the fire of my anger. The rage is already burning off, tears rushing in to replace it, turning me back into my usual weak and pathetic self.

"I don't want to censor your self-expression." Alex leans forward, elbows on his knees. "But we have to be considerate of the other students. Make sure this is a safe space for everyone."

Fury flares in my chest again, chasing the tears away. *Nowhere* is safe, not while guys like Bash are out there taking whatever they want from whoever they want, with no one to stand up to them. My story was fiction, but it was about how the world should be—how it *would* be, if we could turn men's actions back on them. Make them fear us instead.

But Alex can't understand that. Even if he tries his best to be sensitive and caring, he's still a man. He'll never know what it's like.

"Fine," I say. "I'll write something more upbeat for next week."

"Hey, you can write whatever you want. Whatever you need to write." Alex pauses, thinking it over. "But maybe it would be best if you took a break from class."

I shake my head. "It's too late in the semester, I can't—"

"You're one of my best students, you're not in any danger of failing. I thought we could meet privately for a little while during my office hours. What do you think?"

"Every week?" I ask.

"As often as you want." He leans even closer. "As dark as the subject matter was, you lit up while reading that story. I've never seen you like that. So much fire in your eyes."

His eyes rove over my face, and just like at the bar, it seems as if he's on the verge of touching me. The difference is, now I'm sure I want him to.

I slide to the edge of my seat, so my knee nudges into his. "I already started writing my next story. I can bring it to you on Thursday?"

Alex smiles. "I'm looking forward to it, Ms. Schiller."

51

SCARLETT

This can't be happening. I want to peel off my skin, step out of it like an unzipped dress.

As soon as Flynn shuts the door, I take off down the hallway. I'm on autopilot, heading back to the lecture hall, but it's empty, the lights turned out. My chest hurts, a squeezing sensation over my sternum like a fist closing. Mina and the police each have parts of the puzzle, and soon they'll put the whole picture together.

Mikayla. I still need to find Mikayla. Not to discipline her for her outburst in class, but to make sure she's okay. But first I have to get out of this building. The walls are too close, the ceilings too low, I can't breathe.

I push through the front doors but don't realize I'm running until I stumble on the last step, tripping onto the sidewalk. It's cold—too cold to be outside without a coat, but I'm on fire, sweat pouring between my shoulder blades.

"Dr. Clark. Where are you headed in such a hurry?"

Stright. Fucking perfect. He was lounging on the steps, smoking a cigarette. He stands up to greet me with a smile, but it's far from friendly.

"Have you seen Mikayla Atwell?" My voice still sounds shaky and strangled. I hate asking him for anything, but maybe he can be of use in this one instance.

He blows out a plume of smoke. "Not since my office hours last Friday."

So he was meeting with her privately again. Her absence from class on Friday, the way she acted today, it all makes sense. I should have known he was to blame.

"She's a smart one, isn't she?" Stright says.

I don't answer. I'm imagining ripping the cigarette out of his mouth and holding it against his skin until he screams. It's the only thing keeping me from screaming myself.

"Maybe too smart for her own good." He laughs and takes another drag. "No wonder you like her so much."

"Shut the fuck up, Stright."

I didn't mean to say that. But at least my voice has returned to its usual lower register, so I sound like myself again rather than Carly Schiller.

"What the hell is your problem with me, Scarlett?" Stright drops his cigarette. The end smolders orange between our feet. "What did I ever do to you?"

"It was you, wasn't it?" I say. "You told the detectives Kinnear and I were sleeping together."

"*Were* you sleeping together?" Stright asks.

My lips curl with disgust. "Absolutely not."

"You fucking wanted him, though." Stright leers at me, the shadows distorting his handsome features. "I saw the way you stared at him. Like some freshman with a crush."

My surroundings fade into nothing. All I can see is Stright's face, the infuriating smile twisting his lips. I'm going to kill him. I'm going to kill him right here on the steps of Miller Hall. I should have killed him the night of the bonfire, before he'd ever laid a hand on Mikayla.

He steps toward me, and my rage slithers out, coils around him like a snake.

Yes. Come closer. Give me a reason.

I fix him with a poisonous smile. "You don't know anything about me, Patrick."

Stright is looming over me—or attempting to, anyway. He's not much taller than I am, but he's trying his damnedest to make me feel small, threatened. He's so far into my space, I'd barely have to reach out to hit him. To keep hitting him until he's bloodied and disoriented, until he goes down and I'm the one looming, raising my heel to crush his skull into the sidewalk.

"Always a pleasure, Dr. Clark."

Stright smiles as he turns to go inside, and this might be the worst part: letting him believe, even for a moment, that he's won. He stops on the top step to toss one more comment over his shoulder.

"I'll tell Mikayla you were looking for her."

52

CARLY

When the spotlight hits Allison, the rest of the theater falls away.

She's alone onstage, singing into a standing microphone, a black feather boa dripping off her shoulders.

Maybe this time, I'll be lucky . . .

I've heard her sing this song countless times before—under her breath while she's sprawled across her bed studying, at the top of her lungs in the shower stall next to mine—but I never really *heard* it, not until this moment.

Something's bound to begin . . .

She cups the microphone tenderly, like a lover's caress, black hair and green fingernails glinting under the bright stage lights. But her other hand is gripping the stand, white-knuckled. She looks right into my eyes, and it feels like she singing just for me.

Allison belts out the last lyric, throwing her head back so I can see the sweat gathered in the hollow of her throat. As the final note fades, everyone in the audience bursts into applause. It's not until I bring my own hands up to clap that I realize I've been gripping the armrests of my seat, leaving marks in the vinyl.

The rest of the musical rushes by in a blur. I manage to mostly ignore Bash as he slinks around the stage warbling song after song in a cartoonish German accent. When he grabs Allison's hand as they take their bows, I twist toward the back of the theater. I can barely see Wes in the little window of the sound booth—the top of his shaggy hair, the lights reflecting off his glasses.

We haven't spoken since writing class on Monday. He and Allison have both been busy with the musical, but I know he's avoiding me—and I know I deserve it. I can't get his kicked-puppy expression out of my mind.

I know my way around the theater well enough by now to sidestep the crowd in the lobby and slip downstairs to the dressing rooms via the tucked-away stairwell the actors use. The basement of Riffenburg Hall is filled with cast members laughing, hugging each other, the stench of sweat and hair spray thick in the air.

I don't see Allison, so I keep walking, head down, until I get to the last dressing room, which she shares with a couple of the female dancers. Sure enough, she's in there—alone—staring at herself in the mirror. She's already changed out of her costume, though the lace-trimmed black dress she has on looks like something Sally Bowles might wear too.

She doesn't notice me at first. I watch as she tucks her sleek dark hair behind her ears. Her nail polish is already chipped, a big chunk missing from the right thumb. Onstage she was magnetic, mesmerizing—but now her eyes look lost and blank. The same way they did the week after Halloween.

As soon as she sees me standing in the doorway, though, Allison switches back on, her face lighting up with an exaggerated smile. "So?" she asks. "What did you think?"

I smile back. "You were *brilliant*."

Everyone else in the opening-night audience probably thought she was just giving an incredible performance, but I saw the genuine pain in her eyes, the desperation, the heartbreak. Like Alex told me, you can't keep feelings bottled up inside forever—and Allison poured hers out all over that stage tonight.

Allison beams at me. "*Thank you*, darling, I try."

"Is Wes around?" I ask.

"He's up in the booth still." A cruel smile pulls at the corners of Allison's red-painted lips. "He said you were a giant bitch to him in class."

My mouth falls open. "He *said* that?"

I *was* kind of a giant bitch, but I can't imagine Wes calling anyone that.

"No, he just told me what happened. *I'm* the one saying you're a giant bitch." Allison laughs and jabs at my arm. She might intend it to be playful, but it hurts all the same. "You can talk to him at the cast party. I'm heading over there as soon as I fix this mess."

She gestures at the smeared, sweat-blurred stage makeup distorting her features. I assume she's going to wipe it all off so she'll look like herself again, but instead she picks up a sponge and starts applying even more color.

"It's going to be so much fun!" she says, reaching for an eyeliner pencil next. "Bash's roommate designed this show-themed cocktail, 'the Toast of Mayfair.' Isn't that adorable?"

"The party is at Bash's place?"

She can't be serious. The thought of setting foot in that house again makes me sick, and I'm not even the one who was attacked there.

Allison's face hardens. "If you don't want to come, don't. Jesus."

But I don't have a choice. I have to go to the party.

It's the only way to make sure he doesn't hurt her again.

53

SCARLETT

The second my murderous rage at Stright drained away, something worse took its place.

Anxiety. Throat-closing, chest-clenching, debilitating anxiety. I used to live in this state all the time, and I don't know how I survived it. There's only one cure when I feel this way, but I can't risk it, not now. Maybe not ever again.

I can't trust myself. So I've spent the past few days shut up in my house, feigning illness and attempting to get myself under control.

My final interview for the Women's Academy fellowship went by in a blur—I don't know whether I did well; I can barely remember the questions Judith asked me, or what I said in response. Since then, I've had no contact with the outside world, ignoring all of Drew's increasingly concerned check-in calls and Jasper's passive-aggressive emails about the classes he's covering in my absence.

Everything I do to calm down winds me up further. I've resorted to sitting very still on the sofa, sipping cup after cup of chamomile tea, but my head feels like a hornet's nest. Every time I blink, blood lights up the insides of my eyelids.

The harsh peal of the doorbell startles me, and I jump in my seat, clacking the teacup and saucer together so hard I'm surprised they don't shatter. My pulse was already pounding, but now it seems too loud for my body to contain.

I set down the teacup and go to the door, tightening the sash of my robe. I know I look awful: unshowered, no makeup, still wearing my nightclothes, my nails gnawed down to swollen stubs. If Abbott and Flynn see me like this, they'll think the guilt is finally getting to me.

I open the door, and it's not Drew or Jasper or the police standing on my front porch.

"Mina." My relief lasts less than a second. I'm not sure I can trust myself around her either. Not that I would hurt her, but her presence makes me weak in other ways. "What are you—"

"I need to talk to you," she says. I haven't invited her in, but she pushes inside anyway. That wild-eyed obsession is back in her eyes again, and she's clutching a file folder to her chest so hard her knuckles blanch. "But you weren't at work. Are you sick?"

I start to answer, but she's already onto the next thought, too distracted to wait for my response. "I figured it out," she says. "I figured it all out."

She thrusts the folder into my hands. "What's this?" I ask.

"The report. The one Mikayla and I have been working on, on the suicides."

The stapled document includes all the men she'd listed on the whiteboard, and she's found a few others too. So many faces I looked into while they breathed their last.

"Except," Mina says, "I don't think they were suicides at all."

I try to keep my own breathing steady as I flip through the pages, but my pulse is racing, my body betraying me. "What do you mean?"

"I think these men were all murdered." She smiles, dark eyes shining, triumphant, and I think I'm going to be sick. "By the same person."

54

CARLY

Bash isn't at the cast party yet, but everyone else seems to be. The living room is crammed so full of bodies, I can't even tell where they've set up the speakers that are rattling the walls with deafening rap music. No one is dancing, at least, but that's the only aspect of this situation that's not my literal nightmare.

A girl with frizzy red hair and freckles pushes past us, clutching a red Solo cup in each hand. I've seen her around the theater, but I can't remember her name. "You were awesome tonight, Allison!" she shouts over the music.

Allison presses a hand to her chest as if to say, *Who me?* "*Thank* you, darling!"

I thought things would be less weird between us once she was out of costume, back to her real self. But she's not in character or out of it now, she's something in between. Somehow it's even worse.

"You want something to drink?" she asks.

I shake my head. "That's—"

"Oh, right. You don't drink." Her tone makes it clear that she did not in fact forget this. She's being so mean tonight. No, not only tonight—there's been a nastiness festering under every conversation we've had since that morning on the roof.

Allison darts away toward the kitchen, without even a glance back at me. I think about following her, but I'd have to push through the thickest part of the crowd, and it's bad enough where I'm standing right now. I stay as still as possible, pressing my palms into my legs, trying to shrink myself so I'm not touching anyone, but people keep knocking into me. A guy's elbow catches me right in the spine, and I want to clock him in the jaw.

I can't do this. I'm going to scream.

The front door swings open, admitting both a frigid blast of wind and a group of theater department boys. Bash is at the head of the pack. The rest of the guys have scrubbed off their stage makeup, but Bash still has the shadow of liner around his eyes. Instead of rendering him effeminate, it makes him look rougher, like he's been in a fight and is spoiling for another one.

Bash scans the crowd, eyes snagging on each scantily clad girl for a second before moving on. His gaze passes right over me. With my baggy black hoodie zipped up to my throat, I don't even register on his radar. I imagine dragging him out back like a carcass, pounding my fist into his face until his eye sockets shatter.

"See, you *are* having fun." Allison jabs her elbow into my side. She's returned from the kitchen carrying a cup of something brown and noxious-smelling. "I knew you had it in you!"

My violent thoughts blow away like smoke. "Huh?"

She points at my mouth. "You're smiling."

I drop the corners of my lips downward again, filing the fantasy away for later. Maybe I can turn it into a new story for Alex.

"Wes!" Allison calls out.

He was walking past with his head down, obviously trying to avoid us, but Allison snags him by the sleeve. "You two need to kiss and make up," she says. "In fact, I recommend that exact order of events."

She takes a gulp from her cup, then turns to go with a smirk on her face.

"Allison, wait." I reach for her, but she's already slipped into the crush of the crowd. She's not headed in Bash's direction at least; he's still by the front door.

Wes and I are left there staring at each other, and it's so awkward I want to die. At least there's some space between us, but even that's ruined when someone knocks into me from behind, pushing me into Wes's chest.

I back away from him as fast as I can. "Sorry, I—"

"It's okay." Wes smiles. "I'm gonna go grab a beer. You want anything?"

There it is: he was just being polite until he could find an excuse to get the hell away from me.

"I'm good," I say.

"Okay. Be right back."

No, you won't. But as Wes pushes through the crowd toward the kitchen, he keeps tossing looks back at me, the traces of a smile crinkling his eyes. So maybe he really isn't mad at me. He should be. He's way nicer to me than I deserve. To Allison too.

As soon as he's out of sight, I realize I've lost track of Bash in the crowd. I scan the room and find him leaning by the staircase, talking to a girl with jaw-skimming black hair.

Allison.

My heart pounds in my throat as I start trying to push my way toward them.

I bump into someone harder than I meant to, and beer slops out onto my boots.

"Watch it!" the girl I ran into says, and I realize it's Allison. She's here, not with Bash. She's okay, she's safe.

The other girl, though . . . Bash leers at her, tweaking the strap of her dress. She slaps his hand away, but she doesn't leave. She's smiling at him.

Allison touches my arm, and I jump. "Oh my God, relax! You really *do* need a drink."

"S-sorry, I—" I'm shaking, all that spun-up adrenaline screaming through my muscles with nowhere to go. "I didn't know where you went."

She looks at me like I have two heads. "I've literally been standing right here."

The music cranks up even louder, and people start pushing furniture out of the way to make enough room to dance—which means there's even less space to stand. Allison and I back up, bumping into each other and then into Wes, who's just returned from the kitchen with a bottle of Yuengling.

"You want to dance?" he asks me.

I shake my head. I don't care if Allison is annoyed with me, I'm going to stay by her side tonight, no matter what. And keep a close eye on Bash too. He has his arm around the dark-haired girl's waist now, and she's leaning into him, smiling, as he pulls her out onto the makeshift dance floor.

"Who's that girl?" I have to shout the question twice and do some very rude pointing for Allison to understand me over the music.

"Anna Turner," Allison shouts back. "She's a freshman. She lives in our dorm."

Anna actually doesn't look a thing like Allison, except for the length and color of their hair. We've never spoken beyond the occasional hello in the hallway, but I saw her on move-in day: the young woman bidding a tearful goodbye to her father right next to my own family's farce of a farewell.

Bash flips Anna around so he's pressed up against her back, his arm latched across her stomach, and there's a little stutter in the rhythm of her dancing, her body stiffening. She's not smiling anymore.

"We should do something," I say.

Allison frowns. "What?"

"We should *do something*," I repeat, louder this time, assuming she couldn't hear me.

But she just rolls her eyes. "They're dancing, Carly. What do you want me to do?"

Bash's fingers are digging into Anna's hip bones now, his nose pressing against her neck. She's clearly uncomfortable. Why can't Allison see that?

"Are you serious?" I yell. "He's *groping* her, right in front of—"

"Oh my God, *calm down*." Allison drains the rest of her drink. "Just 'cause *you're* so fucking repressed."

I glare at her. "I am *not* repressed."

She's the repressed one—repressing all her feelings about what Bash did to her, pretending everything is fine when it's not. I'm the only person who's treating what happened to her with the gravity it deserves. That horrible doctor, the dean of students—they both dismissed her. I'm the only one trying to protect her from him.

And who's going to protect that poor girl? If he tries to do to her what he did to Allison—well, I don't know what I'll do, exactly, but I can't stand by and let it happen.

"Oh, really?" Allison says. "You're not repressed?"

Then she takes my face in her hands and kisses me.

55

SCARLETT

Mina doesn't even seem to notice how shaken I am. She's pacing back and forth, rattling off names, causes of death. If I weren't already so intimately familiar with the cases she's referencing, I'd find it impossible to keep up with the dizzying pace of her words.

"It's sort of brilliant, actually," she says. "Different murder methods every time, tailored to the victim. But there's still a pattern, there's always a pattern."

Mina takes the report out of my hands and starts turning the pages herself. "Mikayla charted out all the dates for me, and there's been one death like this per year for at least seven years. The first one was this guy . . ."

She stabs the picture at the top of the page with her index finger. A handsome blond boy with bleached white teeth. Dylan—

"Dylan Hughes," she says. "He drugged girls at parties and took naked pictures of them while they were passed out. But he was the son of a major donor, so the university brushed it under the rug. Then he ends up downing a bunch of pills and choking to death on his own vomit the night before graduation."

I was still refining my technique. Luckily the police assumed the haphazard cuts on Dylan's arm were hesitation marks, that he'd considered slitting his wrists before turning to the pills instead. A bit of a rush job—not my best work—but that boy was despicable, and I couldn't let him go off to his bright future earning six figures at his daddy's corporation. The pictures he took are probably still floating around the darker corners of the Internet, but at least I made certain he couldn't victimize any more girls.

"Have you told the police about this?" I ask.

"Not yet." Mina flops down on the sofa, raking her fingers through her hair. Her knees knock into the coffee table, spilling a little of the remaining tea. "I don't know, am I sounding crazy again? This sounds crazy."

I sit down next to her and pat at the spilled tea with a napkin. Mina is staring off into the middle distance, wheels turning behind her eyes, so at least she doesn't see the way my hands are shaking. The police haven't even come close to connecting all these dots. I have to admire Mina's thoroughness, even if it's going to be the end of me.

"I know it's a leap from the data," she says. "I mean, a serial killer? In Gorman, Pennsylvania?"

She might not have the investigative capabilities to trace this all back to me, but once she tells the detectives, it will take them no time at all. They already suspect me of killing Kinnear, or at least helping Drew do it. The fact that I haven't heard from them in days only makes me more paranoid. I'm certain they're watching me, building their case.

"I even wondered if the same person might have murdered Alexander too," she says. "But that death was so sloppy compared to the others—unless the killer finally snapped or something. Do you think that's plausible?"

I have to stop her, before she goes to the police. But how can I do that without hurting her?

Without killing her?

"All those men in the report," I say. "You said they were abusers, rapists."

Mina nods.

"But your ex-husband . . . I mean, he was a bit of an asshole, certainly."

Mina gives a mirthless laugh of agreement.

"Does he really fit in the same category as the others?"

I believe he does. But the truth is, I killed Kinnear for personal reasons, because I hated him and wanted him out of my way. It was revenge as much as justice.

"Well, you know all about him and his students," Mina says.

I've always wondered if I was the first student Alexander Kinnear crossed the line with, or already part of a long series of hapless girls all those years ago. It was a mistake to target him, no matter what awful things he'd done. I see that now. I was too close, my feelings toward him too raw to be reined in. And I'm going to pay for it.

"The whole time we were married," Mina says, "I knew he was cheating on me, all the signs were there, but he'd deny it, tell me I was imagining things, that I should see a therapist for my 'pathological jealousy.'" Her voice breaks a little, rage seeping through the cracks. "He made me feel *insane*."

On impulse, I take her hand. Mina's so caught up in her memories of Kinnear, at first I don't think she notices the gesture. But then she laces her fingers tighter through mine.

"You know what's really fucked-up?" she says. "I used to wish he would hit me."

I'd had this same thought about my father. His abuse was all emotional and psychological; the only marks it left were internal. Impossible to see, easy to deny.

"Alexander could lie and cheat and turn my own mind against me, and everyone still thought he was so *charming*. But if I'd showed up to work with a black eye just once, everything would have changed. They would have had to take it seriously."

You would think so. But there's no guarantee. I've murdered plenty of men who beat their partners bloody and faced zero consequences until me.

"If there really is someone killing all these men, I have to say . . ." Mina looks me right in the eye. "I almost admire them."

"*Admire* them?" It's what I've always wanted to hear. But I'm sure she would feel differently if she knew she was holding the hand that cut her ex-husband's throat.

Mina squeezes my hand, pulling it into her lap. "Whoever they are, they're not standing by, letting men get away with this shit. They're doing something about it."

I want to tell her everything, about Kinnear and Dylan Hughes and all the other men I've killed, about the timid girl I used to be and the way she turned herself into a weapon. I want to look her in the eyes and say: *It's me, I'm the one, and I did it all to protect women like us. I did it, and I'd do it again.*

But I can't tell her any of that. So I swallow my secrets and kiss her instead.

56

CARLY

The second Allison's lips touch mine, every eye at the party turns in our direction.

Whoops and wolf-whistles and even a smattering of applause spike above the music. Bash stops dancing just to leer at us, the freshman he was pawing practically forgotten.

By the time Allison pulls away with a big, theatrical smack, I'm shaking, blinking tears out of my eyes. I've wanted to kiss her for so long. But not like this. Not with everyone staring at us like we're zoo animals, and her lipstick painted on so thick her mouth felt like a waxy facsimile rather than the real thing.

Wes is watching too, clenching his jaw, gripping the neck of his beer bottle. He doesn't look like a kicked puppy anymore, that's for sure. I don't know if he's angrier at me or Allison.

"Why—" I start, but I can't even hear my own voice above the cacophony. "Why did you—"

Allison runs her thumbnail along her bottom lip like she's fixing her makeup, even though it looks totally flawless still. "It's no big deal."

But it is. It is to me. And she should know that.

I have to get out of here. I start shoving through the crowd, and Allison doesn't follow.

No big deal. God, I wish she hadn't done that.

It's exhausting, being in my head. I wish I could stop thinking. I wish I could be like everyone else.

I end up in the kitchen. The air is less saturated with smoke back here, and there's space enough to move, only a couple of people loitering between the crookedly hung cabinets and the dented refrigerator. Every surface seems to be covered with drinks: a precarious assortment of bottles and cans weighing down a card table in the corner, a bowl of punch sitting on the counter, plastic cups strewn across the oven range and the floor next to the trash can. The punch is already half gone, splatters of brownish red like dried blood staining the Formica around it.

Maybe I *can* be like everyone else, at least for tonight.

Before I second-guess myself—before I think anymore at all—I pick up one of the cleaner-looking cups and dip it into the punch bowl, then toss my head back and chug.

It tastes *disgusting*, too bitter and too sweet all at once, burning my throat. But I force myself to swallow it all, and the intensity of my feelings dials down, replaced by a pleasant, floaty warmth. I scoop out a second helping and gulp that too, even faster than the first.

Taking a deep breath like I'm about to swim underwater, I push my way back into the living room. The music has switched to a brutal techno beat that hammers at the base of my skull. I don't see Allison, but at least Anna Turner is clear of Bash's clutches for the moment. She's dancing in a circle with some female friends, arms raised above her head. Wes is out on the dance floor too, pressed up against the redhead who complimented Allison earlier.

Everyone is laughing, smiling, having fun. Everyone but me. I'm in a house full of people, and I'm all alone.

Relax.

But I feel woozy, nauseated. Everything is too bright, too dark, too loud, too much.

And then I see them: Allison and Bash, in the center of the throng.

At first, I think I'm imagining it. A hallucination, a bad dream. But as the other dancers bump around them, bodies separating and slamming back together again, I catch glimpses: his hand spread across her shoulder blades, her breasts crushed to his chest, his hips thrusting into hers. He lowers his mouth to her sternum, his fingers slipping past the fabric of her dress.

No. Not again.

I shove my way to them, elbowing sides, stepping on toes, whatever it takes to reach Allison. If she cries out in pain or protest when I grab her by the elbow, I can't hear it over the music. I drag her away from him, through the roil of bodies and perfume and sweat and smoke, grabbing for the staircase railing, hauling us up, out of the crowd.

On the second floor, it's quieter and cooler, but the music still throbs through me. If I hadn't been there, if I hadn't intervened—

Allison shoves me away from her. My shoulders scrape against the wood paneling, and that's when I realize where we are: the hallway outside the bathroom where Bash took her on Halloween.

"What the hell is wrong with you?" she demands.

"He was—" The images strobe across my mind, speeding up, sharpening. "I thought he was—"

But he wasn't. Bash wasn't grabbing her, forcing himself on her. Not this time. This time Allison's hands were on him. Gripping the collar of his shirt, the back of his head. Drawing him close, not pushing him away.

A sour taste rises in my throat, that revolting punch threatening to come back up.

"You need help, Carly," Allison says. "Don't think I haven't noticed you following me around campus like some stalker creep."

"I was only trying to—to make sure—"

"Well, I never asked you to." She backs me up against the wall again, caging me with her arms. "You know, I tried to be nice to you, tried to include you in things because I felt sorry for you. But you're a total freak."

She's right. I'm not normal. Normal girls don't feel this way. Normal girls don't fantasize about breaking guys' fingers and bashing their faces in. Or about kissing their best friends.

I don't know which one of us starts it this time. One second her lips are inches from mine, her eyes sparking with rage, and the next we're clutching each other, her tongue in my mouth, her hand sliding up under my sweatshirt. She's pinned against the bathroom door now. It swings open and we stumble inside, tripping over each other's feet. She moans into my mouth and steeples her fingers over my spine.

This isn't what I imagined either, all the times I fantasized about kissing Allison. It's frantic and it's awkward and it hurts, and both of our mouths are sour with punch. But at least it's *real*. The strap of her dress slips off her shoulder, and I tangle my fingers in it, tugging it lower.

As soon as her hips hit the edge of the sink, though, she breaks off the kiss, snapping us apart like a broken bone. She says something, almost a whisper, too soft for me to hear. I reach for her, sliding my palms across her skull to grip her hair at the roots, but she holds me at arm's length.

"I said *no*."

A few strands of Allison's hair come away in my hands when she shoves me. I stare at the black tendrils threaded through my fingers, then at her tear-streaked face. She looks even angrier than before. She looks like she hates the sight of me.

She swipes her knuckles across her eyes, smearing what's left of her makeup into a furious slash of black across her temple. "Get out."

I reach for her again. I'm not trying to kiss her anymore, I just want to calm her down.

"Don't touch me." She shoves me even harder than before, sending me stumbling back toward the doorway. "I don't want you to touch me."

My heart is crumbling into dust. "Allison, please, I—"

This time she shoves me so hard, I trip back into the hallway, catching myself on the doorframe to keep from falling over.

"Get out get out get the fuck OUT!" She's shrieking, almost incoherent.

"I'm so sorry," I tell her, because it's the only thing I can think to say.

She answers by slamming the bathroom door in my face.

57

SCARLETT

All the times I allowed myself to fantasize about sleeping with Mina, I imagined her being tender, soft: her pillowy lips, her coils of hair, the curves hinted at under her clothing.

Mina may be soft, but she isn't tender. There's a brisk efficiency in the way she takes off my clothes, like she thought about it in advance and mapped out the most effective method. Once she's stripped me naked, she pushes me down on the bed and removes her own clothing, still standing, letting me watch. Her body makes me think of classical statues, the wide hips and small breasts like ripe apples, the rounded stomach. She's even more beautiful than I'd imagined.

She slides between my legs, kissing my chest, my collarbone, my neck. My hands fit perfectly into the curve of her back, holding her close. She moves on to the sensitive spot behind my ear, whispering something I can't quite make out.

"What did you say?" My voice is soft and breathless, but still sounds too loud in the hushed shadows of my bedroom.

"I said, what took you so long?" Mina kisses my neck again, her lips curving into a smile. "I wanted you from the first day I met you."

The first day I met you. The same thing Kinnear said while he pressed me against his bedroom wall.

I blink the image away. He has no place here.

Mina's lips are soft as flower petals, but there's steel behind them too. She knows precisely the amount of pressure to use, and before I can think or breathe or even moan in pleasure, I'm coming with a startled gasp. I feel her smile again, molding against my inner thigh as she grips my hips, waiting for the waves of my orgasm to subside. She presses a kiss into the pale skin there, making me shiver, then crawls back up to lie beside me.

Immediately we're kissing again, hands tangling in each other's hair. Her perfume, that night-blooming jasmine scent, fills up my senses. I slip my hand between her legs so I can look her in the eyes while I make her come. I want to savor every moment of this, because as much as I want it to be the start of something, more likely it's the end.

All of Mina's reserve melts away as my fingers work inside her. She moans and throws her head back and clenches her thighs around my wrist. She trusts me. She's vulnerable, here in this bed, naked, her throat exposed. But she's not afraid.

I lose count of how many times we make each other come. Our last climax is nearly simultaneous, and we collapse in each other's arms, heads sharing a pillow, slick bodies pressed together.

I haven't slept like this—wrapped up in someone else, mouths so close we're sharing breath—since college, so I'm not sure I'll be able to fall asleep. But I shut my eyes, and when I open them again it's daybreak.

In the pale morning light, Mina practically glows, her dark hair shot through with strands of gold and red, a light dusting of freckles shining like constellations on her bare shoulders. How could Kinnear have cheated on this perfect woman? I never want to let her go.

Mina stirs slightly, and I shut my eyes, pretending to be asleep still. She slips out of bed, slow and careful, obviously trying not to wake me. Does she regret what we did last night? Is she going to sneak out of the house without speaking to me?

I open my eyes a sliver, just enough to see Mina arch into a leisurely stretch like a cat and pick up my robe off the floor. She wraps it around herself, tying the sash at her waist.

She's not leaving. She looks satisfied, happy. She wants to be here. For now, anyway.

Mina heads down the hall, most likely looking for the bathroom, and I roll onto my back. I want to stay in bed forever. Once I get up, I'll have to deal with reality.

My cell phone buzzes on the bedside table. I reach for it, the brightness of the screen stinging my sleep-blurred eyes.

It's Judith Winters. Jesus Christ. Of all the times for her to finally call: at the break of dawn on a weekend, when I'm naked in bed.

I wrap the sheets around my body before I answer, even though Judith can't see me. "Hello?"

"Dr. Clark. I hope I didn't wake you."

"Oh, no, I was up." I cinch the bedding tighter around my chest. "I'm quite an early riser."

"As am I," she says. "I'm sure we'll beat everyone else to the archive every day next year. I'm so pleased to officially extend the Women's Academy fellowship to you."

"I'm—" I'm thrilled, my heart nearly pounding out of my chest, but I'm also seized by the thought: *I could be in jail by then.* I could be in jail later today.

Or maybe not. Maybe Mina won't tell the police what she's figured out. Maybe I can convince her. Maybe they'll never catch me. Maybe I could go to London and spend next year exactly as I planned: working on my book and killing deserving men.

Maybe Mina could come with me.

"I'm thrilled to accept," I tell Judith. "Thank you so much."

"Lovely!" she says. "I'll have my office send over all the paper-work. Enjoy the rest of your weekend. Looking forward to work-ing with you, Dr. Clark."

"Likewise." I hang up the phone and clutch it to my chest, and all I can think is: *I did it*. And then: *I have to tell Mina*. It's strange and wonderful, having someone with whom to share my good news.

I've spent so much of my life wearing a mask: the dedicated student, the impeccable professor. Controlled and remote and iso-lated by choice—but only because I thought there *was* no other choice. Anything else was too dangerous—for my lovers as well as for me.

I almost admire them. That's what Mina said. But did she really mean it?

I slip on the nightgown that matches the robe she took and head down the hall looking for her. The bathroom door is wide open, and she's not in there. Maybe she went downstairs to get a drink of water. I start for the stairs, but then I notice my office door is ajar.

"Mina?" I push the door open the rest of the way.

Sure enough, she's inside, standing right in front of the desk. She turns toward me, and there's something in her hands.

A small book with a red cover.

58

CARLY

I've been walking all night.

Until the sun peeks up over the horizon, I have no concept of how much time has passed. My face and hands went numb from the cold a while ago, but my feet still tingle like I'm treading on needles. I could sit down on a bench and rest. Or I could suck it up and go back to Whitten, try to apologize to Allison. But instead I keep circling the empty Oak Grove, hugging myself against the freezing gusts.

If I kept going, walked past campus, walked past the Gorman city limits, walked until my feet were bleeding and I collapsed into a ditch and died, I wonder who would even miss me.

As my circuit takes me past Miller Hall yet again, a light flicks on inside. I drift toward it like a moth to a flame.

Alex's office. What is he doing here so early?

It doesn't matter. All I can think about is getting inside, getting warm. I try to open the front door, but it's locked. The cold metal of the handle makes my fingers throb.

I pick up a few chunks of mulch from under the bushes, then chuck them at the glass until Alex comes to the window. His eyes widen when he sees the state I'm in: shivering so hard I'm practically convulsing, face red and swollen from crying. He gestures for me to go around to the main entrance.

"What are you doing out here?" he asks as soon as he pushes the door open. He's breathing hard, like he sprinted to get to me. "It's *freezing.*"

The heat in the building is dialed down for the night, but it's so much warmer than outside it feels like stepping into a furnace. The relief nearly knocks me over.

Alex takes my hands in his, rubbing at my ice-cold skin, as he leads me down the hall. The feeling slowly returns, nerves lighting up my fingertips with painful sparks of sensation.

Somehow it feels even more claustrophobic in his office with the chairs we use for class stacked up in the corner. Alex sets me down on the loveseat and wraps a blanket around my shoulders. He must have been sleeping here; he's rumpled, eyes bloodshot, lines from the cushions pressed into his face.

"Let me make you some hot tea," he says.

Alex doesn't try to talk to me while he prepares the tea, but he keeps casting worried glances in my direction. He might be the only person at Gorman who gives a single damn about me. He might even be the only person on earth who does. That thought is enough to make my shivers give way to sobs again.

As soon as he sees that I'm crying, he abandons the electric kettle and tin of tea bags to kneel on the floor in front of me, gathering me to his chest. "It's okay. You're safe."

He stays there as the water in the kettle boils, rubbing his hand in slow circles over my spine. It's strange having a professor hug me, but it feels nice too.

When he hands me the steaming mug, I take a sip right away, not waiting for the tea to steep or the water to cool. It burns my tongue, but the heat rushing into my mouth feels so good I don't mind the pain.

Alex sits down next to me on the sofa. "Okay. You want to tell me why you were freezing your ass off in the Oak Grove at five in the morning?"

I hesitate, pressing my palms into the sides of the mug. He scoots closer to me and covers my hands with his again. Now that I've got all the sensation back in my fingers, I can feel how soft his skin is, even softer than Allison's.

"Just let it out," he says. "You'll feel better."

He's right. I can't keep holding all this inside of me, or I'm going to explode. And Allison already hates me. What difference does it make now if I share her secrets?

So I start talking. I tell him about Bash assaulting Allison, the dismissive treatment we got at the hospital, the dean's shaming speech, the way Allison's been pushing me away even as I tried to protect her. *Because* I tried to protect her.

Alex shakes his head sympathetically but doesn't say anything until I get to the end: my fight with Allison at the party and running away into the night after she slammed the bathroom door in my face. I skip the kissing part; he doesn't need to know *everything*.

"You can't blame yourself, Carly." Alex squeezes my hands. "I know you care about her, but she's not your responsibility. She's just your roommate."

I jerk away from him, sloshing a bit of tea over my knuckles. "She's not *just* my roommate."

He looks at me quizzically, waiting for me to elaborate. But I don't know what to say. Sometimes I think I love Allison. Other times I think I'm not even capable of feeling love.

"Look," Alex says. "I'm sure if you go home and talk to her, you'll be able to get past this. Sounds like she's been going through a rough time, and—"

I shake my head, setting the mug down on the floor. I'm crying again, but it's less intense this time, tears streaming down my cheeks rather than full-body sobs. "I can't go home. I can't."

If I never went back, I bet she wouldn't even miss me. She'd probably be relieved to have the room to herself, to finally be free of my creepy attentions.

"Are you . . ." Alex leans closer.

I keep my hands knotted together in my lap, so he touches me on the knee instead.

"Are you worried this boy might hurt you too?"

My mind fills up with flashes of the stories I've written. All that rage, violence, and blood spilled onto the page is a poor imitation of what I *really* want to do to Bash.

"No," I say. "I'm afraid *I* might hurt him."

"Don't be ridiculous," Alex says. "You wouldn't hurt anybody."

"I want to." I look him right in the eye. The tears have stopped, though my cheeks are still wet with them. "Sometimes, it's all I can think about."

I can tell he'd like to back away from me, but instead he presses his hand harder into my knee, forcing a smile onto his face. "Those are just stories, Carly."

"No." I shake my head, the tears rushing in again. "No, I think there's something wrong with me."

"Don't say that." Alex grips my shoulders, pulling me closer. "There's nothing wrong with you. You're smart, you're a brilliant writer, you have a bright future ahead of you."

That overwhelming sincerity shines out of his eyes again, a beacon in the darkness. He can't possibly care about all his students this much; it would be exhausting. But somehow, he cares about me.

I smile, swiping my face dry with my sweatshirt sleeve.

And then Alex's mouth covers mine, and I can't breathe.

59

SCARLETT

Mina holds out the book. "Where did you get this?"

Viola Vance's diary, the one I took from Kinnear's library. She recognizes it.

I am so screwed.

"I bought this for him," Mina says. "On our first anniversary. I scoured my favorite little shop in London, looking for something special, something that would show him how much I . . ." Her voice is steady, but there's fear in her eyes. "He would never have lent it to you."

"Mina, I can explain." I take one small step toward her, and she freezes like I have a gun aimed at her chest.

"It was you." She's not asking. She's sure. "You killed him. You killed them all."

I try to think of a way to deny this, to smooth it over, to explain away the presence of the diary. *Of course not, I would never have hurt him, I had no ill will toward him, I could never kill someone.* But I know how false it would sound.

"Mina, please."

I move into the room so I'm no longer blocking the doorway.

Mina backs herself against the wall, pointing the book at my heart as if it's a weapon.

"Don't come any closer!"

"I would never hurt you, Mina." I mean every word, but she has no reason to believe me.

"How many?" she asks. "How many people have you killed?"

I want to fall on my knees and beg her to stay, to understand, but I know it's futile. There was never any hope for us. Never any hope for me to have a real relationship, for someone to love me. I was deluding myself, thinking I might be able to take off my mask for her.

"Tell me." Her voice cracks, and now she's clutching the book to her chest like it can shield her. Like it can protect her from me. "Just—"

"I've only ever killed men," I say. "Men who deserved it, like you said."

Mina presses the diary harder into her sternum, trying to steady herself. She's starting to hyperventilate, blood draining from her face, her eyes glittering with tears.

But she hasn't tried to leave yet.

"Just the men in my report?" she asks.

I hold her gaze. I don't want to lie. I never wanted to lie to her. "More."

She stares at me like I'm a wolf about to tear her to shreds with my teeth. I've seen that look before: not just on the faces of my victims, but on Allison Hadley's face, the last time I ever saw her.

When Mina runs out the door, taking the diary with her, I don't try to stop her. I was a fool to think for even a second that she could find out what I was and still accept me.

I'm a monster, just like the men I kill.

60

CARLY

At first, I'm too shocked to do anything except let Alex keep kissing me.

Is this how Allison felt when I kissed her?

Frozen.

Stunned.

Helpless.

Alex hasn't shaved in a day or two, and the feeling of his stubble scraping across my chin finally snaps me out of it.

I put my hands on his chest and push him away. "What are you—"

He tucks my hair behind my ears, cupping my cheeks, smiling gently as he presses me back against the arm of the sofa. Then he starts to unzip my sweatshirt. Slowly, tooth by tooth.

I'm smothered by his body, trapped in place, but I'm also floating away, watching his hands move on my breasts like I'm over in the shadowed corner of the office rather than underneath him. The only thing I can feel is the panic in my chest. It keeps rising until it bursts out of my throat.

"Stop," I say, but his mouth swallows the sound. He's crushing me, sucking all the oxygen out of my body. I push against him, harder this time, locking my elbows. *"Stop it."*

He listens. He stops. But when he sits back on his side of the sofa, he has a look on his face I've never seen before.

Alex is angry.

"I don't—" I curl in on myself, my knees against my chest. "Why would you— What about your wife?"

"I thought we understood each other, Carly." He shakes his head, like I'm a misbehaving child. "I thought you were more mature than this."

Not so long ago, I would have apologized—for coming here alone, for giving him the wrong impression. I would have cried and simpered and tried to smooth things over.

But I'm all out of tears. I stand and zip my sweatshirt back up, all the way to my throat. Alex watches me warily. My calmness unsettles him, and that makes me cling faster to it, fasten it around me like armor. He can't hurt me unless I let him.

"You're not . . ." Alex swallows. I'm the one scaring him now. "You're not going to tell anyone about this, are you?"

He runs his hands through his hair, and he looks so lost. Why didn't I see it before? He's pathetic, with his constant grin, his desperate need for everyone to like him. No wonder he pretends to care so much about his students. We're the only ones still young and foolish enough to fall for his bullshit.

"All right, Carly. I know I shouldn't have done that." He smiles as he says this, staring into my eyes, seeking some hint of compassion. But there's none left. Not for him. "It's just, my wife is leaving me. This job is all I have."

I was stupid to trust him, for even a moment.

"Please," he says. "I'm begging you."

"You're pathetic, Alex."

The smile fades, and a meanness seeps back into his expression. His face looks so ugly now, I can't believe I ever considered him handsome. "No one would believe you anyway, if you told them. Troubled girl like you."

I glare down at him. "I guess we'll find out."

He doesn't try to follow me. I slam my hands into the front door of Miller Hall so hard it scares a small flock of birds into taking flight, retreating to the mostly bare branches of the oak trees. It's much warmer out now, sun streaming through wispy clusters of clouds.

I could march right into the department chair's office on Monday morning and file a report on Alex Kinnear, let everyone know exactly what he tried to do to me. Not only the kiss, but all of it— the private meetings, the lingering touches, bringing me to a bar even though I'm only eighteen.

But who's to say he'd take me any more seriously than the dean of students took Allison? No. I can't trust any of them. If I'm going to give Alex and Bash and all the other men like them what they deserve, I'll have to do it myself.

61

SCARLETT

I planned for this day just like I planned everything else.

My only chance now is to change my identity again—more dramatically this time—and start over somewhere far from here. My suitcase is already packed. I've kept it hidden in the back of my closet for years, standing ready with clothes, a forged ID, credit cards with no ties to my regular accounts. I have a checklist too, of all the things I need to take with me if I'm never coming back. I knew this would happen someday; it's incredible that I've lasted as long as I have in a town as small as Gorman. But I didn't think it would happen quite like this.

I stuff the last few items on the list into my bag and carry it down to the front door. That's when I realize it's snowing outside. It must have just started, but already there's a thick layer on the ground, the roads coated in white. Usually I wouldn't think of driving in this weather. Today, I'll have to risk it.

It would be more prudent to leave my car behind, but the Greyhound bus only stops in Gorman once a day, and I can't wait until its afternoon departure time. They'll have arrested me by then. So plan B: I'll drive to Pittsburgh, taking rural roads only. Abandon the car there, walk to the Amtrak station, and take the first train leaving to a city I've never been before, where I have no ties, no one who'll recognize me. I can do this. I can start over. I can find somewhere else to hunt, and after a while I won't even think of Mina Pierce anymore. Her soft lips or the skill of her tongue or the fear in her eyes.

My hand is on the doorknob when footsteps start to crunch up the snow-covered walkway. I clutch the suitcase handle, heart pounding.

They're here.

62

CARLY

I part my hair and squeeze out a thick line of bloodred dye, smearing it over the mousy brown. I didn't bother laying out trash bags in the bathroom this time, so I'm getting little flecks of red everywhere: in the bowl of the sink, the grout between the floor tiles, even on the mirror itself, making my reflection look gore-spattered.

When I rinse the dye out in the shower, it's even more like a slasher movie, red dripping over my skin, swirling down the drain. Changing my hair color wasn't a strictly necessary part of the plan I concocted after storming out of Alex's office, but I wanted to look different. Like a stranger.

I've felt strange all day—a buzzing in my blood, a sharpness in my senses. I haven't even attempted to sleep. I haven't seen Allison either, and I don't want to. If she knew what I was about to do, she'd probably try to talk me out of it. But it's the only way. I hope she'll be able to see that, once it's done.

Back in my room, I towel off, then take a dress out of Allison's side of the closet. It's black and formfitting, long sleeves and an above-the-knee skirt, crisscrossing straps of fabric binding the waist like a corset. I've never seen her wear it, except in the thrift store dressing room on the day she bought it. She tried to get me to try it on after her, but I was too shy.

I borrow makeup from her too: pale foundation, lipstick the same fiery red as the shade on the dye box, black eyeshadow that dusts onto my cheekbones like soot. My hands are shaking so much I mess up my eyeliner, drawing a jagged line across my lid. Instead of fixing it, I smear it further. Then I set the pencil down on the dresser and step back to assess myself in the mirror.

I look different, that's for sure. Allison's dress turns my body into a series of black slashes, my cleavage swelling over the top. My lips look swollen, my eyes dark and hollow. And my hair . . . even slightly damp, the red glows around my face like flames.

I notice the flaws too: strands I missed with the dye, a smear of red staining my neck, bits of lint speckling my skirt. But as I take in the whole picture, my spine draws up straighter, my shoulders square back. I don't just look different.

I look *dangerous*.

63

SCARLETT

The footsteps stop, and the door shudders with a knock. I want to peer around the curtains to see who it is, but I can't risk showing my face.

"Dr. Clark, are you there?"

Mikayla Atwell. She's the last person I would have expected on my doorstep today. I haven't seen or spoken to her since she stormed out of my classroom, and she's never been to my home before. But whatever Mikayla wants, I don't have time for it.

"Please, I need—" Mikayla breaks off, sobbing. She sounds distraught, desperate.

I have to go—I should be gone already, the police could arrive any minute—but I can't leave the poor girl out there crying in the cold.

Before I can talk myself out of it, I open the door to her.

"I'm so sorry to come here like this." Mikayla's words tumble out in a panicked rush. She's a wreck, skin pallid, eyes bloodshot and shadowed. "I didn't know where else to go."

"It's okay, Ms. Atwell. Come in."

I peer past her, scanning the street outside. Everything is silent, blanketed by the snowfall. The snow is coming down harder by the second. Flakes sparkle in Mikayla's hair, and as soon as she steps into my well-heated entryway, she starts dripping all over the rug. Her coat is buttoned wrong, and she's wearing pajamas underneath, the fleece pants tucked sloppily into a pair of imitation UGG boots.

She notices my suitcase sitting by the door. "Are you going somewhere?"

"Yes, I'm heading out of town," I say. "I need to leave soon, actually, but why don't I get you—"

"Where are you going? You're not going to London already, are you?" She's shaking now, her eyes huge and frantic.

"I'm . . . not sure, I—"

"You can't. You can't leave. I don't know what I—"

She shatters into another round of sobs, legs convulsing like she's about to crumple to the floor. I put my arm around her, and she slumps her full weight against me, crying into the curve of my neck.

This isn't about my sudden departure, clearly. Something happened to this girl. Today, right before she came here. Something devastating.

My time to escape is draining away, sand in an hourglass. But I can't leave Mikayla, not in this state. When I was her age, I went to a professor for comfort in a crisis, and all he did was make things worse. I won't do that to her.

"Come here," I say. "Sit down."

I lead her over to the sofa and take a seat beside her, stroking her back. I'm still listening for the scream of approaching sirens, but there's no sound other than Mikayla's heart-wrenching sobs. I wait until there's a brief lull before saying, as gently as I can manage, "Tell me what happened."

She shakes her head. "You're going to think I'm so stupid."

"The last thing you are is stupid. You're one of the brightest students I've ever taught." *I'm* the stupid one, sitting here chatting while the police are probably racing toward my house to arrest me for multiple murders.

Her delicate features pinch tight with tears again. "I just . . . I thought I had it under control. I thought—but he wouldn't leave me alone."

Stright. I fucking knew it. "I need you to tell me exactly what he—"

Mikayla winces, and I realize I've grabbed her wrist. I let go and try to soften my tone. "Did he hurt you?"

She shakes her head, a shadow crossing her expression. "He tried, though."

"How long has this been going on?" I ask.

"I don't . . . I mean, at first it was . . ."

I've never seen Mikayla so at a loss for words. But I can fill in the blanks on my own. It would have been all too easy for someone like Stright to draw her in. He may be a scumbag, but he's much closer to Mikayla's intellectual equal than any of the boys her age.

"We'd hang out after class sometimes, talk about books, music, that kind of thing. But then, well . . . one time he kissed me, like out of nowhere." Mikayla's tears are fading now. She's getting angry. Good, she'll need that anger. "I always thought if a guy ever tried to hurt me, or control me, I'd fucking destroy him. You know?"

I nod. I know all too well.

"But he started acting all weird and possessive, and I just, like . . . put up with it. I tried to break things off with him a few times, but he wouldn't let me."

"What do you mean, he wouldn't let you?"

"The more I tried to avoid him, the more I started seeing him all over campus. Watching me. Outside my dorm room window even. So . . ." She twists her hands in her lap, avoiding my eyes. "I started carrying around a knife."

"A knife? Where the hell did you get a knife?"

"From the dining hall." She reaches into her coat pocket and pulls it out to show me. It's a steak knife, the standard kind they stock in the campus cafeteria. She lets me take it out of her hands and set it a safe distance away on the coffee table.

"I just wanted to be able to defend myself," she says. "I know it's messed up."

I eye the serrated edge. Not an especially deadly weapon, unless you know the right way to use it, which I sincerely doubt Mikayla does. But sharp enough to do some damage.

"What happened this morning?" I ask her. "Right before you came here?"

Mikayla starts shaking, tears welling up again. I lay my hand over her wrist, more gently this time.

She takes a deep breath. "I'd finally managed to sleep through the night, and then I woke up and—"

I squeeze her arm—still gentle—urging her to continue.

"He was in my *room*," she says. "Standing there, like, *looming* over me. I have no idea how he even got in! I screamed, and he just smiled at me." Mikayla shudders. "He said I looked so pretty while I was sleeping."

My eyes flick to the knife again. The blade is clean, but she could have wiped it off. "You didn't—"

"No, I—I was too scared to even pick it up. But he came at me, and—I hit him."

She flexes her fingers. Her knuckles are red and swollen; I'd assumed it was from walking around gloveless in the cold.

"I think I broke his nose," she says. "He was bleeding a lot. I don't know. I ran out, and I—well, I didn't know where to go, so I came here."

"You did exactly the right thing, Mikayla. I'm proud of you."

Nothing she said before this surprised me, but *this* . . . I knew Stright was a creep, that he slept with his students, but this is something else. I was so obsessed with Kinnear, I overlooked what a monster his protégé has become.

"I don't know what to do now," she says. "I can't go back to my room, what if he breaks in again? What if he tries to—"

I quiet her with a squeeze of her shoulder. "I'll take care of it."

If I run away, Stright will be able to keep right on hurting women with impunity. Just like those football players and all the other men at Gorman University I've held myself back from murdering because I was playing it safe, trying not to get caught. I should have killed Stright years ago.

I should have killed them all.

"R-really?" The hope in Mikayla's eyes slices me to the bone. None of this should have happened to her in the first place. I should have protected her. "But how—"

"He's not going to bother you again, I promise."

Mina's been gone nearly an hour. If she went to the police, they would be here by now. But there've been no more knocks on the door, no sounds outside but the wind. So she hasn't told them yet. I know that doesn't make me safe by any means, but it does buy me some time.

Time enough to deal with Patrick Stright.

64

CARLY

I'm not sure he'll show. Until I hear the creak of the fire escape. His footsteps are steady, relaxed. No hint of hesitation or fear, despite the gathering fog making the steps more treacherous, distances harder to judge. The whole time I've been waiting, my back pressed against the chimney, I've felt like I was floating in a void, the darkness and mist blotting out the rest of the campus like it never existed.

It's given me too much time to think, to second-guess myself. Right now, I'm still just playing dress-up. I could take off Allison's dress, scrub away the makeup, even dye my hair back to brown, and pretend this never happened. Go back to being the shivering, unsure girl who walked into Alex's office this morning, desperate for reassurance.

Bash Waller steps onto the roof of Whitten Hall, squinting against the glare of the string lights wound around the chimney. "Anna?"

When I approached Anna Turner in the Whit bathroom and told her what Bash did to Allison on Halloween, she shuddered like she wanted to run right back into the shower and scrub herself all over again. She thanked me profusely for warning her—and she was all too happy to help with my plan.

"Anna?" he calls out again. "You there?"

It was simple, really: Anna texted Bash, telling him how much fun she had at the cast party last night and asking him to meet her on the Whitten roof at midnight. I was afraid he'd be suspicious, ask questions—why so late, why the roof, why couldn't she come to him—but he agreed readily. Enthusiastically, even.

Now Anna is safely asleep in her room downstairs, and Bash is right where I want him.

He makes one more cursory sweep of the roof before plopping down near the edge to wait. There's a flash of flame as he lights a fresh cigarette.

I take a deep breath. Then another. No turning back now.

"Looking for someone?" I say as I step out from my hiding place.

Bash shoots to his feet, spinning to face me. He loses his grip on his cigarette, and it goes plummeting over the side of the roof, swallowed by the fog.

"You're not Anna," he says.

I shake my head. Bash looks me up and down. It takes him a few seconds of focusing on my chest before he finally recognizes me.

"You're Hadley's friend, right? Karen?"

I don't bother to correct him. It's probably for the best if he doesn't know my real name.

"Yeah, I remember you." Bash grins wolfishly. "That kiss last night—that was hot."

I want to put my fist right through his shiny white teeth. He's almost close enough now.

Close enough for me to lift the canister of mace clenched in my right hand and spray him in the face. When he collapses to the roof-top, howling, I'll kick him in the balls with the heavy toe of my combat boots. Then in the stomach. Maybe even in the nose.

He'll scream and he'll bleed, and the next time he even *thinks* of touching a girl against her will, he'll remember tonight like it's happening to him all over again.

"What are you doing here?" he asks, still staring at my cleavage. "Where's Anna?"

There's not even a hint of worry in Bash's voice. We're several stories up, alone in the dark, I lured him here under false pretenses, and it *still* hasn't occurred to him to be the least bit concerned about my intentions. If anything, he seems amused by this whole thing. He doesn't see me as any kind of threat.

"Well." I'm trying to move slowly, seductively, but my legs are shaking, and I don't know if it's from nerves or rage. "Anna and I, we played a little trick on you."

Bash raises his eyebrows. "Oh yeah?"

"I've been watching you," I say. "All semester. I wanted to tell you but I was too . . ." I avert my eyes, acting shy when really I'm just avoiding having to look at his arrogant face. "So Anna said she'd help me."

Bash's eyes rove over me again, following the seams of my dress like a road map over my curves. "You don't look like you need any help."

He's right: I don't need any help. But in a second, he will.

65

SCARLETT

On the drive to campus, I keep expecting police cruisers to roar up alongside my car, cut off my route, drive me onto the shoulder. But the road is deserted, my tires the first to cut tracks through the fresh snow.

I dropped Mikayla off at Whitten Hall on the way and told her to wait there until she heard from me. Of course, I doubt I'll be able to contact her afterward. She'll hear about my arrest or Stright's death or both later today, and she'll get the message.

At my instruction, she sent him a text asking him to meet her at Miller Hall so they could talk. She received a reply within minutes, telling her he'd be there soon.

I expect to find the front door of Miller locked since it's the weekend, but it swings open. Someone else must be here already, which is not ideal. I still have a bit of time, though—in the snow it should take Stright longer to make the trip to campus. In the meantime, I can find whoever's here and try to convince them—nicely, or otherwise—to leave.

As I walk down the hall, past the darkened classrooms and locked-tight faculty offices, I'm all too aware of the cold length of the blade pressing into my leg. I scrubbed Mikayla's fingerprints from the steak knife before slipping it into my boot. On the slim chance that Mina hasn't turned me over already, I want to take out Stright using a weapon with no personal ties. The knife is perfect: totally generic, one of thousands in circulation in the campus dining hall. I'm wearing gloves too, to ensure I don't leave any of my own prints behind.

The entire first level is empty, so I head up to the second, where I find only one room illuminated on the whole floor.

Mina's office.

When I appear in her doorway, she starts, then exhales, pressing her hand to her chest. "What are you doing here?" she asks. "Did you follow me?"

It looks like she's been hard at work—though it also looks as though she stopped off at home after she fled my house. She's wearing a white sweater and jeans, her hair piled high on her head, and she even swiped on some mascara. Not exactly the actions of a woman fearing for her life.

"I had no idea you'd be here." I step inside the office, and Mina stays completely still. She doesn't look happy to see me, but at least she's not backing away or screaming for help.

She has a spread of file folders on the desk in front of her, arranged in neat stacks. Viola Vance's diary sits on top of the center pile. The whiteboard on the wall still contains the list of men's names, but she's added another at the bottom.

Alexander Kinnear.

"You haven't contacted the police yet," I say.

Mina presses her lips together. "You shouldn't be here."

She's right, I shouldn't. If I were smart, I'd be long gone by now. But then Stright would keep right on terrorizing Mikayla—and the next girl, and the girl after that. I promised to take care of this, and I will. It might be a stupid thing to do, but it's the right thing too.

I take another step toward her. "Why did you decide not to—"

"I haven't decided anything yet," she snaps.

"Well, what are you waiting for?" I meant to sound forceful, but the question comes out pleading instead. "You know what I did. What I am."

"I have no idea what you are." She arches her fingers on top of the file folders. "I don't have all the data yet."

"Mina, I'm sorry, but I don't have time to explain. I need you to—"

"Tell me about the others," she says. "Did you always make the deaths look like suicides?"

No point in keeping secrets from her now—especially if answering her questions will get her out of here faster. "Some of them were staged as accidents."

Mina's eyes light up a little at the pleasure of having deduced right. "How did you decide?"

"I studied them," I say. "For months sometimes."

This entire conversation seems surreal. After Mina ran out of my house, I didn't expect to see her again unless it was in a courtroom, testifying against me. But she's here, and she's listening.

"Do you remember that adjunct who died in a DUI two years ago?" I ask.

She nods.

"He used to drive home from this bar another town over late at night. Always on the same road, nothing but cows and trees for miles. And as soon as he got home, he'd go into his stepdaughter's room."

Mina's eyes are still bright and curious, but she looks a little queasy too. She wants to know, and she doesn't. "So he wasn't drunk when he crashed?"

"Oh, he was. But I slipped something extra in his drink to make absolutely sure."

She looks more fascinated than horrified, and a tiny flare of hope lights up my chest. Maybe I'm getting through to her. She'll still report me, I'm sure, but if she can understand why I've done the things I've done, that's more than I've ever dared to hope for.

Mina taps her fingernails against the cover of the diary. "But something went wrong, didn't it? With Alexander."

I want to tell her every last detail: how long I waited to kill him, how furious Kinnear made me that night, how the knife felt in my hand. The pure relief that flooded through me when I cut his throat. Almost as sweet as the very first time.

"You know," Mina says. "I used to think about killing him."

At first I think she's joking. But her expression is deadly serious.

"All the time. The last year of our marriage especially." She walks around the desk so she's standing right in front of me. "He'd come home smelling like some college girl's cheap perfume, and he'd sit across from me at the dinner table, like nothing was wrong."

She has a faraway look in her eye, caught up in the memory. "Every time he'd slurp his soup I'd imagine jamming his spoon down his throat, or wrapping his tie around his neck and throttling him. And later, when we were in bed, I'd close my eyes and just—" She shakes her head. "But I knew I could never have gone through with it."

It's easier than you think, I want to say. But I stay silent, watching Mina, tracking the subtle shifts in her expression. I long to reach out and touch her—we're close enough now, I could—but I'm afraid to.

"When I heard he was dead, all I could think was *He finally did it*. He finally pushed someone too far, and they snapped."

"I was his student, you know."

The words tumble out before I can stop them. Mina tilts her head, confused. "I thought you went to Swarthmore?"

"I did," I say. "But I transferred there from Gorman. I was in his writing class, my first semester of college."

"Did he . . ." She swallows, like she's trying to keep from throwing up. "Back when you were a student, did—"

"He tried."

Mikayla told me the same thing. *He didn't hurt me. But he tried.* The world is a better place without men like Kinnear and Stright.

If I'd killed Kinnear that cold morning in his office, when I came to him in crisis and he tried to fuck me, I could have saved myself and who knows how many other women so much pain.

This time, when I move toward Mina, she does back away, but there's nowhere for her to go. Her hips bump against the edge of the desk, and she puts her hands back to steady herself, messing up the stacks of folders.

I look her right in the eyes. "These men are *predators*, Mina."

She meets my gaze, unyielding. "So are you."

She's right; I am. I enjoyed every second: their screams, their blood, the life draining from their eyes. She's still afraid of me, and she should be. I belong in a cage.

"I mean, you're plotting their deaths," Mina says. "*Hunting* them. It's . . ."

She trails off, but I can guess what she's about to say. *Sick, twisted, appalling. Evil.*

"It's brilliant."

I blink at her, not sure I've heard her right. She runs her hand over my cheek, pulling me closer, staring into my eyes. Not with fear now, but with fondness, desire.

"*You're* brilliant, Scarlett."

When she kisses me, I'm so shocked, it takes me a second to respond. But then I melt into her, gripping her waist like a lifeline. *Brilliant.* She thinks I'm brilliant.

I've finally found someone who accepts my monstrous side, and now I'm going to lose her. I can't let Stright live, and I can't let her go, but I can let the rest of the world fade away for this one brief moment.

I squeeze my eyes shut and keep kissing her. When I open them again, there's a man standing in the doorway, watching us with a wicked smile on his face. But it's not Stright.

It's Jasper.

66

CARLY

I imagined every detail of my revenge on Bash. But now, here, with him advancing on me and the wind whistling through the fog, I find myself frozen.

My hair lashes around my face, and he brushes some of it back. But he doesn't let go. Instead, he winds a curl around his finger, tugging at the root. My throat grips with fear, tighter than my fist around the pepper spray.

"I like the new look," he says. "The red suits you."

My thumb slides over the safety on the canister.

"You have no idea how pretty you are." He takes my hair in his fist and presses his mouth to the spot where my neck meets my shoulder. "Do you?"

"Wait," I say, but Bash wraps his arms around me, pinning my elbows at my sides. My finger is on the trigger of the mace, but I can't lift it. I can't move at all. "Stop it, I—"

This was a mistake. I shouldn't have tried to face him alone. I'm stupid, I'm so stupid.

Bash's mouth creeps higher, next to my earlobe. His lips are cold, and so is the breath that pushes past them, slithering all over me, reptilian.

I struggle against him, but that just makes him clamp down tighter, digging into my arms, the same place where he left those bruises on Allison. I think of my fantasy, my story for Alex's class, but it seems pathetic now.

I could still kick him in the crotch. I could scream—loud enough to wake up Samantha, to rouse the whole dorm. I'll tell them he tried to force himself on me. I'll tell them he's done it before.

But I'll get all the blame, just like Allison did. More, probably, because I dressed up like this. I lured him here. I asked for it.

"Relax," Bash whispers against my skin.

It's not enough. It would never have been enough, to spray mace in his eyes or kick him in the teeth or even to scream that he's a rapist for the whole campus to hear. He deserves so much worse than that.

And then I'm imagining something else: Bash stumbling over the edge of the roof, screaming as he falls.

He takes my face in his hands, fingers jabbing under my jawline. Freeing my arms, because he thinks he has me under his control. He thinks I'm not a threat, I can't hurt him, I wouldn't dare, I'm just a scared girl like all the others. I have no idea how many there have been. But I intend to be the last.

Maybe he'd be so surprised, he wouldn't even have time to scream. His body would still make a sound, though, when it hit the pavement below. A sickening wet crunch. Then silence.

I press my palms against his chest. There's a rumbling in my ears like an approaching storm.

"Stop."

I say it even though I know he won't. Men like him, they don't stop. Not unless someone stops them.

The sound thunders louder, until it's all I can hear.

This should have been my plan all along.

67

SCARLETT

I'm not sure how long Jasper was standing there in the doorway, how much of my conversation with Mina he overheard. His nose is red, dried blood scabbed around his nostrils, and suddenly I understand.

He's the one who broke into Mikayla's room this morning. The one she hit, the one she hid a knife under her pillow to protect herself from. It was him, not Stright. It was him all along.

"I knew you were behind that text." Jasper looks haggard, his hair lank and greasy, and his white oxford shirt wrinkled like he slept in it. Mikayla must have gotten him with her nails too: raw red lines mar the skin above his collar. "She would never have done that on her own."

Mina looks back and forth between the two of us. "What the hell is he talking about?"

"I don't know what Mikayla told you," Jasper says. "But that little bitch is so obsessed with me."

Mina bristles. She may not know the whole story, but she won't put up with him talking about Mikayla that way any more than I will.

All the pieces are coming together in my mind, the signs I missed because I was so focused on Kinnear and Stright: the petite figure by Jasper's side the night I tailed Kinnear to the Gorman Tap. The lock-picking skills that must have gotten Jasper into Mikayla's dorm. The way she reacted when he touched her arm in class. He was the only one in the room not disturbed by her outburst— because he knew it was about him.

"To be fair, though, Mikayla's pretty obsessed with you too," Jasper says, sidling closer to me. Mina shifts back a step as he approaches, but I force myself to remain completely still.

I could have killed Stright without remorse or hesitation. With Jasper, it isn't so simple. He's much larger than Stright, and I'm all too aware of the sinewy strength in those arms. If we were alone, I could seduce him. It would have been easy to pretend to reconcile, to get him down on the floor underneath me, where he's been so many times before, and choke the life out of him.

"She talks about you all the time. *Dr. Clark* this, *Dr. Clark* that. *I wonder what Dr. Clark will think of my term paper.*" He traces his finger down my arm and around the point of my elbow. "I bet she'll be so disappointed to find out her role model is a fucking *murderer*."

Mina sucks in a sharp breath. I just stare at him. He wants a reaction, and I'm not going to give it to him. I'm saving all my energy to take him down.

Jasper grips my shoulders and hunches lower to stare me right in the eyes. "Why didn't you tell me?"

"Excuse me?" I try to pull away, but he holds firm.

"I wouldn't have told anyone. I *haven't* told anyone. I could have ratted you out to those detectives, but I didn't. Doesn't that count for anything, Scarlett?"

He's squeezing me so hard now it hurts. I want to slap his hand away, but I know if I touch him I won't be able to stop until he's bleeding.

"I followed you to Kinnear's house that night, you know."

I didn't know. I had no idea. He's held the nails to my coffin all this time. So why didn't he hammer them in? Why did he lie for me, tell the police I was with him all night? Jasper always did love to back me into a corner, but in his own twisted way, he does care about me. That doesn't change what he's done, though—or what I have to do now.

"I hated that bastard too," Jasper says. "I could have helped you."

No, he couldn't. He disgusts me. He's just like every other man I've murdered.

Jasper shakes his head. "But now . . ."

I can't kill him yet. Not in front of Mina.

Keeping my eyes trained on Jasper, I reach back for her hand. "Mina. You need to leave."

"No," she says. "I'm not going anywhere."

"I don't want you to see this."

I still can't believe Mina is as understanding as she claims to be about my secret life. But knowing I've murdered dozens of men is one thing. Actually witnessing me take a life right before her eyes is something else. I don't want her last memory of me to be with blood on my hands.

"I'm not leaving you alone with him," she insists.

Jasper lets go of me but only so he can turn on Mina. "I've been *alone with her* more times than I can count." He looms over her, lips stretched in a lascivious grin, and she shrinks away. "The things we've done, you have no idea."

"Jasper," I warn. "If you touch her—"

He laughs. "What, Scarlett? You'll kill me too?"

68

CARLY

"Get your hands off her!"

Wes. He's here, on the roof. He's running toward us, Allison right behind him.

That thundering sound I heard wasn't just in my head: it was the two of them racing up the fire escape.

Coming to save me.

Bash turns languidly, like he has all the time in the world. My palms are still pressed into his sternum. The fog is so thick now, it's hard to see where the roof ends and the open air begins.

"Hey, man," Bash says to Wes, a lazy smile stretching across his face. "Chill."

Wes responds by punching him in the mouth.

Allison shrieks, and Bash reels down, catching himself on the heels of his hands. He's so close to the edge of the roof his fingertips wrap over the side. He scrambles backward, eyes wide with panic. It's the first time I've ever seen him truly afraid.

"She tricked me into coming up here!" Bash points a trembling finger at me, his voice keening unnaturally high. "She wanted it!"

"Just like I wanted it on Halloween, right?" Allison says. She's trying to look strong, hips cocked defiantly and arms folded across her chest, but I can see how shaken she is.

Bash spits a mouthful of blood onto the roof, then glares up at Allison. "You *did* want it, you were practically begging—"

Allison kicks him hard between the legs, the same way I imagined doing. Bash doesn't howl with agony like in my fantasy, though; he just curls up in a ball, hugging his knees to his chest.

"Shut the fuck up!" Allison screams, even though his pathetic whimpers are barely audible above the wind. It's picking up, growing wilder now, like her anger is summoning a real storm.

She rears back, but before she can kick him again, he hauls himself to his feet. "Crazy bitches," he mutters under his breath. He looks at Wes. "They're all yours, man."

Bash stumbles toward the fire escape, as fast as he can while still bent double with pain. Allison looks like she wants to go after him, land a few more hits, but she stays rooted in place, glaring at his receding back.

"It's okay," Wes says, putting his arm around me. "He's gone. It's okay."

But the last thing I need is comfort. Wes made Bash bleed, Allison made him cry, and I did nothing. I failed, and Bash just walked away. He has a split lip, maybe some bruises, but that's it. Nothing permanent, nothing truly damaging.

"What are you guys doing here anyway?" I shiver, and Wes draws me closer. But I'm not cold or scared. I'm vibrating with unspent rage.

"We couldn't find you," Wes says. "And Anna Turner told us—"

"Nice dress, by the way. I told you it would look good on you." Allison gives Wes a pointed look, and he tightens his grip on my shoulders. "Didn't I tell her?"

"Allie," Wes warns.

"Did Bash like it too?" Her voice is dripping with venom. "I bet he did. I bet he couldn't stop staring at you. Just like on Halloween, right?"

I'm confused at first: Is she *jealous*? Or just upset that I tried to get revenge on my own, without involving her?

But that's not what this looks like. It looks like I stole her dress and dolled myself up and tried to hook up with her attacker, less than twenty-four hours after we got into a nasty argument on this very subject. After we kissed and she slammed a door in my face. This looks like revenge against *her*, not Bash.

"How could you?" Allison asks. The same thing I said to her when I dragged her away from Bash last night.

"You don't understand," I say.

And she never will. My plan seemed perfectly reasonable when I was thinking it up, but now even in my head it sounds completely unhinged. I was going to pepper-spray him and rough him up a little—and then when that didn't work, I seriously considered pushing him off the roof to his death? I can't tell her that. I can't say that out loud.

"No." The fire of her rage is fading already, her blue eyes icing over. "I really don't."

69

SCARLETT

Jasper holds my gaze as he seizes Mina by the shoulders. Daring me.

I lunge at him, but Mina doesn't need me to defend her. By the time he slams her up against the whiteboard, she's already shrieking and clawing at his neck and wrists. Then she rams the heel of her hand up into his nose.

He wheels back, letting go of her to clutch at his own face. She didn't hit him all that hard, but with the damage Mikayla did earlier, it doesn't take much to make him bleed.

While Jasper is still reeling, red pouring down his chin, I drive my boots into the backs of his knees, knocking him to the floor. He's thrashing, furious, trying to throw me off as I climb on top of him. I jam my knee against his throat and slip the steak knife out of my boot.

Jasper's eyes go wide when he sees the serrated blade aimed at his face, and he finally falls still. I tighten my gloved fingers around the handle, lining the knife up under his jaw.

"Stop!" Mina shouts. "Scarlett, don't—"

She's down on the floor with us, and she keeps grabbing at me, trying to pull my hands—and the knife—away from Jasper's throat. For a second I think she's bleeding too, but it's only the red marker from the whiteboard, smeared over the back of her sweater. The list of names has been scrubbed into oblivion.

"Let me take care of this." I press the knife down hard enough to draw a thin line of red from Jasper's neck.

Why did I think it would be difficult to kill him? It's so simple. It's always simple, no matter how much careful planning and preparation I have to do. Cut them, and they bleed. Choke them, and they stop breathing.

Jasper gulps in a panicked breath, and the knife slices him again, a little slit over his Adam's apple.

"You can't," Mina says. "You'll go to jail."

She's desperate, pleading, tears running down her cheeks. But I know it's hopeless, and, deep down, Mina must too. I'm going to jail no matter what I do now. I killed my boss, I'm attacking a student with a knife.

But I can do this. I can take care of him so he doesn't hurt Mikayla anymore, so he doesn't have the chance to hurt anyone else. I can't kill them all, but I can kill Jasper.

"Please." Mina wraps her fingers around my elbow. "Please."

Jasper bucks against me again, knocking me to the side. The knife flies out of my hand, clattering to the floor, and all three of us dive for it. When we scramble back to our feet, I'm between Jasper and the exit. But he has the weapon.

He edges toward me, nostrils flaring, blood covering his face like a death mask. "Move, Scarlett. Now."

I stand straighter, taking up as much space as possible. He'll have to go through me. Mina tries to make another grab for the knife, but Jasper jabs his elbow back, cracking her in the cheekbone and sending her careening to the floor.

She smacked her temple against the corner of the desk on the way down, and she's not getting up. I can't tell if she's unconscious or just stunned. And I can't get to her, because Jasper is between us, brandishing the knife.

"Move," he says. "Or I'll fucking kill you."

He levels the blade at me, but his hands are shaking. He's not capable of this. He never was. He's nothing but a cornered animal, and even without a weapon, I'm the dangerous one.

Mina stirs, propping herself up, pressing her fingertips against her forehead. They come away stained red. But she's conscious, that's all that matters. *She's* all that matters to me.

Jasper is trembling more by the second. Pathetic. He has no problem intimidating a woman, violating her, but he can't bring himself to commit actual violence. Like Mikayla said in class, though, it's all the same crime.

"You're a psychotic *bitch*!" He spits it in my face, his voice as serrated as the knife.

My mouth curves up in a smile. "Yes, I am."

"Get away from her!"

Jasper's grip was already tenuous, and the sudden scream startles him into losing it completely. The knife slashes down across my collarbone and falls at our feet.

What the hell is Mina doing? I told her to let me handle this, she's in no shape to—

But then I see her, out of the corner of my eye. She hasn't gotten up, she's still prone on the floor. Only now she's staring up in horror as Jasper stumbles away from me, clutching at his chest, his white shirt rapidly staining red.

70

CARLY

The receding stomp of Allison's feet as she storms down the fire escape sounds like rocks tumbling down a well. I've really lost her this time.

I shudder, swallowing a sob, and Wes rubs my back.

"It's okay," he says again, like if he repeats it enough times it will magically become true.

None of this is okay. Allison is never going to speak to me again. Bash will never be punished. Everything is fucked-up and broken, and I can't fix it. I'm a freak and a failure, and I shouldn't have tried in the first place.

"You must be cold," Wes says.

I'm hot, actually, burning up like I have a fever, hair sticking to the back of my neck with sweat. But he's already draping his heavy coat over my shoulders.

Wes slips his arm around me again. "She'll calm down. She always does. She and her roommate last year fought a lot too, but they always made up."

"Really?" I say.

"Yeah, there was a whole month last spring when they couldn't even be in the same room without trying to kill each other. So Allison crashed in my room."

"Is that . . . allowed?" I try to imagine them in bed together, Allison pillowing her cheek on Wes's chest like I did during that strange night I spent in his room, but I can't quite picture it.

Wes laughs. "No way. But you know rules never stop her. She snuck in and out through the window every night for weeks." He shakes his head and laughs again, but it's a harsher sound. Almost bitter. "All our friends thought we were sleeping together. Isn't that funny?"

It's not funny. And it's not the same thing at all. Allison hates my guts, and she doesn't even know the half of how fucked-up I am.

"Why were you up here with Bash anyway?" Wes asks, that bitter note lingering in his voice.

I can't tell him about my ridiculous revenge plan either. I don't even have the canister of mace anymore; I must have dropped it. It doesn't matter now.

"It's a long story," I say instead.

"And you and Allison kissing at the party last night? Is that a long story too?"

I know he's referring to the kiss on the dance floor, but my mind immediately goes to our other kiss—the real one. Her hands on my spine and her tongue in my mouth and her breath in my throat.

Wes doesn't notice the tears filling my eyes, not even when he cups my face in his hands. "You deserve so much better than her," he says, planting a kiss on my cheek. "You know that, right?"

He kisses my other cheek next, close to the corner of my mouth, but I barely feel it. My thoughts are racing, chasing each other in circles.

Then Wes leans in and kisses me for real.

It's far from a friendly peck this time. His tongue is already past my teeth, his hands tangling in my hair. I manage to pull away long enough to say his name. "Wes, I—"

He kisses me again—even harder now—and I feel sick, I can't breathe, I want to scream, but his mouth is covering mine, and how can he think I'm enjoying this? My body is rigid, my hands wrapped around his wrists like manacles, my face wet with tears.

"Stop it." It's not a plaintive whisper like in Alex's office. I shout the words, shoving Wes off me so hard he stumbles back. *"Stop."*

I'm expecting him to apologize, to say he got carried away, he's so sorry, he doesn't know what came over him. This is all just a misunderstanding. Of course he wouldn't want to make me uncomfortable. Of course he'd never pressure me to do anything I don't want to do.

Instead, his eyes turn hard and his mouth twists with cruelty.

"Are you fucking kidding me?" he says.

71

SCARLETT

"You bitch, you fucking bitch!"

It's not me Jasper is screaming at, or Mina.

It's Mikayla.

After all, she is the one clutching the steak knife smeared from tip to hilt with his blood.

Jasper falls to his knees, a circle of red already spreading on the floor beneath him. I'm vaguely aware that I'm bleeding too, a pulsing sting below my throat where the blade bit in as he dropped it, sticky warmth soaking into my shirt.

Mikayla is shaking all over, gripping the knife so hard her knuckles turn pale. Her angelic face is a mask of horror, eyes unfocused.

She must have followed me here instead of staying in her room like she was supposed to. She shouldn't have had to see this. She shouldn't have had to *do* this.

"Mikayla." I step toward her. "Give me the knife."

"He was going to kill you." She can hardly get the words out around the panicked gasps gripping her throat. "Wasn't he?"

The pool of gore around Jasper swells, his skin looking more waxen by the second. Incredible that such a small blade could draw so much blood. She must have hit a vein.

Beginner's luck.

"He was going to kill you, I had to, I had to . . ."

She collapses into sobs, clutching the knife dangerously close to her chest. I wrap my hand around hers, prying her fingers loose so I can take it from her. The blade nicks her under the chin as I pull it away, but she doesn't even flinch.

"It's okay, Mikayla," Mina says. She's pulled herself up to standing now, though she looks more than a little unsteady, blood smeared down the side of her face from where her head hit the desk. "Just try to breathe."

Jasper is still clutching at his chest, eyes wide with terror, like a little boy desperate to wake up from a nightmare. That darkness I've always sensed in him, it's not like my urge to kill. It's something else: an urge to control, to possess.

I don't feel guilty, not in the least. But I will take the blame.

"Listen to me carefully," I say to Mikayla. "When the police get here—"

She whimpers, clutching at her own coat sleeves for comfort.

"*When the police get here*, you're going to tell them I stabbed him."

Mina grabs my hand—the one holding the knife. "Scarlett, you don't have to do this."

Mikayla looks so scared, so lost. I want to put my arms around her, but Jasper's blood is all over my gloves. Her hands are covered in it too, and she has a smear across her cheek. We'll have to clean that off, before the police arrive.

"You did the right thing, Mikayla." I scrub the knife on my shirt, wiping away her fingerprints. "You protected me. You protected yourself. You still have a bright future ahead of you." I tug off my right glove and toss it on the floor, then wrap my fingers around the knife handle, pressing my own prints in. "I told you I was going to take care of it, didn't I?"

Mikayla gives me a trembling nod, but Mina is shaking her head. "Scarlett, I'm telling you. Don't do this."

She puts her hands on my face, forcing me to turn toward her. She looks so beautiful, even with her swollen eyes, the blood matted in her hair. I want to carve this moment into my mind—the way she's looking at me, the feel of her fingers on my skin. If this is one of my last moments with her, I'm determined to remember every detail.

"It's okay," I tell Mina—the same words she said to Mikayla. "It's my choice."

She has to know it's too late for me. At least if I can save Mikayla, some good will come of this situation. Jasper has gone still now, his hands sprawled at his sides. He's breathing shallowly, the barest rise and fall of his red-stained shirt, but he won't last much longer.

"Fine, but it's not your only choice." Mina isn't pleading or desperate anymore. She's strangely calm, looking at me with that loaded-gun intensity again. She holds out her hand. "Give me the knife."

"What?" I jerk away from her. "No way, you're not—"

"Do you trust me?"

I stare back into her dark brown eyes. She could have turned me into the police today, but she let me explain myself instead. She listened, and at least on some level, she understood. I do trust her. Mina might be the only person in the world I trust.

I let my grip fall open. Mina plucks the knife out of my palm, deliberately pressing her prints in over mine. Then she picks up Jasper's limp hand and wraps his fingers around the handle too.

"W-what are you doing?" Mikayla watches us, blinking like she's just woken up.

Mina smiles at her. "Everything's going to be okay, honey."

That poor girl is going to need a lot of support to keep this secret, to keep herself together in the aftermath. Whatever Mina's plan is, I know she'll make sure Mikayla is safe. That's what matters now.

Still clutching the knife, Mina picks up her cell phone and dials 911. As she waits for the operator to pick up, she looks thoroughly, terrifyingly calm.

"Nine-one-one, what's your emergency?"

"I'm at Miller Hall on the Gorman campus," Mina says into the phone.

Her eyes stay steady and unblinking, but her voice transforms entirely. She sounds genuinely panicked, her breathing shallow and gasping like she's running for her life. Her grip tightens around the knife, flicking more of Jasper's blood off the tip onto the floor tiles.

"You have to come right away! He's—he's going to kill us."

72

CARLY

I feel the cold now, all the way down to my bones.

"I—I really like you, Wes." I lick my lips. They feel bruised from the force of his kiss. "But—"

"But what?" he demands.

"It just doesn't seem— I mean, with Allison, and . . ."

I can't find the right words. I sound like an insecure little girl, and I hate it. I hate myself.

"Why?" he says. "Why are you so obsessed with that fucked-up bitch when I'm *right here*?"

I really thought Wes was different. The way he listened when I told him about my father, the respectful distance he maintained between us when I slept in his room. Even the weight of his coat on my shoulders now. I thought we were friends. I thought he cared about me. But I never really knew him at all.

"You act all innocent." He's scowling, and he looks like a complete stranger. "But you're just as manipulative as she is. I mean, I just punched a guy for you, I *saved* you, and now you're like *Oh no, don't touch me, how dare you.*"

I wince at his high, mocking impression of me, pulling his coat sleeves over my palms. "I'm sorry if I gave you the wrong—"

Wes scoffs. "You're not sorry."

He's right: I'm not. He doesn't deserve an apology, but the words keep rising in my throat, hot and urgent as vomit. *I'm sorry I'm sorry I'm so sorry.*

I shrink away from him, wrapping my arms around myself as another gust of freezing wind rips over the roof. He's pacing right in front of the fire escape so I can't leave. I'm trapped, and no one's coming to save me this time. If I shouted for help, would anyone even hear me?

Wes puts his hands on my shoulders, rubbing up and down like he's trying to warm me up. "I could make you happy. I know I could, Carly." He smiles, suddenly his sweet and pleading self again. "If you'd just give this a chance."

Maybe a boy like Wes could have made me happy. If I were a different girl, a normal girl, not a freak with a head full of revenge fantasies. If I'd never seen behind his nice-guy mask. He's never given a damn about me, or about Allison. He thought if he was nice to us, eventually we'd fuck him. He thinks we *owe* him that.

This time, when he leans in to kiss me, I don't say *stop*. I don't push him away. Instead, I grab him by the shoulders, fingers digging in around the bone.

Wes takes my aggression for passion, groping at me, pushing his coat off my shoulders. He thinks I want him, when all I want is to hurt him. I want to hurt him so much it overwhelms me, blood shrieking in my ears, louder than the wind, louder than the small, pathetic noises of pleasure he's making at the back of his throat.

He's just like the rest of them. Bash, Alex. My father. They want us to bend and bend, let them say and do whatever they want to us. They get away with it, over and over again.

Wes is so close to the edge now, I don't even have to push.

All I have to do is let go.

73

SCARLETT

The sirens scream up minutes later, but Mina waits until we hear the stomp of police boots pounding down the hall to start crying again.

"Oh thank God," she sobs when Abbott bursts into the task force office, her weapon trained at Jasper's unmoving form on the floor. "Thank God you're here."

Abbott is flanked by her partner and several Gorman Township officers, but only one of the uniforms follows her into the room; there are too many of us crowded in here as it is. He stoops down to feel for a pulse, then looks up at Abbott and shakes his head.

Abbott holsters her weapon, surveying the scene: Jasper in a pool of his own blood, the knife abandoned on the floor next to him. Mina, Mikayla, and I standing in a row, red-stained hands clasped.

"You want to tell us what happened here?" Abbott asks.

"Scarlett *saved our lives*, that's what happened." Mina swipes at her tears, Jasper's blood striping under her left eye like war paint. "He just showed up here and attacked me out of nowhere."

She looks to me—waiting for me to pick up the next part of the story we decided on while waiting for the police to arrive. I wish we'd had more time to work out our plan, but any further delay would have invited questions about Jasper's time of death.

"I was— We were in my office downstairs. Ms. Atwell and I." I look at Mikayla.

She nods, biting her lip. We agreed it would be best for her to stay silent as much as possible.

"And we heard Mina screaming—"

"He had a knife," Mina says. "If she hadn't been here, I don't know . . ."

She breaks down again, burying her face in my neck. I wrap my arm around her. I wish I could force myself to cry like that. I can only hope the detectives take my relative stoicism as an attempt to stay strong for Mina and Mikayla.

Abbott crouches down to make a closer inspection of Jasper's body. "Looks like one of you has an impressive right hook."

"That was me," Mikayla says. Her voice is shaking. I put my arm around her shoulders too, drawing her against my other side. "He came at me, I didn't know what—"

But Abbott's already moved on, pointing at the marks on Jasper's neck. "And these?"

The slices from when I held the knife to his throat overlap with the scratches Mikayla gave him earlier, and the fresher gouges from his altercation with Mina. I usually try to erase all forensic evidence from the scenes of my crimes, but in this case the messier the better. We just have to stick to the story.

"We were all struggling," I say. "Trying to get the knife away from him."

Mina nods. "And then he rushed toward us, and—"

Abbott raises her eyebrows. "He ran into the knife?"

"It all happened so fast." Mina's eyes fill again. Abbott appears dubious, but Flynn is looking at Mina with far more compassion. Men never can resist a pretty woman in tears.

Another man bursts through the doorway—not one of the cops,

but Drew, responding to the frantic text I sent him after Mina's 911 call.

He stops on the threshold, taking in the body, the blood. "Dear God. Are you—"

"Please wait in the hall, Dr. Torres," Flynn says.

Drew backs up as instructed, but his eyes don't leave me. "Are you okay, Scarlett? I got here as soon as I—"

"Dr. Torres." Abbott gives him a warning look. "Actually, if you could all go outside. And watch your step."

She herds us out of the office, sidestepping the viscous seep of Jasper's blood. As soon as we enter the hallway, Drew moves in to embrace me. Abbott surges forward to stop him.

"Don't touch her," Abbott snaps. "Don't touch any of them."

Drew backs off further, shoulders against the wall, hands in his pockets. "Sorry."

"I'm okay," I tell him. "But she's bleeding." I motion to Mina's head injury.

"Where's the ambulance?" Drew asks. "She might have a concussion, or—"

"They're right behind us," Flynn says. "Dr. Pierce, why don't you sit down."

Mina waves him away. "I'm fine. Scarlett's the one who needs medical attention."

She gestures to my throat. I'd almost forgotten about the cut; the pain has settled into a dull throb. But while the nick on Mikayla's chin has already started to coagulate, I'm still bleeding freely. The knife must have sliced deeper than I thought. Drew reaches out like he wants to wipe the blood away, but then he sticks his hand back in his pocket, remembering Abbott's warning.

Abbott squints at my wound. "Mr. Prior did that?"

I start to answer, but Mikayla steps in. "He tried to cut her throat. I saw it." Her voice is sounding steadier. She's better at this than she thinks.

"Scarlett was just trying to protect me," Mina says. "I thought he was going to kill her too. I thought he was going to kill all of us."

Drew shakes his head in horror. Abbott looks less credulous. "Any idea why he would attack you, Dr. Pierce?"

Mina shakes her head. "I barely knew him. But . . ."

She pauses, letting the detectives see her think this through, so it seems like the idea has just now occurred to her. Mina called me brilliant, but I pale in comparison to her.

"Jasper always hated my ex-husband," she says.

"That's true," Drew says. "Jasper used to be Kinnear's graduate assistant; did he tell you that? They never got along, they argued constantly. That's why he was reassigned to Scarlett."

The detectives exchange a look. "He didn't mention it to us, no," Abbott says. "But we were aware."

Mina's eyes widen, her hand flying to her mouth. "You don't think he might have had something to do with—"

"It's possible," Flynn says. "We have reason to believe Mr. Prior visited Professor Kinnear's residence on the night of his death."

"Then why the hell hadn't you arrested him yet?" Mikayla's voice is brittle with anger. I tighten my grip on her shoulders. *Careful.*

Abbott shoots Flynn a glare; clearly he wasn't supposed to volunteer this information. "Let's discuss this down at the station—after you get those injuries looked at, of course." She nods to Flynn. "Make sure forensics gets pictures of everything before the EMTs treat them. Dr. Torres, if you don't mind sticking around? I have a few more questions."

Flynn motions for Mina, Mikayla, and me to come with him. I catch Drew's eye, and he smiles, trying to reassure me. He has no idea the hell he could find himself in if he says the wrong thing to Abbott. But he's on his own for now. He'll tell nothing but the truth, so I just have to hope they believe him.

Mikayla follows us obediently at first, but then comes to a standstill, staring through the office door at Jasper's body. She's been avoiding it until now: actually looking at what she did. Jasper's eyes are still open, wide and blank and impossibly green.

I steer Mikayla away before anyone can get a look at the stricken expression on her face. Abbott seems skeptical, but we just have to stick together, keep repeating the same story. Jasper's not here to contradict us, and thanks to Mina's quick thinking, he could even end up taking the fall for Kinnear's murder.

I might have a future after all. A future with her.

74

CARLY

I rush down the fire escape, like I can still save him. But I know it's too late.

Wes landed on the pavement beside the building. His neck is bent at an uncanny angle, blood pooling around his skull, eyes wide and empty behind the spiderwebbed cracks in his glasses.

He's dead. I killed him.

I don't cry, or scream. Instead, as I stare at his lifeless body, my heart rate slows and my breathing steadies. That strange calm settling over me again.

The door slams open. Samantha comes outside, her boyfriend right behind her, rubbing sleep out of his eyes. She glares accusingly at me. "Schiller. What the hell are you—"

She sees Wes, and her eyes bulge in horror.

"Jesus fucking Christ!" her boyfriend shouts, rushing over to where Wes lies. He crouches down, sliding his arm underneath Wes's shoulders as if he's going to pick him up and cradle him like an infant.

"Don't move him!" Samantha shouts. He turns to her with a helpless look. The front of his Steelers sweatshirt is already soaked with Wes's blood. "Call nine-one-one."

Her boyfriend gently lays Wes down on the bloodstained concrete before rushing back inside to get his phone. Samantha stares at me. I know I seem way too calm. I should be freaking out, shrieking, sobbing. I should—

"We were up on the roof," I tell her. "And—"

"What the hell were you doing up there?" She's trying to sound like her usual bossy self, but her voice is trembling. "I *told* you idiots never to—"

"I know," I say. "I'm sorry."

You're not sorry.

The door swings open again, and Samantha's boyfriend runs back outside, his flip phone pressed to his ear. Several other students file out behind them—including Anna Turner, in her bare feet, hair wrapped up in a scarf. She gasps at the gruesome sight, clutching the girl next to her.

Then Allison appears in the doorway, pushing past everyone. When she sees Wes, she wails louder than the approaching sirens.

She turns on me, eyes red and wild. "You did this!" she screams.

"Hadley." Samantha huffs out a breath, white steam obscuring the strange, blank look on her face. I can't tell if she doesn't believe my story, or she's just in shock.

"It's all your fault!" Allison shoves me so hard I stumble back. "You bitch, you did this, you killed him!"

She shoves me again, and I fall to the pavement, scraping my palms raw.

She's right. This is all my fault. But I don't feel guilty. I feel the way I expected to feel after taking revenge on Bash.

I feel *satisfied*.

Allison keeps screaming out accusations, but now she's almost as incoherent as she is inconsolable. Some of the other girls, Anna amongst them, close around her like a protective shell and lead her back inside.

Samantha stays to help me up. "This isn't your fault, Carly," she says, sounding so warm and maternal I almost don't recognize her. "It was just an accident."

I can't believe it's that simple. But when the authorities come, I repeat Samantha's words to them. We were on the roof, and it was dark, and neither of us could see the edge clearly. Wes got too close, and he slipped and fell. There was nothing I could do. We shouldn't have been up there. We should have known better.

I manage to make myself cry for them too—gradually, slow tears leading to hiccuping sobs, like the shock is wearing off, like reality is hitting me. The paramedics give me tissues and wrap a blanket around my shoulders. The detectives let Samantha sit with me in the back of their car while they ask me a lot of questions, about my relationship with Wes, whether we'd been drinking, why we were up there in the first place. One of them writes down every- thing I say in a little notebook, while the other focuses on my face like he's trying to memorize it.

But they never ask the question I'm dreading: *Did you push him?* They have no reason to suspect me of doing something so awful. Samantha keeps her arm around me the whole time, holding me in place like an anchor.

When my parents get word of what happened, they want to pull me out of school the very next day. I talk them into letting me stay until Thanksgiving break, but they won't hear of me coming back in the spring.

Within hours, Allison has cleared out her closet and gone to stay with some theater department girls in a house on the other side of town. I expect her accusation to spread across campus just as fast as the shocking story of Wesley Stewart's death. I steel myself, waiting for the whispers to start: *crazy, psycho, killer.*

But instead of avoiding me, people seem drawn to me. They approach me in the cafeteria, the hallways of Miller, the middle of the Oak Grove, just to tell me how sorry they are for my loss. They tell me what a sweetheart Wes was, what a good friend. I smile and thank them, and all the while I'm thinking of that ugly sneer on his face when I told him to stop touching me. I wonder how many other girls got to see that side of him. I wonder if Allison's ever seen it.

I don't see her again until the day before Thanksgiving, when I'm standing outside Whit waiting for my parents to pick me up. The sky is dark, the first flakes of a coming snowstorm starting to fall. I see a car lumbering down the drive, and I pick up my bags.

The car gets closer, tires skidding over the slippery pavement, and I realize it's not my parents' vehicle at all. It's a giant brown boat of a thing, with a big dent on the driver's side door and Indiana plates.

Wes's car.

Allison gets out and starts walking toward Whitten. She looks awful: pale and thin, her eyes shadowed and her cheeks hollow. She's changed her hair again. It's red now—much brighter than mine, the blaring red of alarm lights.

I set down my bags. When she sees me, her expression turns stone-cold.

"Don't you dare," she snarls. "I have nothing to say to you."

It sounds like a line from a play, her voice ringing out as if we're onstage. The snowflakes swirling between us make the scene feel even more unreal.

"It was an accident." The words come so naturally now.

"No." Allison shakes her head. "He wouldn't have even been up there if it weren't for you. Wes was careful, he was responsible, he was—"

"I was there," I say. "I saw it."

Allison's gaze drops to the pavement under my feet. I'm standing right on the spot where Wes died. The campus grounds crew tried for days to scrub his blood out of the concrete, but the red is still there if you know where to look.

Her eyes narrow. "Did you."

Panic flares in my chest, but I squelch it. I'm getting better at that every day.

What did I ever find so fascinating about her? She's just a girl. A girl who has no idea who she is, who changes her hair color like she changes her underwear, who's so desperate for attention she'll accept it from men who hate her. I wish I could have done more to protect her. But she made her choice, and I've made mine.

"Fuck you, Carly," she says.

I smile at her, so cold she actually shivers. "I'll miss you, Allison."

Whatever she came to Whitten for seems to be totally forgotten. She doesn't take her eyes off me for a second as she backs up to Wes's car and gets inside.

I watch her pull away. Even when the car gets to the end of the drive, I can see her red hair through the scrim of the snowflakes, bright as a flame.

By the time my parents arrive, the snow is coming down hard, drifts covering the ground.

My mother jumps out of the passenger seat before the car has come to a complete stop and runs to me, gathering me in her arms.

"Oh, sweetheart," she says. "How are you? Are you all right?"

"I'm fine," I say, and it's the truth, even though it shouldn't be. Since Wes died—since I killed him—I've been sleeping better than ever. No bad dreams, no waking up with all my muscles clenched.

"Your hair," she says, touching the red ends. I know what she's thinking: my father will hate it.

Good.

She takes my bags and loads them into the trunk. Before I get into the back seat, I scrape my boot over the pavement until the red stain on the concrete is visible again.

My father doesn't say a word as he steers the car away from Whitten Hall, but I can sense his ire just from the set of his shoulders, the way his hands grip the steering wheel, the flash in his eyes when they find mine in the rearview mirror.

I meet his gaze—steady, unblinking—and I think of the way that girl at the restaurant in Pittsburgh laid her long manicured fingers over his knuckles and laughed. He might be able to fool her and my mother, but he can't fool me. Not anymore.

A smile spreads across my lips, even colder than the snow.

You're next, motherfucker.

Epilogue

SCARLETT

"Hold still," Mina says.

She tilts my head to the side so she can wind the braid tighter. I lean back against her legs, shutting my eyes. I'll never tire of the sensation of her hands in my hair.

We're still settling in to our new home in London, boxes of books waiting to be unpacked into the built-in shelves around the fireplace. The one-bedroom flat is cramped and drafty, with pockmarked plaster walls and a scenic view of a soot-stained brick chimney, but it already feels like home. Because we're here together.

Abbott and Flynn spent months investigating, trying to re-create the exact sequence of our struggle with Jasper. But in the end, they couldn't prove who was holding the knife at the moment it went into his chest, whether it was accidental or intentional—at least, not conclusively enough to hold up in court.

Following Jasper's death, it seemed like half the campus came forward with their own damning anecdotes about him. Even Stright proved oddly useful: he took every opportunity to regale the police with tales of Jasper's creepy behavior and the protracted grudge he'd held against Alexander Kinnear.

Because Jasper followed me to Kinnear's house on Halloween, his cell phone records placed him right at the scene of the crime—circumstantial at best, but with most of the concrete evidence compromised by the fire I set, and Jasper no longer around to tell his side of the story, it was enough to pin the murder on him, for the sake of the paperwork anyway.

By the time both cases were officially closed, Mina was practically living with me—spending every night in my bed, her clothes crammed next to mine in the closet, her favorite brand of tea sitting by the stove. So when I was free to travel to London, I didn't even have to ask her to come with me: she resigned immediately and booked a ticket on a flight a few days after my own.

There were many times over the past few months when I thought I was doomed, that I was going down and taking Mina with me—or even that the police would refocus their suspicions on Drew again and I'd have to confess to clear his name. He was promoted to department chair at the start of the spring semester, and he's already proving himself the capable leader I always knew he could be. One of his first acts as chair was introducing a stricter code of conduct to protect students from predatory faculty and staff. It's not enough, but it's a start.

I know Sharon Abbott suspects what I am, even if she can't prove it. If she discovers any of my other crimes, I could still face consequences. Mina knows that too, but she's stayed by my side through all of this, unwavering. For the first time in my life, I didn't have to account for every detail on my own.

Mina finishes tying off the braid and starts coiling it at the base of my skull—her improvement on the hairstyle I used to wear for my kills. She's right: it does stay in place better, even with vigorous movement.

"I wrote in the Great Court at the British Museum for most of the day," she says as she sticks pins through the knot. "I stopped off at Sainsbury's on Tottenham Court Road to buy wine."

"I was at the archive until five fifty-two p.m. Then I took the tube straight home."

While I work at the Women's Academy, Mina's making progress on a research project of her own involving statistical analysis of domestic abuse reports to predict future offenses. Despite the distraction of the police investigations, she managed to wrap up the task force's work before joining me in London—though, of course, her final report to the university administration made no mention of the fact that some of the campus suicides weren't suicides at all.

Even though we're across the ocean, we make sure to check in on Mikayla weekly, and she's doing as well as can be expected under the circumstances: still excelling in her classwork and seeing a therapist who's proving very helpful even though Mikayla can't share the full story.

Mina slides in another pin, tamping down a few stray hairs on the side of my head. "We had lamb vindaloo for dinner. I had a cup of tea and you had wine, and we watched a documentary on Netflix about Egyptian tombs."

I nod. We've been over all this before, but we agree that you can never be too prepared. "We fell asleep by eleven."

She leans over my shoulder, looking down at me. "Will you be home by then?"

"I don't know," I say. "I'll do my best."

She smooths her hands over my hair. "Take the Piccadilly line back. It'll be faster that time of night—and fewer passengers."

Mina is the one who brought me this latest target: Edward Victorson, a Southwark barrister she saw screaming at his wife in the middle of Potters Fields Park.

The last time I followed the not-so-happy couple, the weather was warmer, and Mrs. Victorson wore a sleeveless dress that showed off the bruises encircling her upper arms like grotesque jewelry. He kept telling her to cover herself up, but she refused. Whenever his back was turned, she glared at him like she wanted to throttle the life out of him.

But she doesn't need to worry; I'm going to do it for her. Tonight.

I cinch the belt of my black trench coat around my waist, then check my bag to make sure I have everything I need. Mina watches me, her brow pinched with worry. She always worries when I go out hunting. She never wants to discuss the details afterward; she just asks, "Is it done?" And I nod, and we go right back to our cozy academic life—until the next one. For me, this work will never truly be done.

She opens the door, letting the misty night air seep into our entryway. The fog is so thick, you can barely see a foot in front of you. Exactly why I chose to strike tonight: Edward always goes out drinking with his colleagues after work and walks home alone along the Thames. He'll never see me coming.

Mina pulls me in for a kiss, fingertips ghosting over the serrated pink scar across my collarbone—my lovely parting gift from Jasper Prior.

"Be careful," she whispers against my mouth.

She looks so gorgeous, leaning against the doorframe, eyes glowing in the dim light, ringlets wreathed in fog. Sometimes I can't believe she's real. I can't believe Mina can look at me and see everything—the woman and the monster—and love me anyway. Since the night I pushed Wes off that roof, I thought I had no choice but to live my life in jagged pieces. But for the time being, at least, I can have it all.

"Don't wait up," I tell her.

Mina smiles. "You know you can't stop me."

Acknowledgments

I have to start by thanking my friend and fellow Pitch Warrior Emily Thiede, without whom this book would never have existed in the first place. I should really frame that tweet of yours!

Massive gratitude of course to my editor, Kate Dresser, and my agent, Sharon Pelletier. Kate, not only have you made my writing better, you've made *me* better. Thank you for being both a brilliant teacher and a fierce advocate. And Sharon, when I signed with you, I thought you were my dream agent. Now that it's been a few years, I can say for certain: working with you is well beyond my wildest dreams.

Thanks as well to Molly Gregory, Jessica Roth, Jen Bergstrom, Abby Zidle, Anabel Jimenez, Caroline Pallotta, Christine Masters, Anne Jaconette, Erica Ferguson, and everyone else at Scout Press. And to Laywan Kwan for the stunning, spooky cover—I may never stop staring at it!

Wendy Heard, thank you for helping me become a better (fictional) murderer and being the best goth sister-wife a girl could ask for. Halley Sutton, I believe fate brought us together, and I look forward to both your sure-to-be-phenomenal writing career and our future feminist world domination. And a shout-out also to

Hannah Whitten, Bibi Cooper, Lisa Catto, and everyone else who read early snippets of *They Never Learn* or offered advice as I was working on it. I wrote *Temper* mostly alone, but this book I wrote surrounded by a community of incredibly smart, funny, and all-around badass women, and that's made all the difference.

Finally, thank you to my family: my mom, my grandparents, my "aunt" Patty, and my faithful writing assistants, Finn and Tallie (who never fail to sit on my keyboard when they think I'm working too hard). And to my partner, Nate: just when I think I can't possibly love you more, you go and prove me wrong. You deserve everything you want in life and then some.

Made in the USA
Columbia, SC
20 July 2022